Joanna Adam was born in Edinburgh and grew up on the West Coast of Scotland. She now lives outside London. Trust is her second book. Her first book Kept was published in 2023.

TRUST

Joanna Adam

ISBN 978-1-7395131-7-7

Cover design: Primrose Adam

for Michael

Charlotte, James, Lizzie & Prim

for without family, I have nothing

The Wedding Guest

Mr & Mrs Semple
request the pleasure of your company
at the marriage of their daughter
Jennifer Anne
to
Capt. Jack Robert Weatherstone
on Saturday the 5th June 2004
St Mary's Radcliffe

Jenni's Wedding

She shouldn't have come. She knew it would be a mistake, too many happy people. And yet, here she was.

Margot followed other guests through the house towards the reception line, hugging Jenni, who wore a column of ivory silk, and shaking hands with her dashing new husband, Jack. Then she greeted both sets of parents and descended the short flight of steps to the marquee, accepting a drink from a proffered tray on the way.

It was hot for early June and getting hotter. Margot slid her hand down the stem of her champagne flute to prevent her Prosecco from warming.

People were flooding into the reception, a flow of grey suits and pastel dresses, dipping heads and gushed greetings, friends and relations pooling together and rippling on. Margot, alone in the crowd, wasn't expecting to recognise anyone, and she didn't. She swallowed some of her Prosecco.

She hadn't seen Jenni since they shared a flat nearly five years ago. When the invitation arrived, Margot had wondered whether to accept. They had been close once but Jenni knew what Margot had done and as she tried to forget and move on, Margot had pushed Jenni away. Shortly after that, Jenni decided to apply for teacher training in Manchester and returned to live with her parents. While Margot had stayed in London, landing a junior role at a gardening magazine off Covent Garden.

Curiosity had brought Margot north, and, of course, it was lovely seeing Jenni again, and on such a joyous occasion. Jack seemed charming and looked exactly like the sort of man that Jenni would marry. Margot gathered he was in the army and had recently made Captain. When she looked around the room, she saw many tall, young men of military bearing amongst the guests. She should make an effort.

The air in the marquee shimmered with buttery light as the sun shone through the canvas onto the lemon flowers and golden ribbons. Small bridesmaids in yellow dresses ran like chirping canaries between tables. Margot teetered through the throng, looking for another glass of Prosecco and something to nibble. She drifted around the room, cutting in and moving on quickly if necessary. She had fun flirting with the soldiers, all charming boys, but not what Margot was looking for in a man.

She tried to guess bride or groom, before breaking into conversations, but Margot quickly deduced that the groom's side were considerably smarter, which made guessing too easy and her game less interesting. Then she was cornered by Jenni's aunt in floaty, coral chiffon, who placed an apricot hand with blood orange nails on Margot's arm. Apparently, the newlyweds had met in Windsor Castle not even a year previously.

‘She didn’t want to go, but Louise, her maid of honour, do you know her? She’s one of Jenni’s teacher friends from the school. I can’t see her now. Must be in … upstairs,’ said Jenni’s aunt, her head bobbing back and forth looking for the absent Louise. ‘Well, anyway, Louise wanted to go, but she wanted to have someone along with her, you know, to hold her hand. Jenni thought the Ball would be full of posh boys and didn’t fancy going. I mean it wouldn’t be called a Ball if it wasn’t posh, would it? But I told her, that’s why you should go! Go and meet someone nice – and look what happened. I knew I was right. She borrowed a dress and found her prince. It’s a fairy tale, that’s what it is.’

‘Excuse me,’ said Margot. ‘I must move on.’

It was already too hot, and Margot’s clothes, which had been easy when she dressed and loose in the cool of the church, were beginning to feel tight. Her large hat felt awry, but she had a glass in one hand and her bag in the other, so she couldn’t do anything about it. She wobbled, catching her fancy heels in the coir flooring. She felt tawdry, her glass marked by smudged lipstick and her fingers sticky from the drink.

She felt she needed a break. She spotted an ancient man abandoned at a table in a corner and was on her way to introduce herself and take a seat next to him when she was accosted by a small bridesmaid.

‘I’ve lost my mummy,’ said the little girl, staring up at Margot.

‘Oh dear,’ said Margot, wobbling as she flexed her knees and lowered herself, so she could be face to face with the bridesmaid.

‘How can I help?’ Margot slipped a fallen blonde curl around the girl’s ear. ‘Everyone here is wearing such pretty dresses. What colour is your mummy’s dress?’

‘Purple, like yours. That’s why I thought you’d know my mummy.’

‘Shall we go and see if we can find her?’

The bridesmaid put out her small hand. Margot took the warm, damp fingers, tiny in her grasp. As she righted herself, Margot brushed back a tear. This little girl must be around five, about the same age as her baby would have been.

Margot scanned the tent. By the tea urn, she could see a young woman in a deep mauve outfit talking to a man wearing an impressive moustache.

'I think I can see your mummy,' she said.

After returning the bridesmaid to her mother, Margot retreated, swallowing a sob. She didn't know why she still felt like this. It was years ago, but she couldn't stop herself from wondering what might have been. Margot hurried into the house and ran upstairs, abandoning her tacky glass on a radiator cover in the hall.

'Ladies, up the stairs, on the right.' Margot heard someone say.

Opening the first door at the top of the stairs, Margot quickly realised her mistake. There was a shriek and a scuffle under the coats on the bed. Margot saw a pale pink coat slide off the edge of the silky eiderdown onto the floor and retreated, eyes down. As she closed the door, she heard a deep laugh. Margot wasn't sure why she felt ashamed.

The bathroom was through the next door on the right. There was a large sign.

'I don't really need to go, but I never pass up the chance,' said a middle-aged woman in floral, pastel blue in front of Margot in the queue. 'You wouldn't know yet, but there comes a time… and who knows how long the speeches will be ... I do like your hat, by the way, fuchsia, isn't it? It's quite a statement. I mean … it's lovely.'

Uncomfortable in her high heels, Margot tried to wriggle her toes to ease the pinch.

'Such a fabulous occasion. So great to have all the cousins together. I do love a big family gathering, don't you?' said a woman in pale yellow who was behind Margot, edging nearer as the queue inched forwards.

Finally, it was Margot's turn. She washed her hands in cool water and looked at herself in the mirror. She tested removing her hat. A livid line stippled across her forehead like narrow railway tracks. It looked as if she had stapled the hat to her head, and her hair, covered by the crown, had been squashed flat, damp in the heat.

Her aunt always said you should wear a proper hat to a wedding but next time, Margot would choose something more discrete. She pulled a tissue from the box by the sink, dampened it under the tap and patted the mark on her forehead. It was useless. She undid the top button of her dress and pressed the cool tissue to her chest. It was too hot to be smart. She fluffed her hair, forking her fingers through it to give it lift, but the life had gone out of it.

Margot took another tissue and blew her nose. She stared into the pale grey eyes in the mirror. She was twenty-nine. Everyone had said she had time, but here she was at Jenni's wedding, and she was single again. It was true, Jenni was golden blonde, tall and thin, and looked amazing in her wedding dress, but Jenni didn't have the curve and flare that Margot did. She just didn't.

There was a knock at the door.

'How are you doing?' said a thin voice.

Margot shoved her preposterous hat back on her head, applied some lipstick, and took a final look in the mirror. Her dress was too severe, too formal, she undid another button and loosened the collar before heading back to the party.

She could hear the rising din as she descended the stairs. It was like a sauna in the marquee. Margot stepped into the crowded room, picking up some bubbles on the way. The bride and groom were just arriving at the head table. Margot glanced around for somewhere to sit, most of the tables were full. She sidled along the edge of the tent and slipped into a chair by the elderly man she had seen earlier. She kicked her shoes off under the table.

The centrepiece had wilted already, petals dropping from the yellow roses and the tiered cake stand was empty. Margot was desperate for a cup of tea, but the urn was on the other side of the tent, she had missed her chance. The speeches were about to begin, and she could hardly get up and cross the room now.

The father of the bride stood. He tinged his glass with a teaspoon. He talked about Jenni, how she was the light of their lives and how he felt confident that Jack, with his promising career in the army, was the sort of man who could be trusted with their only daughter. The guests all raised a glass. The groom then rose to jeers. He really was remarkably good-looking. He made an acceptable speech, thanking everyone and the bridesmaids were toasted.

Then the best man spoke. Margot strained to hear. He was mumbling into his shirt. The elderly man sitting next to Margot placed a dry hand on her arm and leant towards her.

'Can you hear what he's saying?' he bellowed. His breath smelt of stale biscuits and cigarettes. 'Can't catch a word.'

'Me neither,' said Margot.

Several people nearby turned to shush. Ribald laughter came from those sitting closest. The speech must be hilarious. The groom looked down at his plate, smiling and shaking his head. Jenni stared straight ahead with a fixed grin. The best man rambled on. Finally, reaching a toast.

'I like your hat,' the old man said, leaning towards her again.

Margot shifted her chair, as she did so, the spindly legs caught in the coir matting and threatened to tip her up. She put her hand on the arm of the man sitting on her other side to stop herself from tumbling into his lap. He turned to catch her.

'Hello,' he said, smiling. moving his chair over to give her more room.

‘Thank you,’ said Margot. Her neighbour looked like the groom, with the same dark hair and blue eyes. If they stood next to each other, this man would perhaps be a little shorter, and a little broader. He seemed grounded, with none of the bravado that had characterised Margot’s brief exchange with the groom in the reception line.

‘I’m Patrick, Jack’s first cousin,’ he said, holding out his hand. ‘Whose side are you on?’

Jack’s Wedding

After the stag night, Patrick almost didn’t attend Jack’s wedding. As children, they had been like twins. Their mothers were sisters and, when they were young, Patrick and Jack often met up after school and on weekends. Also, there were the family holidays to Wales, a glorious time, outside all day building dens in the woods and playing board games in the evenings. Although Jack was two years younger than Patrick, he was tall for his age, and the gap between them soon counted for nothing. Their friendship had survived them being sent away to different prep school, but when Patrick went to boarding school at thirteen things changed.

Patrick had been slow to settle into his new school but managed to carve a niche for himself. He was not unpopular, but he was not one of the uber-successful boys either.

Jack, two years younger, had made an immediate impact at Winton. He instinctively understood the hidden hierarchy and made friends with ease, always in charge, always in trouble but never first in class. Patrick couldn’t understand why. He knew Jack was clever, but Jack was doomed to be labelled naughty. His saving grace, from the point of view of the staff, was his sporting ability. With Jack at the crease or with the ball, the school teams excelled.

In contrast, Patrick had never been able to catch or throw a ball. Being academic was something, but you didn’t want to be known for being a geek. He had learned to conform, to be inconspicuous, disappearing into the miasma of boys.

In his mid-teens, just as Patrick was emerging from the constraints of childhood and it was his time to shine, Jack became taller, funnier and more charismatic. Patrick tried not to be offended, but he found it hard to hold the high ground. Jack wasn't outshining him on purpose, he was just being Jack, but even so, for a time, Patrick avoided family events. Tolerating Jack's effortless bonhomie had become easier once Patrick had gone to university and Jack had joined the army.

For the stag night, the best man had booked a table at Quaglino's. There were eight of them for dinner. It seemed quite civilised. Perhaps Patrick would enjoy the evening after all.

'Good to see you,' said Jack, smiling as they shook hands when Patrick arrived. 'Sorry about the divorce. Good of you to come.'

'Wouldn't miss it for the world,' said Patrick, handing his coat in at the cloakroom. 'Yes, it's final … I'm a free man.' All in all, he had been with Vi for nearly ten years. Now, he was thirty-four and divorced, Patrick wasn't sure if it was a matter to celebrate or to lament.

'Onwards and upwards,' smiled Jack, clapping Patrick on the shoulder as they walked to their table. 'You're the only family here tonight, so you'd better be on good form.'

'Knowing you, Jack,' said Patrick. 'You'll be able to hold your own without any help from me.'

Old-fashioned's were ordered and introductions made. Patrick had met most of the other guests or heard of them, the friends from school and the army colleagues. Their table was on the first floor in a private room overlooking the vast hall with a central bar and live music.

After dinner, more of Jack's guests arrived and they moved to the noisy, downstairs bar. Detached, and more sober than his companions, Patrick found it hard to hear what anyone was shouting about over the background noise. When the party relocated to a club, and the chance of civility declined, he shook Jack's hand and slipped away. Patrick hadn't met Jack's fiancée, but he hoped she was up for the challenge.

Of course, Patrick did go to the wedding. He drove his parents, they didn't want to miss the party, and it was a chance for Patrick's boys to see their cousins.

Arriving at the reception, Patrick's mother stopped to chat with friends, so Patrick settled his father, who was becoming hard of hearing, at a table at the edge of the fray. Nearby, there was a gap in the marquee flaps, so if his father fancied one of his filthy cigarettes, as his mother called them, he could make a sneaky exit and have a smoke.

Patrick then took Ollie and Toby to the children's table, where there was a girl dressed as a clown who was babysitting for the afternoon. She soon had the boys colouring in printed sheets alongside some of the younger bridesmaids.

He saw his mother working the flower-filled room, flitting bird-like from group to group, but as the tent filled and became warmer, his mother took a seat by one of the elderly cousins and Patrick went to get them both some tea.

In a queue, shuffling forward, scanning the crowd, trying to identify all the family he should speak to, Patrick saw a striking woman poised at the entrance to the marquee. He hadn't seen her in the church. She must have been sitting at the back. He didn't recognise her, she must be on the bride's side, not that he knew all of Jack's extended family and friends.

There was something about the way she hesitated at the edge of the room as if to step into a fast-moving river that resonated with Patrick. She had a vulnerability that defied the bold colour of her dress. She wore a large hat, a statement piece his mother would call it, and as she scanned the room, he caught a glimpse of an earring as her hat tilted one way and a curl of light hair when she turned the other. It was impossible for him to see her face properly. He hoped she wasn't one of Jack's many exes.

Patrick reached the urn, collected the teas and took them back to his mother and cousin.

'You don't happen to know who that woman in the purple dress is, do you?' he asked.

'I don't know anyone who would wear purple to a wedding,' his mother said.

'She was by the door.'

They turned to look, but the woman was gone.

'Bride looks a lovely girl,' said the cousin.

Patrick left them and moved around the hot tent to find family or friends he could bring to talk to his mother or father. By the time guests were due to be seated, his mother's table was full. Patrick swept by the children. Ollie was counting smarties with one of the bridesmaids, and Toby seemed to have fallen in love with the babysitter. There were no free chairs nearby. Patrick was surprised. You could usually get a seat near the children's corner.

There were still some empty places at the table where his father was sitting. Patrick joined him, nodding a greeting. He angled his seat so he could keep an eye on the boys. He hadn't seen the woman in purple again. Perhaps she was a disappointed ex after all and had left early.

Just as a glass was being tapped to call for silence, someone slipped into the vacant chair between Patrick and his father. Patrick caught a haze of purple out of the corner of his eye as he turned towards the head table as the speeches began.

When the best man rose, Patrick noticed his father lean into the woman in purple. Amongst the ribaldry of the speech, Patrick turned and introduced his father and himself.

'I'm Margot,' she said, whispering from under her hat brim.

Her breath was soft on Patrick's ear, and he felt a prickle of a smile as they all rose to toast the newly married couple. He didn't know this woman at all and yet he felt a warmth. He hadn't smiled like this, a secret inner smile, for a while. He laughed all the time with the boys. They were his joy. But this was something different.

As they returned to their seats, Patrick pivoted his chair towards her. She looked cool and chic and was wearing that huge hat. It covered half her face. Perhaps Margot had something to hide.

'Lovely name. French, isn't it? Are your parents from France?'

'No,' she said, leaning towards him to whisper. 'They're dead.'

'O-oh. I'm sorry.' The skin of her throat was so pale it looked like she was made of living marble. He tried to keep his focus on her face. He could now see her eyes were a cool, calm grey.

'No, I'm sorry. I don't know why I said that. I mean, they are … a long time ago now. It must be being surrounded by all these happy families.' She glanced at the room before shaking her head as if to toss away the memory.

'A-ah.' Patrick didn't want to be tongue-tied now, but this wasn't going as smoothly as he hoped. Her eyes were veiled by the shadow of her hat brim again, but her pink lipstick formed an amiable semi-circle. He wanted to smile back and say something amusing but ended up wriggling his mouth around words that stuttered out before being fully formed. She probably thought him a lunatic.

He felt a tugging at his sleeve.

'Daddy, Daddy.' Toby appeared by Patrick's chair.

'Children,' he smiled at Margot. The boys had been so good all afternoon he could hardly complain if they needed his attention now.

'Ollie took my balloon,' said Toby, moving between Patrick and Margot's chairs.

'Duty calls. I'm sorry to abandon you, but Toby and I must go and solve a miscarriage of justice.'

'The case of the misappropriated balloon,' she said.

'Exactly. I have become chief investigator since, er, since … since my divorce.' God, he was welling up. It was as if it was the first time he had said the word. He looked down at Toby, trusting, waiting, then turned back to Margot. 'Toby, this is Margot.'

'Hello.' She shook Toby's hand before turning back to Patrick with a broad smile. 'You had better go then. We can continue our inappropriate and far too familiar conversation once the case has been solved.'

Patrick felt his hands become sweaty.

'A-ah, um, well, I'm afraid the boys and I will be leaving promptly after the cake is cut. We have a long drive, and we are taking my parents' home.'

'Another time then, in London, perhaps.'

'Yes, that would be lovely.'

'Daddy!' Toby was pulling on his sleeve again.

'Time to go,' Patrick said, and retreated into father mode, took Toby's hand and went in search of the lost balloon.

'I only took it 'cause I knew he'd lose it. And anyway, he ate my smarties,' said Ollie, scuffing his shoes along the road. 'I was going to bring it to the car.'

Toby snivelled. They were on their way to the church car park. Patrick smiled as his fingers brushed against the note in his jacket as he rootled around for a tissue for Toby. The boys were exhausted. His father was coping manfully with the walk, his mother was slowly tottering along in her heels, but in his pocket, Patrick had hope.

'You could have brought the car to the reception. I could have kept an eye on the boys while you collected it,' said his mother.

'That would have been sensible,' he said, but also impractical. It had been difficult enough extracting himself and the boys, let alone his parents. While he collected Ollie and Toby's bits and pieces, his mother had darted off to kiss another cousin goodbye and disappeared into the throng and his father had staggered outside for a smoke.

'I must pop upstairs,' his mother had said when Patrick had finished packing the boy's pictures into a holdall and was ready to leave. When she returned, Toby tugged his sleeve.

'Daddy, I need to go too.'

'Ollie?'

'No!'

'I think it would be a good idea,' said his father coming to find them.

'Perhaps we should all go …,' said Patrick. 'It's a long drive home, and we need to drop Grandma and Grandpa off first.'

By the time they returned to the hall, his mother was gone.

'I haven't said goodbye to the clown lady,' said Toby, on the verge of tears. Patrick hesitated but didn't want Toby crying all the way home in the car, so he left his father with Ollie and headed back into the marquee with Toby. On the way back out, Patrick spotted his mother by the door talking to Margot.

'Marvelous,' he said to her. 'You've found my mother. We've been leaving for half an hour.'

'Don't exaggerate, Patrick,' said his mother.

Margot laughed and said goodbye to them all. As she kissed Patrick on the cheek, he felt her hand in his jacket pocket.

The Follow Up

The First Note

Margot, Maaa-go, Patrick loved the way the first syllable stretched out and the second clipped short. A name with a hint of Gallic sophistication. Maa-go. He moved the note from his morning suit to the bedside table, wedging it under the light so it didn't get lost. On Monday morning, he transferred the number to his work suit.

It gave Patrick hope that someone, somewhere, thought he was interesting - even with two small children in tow. Today would be the day he would call her in his lunch break.

He walked out of the car park into the early sunshine. The day was bright. The high, pale blue sky beamed at him between the tall buildings. Maa-go, she had looked amazing at the wedding, and her hat had been spectacular. It took a person of character to carry off a hat like that.

He turned into Horse Guards Avenue, past the machine gun toting police, through security and bounced up the slick escalators to the corridors of power. By lunchtime, the promise of the day had faded, and Patrick was still reading through reports that needed to be précised before that afternoon's meeting. He wouldn't have time to call Margot. It wouldn't matter, he didn't want to be rushed and, anyway, he didn't want to seem too keen either. A woman like that would expect him to be cool.

By Thursday, time's pendulum had reached its zenith, pausing before it began its descent. This was the moment. If he left it any longer, he may as well not call at all.

On his lunch break, Patrick walked towards the river and turned left up the few steps to the Embankment Gardens. He settled on his favourite bench facing the sun and took out his lunch. Across the river, the arc of the London Eye rose above the green of the trees along the embankment, the cabins moved imperceptibly slowly. He finished his sandwich, wiped the remnants from his lips with the back of his hand and pulled the note from his jacket pocket. He ran his thumb across the number before reaching for his phone.

Patrick began typing Margot's number but paused before he was halfway through. He wasn't sure of the etiquette. If he rang, she might be busy. He decided to message first. That way, if she wasn't interested, she could let him down gently. He was pathetic, after almost a week of procrastinating, he wasn't even going to ring her.

Afternoon ...too formal.

Margot, you passed me a note... accusatory.

Hello Margot, we met at Jack and Jenni's wedding last weekend. I wondered if you might be interested in meeting up sometime... not quite.

Hi, we sat next to each other at the wedding. I found your note. Would you like to meet up? Patrick.

That would do, he pressed send.

Before Patrick had put the note and his mobile away, it rang. He flipped his phone over so he could see the screen. It was Margot. For a panicky moment, he wondered what he could possibly say. What an idiot, this was what he wanted. He packed up his things and took the call.

'Hello,' he said.

'Hello, Patrick.'

'It's a lovely day.' He should be able to talk about something other than the weather. He should have thought this through.

Margot laughed and agreed, it was a beautiful day. She asked him about his family and how he was related to Jack.

'First cousins,' he said. 'Our mothers are sisters.'

With his phone at his ear, Patrick set off to walk around the gardens, throwing his sandwich wrapper in a bin on his way. He passed the contorted bean trees, stretching out for the sun, their heavy limbs propped up with huge metal stakes. He circled Sir

James Outram, back from India, immortalised in bronze, and returned by the beds of red canna lilies, standing to attention like sentries, to the statue of William Tyndale, all the while talking to Margot above the blur of the traffic.

By the time the call ended, he was back at Whitehall. They had started with the weather, and moved on to the wedding, finding out how they were connected to either Jenni or Jack and the history that involved. Then Patrick told Margot about Ollie and Toby and by then he was at his office door, just short of the armed police officers who patrolled the entrance.

Somehow, they had talked about everything and nothing, nothing at all, not even about when they might meet. But the relief of having made contact, and not being rebuffed, and the ease of their conversation left Patrick with a rosy feeling as he headed back into Whitehall, running to catch up with the rest of the day.

Patrick walked tall. After all the years of dealing with Vi, he suddenly felt light. He wanting to find someone to share his life with, someone to make a home for the boys, someone congenial to return to at the end of the day. Perhaps Margot was the one.

After work, as Patrick strode past the jostling tourists on Horse Guards Parade to the car park, he thought back to their lunchtime conversation with a smile. But what a fool he had been not to secure a time and place for a date. That was the main purpose of the call. He had fluffed it. He needed to call her, or at least message.

Patrick had left his car in a corner bay; it had been the only space available that morning. A beam of sun must have slanted in; the car was boiling. Opening the door, the smell of the leather seats was overpowering.

He recalled returning to prep school, sitting in the back of his father's old Jag. Ripe leather and cigarette smoke, anxiety and misery souring his mouth. His father would have the front window open an inch or two, one hand on the wheel, a cigarette between the fingers of the other, lifting to tap the ash through the gap.

Patrick could hear the murmur of his parents talking from the front of the car, distant, undecipherable, while he fought nausea in the back. They were probably discussing what they would get up to when they had dropped him off. He wasn't ready to return to school. The weather was still fine, the air fresh. There were still camps to build, games to play and trees to climb. Instead, he must sit in the car shrouded in the ominous smell of leather and cigarette smoke.

Patrick got into his car, leaving the door open while he turned on the ignition and let the windows down. He sighed as the breeze curled around him and carried away disheartening memories. He pulled out his mobile. He should write something to Margot that referenced their earlier call but was also witty and engaging. His fingers hovered over the keys. Once or twice, he started, then delete, delete, delete. He started again.

Good to chat today. Shall we meet up for a drink?

In the end, banal and to the point. How should he finish? She might think it presumptuous if he signed off with a kiss. Undecided, he left it as it was.

It had been so long since he had dated. He had forgotten how these things went. At home with the boys, he spent every minute organising outings and activities, retrieving socks and soft toys. At work, he made decisions based on research so thorough and so carefully shaded that the answer was often identified before the question had even been asked. Overthinking was what he was paid to do. None of these skills were helpful now.

His relationship with Vi had covered ten years, give or take, seven years of marriage. Then the amicable, quick divorce from the acrimonious, often absent Vi. Now, trying to move forward, he was finding it hard to remember how he was supposed to communicate, to behave. He wasn't even convinced that texting was appropriate. He pressed send and hoped Margot might have replied by the time he got home.

Patrick was manoeuvring through the carpark exit ramp when his phone pinged. He paused to check his messages.

Great! Tmrw, Fri 6.30 American Bar, Savoy c u there xxxx

Marvellous! Fabulous!

He must let the nanny know he would be late.

A car horn broke his reverie. A queue was building behind his stationary car.

The next day, he got to the Savoy early and secured a table. Margot wasn't much later. He looked up from the complicated cocktail menu to see her crossing the bar towards him. She was wearing black trousers, a silky shirt, and black heels that added an enticing swish to the way she moved. He rose to greet her.

'Am I'm late,' she said, kissing him on the cheek.

'No, no, I was early.' He brushed the cheek she had kissed with his forefinger, as if to hold on to the moment.

She took the chair opposite him, shaking her abundant, fair hair behind her shoulders as she did so, a stray strand, slightly shorter than the rest, fell over her eyes, she brushed it back. Her hair wasn't too long or too short, it wasn't a brassy or golden blonde, it was a silky, silver fawn. A swish and a shake and Patrick was mesmerised.

'What can I get you?' he asked.

'Have you had a look?'

'I'm rather bewildered by the choice,' said Patrick, passing her the menu. 'I shall probably go for an Old-fashioned.'

'A Marguerita for me, thanks,' she said snapping the menu book shut.

Over the tinkling of jazz, Margot asked him about himself, but Patrick was adept at turning the conversation back to her. He knew him, she was the mystery. She knew he was divorced with two young sons. There was nothing else to him. He was rather boring. He hoped she wouldn't find that out too soon.

They arranged to meet that Sunday. Margot suggested the Hampton Court Flower Show.

'I missed Chelsea this year,' she said. 'And I have tickets through my work.'

Patrick couldn't think of anything he'd rather not do but found himself agreeing it was a splendid plan, while busy calculating how he would manage. Vi was off on one of her jaunts, so he had the boys. The nanny didn't work weekends, he would see if Mrs Stapleford was free. Patrick wouldn't ask his mother. No need to go there yet. Margot was his to discover alone.

They met at the train station and joined the throng heading across the bridge. Patrick wanted to hold Margot's hand in case he lost her, but fearing that might be construed as too familiar, he walked beside her, as close as he dared, taking sideways glances to make sure she was still there. She was wearing a pale-pink floral dress and a white cardigan and carried a wicker basket. It had an open top. Patrick hoped there wouldn't be any pickpockets.

The show was hideously crowded, but the weather was good. Margot wasn't bothered by the hordes but flitted from flower display to gardening stand and back again, chatting to the stall holders and lingering over bountiful exhibits of roses or delphiniums, or whatever caught her eye. Even Patrick had to agree that the display gardens were impressive.

It had been a long morning, and his stomach was beginning to grumble, when at last Margot turned to him.

'Ah, Patrick, thank you for indulging me. I'm having such a lovely time. I hope you haven't been bored.'

'Not at all,' said Patrick. He had enjoyed watching Margot dart like a pink butterfly around the stalls, her dress floating behind her in the breeze. He had been impressed by how lovely she was to all the stall holders, and how her enthusiasm for plants of every variety made her everyone's' instant new best friend. 'Shall we get some lunch?' he added.

They bought outrageously expensive sandwiches and sat on a bench drinking rosé looking out over the Long Water. They could hear music from a distant band stand. Patrick made a daft joke about the ducks that were paddling nearby, and Margot was good enough to laugh. It was glorious. With her, suddenly it seemed, anything was possible.

Margot was charming and attractive – no beautiful – no, that wasn't quite right – he found her shockingly desirable. And miraculously she appeared to want to be with him. Beside her, he felt more himself. He wondered what the boys would think of Margot, but he was getting ahead of himself. It seemed a miracle he had found her, but, as yet, they hardly knew each other.

It was after four before they rose to leave. As they wended back through the show towards the exit, Patrick was surprised when they stopped at various stands they had visited before. Margot was collecting plants. He was astonished.

'Sometimes, they sell off plants at the end of the day. I reserved a few earlier.' Margot placed the pots in her wicker bag. 'I don't have a garden at my flat, but these will do nicely as house plants and flower all summer on my windowsill,' she added.

Patrick Before Margot

Starting Out

When they first met at a talk at the Oxford Union in the spring of Patrick's final year of university, Vi had been so vibrant, she fizzed. Her vivaciousness brushed off on him and, standing beside her, he felt more the man.

After graduation, they rented a flat in north London. Vi grew herbs in the window boxes. Patrick worked behind the bar at their local pub while he applied for jobs. On the way back from an exhausting interview in Whitehall, he passed a bookshop and, on a whim, bought a book, *Coding for Beginners.*

'There's no need to rush into a serious grown-up life,' said Vi, coming back from Camden Market with a bunch of carrier bags and wearing some sparkly eyeshadow.

'Had fun?' said Patrick, looking up from his computer. He wondered if they could afford quite so much shopping.

'We should take a year off, explore the world. Have you ever climbed Snowdon?' she said.

'Er, no,' said Patrick.

'Me neither. Let's go.'

'What now?' he said.

'Yes.'

They had gone right there and then, bundling their stuff into the clapped-out Polo that Patrick's mother had given him when he had passed his driving test. As they drove up the M40, Patrick wondered what they had forgotten and about the efficacy of the ground sheet and whether they had enough waterproofs.

'Wasn't the weather amazing,' said Vi on the way back.

'There were too many people,' said Patrick.

'We should go on an adventure every weekend,' she said.

When they got back, the plants in the window boxes were dead, and there was an envelope for Patrick from the Ministry of Defence. He was chuffed.

'Really, Patrick?' said Vi. 'We talked about this. You said you were going to teach yourself programming and start your own business. I thought you wanted to be an entrepreneur.'

Although the interview had gone well, no one was more surprised than Patrick when he received an offer from the MoD. He inquired if they had made a mistake.

'We don't only want highflyers. We also look for people who can keep tabs on our personnel abroad and deal calmly with any issue that might rear its head. You fit the bill. You will be our glue,' was the reply.

'But I want to be married to an entrepreneur,' said Vi. 'Someone more romantic than mere paste.'

'Really?' Patrick smiled. He loved her, but he hadn't asked the question. He hadn't thought his exotic, bohemian Vi would agree to anything so formal and binding as marriage.

He had been nervous about gambling with his future, but if Vi was ready to commit to him, anything was possible. She hauled him out of the rut he worked so hard to maintain. With Vi, he would put aside the offer from the MoD. It was exhilarating. For the first time Patrick was living in the moment.

He telephoned his parents with the good news.

Patrick and Vi were invited to Sunday lunch.

'Congratulations,' said his mother, kissing them each in turn as they arrived. 'What an exciting turn of events.'

'Lovely surprise could have knocked me over…,' said Patrick's father, as he struggled to open a bottle of champagne.

At lunch, when their plates were filled with roast beef, vegetables and crisp Yorkshire puddings, and the gravy boat had been passed around, Patrick's mother said. 'We always hoped when you left university, you might step up a gear. Are you sure you want to throw everything away before you've even started?'

'You're only young once,' said Patrick, rocking slightly in his chair like a roly-poly toy, hoping to express confidence, but spouting cliches like his father.

'Patrick has some fabulous ideas and is working really hard to create something exciting and individual,' said Vi.

'Well how lovely.' His mother arched her eyebrows before turning to Patrick. 'We were amazed when you bagged a first and then passed those tricky Civil Service exams. It is an exceptional achievement.'

'If you feel so strongly, perhaps they will allow me to defer for a year,' said Patrick. 'Then I can try out my idea… and see how it goes.' He had already bought several pads of lined paper and some gel pens and cleared an area of the kitchen table for his new project.

'Your father will be so disappointed if you turn down this opportunity.'

'No need to kick the gift horse in the mouth,' said his father as Vi helped his mother clear the table.

Patrick had not realised that his life had been planned out for him, and he was not going to be allowed to career off script. His parents had never believed in delaying the inevitable, but Patrick had hoped they would be happy for him to forge his own path.

'It would be foolish to dither,' said Patrick's mother as she spooned up the blancmange. 'You have this unexpected offer. You should accept graciously.' She passed Patrick a bowl of the jelly-like goo. 'But, of course, you mustn't feel you have to take our advice. It is just that … advice.'

'We wouldn't want to change your mind if your heart is set on this entrepreneurial nonsense,' said his father. 'But a bird in the hand … think of the pension … and there is always the possibility of an honour.'

'We may be getting ahead of ourselves here,' said Patrick, but he knew when they married, Vi would want a home and a garden and the finances to travel.

'I rather wonder if my father isn't well, and my parents would like to be assured I'm sorted,' he said to Vi on the way back to their flat stuck in traffic on the North Circular. 'They seem very set on my joining the Civil Service.

'They're just old and insecure and come from a generation where a job is for life. Then, you signed up for some boring, dead-end career and kept going till the bitter end.'

'My father has slowed down. I think his leg might be giving him problems, balance is the key.'

'And you working for the MoD is something they can brag to their friends about,' said Vi.

They married. With the promise of employment at the MoD and a loan from his mother, which he tried not to think of as a bribe, Patrick and Vi secured a huge mortgage and bought a tiny run-down terraced house at the bottom of Wimbledon Hill.

'Well, this confirms it,' said Vi, giving him a peck on the cheek as he set off for Whitehall on the first day of his new job. 'I never thought it would come to this, Patrick, but now, you are to be a cog in the machine.'

Looking back, Patrick wondered if it was then, so early in their relationship, that she had started to doubt him. But he knew he wasn't really a risk taker, and being married to Vi was as exciting as he wanted life to be.

He needed structure to shine. At the Ministry of Defence, bit by bit, Patrick excelled at being the glue. From behind his desk, he held the ships and planes and tanks together. He began to be recognised within his department for his cool head. His skill was seeing clearly when too many people had too many ideas. With his calm manner, Patrick could divide a problem into constituent, manageable parts and prioritise. It was a critical ability within his group.

Quite quickly, Patrick began to climb the greasy pole.

A Beginning

One night, Vi, snuggling up to Patrick, said. 'Let's have a baby?'

Patrick pulled Vi close and kissed the top of her head. He didn't know he had been waiting for this moment, but he felt a warm glow. Lucky he was doing well at work, they could move up the hill to a bigger house with a proper garden and they would need to get a four-door car. He felt his chest puff. He would give Vi all she needed to make a new home. A new love for Vi washed through him as he thought of the family they were going to make together.

Pregnancy had made Vi furious.

'This is a terrible mistake,' she wailed. 'I'm being reshaped from the inside out. I'll never be the same again.'

Patrick loved her new rounding body and the way she rolled when she walked. Vi had been small and wiry, a coiled spring ready for action, her transformation delighted him. He saw the mother emerging.

'You look rather gorgeous,' said Patrick, supporting her head on his shoulder as she sat beside him on the sofa with her feet up. While she cradled her stomach as they watched TV, he stroked her hair, pulling his fingers through her curls, feeling the resistance.

They drove over to Queen Mary's Roehampton when Vi's contractions began. Patrick held Vi's hand during her awkward labour, taking the blame. After the birth, Vi lay exhausted. When she had had enough, the midwife took the baby from Vi's limp grip and placed the child in Patrick's arms.

'He's an Oliver, don't you think?' said Vi.

'Whatever you like,' he said.

Patrick looked down into the sleepy, inchoate face, eyes struggling to focus. His heart swelled to think that such a tiny being should have come from him and Vi. How was that even possible?

Ollie was a beautiful baby who didn't need much sleep, or any at all.

'I suppose we'd better have another one. Otherwise, he'll be spoiled rotten,' Vi said almost a year later.

'Are you sure?' said Patrick. She couldn't be thinking clearly, cloaked in the fog of early motherhood. Vi had only just stopped breastfeeding. She was only just beginning to resurface.

'Quick,' she said. 'Before I change my mind.'

Toby arrived eighteen months after Ollie. It was another difficult birth.

Patrick was amazed. Vi had done it again, another miracle, a bundle of cells had become a baby that would grow to be a man.

The new addition charmed everyone all day and screamed all night. Ollie was a happy, burbling toddler who still wasn't interested in sleeping. Patrick and Vi limped through their lives. At least Patrick could escape to the office, saving all his able brain cells for the working day.

'I think you need some help,' said Patrick's mother. She had come over for tea one Saturday to meet her latest grandson. Perched on the sofa's edge amongst muslin cloths and unpaired socks, she held her mug high, out of Ollie's curious reach.

'That would be kind,' said Patrick, leaning back into the pile of ironing on a matching armchair. His mother and Vi didn't always see eye to eye, but he was sure they could work something out. 'A couple of afternoons a week would make a real difference to Vi,' he added.

'I don't think *I* could be much help.' His mother's eyes roamed over the mayhem. 'I was thinking more of a nurse who could establish some kind of routine. I shall look in my book. Somebody will be able to recommend someone.'

A live-in maternity nurse arrived for a month courtesy of Patrick's mother.

'I hate having someone else living in my space,' said Vi.

But the new house at the top of the hill had plenty of room, and order was restored.

Back on her feet, Vi had the energy to enjoy the children and seemed to thrive on the chaos the two small, demanding boys generated, as long as somebody else was there to tidy up after them. After four weeks, the nurse left, and Patrick found a cleaner, Mrs Stapleford.

As the boys hurtled through their days, Vi ran the house like a ship heading towards the rocks and Patrick felt the need to be a steadying force. He relied on the routine of work, his hours of calm analysis and adult engagement to keep him sane, then he would race home to be an anchor of sorts against the storm. He would help with the boys' bathtime and read them a story before bed.

Patrick's own childhood had been sedate and organised. His time was spent reading books and playing with building bricks. Ollie never sat still and was much more like Patrick's boisterous cousin Jack had been. Of course, Ollie was only a toddler, and Toby was just beginning to move, rocking back and forth on his knees, getting ready to crawl. They would calm down when they were older.

Patrick would get involved at the weekends, if Vi let him, though sometimes it was hard to know where he could be of most use.

He followed her through the house, but she brushed him off. Vi buzzed, moving mail from the kitchen table to the desk in the study. She put Ollie's shoes at the bottom of the stairs, returning to the kitchen to turn the sausages. Then went back into the hall peeking through the door to the den to check on the boys who were sitting in front of cartoons.

Patrick chased after her like a puppy.

'Do you think the boys are watching too much TV?' he asked.

'Really?' Vi stopped in her tracks. She turned to stare him down, before continuing with her chores. 'For goodness' sake, Patrick, stop trailing after me like some stray. You are worse than the boys.'

'I'm trying to talk to you, but you won't stand still.'

'I have things to do, Patrick. And what about anyway? What's more important than feeding your children and keeping your home? Can't it wait until lunchtime?'

She carried a bundle of the boy's muddy clothes through to the utility room. From the door, Patrick watched as she pushed the laundry into the machine.

'I want to talk, connect… we should do more together,' he said.

Vi rolled her eyes.

'If you helped more around the house, we would be doing things together,' she said with a thin smile as she pushed past him back into the kitchen.

'Let me take the rubbish out,' he said. That would be a good contribution, a man's job, but as he spoke, Patrick knew his tone was all wrong, too noble, as though he was doing her a favour.

'It's lunchtime now - do it later,' said Vi, pressing the water jug into his arms. 'Can you fill this? And get the boys.'

Patrick couldn't understand what had gone wrong. It was true, Vi's life had changed beyond recognition, while he loved his job, and his routine had remained the same, but it was Vi who had wanted a baby.

'I'm bored, bored, bored,' she said. 'I thought this would be fun, having children, but it is dull and monotonous. I've decided to go back to work. I want to talk to other adults. I want to be me again, Patrick. The old me is somewhere. I will find her.'

'Why did you want children if you don't want to be a mother?'

'Oh, Patrick, I want it all! I want to be a mother, have a career, and be free to do what I want, when I want.'

'But what about us … as a family?'

'There is something you could do for me, Patrick. You won't notice a difference – but it would make me happy,' said Vi.

Patrick wasn't sure that Vi's idea of what was good for them as a family was good for him as a man, but he was willing to make the effort. He saw a doctor and booked an appointment for the end of the summer.

The Snip

'Just a small prick,' said the doctor as she readied the syringe. Patrick saw her exchange a smile with the attending nurse, a running joke no doubt in this department, before she explained. 'This is the local anaesthetic.'

Patrick braced himself. His palms were sweaty against the edges of the plastic mattress of the gurney as his grip tightened and his heart quickened. He hadn't told the doctor. He didn't want to make a fuss, but Patrick was terrified of needles.

At school, queueing for his BCG injection, Patrick had been petrified. The tension rising the closer he inched towards the door and Matron waiting with the syringe. Of course, at school, he had to be macho about the whole thing and couldn't let on. He would never have heard the end of it.

'All numb? Here we go,' said the doctor as she readied the scalpel.

'Shit,' said Patrick. 'Sorry.' Argh - he shouldn't apologise. It showed weakness, and what did he have to be defensive about. Sorry for being here, lying exposed on this table, while someone chopped at his bits. This was the oddest thing he had ever agreed to do.

'You've made a good choice,' said the doctor. 'We'd like more men to sign up for this procedure.'

'It was my wife's idea,' said Patrick, sounding even more pathetic. What a wimp he was. Patrick couldn't look at the doctor.

He had almost asked for a male surgeon, but it had seemed childish, and Vi would have scoffed. So here he was, prone on a gurney in an impersonal clinic, covered in a modesty sheet with a rectangular window in the relevant area to allow access. Patrick listened to the sounds of the surgical instruments clanging in the stainless-steel kidney dish on the medical trolley wheeled close by. He could smell the antiseptic and caught sight of a purple-tinged iodine swab pinched in surgical scissors as it made an arc from dish to wound. Patrick sighed and concentrated on the plain white ceiling without even a crack to distract him.

Doctor and nurse barely exchanged a word. Patrick was glad there was no more small talk, and they were concentrating on the job at hand. This procedure which must be so mundane for them was life-changing for him. A small cut, a chop here, a chop there, sew it up and we can all go home. Patrick tried not to think about the weird tugging and pulling that was going on.

At the pre-op appointment, the doctor had grilled them both.

'Current ideas of masculinity generally preclude voluntary infertility. You are thirty-two, quite young to have this procedure. It is ninety-nine percent effective. So, we need to confirm that you are both in agreement. It is reversible, but reconstruction is not always guaranteed to be successful.'

Patrick barely listened and had been unable to look the doctor in the eye, and that was before she became so well acquainted with his equipment. It didn't make a difference. He wouldn't have chosen to do something so intimate, so permanently emasculating. A vasectomy didn't fit in with his idea of who he was as a man. But Vi had pushed for it, and he had agreed.

They had the two boys, aged two and six months now, and that was plenty. Children were expensive, and now was the moment for him to concentrate on his career.

Since her last pregnancy, Vi hadn't wanted him to touch her. He had been worried she might have postnatal depression. She said she was sick of the pill, it gave her headaches and bad skin, and she didn't like the messy alternatives; found them a turn-off. If having a vasectomy encouraged Vi to welcome him back into bed, he was up for it.

But this was something he would never want to talk about. He wouldn't tell anyone about this ever. Not having to think about fertility was supposed to set you free, but Patrick did not feel emboldened, he felt ambushed and diminished.

On his way out, the nurse gave him some ice packs.

Vi was waiting for him outside the Urology department. Patrick shuffled across the car park.

'There you are,' she said, as though he had been playing truant. He checked his watch. He had been gone for less than an hour.

Vi helped Patrick manoeuvre himself into the car. On the journey home, he sat on one of the ice packs wrapped in a towel. He wondered if he was destined to waddle forever like an old cowboy, saddle sore and bow-legged. He was glad the boys were with his parents for the afternoon. He didn't feel like engaging in rough and tumble. A bit of sport on TV and a cup of tea might begin to restore him.

The doctor had said there would be no difference in performance. Patrick had wanted to believe her and to his relief she was right. Once Patrick got over the initial unease that he would be firing blanks, he was back on form.

'So, how is it?' he asked Vi when he was, at last, allowed onto her side of the bed.

'Well,' she said. 'How does it feel for you?'

'I'm not sure yet. You?' Were they going to bat away at the issue indefinitely.

'Oh, nothing changes with you, Patrick. You are always the same.'

He wasn't sure if this was a compliment or an insult. It was admirable to be steady, but he suspected Vi thought their sex boring.

Unravelling

That autumn, Vi went back to work part-time and an au pair came to live in. An Australian on a gap year, travelling and working.

'I miss it, travelling. Even, not the travelling, but the ability to be spontaneous,' said Vi, sipping her second glass of wine while Patrick got supper together.

'Are you jealous of the au pair? You were that age once. We've had our turn.'

'Always so helpful, Patrick. I don't know why I didn't think about how much of a difference having the boys would make. But your job is the worst. Such long hours and lousy holidays.'

'If I get in early, I get back to see Ollie and Toby in the evening. Anyway, I'm just trying to put things into perspective. It will get easier with the boys. It already is easier with the au pair here. And I'm qualifying for more holiday every year. And where I am is much better for time off than the private sector.'

'Thanks, Patrick. I feel much better already.' Vi chugged down her wine.

'Is there any more of that,' said Patrick, looking in the fridge.

After six months, the au pair left to go travelling. Vi stood on the doorstep and watched as she packed the bulging rucksack, almost bigger than herself, into the boot of her taxi and jumped in the back seat on her way to the airport.

'I wish I could go too,' Vi said to Patrick, who was diverting the boys with juice and biscuits in the kitchen.

A new Danish au pair arrived.

Shortly after, one Friday coming home earlier than usual, Patrick bumped into Vi, rushing out the door.

'Oh Patrick, there you are. I'm off, remember … spa weekend.' She gave him a kiss.

'I don't remember us talking about that,' said Patrick, but she was already gone.

It was a good idea. Vi should take time out. She deserved to be pampered.

Vi was back on Sunday evening.

'It was just a weekend with the girls, Patrick. Keep your hair on,' said Vi when he asked where she had been.

The next time it happened, Vi was gone when he got back from work. There was a note on the kitchen table.

'She didn't say. It is normal, no, for the wife to … take off?' The au pair was amused by his bewilderment.

Patrick didn't like this girl so much.

When Vi reappeared, she refused to say where she had been or who she was with.

'It's not *me* time if I share the details with you,' she said rather smugly.

This was a step too far. They were a couple. He didn't want to seem demanding or jealous, but he was. And he had missed her. But she seemed to have taken to provoking Patrick rather than challenging life.

He didn't want to demean the effort that looking after children entailed, but he had done his bit. He had looked after them all weekend and he had had the vasectomy when she asked. What more was he supposed to do?

'So, what is it all about, this need to get away?' He said when the boys were settled, and the au pair had retired to her studio bedroom in the loft extension.

'I really think yoga might be the thing. I've been going to a new class. Wine?'

'Thanks.'

She refilled their glasses.

'I wondered if you were having an affair.' Patrick laughed to soften the blow. He hadn't meant to say it, but it was all he had been thinking about.

'For goodness' sake, Patrick, are you trying to pick a fight?'

'I just couldn't think what would take you away from us, the boys, me.'

'I need to have time to be myself, Patrick. I can't be a good mother if I don't know who I am anymore.'

Patrick thought it would be unwise to mention the cleaner and the au pair, but as usual, Vi was one step ahead of him.

'I don't want outside help. I want you. You say we are a couple, but how involved are you really in our family? I want you to be part of their lives. Share the grind. But no, you have chosen to prioritise work.'

'Well, someone has to. And that's unfair, Vi. I'm home to see the boys most evenings and I've been with them all weekend …'

'So, who do you think I was going off with?' Hmm? Just the girls, of course! Though, now I think about it, I've always thought Jack was juicy. Maybe I should give him a ring. A more exciting version … of you.'

'Jack?' His head jerked involuntarily. 'My cousin?' Patrick tried to look nonchalant. 'You have been having an affair with Jack?'

'Oh, keep your shirt on, Patrick. I'm only teasing.'

Patrick gave a shrug and finished his wine. He didn't believe it for a moment. He had never seen Vi and Jack exchange a word or ever look like they were interested in each other. But he had once told her about the time Jack came to stay with him in his first year of university and ended up sleeping with Patrick's girlfriend. Vi was just prodding old wounds.

Their sex life dwindled and was now all but non-existent. Patrick didn't like to bring it up, but it seemed a shame after all he had been through.

The next morning, Patrick woke up next to Vi. She was still asleep, her breath verging on a snore. Watching her, he felt no tenderness, and it came to him that he didn't want to share a bed or a room for that matter with Vi anymore.

He got up and drove to work. He liked to get in early and get a head start on the day. He had files to read and statistics to make sense of, but the whole day, he struggled to concentrate. He tried to summon up the reasons he loved Vi, but he couldn't think why he had married her in the first place let alone why he loved her now. By the end of the afternoon of engrossing research on the new American iteration of the M270, Patrick knew he needed to consider his marriage thoroughly. Yesterday, he loved Vi, or at least he thought he did, and today, he didn't want to go home. The filaments that held him to her, those bonds as strong as cobwebs, had been blown apart by … by something small … by a single mention of Jack's name.

Patrick tried to pay attention to the traffic on the way home. It was too late for the rush hour, but cars slowed to a snail's pace. There was maintenance work on Battersea Park Road. Patrick mulled over the events of the last few years. Life with Vi was exhilarating, but he had been living too close to the sun. Patrick felt scorched and singed. As the car crawled along, he tried to think what would be best for the boys. Vi would be furious. If it came to a fight, she would be awarded custody. Patrick wouldn't like that, so he had to be careful. He had to be calm and reasonable.

He eased through the final set of lights and sped homeward. Suddenly, he felt light as air. While he had been thinking about the practicalities, his subconscious had imagined it already so and he knew it was over now. He would tell Vi as soon as he got in.

Patrick pulled up onto the driveway. He sat in the car for a moment, taking in the quiet of the evening. His mind was made up. He got out of the car. The house was a dark bruise in the soft night air. There were no lights on. It was the au pairs night off. He paused his key in the air, ready for the lock. Had Vi been due to take the boys somewhere. Had there been a sleepover planned, he couldn't recall.

He let himself in. The house was tidy. Everything as it should be. Only with the boys, nothing was ever as it should be. Patrick wandered through to the kitchen, suspicious of the calm. On the table propped against an empty bottle of wine was a note.

The boys are with your mother. I am on a flight to India. I'm not coming back. Vi

Patrick looked around the clean kitchen. He had been abandoned. He stared at the note in disbelief. Vi had outdone him again.

A Reasonable Man

Just when Patrick thought things might go further with Margot, Vi came back, and this time to stay, or so she said.

The first time Vi had gone to find herself, had he enabled her to leave? He had been happy to no longer have to deal with the vacillating, the tears and the tantrums, but sometimes, he wondered if he should have done more to try and keep his family together. That might have been better for the children. Vi had probably been suffering from postnatal depression.

After two minutes on the phone with her, he no longer felt guilty.

'I had to get rid of the toxins. Clear my mind of all those bad memories, the bad experiences,' Vi said. 'You, Patrick, know best of all what I went through.'

'Really?' he said, with an uncharacteristic note of sarcasm. His heart was beginning to pound. She made him feel so angry. Breathe.

In that first six months that Vi had taken to travel around India, Patrick had just about managed to get his life straightened out and the boys settled into a routine without their mother. Then for a year or more after that, while the divorce was running its course, she continued to travel. Sometimes for weeks, sometimes for months. Then she would turn up with little warning to sign papers and take Ollie and Toby out for the day. Patrick didn't know where she stayed.

This time, there was a permanence to her plans.

'Well, I'm back. I had a great time, thank you for asking. I've learnt so much about myself. About what was wrong in my life. That would be you, Patrick, in case you were wondering. Now the divorce is finally settled, I feel like a new person. All the yoga and relaxation techniques really helped.'

'I'm so glad you feel well rested,' Patrick said. His jaw was so tightly clenched he was surprised any sound came out at all.

'I've bought a house in Raynes Park, in fact I've moved in. So, we're neighbours,' she said. 'You, Patrick, I notice, haven't moved an inch. Still in the same house, with the same routines.'

'You know I didn't want to move the boys, what with so much uncertainty in their lives.' Why was he even bothering to explain. A bequest from Patrick's Godfather had come through just in time to pay the divorce settlement. It had been a relief not to have to sell up.

'You always were touchy about money. You must be doing better than I thought if you can hold onto the house. Anyway, I'll be around for a while,' she said. 'I'd like to see more of my boys.'

'They will be excited to see you,' said Patrick.

He put down the phone and took a deep breath. Sores, he thought had healed over, were weeping, ripped open by the sound of her voice.

When he took the boys round, Vi was standing in the doorway of her new house to welcome her sons. She did look very well, back to her svelte self. Patrick didn't want to be accused of staring, but she was wearing more Lycra than he was used to seeing outside of a gym. He turned away quickly, studying the weeds in the path up to the house. Ollie and Toby were thrilled to see their mother and ran to give her a hug. The boys disappeared into the house with Vi. The front door closed.

Their first visit at the new house was short. Patrick did a supermarket shop and then waited in the car until the boys were ready.

'I want to see the boys regularly,' said Vi as she brought Ollie and Toby out. 'I don't want some strange woman looking after them.'

Vi must have meant the nanny. She didn't know about his new relationship. Nobody did. The thought of Margot cheered him up. He managed a smile for Vi.

'Of course,' he said, getting out of the car to fasten the boys into their car seats. 'You are their mother.'

This could work out well for him. Patrick would be able to see far more of Margot if Ollie and Toby went to stay with their mother. But Vi had conditions. She only wanted the boys, every other weekend. Patrick would not be getting rid of the nanny any time soon. Vi had phoned him wheedling, but he wouldn't have to give Vi an allowance if Ollie and Toby weren't living with her. There was some satisfaction in that.

'Don't be ridiculous. I'm not paying you to look after your own children for a weekend,' he said.

'Feeling parsimonious, are you, Patrick?' she had laughed down the phone.

Parsimonious! The house she had been able to buy with her share of the divorce settlement was within walking distance of the school, had four bedrooms, and a good garden. It was bigger than Vi needed. He hadn't been mean, he'd been fleeced.

Patrick slammed down his phone and paced his study, trying to steady his breath. He didn't owe her anything anymore. He tried to relax his hands which had tensed into balls as he marched up and down the small room. He could still hear her cackle in his head.

He wasn't tight-fisted. Patrick had a sense of duty, but his biggest weakness was that he always wanted to be the good guy. Of course, Vi knew all his failings and fragility. She had studied them for years. It made him so furious that she could so easily get under his skin.

Patrick got back early from work that Friday and helped the boys pack some clothes and toys to take with them when they went on their first sleepover at Vi's. Ollie had been excited about staying over at his mother's new house but became quiet as the weekend neared.

'Will I still be able to do football on Saturday morning?' he asked.

'Don't you worry. I've told Mummy exactly where you need to be when. I wrote it down for her on a piece of paper, so she wouldn't forget.' Patrick reassured him.

Toby was still feeling his way. He was only three and wasn't sure he wanted to sleep somewhere different. He was confused that he would need to pack anything at all. Patrick gave him a new backpack covered in a dinosaur print and he became more enthusiastic about choosing what to take. Then Patrick drove them the short distance to Vi's. Toby chattered away, but Ollie was silent. Looking at his sad, little face in the rearview mirror, Patrick understood how he felt.

'It's going to be such an adventure,' Patrick said, trying to sound cheerful. 'And it will only be two days and two sleeps, and you will be back home.'

At Vi's house, Toby clung to Patrick's trouser leg. Patrick sympathised. It had been two years since Vi had left that first time. She had yo-yoed in and out of the boys' lives since then. It was hard to keep up with her, but Patrick had to give Ollie and Toby a chance to have a normal relationship with their mother.

Patrick waved jauntily to the boys as he pulled away. Around the corner, he slowed the car as, fighting with the tightness of the seatbelt, he pulled a tissue from his trouser pocket.

Back at the house, there was an eerie peace. Patrick wandered from room to room, picking up abandoned games and putting them in the toy box. He went outside and wrangled the mower from the garden shed and cut the grass, righting Ollie's goalposts when he had finished. Inside, Toby's floppy bunny lay on the large sofa they would all cuddle up on to read stories. Patrick sat down next to the rabbit. His reflection in the blank television screen stared murkily back. Patrick fetched a cup of tea and wondered if there was any sport he could watch.

He flicked channels, but nothing suited his mood.

His phone buzzed.

'I imagine you are already enjoying yourself with adult pursuits, but if it is not too much trouble could you bring that blue bunny over? I don't think I'll get Toby to sleep without it,' said Vi.

'No problem,' said Patrick. 'I'll be able to get to you and back before the stripper arrives.'

He could hear Vi's intolerant sigh. 'Just leave it on the doorstep. I don't want you upsetting the boys.'

When he returned, Patrick felt lonely sitting on the sofa without his stuffed friend. But Toby's need was greater than his. Patrick was just thinking he should do something about supper when he noticed he had a text. It must have come through when he was driving. It was from Margot. He was surprised, it was her niece's birthday, and Margot was away in the Cotswolds with her sister and her family for the weekend.

I'll be back in London earlier than expected tmrw. Want to get a late lunch? x

Patrick's heart lifted.

A Proposal

The Old Vicarage

In her early teens, Margot's parents had died in a car accident. At the time, Margot and her older sister, Lily, were away at school. Margot couldn't grasp the sudden absence in her life. In January, when she had been dropped off at boarding school, she had two parents, by half term, she and Lily were orphans. Margot didn't cry. She knew what she had been told couldn't be right. As the term progressed and the truth sank in, she was lost. It was like the longest, emptiest Sunday afternoon … forever.

For years, the feeling stayed with Margot that her parents had no right to leave, and her mother and father lingered in the corridors of her mind. If her thoughts took a wrong turn, old memories would engulf her in an avalanche of loss. Margot wobbled when she thought how easily her future was tipped on its head. It scared her that some mere moment in time could change everything she took for granted. As time passed, she realised that what she needed to do, was build a new family of her own.

By the Easter holidays, a decision had been made and their father's only relation, a much older half-sister took both girls in. Aunt Angela came to collect them from school, driven in her old Humber by her gardener Burr. Their aunt must have been in her sixties. She seemed ancient to Margot, covered in soft, powdered wrinkles that smelt of lavender. The car smelt of earth and petrol and crawled through the lanes to West Clandon.

As they had driven up the short drive, Margot noticed that the house was made of the same pale, cold stone as the nearby church.

'Welcome to The Old Vicarage. The vicar no longer lives here. He now resides on the other side of the village in a more convenient modern house, in a much less convenient location,' said their aunt when they arrived.

The sisters hesitated in the hall, listening to the steady click of the long case clock, clutching their bags as their aunt took off her mauve tweed coat. She turned to look at them.

'This is your home now.' said Aunt Angela.

Margot and Lily exchanged a glance.

Of course, they had been to The Old Vicarage before, but the house felt like a stranger now they couldn't leave with their parents at the end of the day. The house was the same, but the curtains and furniture seemed heavy with their loss.

Lily was a few years older than Margot and was more able to move on. She already had plans for her life and had been thinking about university, but Margot, trapped by age and circumstance, needed love.

Aunt Angela didn't have children and seemed ancient and busy. The Old Vicarage was large, but Margot didn't think there would be room for two teenagers in her aunt's organised life.

Their aunt spent ages in her garden and was a member of the local bridge club. She did flowers for the church and helped with the tea and coffee after the Sunday Service. She encouraged Margot to get involved and engage with the local community. Margot didn't want to, she didn't want to like her aunt, and she didn't want to do old people things.

Aunt Angela persisted, and as the months passed, she became Margot's mainstay. Margot learnt that despite any difficulties or misunderstandings between them, her aunt's love was unconditional, and her hugs healing, and Margot began to mend.

So, when Margot decided Patrick must be the one, she took him to The Old Vicarage to seek her aunt's approval. They arrived promptly for lunch.

'So lovely to meet you,' said Aunt Angela, taking Patrick's hand. 'Could you sort some drinks?' she added, wafting a lavender-scented, trailing arm in the direction of the drink's table.

'We've only just met,' said Margot under her breath to her aunt as Patrick crossed the room to the side table where a range of different sherries in rich golden and amber hues glowed in crystal decanters.

'Well, you must be serious, or you wouldn't have brought him home to meet me. You look quite the couple.' Aunt Angela hissed back. 'You mustn't let him get away.'

'Don't worry, I don't intend to,' said Margot, smiling. 'I really think he is the one.'

'Good for you.' Her aunt patted Margot's arm before joining Patrick at the sideboard. 'Have you found everything you need?'

'Yes, thank you. What would you like, Miss Parrish?'

'Oh, something sweet, please. And call me Angela.'

Her aunt was right; Margot had never brought anyone else back to The Old Vicarage. Patrick was different. She had not been considering a divorcee as a partner, but seeing Patrick with his boys at Jenni's wedding, she saw what an excellent parent he was, and that was partly what she was looking for, a family man. It didn't hurt that Patrick was tall and dark, with those soft, blue eyes that would make any heart melt.

She watched her aunt and Patrick chatting in the sunshine of the bay window. Aunt Angela liked the company of men.

'You know, I never intended to remain unmarried after Charles died .... somehow, I didn't have another opportunity,' Aunt Angela had once told Margot, who found it hard to believe her aunt had ever been young or in love.

'But if you wanted to, you could have married someone else, couldn't you?' Margot had said, young enough to think boys grew on trees.

'Well, you would have thought, but those were different times. I was one of many young women made old by the war. Afterwards, there was a shortage of eligible young men. In truth I was a little lost. And then, much later, you girls came along and brought me such joy.'

Patrick handed Margot a glass of tawny sherry, thick and heady. The cut glass detail on the bowl made her think of acorn cups for fairies.

Aunt Angela served venison and game chips for lunch. The meat was tender perfection, but the chips needed hunting down. Margot watched as Patrick chased crisps around his plate. She caught his eye over the table display of roses, alchemilla and lavender. She swallowed a chuckle along with a forkful of carrots.

'So, what do you do, Patrick?' asked Aunt Angela.

I work at the MoD in Whitehall,' said Patrick. 'An admin job in logistics.'

'How fascinating.'

They had apple crumble for pudding. As she dipped her spoon into the crunch of oats and the soft fruit, Margot remembered how in autumn, when she was back from school, she would help pick the apples from the trees in the old orchard. Her aunt had shown Margot how to store the fruit on the wooden slatted shelving in the garden shed. Apple crumble had been a staple pudding in the winter months of Margot's adolescence.

After lunch, they returned to the drawing room and drank coffee from demitasses. Margot's aunt offered Patrick a cigarette from the silver-plated case that lived on the mantelpiece.

'No, thank you. I've never smoked,' he said.

'No one smokes any more. Do you remember my bridge afternoons, Margot?'

'By the end of the afternoon, I could hardly see out the windows. Are you still playing?'

'Not as often as I'd like, only two or three times a week. It gets harder and harder to make up a four … people do keep becoming … unavailable.'

'I thought nothing would keep your friends from bridge,' said Margot.

'Well, it's hard to keep a good game going from beyond the grave.' Aunt Angela laughed.

'Oh, I'm sorry,' said Margot. 'How crass of me.' Aunt Angela, who had once seemed so old, now seemed quite sprightly, but she was nearing eighty.

'But you are obviously still enjoying gardening,' said Patrick, saving the moment.

'Oh, yes, the wonders of the natural world never cease to bring me joy.'

On the way back in the car, Margot congratulated Patrick.

'Wow, you really can turn on the charm.'

'I have an aunt, myself, you know,' he said. 'Or are you complaining that I haven't used my charms on you … yet?'

Margot knew what she wanted to say but not how to say it, the moment passed, and Patrick filled the silence.

'You'll know something is seriously wrong if I ask you about your roses.'

Margot laughed. All the giggles that had been swallowed bubbled out of her. She felt released from her childhood. Patrick had set her free. She loved Aunt Angela and was appreciative of all she had done, but Margot's childhood had been stained by her parent's deaths. Now, when she went back to her aunt's house, it would be just that, Angela's house. Margot would be a visitor, no longer haunted by the past.

Patrick laughed with her. That was when she knew she would say yes if Patrick asked.

He didn't.

Vi's husband

'Has he asked?' said Jenni, bright and poised, folding herself into a leather carver when they met for lunch one weekend at a country pub outside Guildford. 'I can see it in your face. You're beaming. You've been going out for what, nearly six months?'

'Not quite, just over four,' said Margot, still thinking she could hold the joy of her growing love for Patrick to herself.

'I'd only known Jack for three months when we got engaged. We just knew we were made for each other. So, what's holding you back?'

'It's way too soon. I haven't met the boys yet, apart from briefly at your wedding.' Four months was nothing, but Jenni was right. Patrick was wonderful. Margot couldn't stop smiling.

'He's perfect for you,' said Jenni. 'I can't believe you of all people would be so forward as to drop your number in a stranger's pocket. I told Jack. He thought it was wild. He said he never thought posh Margot in her big hat would be so forward.'

'Posh?' Margot tore into the bread the waiter had brought over. 'Jack's the posh one, isn't he? How's married life? Pregnant yet?'

'Touché,' said Jenni, finishing her gin and tonic. 'Honestly, it's great. I couldn't be happier. But it's not a year yet and what with Jack being away so much and my getting used to army quarters.'

'How are they?'

'It's the people rather than … I mean everyone's very friendly, but you know how it is … I just need to find the like-minded ones.' She waved to the bartender for another round. 'So, what's up with Patrick?'

'I guess he doesn't want to complicate his life too much just now, or at least Ollie and Toby's. You might have heard, Vi's back.'

'Is that really a valid reason? Just saying. I mean, you don't want to hang around, do you? Have you met her?'

'No, not yet.'

'I've only chatted to her a couple of times. Their marriage was already over when I started going out with Jack. But she has this reputation for popping up unannounced at family dos. Have to say,

I kinda like her verve. Vi always struck me as one of those people who is really engaged with life. On it, you know.'

'Actually, I don't really want to hear anything positive about the woman.'

'I'd like to tell you she's a harridan, but she's good fun, up for a laugh.'

'But mad as a hatter.' Patrick had told Margot Vi was unbalanced.

'That's not fair,' said Jenni, taking the drinks from the waiter. They placed their orders. Fish and chips was Margot's go-to pub lunch, Jenni went for the Caesar salad.

'I was trying to be nice about Vi,' said Margot. 'Nag, scold, absentee, were the other words that came to mind.'

'I'd say she just wants to embrace all of life, doesn't want to miss anything.'

How could Jenni even try to persuade Margot that Vi was interesting? It was the last thing Margot wanted to hear. She needed Vi to be in the wrong so Patrick could be in the right.

'Cheers.' Jenni raised her glass. 'Vi likes an adventure. Likes to travel, she's a free spirit.'

'Cheers. But, if she didn't want to settle down, why did she marry and have children?' Margot couldn't think of anything more wonderful than belonging - making a home, being wanted, caring for someone and having a purpose.

'I think she thought it would be an adventure of a different sort.'

'Isn't it?' said Margot, crunching on the battered tail of her fish.

'Honestly, everything's an adventure with Jack, but so far I can only vouch for the married part of the equation.'

'Well, you seem to have worked that out,' said Margot, smiling at her friend.

'He'll be away again soon, on manoeuvres or something. It's a bit stressful, to be honest. Anyway, if you've made up your mind, you could always ask Patrick,' said Jenni.

Four months was hardly any time to build a relationship. Patrick wouldn't want to rush, with one failed marriage behind him. But, for Margot, time was passing. Though what was a couple of months, compared to all the wasted years in her twenties, failing to find a partner with whom to have a child. She should pull herself together, she was not yet thirty, she still had plenty of time. She was sure Patrick would propose soon. Margot just had to convince him that she was the right one and now was the right time.

'You've seen the house?'

'Yes, of course. Patrick took me one Saturday when the boys were with Vi.'

'It's good?'

'Needs a little work.' She would not betray Patrick, but her mind returned to that first visit to the house.

It had been early in September when Patrick finally invited her home to the house where he had lived with Vi. Margot had been curious and excited. She had thought very carefully about what to wear, not just her dress or her shoes. As she rummaged through her cupboard, one of Aunt Angela's odd phrases popped into Margot's head, always wear clean underwear in case you get hit by a bus, not that Patrick was a bus. In the end she chose a soft silk shirt loose over jeans.

Very sweetly, Patrick had picked her up from the station.

'I could have walked,' she said, feeling almost breathless. She felt that Patrick must be able to sense her excitement, but he seemed his normal calm self.

'But it's uphill,' he said, though he must have done the walk many times.

The front door was dark wood with brass fixtures and stained-glass rectangular panels. The hall still had the original tiled floor.

'Let me get you a cup of tea,' said Patrick leading her through the house to the kitchen.

Vi's choices, dark cupboards, dark walls, too much terracotta paint and tiles. Margot could see that once perhaps the room had had a Mexican theme, but it had been neglected and aged horribly.

There was a seating area beyond the kitchen island where an over-stuffed rattan sofa and chairs with stained cushions looked uncomfortably large squeezed into the corner of the room. Margot noticed a curl of rattan unravelling from a sofa leg, pooling spaghetti-like on the floor.

'Actually, I'm not thirsty,' said Margot as she took in the heat-stained, once cream, melamine toaster in a puddle of breadcrumbs and the unwashed juicer in the kitchen sink. It was clear, just from this one room, that since Vi had left, Patrick had been living day to day.

Patrick told her the cleaner, Mrs Stapleford, was wonderful and came twice a week, but Margot could see she was a smearer, not a cleaner. Her feet were sticking to the floor.

'The cleaner comes twice a week?' she asked, with more disbelief than she had meant.

'Yes, that's right Monday and Thursday mornings. Sometimes she'll come at the weekends, if I need extra help, but now Vi is around it should be easier to have more time for myself without bothering Mrs Stapleford. She is a treasure,' said Patrick, perhaps sensing her scepticism.

Patrick led her through a dark, untidy room, that seemed to have become a repository for Ollie and Toby's toys.

'Dining room?' she suggested.

'Snug, for the moment,' he said. 'Till the boys are older. This is the sitting room.'

He led her into a big room with dual aspect. At one end, French windows opened out onto a deep, back garden, which wasn't overlooked. At the other end of the room tall windows framed the front garden. Margot moved into the bay window and saw a man walking his dog pass the open gates, he looked back at her as his dog wandered into the garden and lifted its leg against a bush.

She looked back into the room. Patrick stood with his hands in his trouser pockets in the centre of the room by the coffee table, rocking on his heels, looking like a schoolboy seeking her approval.

'This is a lovely room,' she said, kissing him lightly on the cheek as she passed him on her tour. 'Such a good size and so light.'

Patrick visibly relaxing, took his hands out of his pockets and smiled.

'It's very tidy,' she said.

'We only come in here to watch television,' said Patrick. 'Let me show you the bedrooms.'

Margot's breath caught in her throat. 'Good idea,' she said, following him through to the hall.

Upstairs there were five bedrooms, one in a loft conversion with a bathroom for the nanny that they didn't visit.

'Is she here?' said Margot quietly, as she peered up the narrow stairs to the attic.

'Who?'

'The nanny.'

'No, no,' said Patrick. 'Her weekends are sacrosanct, she leaves promptly when I get home on Friday and we don't see her till Sunday evening, though she doesn't start work until Monday morning.'

The boy's rooms were as expected; Toby's was painted baby blue with white stencilled rabbits at dado height. The single bed was unmade, and soft toys guarded the perimeter. Not that they needed to, it would have been misplaced to spoil the innocence.

'The boys are with Vi all this afternoon?' she asked.

'Yes, all afternoon.'

The adjacent room, Ollie had made his own, the floor was covered in games kit and Lego, and it smelt of little boy. Margot picked her way across the floor to the window. It didn't look as if it had ever been opened. Patrick hovered at the door.

Through the drizzle, Margot gazed at the garden. At the far end was a football net floating on a battlefield of mud and tufts of grass. The flower beds were shaded by overhanging dripping trees and were empty of life but for the odd, skinny, leafless rose reaching for some sun.

'Not the best time of year to see the garden,' said Patrick, surprising her, suddenly at her shoulder. 'I cut the grass most weekends for the boys.'

'If the trees were cut back, the garden would get more sun,' said Margot, feeling the warmth of him beside her. She turned to look into his blue, blue eyes.

'You are probably right,' he said. 'Let me show you the other bedrooms.'

Margot put her hand in his and let him pull her across the room to the hall.

'This is where … I sleep,' he said.

Margot paused, feeling herself blinking against the pink, floral wallpaper, her body drew back, instinctively she could go no further.

'It's very bright,' she said. 'How on earth do you manage to get to sleep?'

Patrick laughed. 'Like a log,' he said, but he didn't take her in. 'There's an ensuite.' He waved across the room before closing the door.

Next, was a small spare room with a single, old-fashioned, high bed. There was an air of something watchful, waiting to happen, and a thick layer of dust. Margot sneezed.

'It's not too bad, really, is it?' said Patrick as they returned downstairs.

Margot felt relieved and disappointed. They had the whole house to themselves and yet nothing was quite right. It didn't matter, but Margot had hoped, and even perhaps expected, that this might be the moment that Patrick made his move. But he seemed to be paralysed by the ghost of Vi who had left her mark everywhere.

'No, it's all rather lovely,' she said.

To the right of the front door was a final room, Patrick's study.

It was a good size, green walls with a window that also overlooked the front garden, but with louvered shutters on the lower half. Apart from the desk and chair in the rectangular bay, there was a fireplace with bookshelves on either side, a small TV, and a leather chesterfield sofa against the opposite wall. It seemed the only part of the house that was entirely Patrick's.

'And Vi, does she still have a key?' Margot asked.

'God no! I had the locks changed, not that she's ever come over, or at least not that I know of,' he said with a laugh.

'And what time do you expect the boys to be back?' she said drawing him inside the green room.

'Um … not till five,' he said. 'Almost an hour.'

Margot playfully grabbed the front of his shirt and pulled him to her. She took him in, his dark hair, the round face with slight stubble, his end of summer tan, and those blue eyes that looked as though he didn't know what was coming, that made her smile. She kissed him. She was relieved when he responded confidently.

She was impatient, he had made her wait far too long, but he stepped away.

'I want to enjoy this,' he said. 'I mean, we should take our time, so we can both… perhaps I should close the shutters.'

Margot shook her head, pushed him onto the sofa and began to unbutton the top of her shirt.

They had ended up breathless and in a tangle. The sofa wasn't really big enough for what they had in mind, and the Chesterfield leather was cold, and the buttons were comically uncomfortable, but it had served her purpose.

'So, you liked it?' said Jenni.

Margot snapped out of her memory and felt her cheeks flush. 'What? Oh, the house, yes, sorry. My mind wandered there for a moment.'

'Yes, Vi's house, what did you think?'

'It has so much potential,' said Margot. 'And it will have to do whatever happens as Patrick won't want to move the boys. Their happiness is his priority.'

Patrick had set a date for Margot to meet Ollie and Toby. What cute little boy names they were. She was sure she would love them, but she couldn't know if they would take to her. That would be a dealbreaker for Patrick.

'I'm sure you will take precedence soon,' said Jenni.

'So, you think I should do the asking?' said Margot.

'Unfortunately, you have just missed a leap year. Only another three and a half years to go until the next one.'

On the train back to Clapham, Margot watched the world whizz past the window, how slowly her life was moving in contrast. She loved Patrick's vulnerability and the care he took over Ollie and Toby, but he was cautious. Perhaps she could try to force Patrick's hand as Jenni suggested, she didn't want to waste any more time.

Vi's boys

'Hi,' said Ollie and Toby in unison. They sat side by side, opposite Margot, hunch-shouldered, watching her through long, straight, dark lashes as they waited for their burgers. She had come to meet them after their football practice at their favourite lunch venue.

'Just a run around on a Saturday morning, really,' Patrick had said.

The boys were gorgeous dark-haired, blue-eyed, mini-mes of Patrick. As Margot smiled at the boys, she felt she might fall into any one of those four deep, blue pools framed by dark bullrush lashes that looked up at her expectantly. As their father's new girlfriend and the grown-up, the boys were waiting to be entertained. She felt like a stand-up comic, who had forgotten all her jokes.

'Um … so, how old are you?' she asked.

'Six,' said Ollie.

'And when is your birthday?'

'I'll be seven in March.'

'And you Toby?'

'Nearly five. You're very pretty.'

'No, he's not!' said Ollie.

'Yes, I am.'

'He's only just four. Are you going to marry Daddy?'

'Well … he hasn't asked me.'

'Will you if he does?' said Ollie.

'What do you think I should do?'

'Say yes,' said Toby, kicking her under the table as his legs flailed in his excitement.

'Well, we'll see … do you like football?'

The boys nodded in unison.

'What team do you support?' Like the opened sluice gate of a mill stream, the boys gave her a flood of information about which teams they backed and why. She was rescued by Patrick, who returned to the table with their food.

Ollie pounced on the trays, dividing up the order, making sure everyone got what they wanted. Patrick, who had spent the morning in the cold watching the boys chasing the ball across a muddy patch of grass, tucked into his lunch with as much gusto as his children.

Margot, if she had to choose, was a chicken nugget girl, but wishing to bond, had agreed to have what everyone else was having. She opened her burger, pulling at the packaging with manicured fingers. She laid the burger on its grease-proof wrapper on the table in front of her. This was going to be messy. She watched Ollie and Toby tear into their food before tackling her own bun. Elbows on the table, Margot leaned forward, picked up her burger, which was shedding garnish like autumn leaves, and took a bite.

While they ate, Margot watched the boys. She felt an absence. There was an empty seat at the table. She did the calculation; her baby would be maybe six months younger than Ollie. Still, she felt the sadness. Still, the tears could rise. Her child could have been a real person like Patrick's sons.

Margot finished her burger and reached for a napkin with greasy fingers. She must stop thinking like this. All the maybes and what-ifs were so destructive. She needed to think of the future, of what could be.

At that moment, as if he sensed her mood, Patrick smiled at her and leant across the table to squeeze her hand, a calm washed over her, and she smiled.

Back at the house, Patrick took Ollie and Toby upstairs to wash and change. Downstairs, Margot wandered through the house. She moved a chair, used the curtain ties, and puffed up the cushions. It didn't take much to make the place look more like a home. She reached the kitchen and cleared the sink so she could fill the kettle.

'The sitting room looks different,' said Patrick, joining her.

'Oh, I moved one of the armchairs into the bay,' said Margot, not looking at Patrick. Perhaps she had overstepped. 'I thought it would give a bit more room around the coffee table if we were going to play games later.'

'I thought something was different,' he said.

‘And I may have moved some of the framed photographs around when I was having a look. You have some lovely pictures of Ollie and Toby.’ Margot concentrated on finishing the washing up, leaning over the sink, not catching his eye.

Pictures of numerous members of the family were on display in the sitting room. Looking through them, Margot had moved any of Vi to the back.

‘It all looks good. And much cleaner in here, thank you,’ said Patrick. He moved close to her as she put the last of the cleaned dishes on the drainer and emptied the sink. He stood close to her, brushing that slightly shorter pale curl of hair behind her shoulder and kissed her neck below her ear.

‘Thought I’d keep busy, while you were dealing with the boys.’ She dried her hands and turned to lean into him.

‘I’m sorry I need to give them so much of my attention,’ he said, slipping his arms around her.

‘But, so you should.’

Patrick smelt of soap and aftershave.

‘I’ll light the fire, get the room toasty,’ he said, releasing her. ‘I washed the boys’ hair. They’ll be down in a minute. Do you want to see if you can find some biscuits?’

There were two digestives in a tightly twisted wrapper, but Margot found some flour, sugar, butter and eggs and made some rudimentary cookies. She chopped and mixed in some dark chocolate she found at the back of the fridge. She hoped it wasn’t Patrick’s secret stash.

It rained all afternoon. They played ludo in front of the fire. Ollie played competitively, looking to his father for praise. To prevent arguments, Patrick played with Toby as a team. Margot lost graciously.

The cookies had been polished off, and the games put away. Margot had agreed with Patrick that, as this was her first formal introduction to the children, she would head back to her flat at the end of the day.

'Where is Margot going?' asked Ollie as Margot was pulling on her coat.

'I'm going back to my flat,' she said.

'Why?' said Toby. 'Why don't you stay here?'

'Come on, boys, we have fish fingers to cook. We need to let Margot get back. She has her own home and things to do there,' said Patrick.

'You could ask her to marry you, and then she could stay here forever,' said Ollie.

'She said she'd say yes,' said Toby.

'Well, stone me.' Patrick, looking alarmed. 'Boys will be boys,' he added, as if he could hide behind a plethora of proverbs.

Margot was aghast and quickly looked away. She didn't want him to think she had been talking to the boys about something so sensitive and for themselves alone.

'I, I, we didn't …' Margot felt trapped in a situation of her own making. She was even more embarrassed because she had wanted this to happen.

Margot glanced at Patrick again. He didn't look quite so pale. He chuckled and at last looked her in the eye.

'I guess this is what being part of a family means, out of the mouths of babes and all that,' he said. 'Proposal by committee.'

She knew that he loved her, and she loved him. It would all work out. They were going to get married, and she would have a new baby and bury her ghosts in the happiness of her new family.

Commitment

The First Misunderstanding

'Do we need to talk about this now?' said Patrick.

'Yes,' said Margot, bringing his coffee and sitting across from him at the breakfast bar. He was staying over in Clapham at Margot's flat for a couple of nights. The nanny was holding the fort back in Wimbledon.

Patrick looked at the brimming mug. He had been trapped by a cup of coffee.

'I know you have the boys, but if we are serious about our relationship, I need you to know that I think it would be lovely for us to have a child together,' she said.

To reassure her he was taking her seriously, he smiled, stalling. He took a sip of coffee. God, it was scalding. He patted his chest and gulped for cool air. 'Yes,' he coughed. 'We are a ready-made family.'

'But a little girl would be darling,' said Margot, handing him a piece of kitchen paper.

'You do know that you don't get to choose upfront. And the boys can be a bit of a handful as it is.'

He had wanted to talk to Margot about all this before he proposed, but the boys had ambushed his measured approach. They had been so excited. It had been a wonderful family moment, but he hadn't had the chance to talk through any issues with Margot, and she hadn't had the chance to step back. He took a second, careful sip of his coffee and glanced at his watch, disguising the movement as if he was arranging his cuff. He would need to finish up quickly or he was going to be late.

'But for me, you'd be willing to try?' Margot twisted her new engagement ring and tiny shards of reflected light spun around the kitchen.

This conversation was too complicated for a workday breakfast. He would sit with her this evening and discuss the reasons this wasn't going to happen. Patrick had never wanted to speak about it again. He sighed. He should have been clear with Margot from the start, but there was never an appropriate moment. Before committing, it would have been presumptuous, but after the event, he could be accused of having withheld information. God, he was in a bind. Patrick didn't want to ruin what he had. He loved her too much. He reached across the table and took her hand.

'Margot, darling, I'm sorry, but I don't have time to go through this now, but it's not something ....' He stroked her palm with his thumb before he got up from the table. 'Let's talk about it this evening.' He gave her a kiss. 'Now, I really do have to go. Do you want a lift?'

'No thanks, I don't have to be in till ten.' She followed him into the hall and gave him a hug.

'We could wait and see …,' He heard her say as the door closed behind him.

Shit! He didn't think she would leave him over such a small detail. He would talk to her properly tonight. He fled down the stairs from her first-floor flat. Out on the street, he turned but couldn't see if Margot was standing in the window. He gave a cheery wave just in case. Then he got in his car, turned on the ignition and tried to think of the day ahead. Patrick pulled out into the traffic and made his way to the Wandsworth Road. If he was lucky with the lights he should still be in the office before eight.

When he had agreed to the vasectomy, he had not thought through all the consequences. Then he had still been loyal to Vi, he could not have foreseen that she would leave him. Now, he suspected it had all been her idea of a joke. She knew he had an aversion to anything medical. She had pressed him to go through with it and he had done whatever she wanted to keep their family together. Now he thought her a malicious witch.

He crossed the river at Lambeth and drove up Millbank. Margot had appeared to be career-minded, busy at the magazine where she worked, and hadn't seemed as though she would be fussed about having her own baby. He had thought she would be happy with the children he had. Of course, it was naïve of him to assume that was what Margot wanted just because it fitted in with his ideas. Patrick would speak to her this evening, and then she would know. It would either be over or perhaps she could love him despite himself. Either way, this needed to be cleared up before they went any further.

His preferred parking spot had been taken by some even earlier car, so Patrick had to circle the lot to find an empty space. Having shoehorned the car into a narrow bay by a pillar, he walked to work, passed through security and swept up the escalators into the heart of Whitehall.

He picked up a coffee from the machine on the third floor and walked up the final flight to his desk. Work was containable, consistent and a relief from the unpredictability of the outside world, figures and forms were a thing he could deal with, managing people and their expectations required an entirely different set of skills.

At home, he had been a master of dissembling, a useful survival technique with Vi, but with Margot, he wanted to be upfront and honest.

At his desk, Patrick had things to do, emails were gathering. He prided himself on being analytical and objective. There was an order to things, research to be explored, costs to be scrutinised, systems to review, meetings to attend and decisions to be made.

At lunch, Patrick was meeting his cousin. They tried to see each other every year or so, a testament to their shared, happy childhood. Patrick was not sure if they met because they were friends or simply because it had become a habit. Oddly, Patrick liked to keep an eye on Jack, to see what it might mean to be a slightly younger, slightly wilder, slightly taller version of himself.

This time it was Jack's turn to choose a venue. They were meeting at the In and Out in Piccadilly. Patrick waited in the foyer, bouncing on his toes. He was early. He had a meeting at two and would need to leave promptly.

'Good to see you,' said Patrick.

'Hello there. I'm not late, am I?' said Jack, glancing at his watch. Jack was always on time.

'Of course not. I am just rather punctual.'

'Congratulations, by the way,' said Jack. 'You are a lucky man.'

'Very,' agreed Patrick. 'Thank you.'

The cousins went through to the dining room.

'You're looking well,' said Patrick as he took his seat. Jack looked tanned and relaxed. He always looked as though he was just back from a holiday. Patrick was as pale as his job suggested he might be.

'Just back from training for the Middle East.' Jack had already been involved in a couple of operations in the region. 'On Salisbury Plain, not Jordan. No substitute for being out there, but it's good to know what we are supposed to be doing, even if the experience on the ground doesn't always match the planning.'

'They were onto coffee before Patrick had the nerve to ask the question that had been torturing him.

'So … this is a bit tricky, but there is something I need to ask you…'

'Spit it out.'

'Well, before you married Jenni, er …. You had quite a reputation and er …'

Jack yawned like a ham actor from Drury Lane.

'Did you ever sleep with Vi?' said Patrick in a rush.

Her jibe from before their divorce had been troubling Patrick. He had tried to ignore it, but sometimes, when he woke early in the morning, he would wonder. Now that he was starting over with

Margot, he wanted to clear this unresolved remnant from his previous marriage. He needed to tidy up the past.

Patrick found he was right on the edge of his seat, leaning over the table, searching for the truth. Jack had been sitting back relaxed but tapped his fingers on the edge of the table and sat upright.

'Well … you know I like a challenge and, I'm ashamed to say, I have never let a woman's marital status stand in my way. I find it adds to the allure. But Vi always has her own agenda and that tends to lead to complications. I like to keep my love life simple, it's more fun that way.'

They eyeballed each other.

'That, well, that's … great, a great relief,' Patrick said at last backing down, not entirely reassured.

'Not that I'd admit it if I had,' Jack laughed, but glancing at Patrick he stopped. Jack looked at his hands and smiled in a way Patrick didn't much like. 'Margot, on the other hand …you have a gem there, Patrick.' Jack was serious again and then added. 'Vi, tricky bitch. Sorry, you married her.'

'Yes, well, she was slinging around insults and that sort of thing sticks. Hard to forget,' said Patrick.

'Can't blame you for asking. We both know what a cad I am,' said Jack, laughing.

Patrick rose. 'Sorry to dash.'

'Your shout next time,' said Jack. 'Let me know where and when.'

They shook hands. 'Safe travels,' Patrick said. Over the next few months, he must remember to phone Jack's mother. The family always worried when Jack was deployed overseas.

Back in Whitehall, Patrick had a meeting on weapons procurement for the war in Afghanistan. Sourcing the right equipment was always a priority. It was vital to keep the troops supplied. Strange to think something he signed off might be used by Jack, might even save his life.

Work ran late. The accounts team wanted an update. People again, Patrick thought, unpredictable. He had some papers to run through for a meeting in the morning, but no, the accounts team had to see him now.

By the time Patrick got back to Clapham, Margot had started watching a movie. She rewound the film to the beginning so Patrick could catch up while she got supper together. Margot brought him a glass of wine.

'Relax,' she said with a smile before returning to the kitchen.

Margot was a sweetheart. When she joined him and they were cosy together, he would explain everything and give her an out. That was only fair. To him, they were already a perfect family, unbelievably, she loved them all. And he loved her. He didn't want to lose her, but he had to give her the option to walk away.

Patrick couldn't concentrate on the film or enjoy his TV supper. All he could think about was the upcoming conversation they were going to have.

'We should talk,' said Patrick when the credits rolled, and they were tidying up the kitchen.

'Oh, not now,' said Margot, putting leftovers in the fridge. 'It's too late to think about anything that makes you look so earnest.' She wrapped herself around him from the back. 'I have a much better idea about how we can spend the rest of the evening. Besides, how can I take a man seriously who is wearing pink marigolds.'

Another Misunderstanding

Ollie and Toby were waiting for him. The nanny strapped the boys into their car seats in the back of his car, gave them all a cheery wave and headed down the hill to the tube and her night out. Patrick ran the boys over to Vi's.

'I guess she'll be there when you get back,' said Vi. 'You'll want to seize the moment, I'm sure. On your own without the boys.'

‘What? Who?’ he said.

‘Don’t be an ass, Patrick. Your new woman!’ she hissed.

‘You mean Margot?’

‘Margot’s nice, isn’t she, Daddy?’ said Toby.

‘She’s going to come and live with us. Daddy’s going to marry her,’ said Ollie, tugging at Vi’s sweater. ‘Can we have ice cream, Mummy?’

‘Later,’ said Vi, hustling the boys into the house. Then she turned back towards Patrick and whispered. ‘Marrying her? Are you taking that woman into my bed, Patrick?’ She glared at him before slamming the door.

Patrick rolled his eyes and shook his head, laughing, as he went back to the car. What was Vi on about? She had betrayed him and had twisted his future. Taken the choices from him. Revenge, but for what? Loving her in the first place? And now she was having a hissy fit because he had found someone better to love.

Anyway, he had totally redecorated the bedroom after that momentous day when he had shown Margot round the house. Now, there was no trace of Vi, it was no longer hers and the old bed was long gone.

He had been so nervous about Margot’s reaction, but in his naivety, he had thought things were going rather well, until he opened the door to the main bedroom and seen her hesitation. Suddenly, the house and everything in it seemed so neglected and tawdry and reeked of Vi. What a mistake it had been to think that Margot would like it. Thank heavens she had ignored his distress and lured him into the haven of his study and made sure he understood that there was nothing wrong with him. He chuckled, she was a dream, he had loved the way she had taken control. She was wonderful.

Ollie and Toby loved Margot, and Patrick was looking forward to them all becoming a family.

There was just this one thing to straighten out before the wedding. He must talk to Margot. He *would* talk to her, tonight.

Patrick struggled to even think the word, let alone say it out loud. 'Vasectomy, vasectomy, vasectomy!' he shouted in the safety of his sealed car. There, he could say it.

On the way home, he pulled into a petrol station to fill up the car. As he went in to pay, he picked up some flowers from the forecourt. He was clutching at straws, but Margot liked flowers.

Stopped at traffic lights on the High Street, in a flash, it came to him. He could have a reversal. The lights turned green, but as Patrick accelerated, he brushed away the thought. Two was plenty. What would he do if Margot reacted to having a baby like Vi had? Vi wanted children and then turned into a witch, he couldn't bear it if that happened with Margot. He couldn't go through all that again.

He loved his sons. Patrick had been blown away by the miracle of their births and he had been there for Ollie and Toby when Vi had gone AWOL. They had come first. But life moved on. It wasn't where or who he wanted to be right now. Ollie was six, and Toby nearly five, caring for the boys was much more straightforward. Patrick didn't want to go back to the nappy days. Margot loved her job, he hoped he could persuade her that was enough.

His work was absorbing too, and he was building something significant. Patrick wanted to move up and move on. He had never thought he was ambitious, but the more involved he became at the MoD, the more determined he was to do well. He didn't like to think of war as a good thing, but the situation in Afghanistan was an opportunity for him to prove his worth, but it would be demanding of his time. He wouldn't be able to help with a baby at this point in his career.

Anyway, he had had a vasectomy. Of course, he wanted to make Margot happy, but having a baby wasn't going to be an option; he would be clear. It must be tonight. He was not going to leave it any longer.

Patrick pulled onto the drive and switched off the ignition. He wondered how he had got home. He couldn't remember anything about the journey. He hoped he hadn't jumped any red lights or run anyone over. Patrick pulled himself together, gathered his bits and pieces from the car seat beside him. He was ready to start the weekend.

As soon as he opened the front door, he could smell something delicious and exotic. Margot was cooking supper. Something much more adventurous than he would attempt. He sniffed the air, garlic and ginger, something sharp and sweet; Chinese, it must be Chinese. This was something new; having someone who cared for you, expected your arrival, looked forward to seeing you, and created something special for you. Margot warmed his heart.

'Good evening, my darling,' he said, giving her a kiss and presenting her with the plastic-wrapped flowers. She was wearing that slate-coloured, silky shirt that deepened the colour of her eyes.

'Oh! Thank you. Carnations, how lovely,' she said, returning his kiss before fetching a vase.

Over supper, Margot said, 'You seem a bit nervy, Patrick. Is everything alright at work?'

'Yes, fine,' said Patrick, jabbing away at the slippery noodles with his chopsticks. This evening, vegetables, words … nothing was holding together. 'But that thing I mentioned last week … there is something we need to talk about.'

'Oh, it sounded serious then and ominous now. Wait a mo.' Margot got up from the table and fetched them both forks, handing one to Patrick. 'Perhaps using chopsticks was ambitious.'

'It's about something that happened when I was still with Vi.'

'I'm not sure I'm interested in anything you got up to with her,' said Margot, tucking into her food. 'That is your past, Patrick. I am your future.' She swivelled her fork around the bowl. 'We are going to have a fresh start. Everything is new from now on.'

Patrick stared at the bottle of wine between them on the table. He knew the words but didn't seem to be able to spit them out in a coherent order.

'Well, this affects us both, will affect you, and our future,' he said. Patrick picked up the wine and topped up their glasses.

'Goodness', you are too serious.'

'Margot, this is real.' He unclenched the fingers of his left hand that had unconsciously formed a fist. He carefully placed his open palm down on the table, slowly letting each finger drop, and took a deep breath.

'Okay.' She settled down and took a sip of wine. The tone of her voice dropped. 'What is it?'

'The other day, you brought up,' Patrick swallowed. He watched her, careful to spot any change in her expression. 'That you wanted a, a -,'

'A baby, yes.'

'Yes, a baby.' There it was, a hopeful, fresh light in her eyes. He was about to dash it out.

'You didn't seem very keen,' Margot said.

'Well, there is a reason …the reason is …. If I could give you what you wanted, I would, but I ….' Patrick wasn't sure he could say the actual words despite practising in the car, not out loud, not in front of Margot. He looked at his plate of half-eaten noodles. Vasectomy, it was such a callous, empty word. He couldn't help but think that this would be the moment Margot's grey eyes would turn leaden, and she would throw down her napkin and leave him for good.

'Spit it out, Patrick, for goodness' sake.'

'Right, um … simply … I already have the two boys. I can't have any more.' There, he had said it. He thought he should repeat himself to be clear. 'I won't have any more. It's not going to happen.'

There was a silence. Margot looked confused. 'What do you mean you can't … won't have any more?'

Her head tilted in askance. Two frown lines had appeared on her otherwise beautiful, smooth face. Patrick searched the tabletop for an answer. Nothing was going to save him, not the scarlet carnations, so upright and stiff in the vase, nor the bottle of soy sauce with its jaunty red hat. He looked up at her.

'I don't want you to misunderstand.… But, well, there are Ollie and Toby to think of, and that's … well, we are a ready-made family. We are complete. Do you see? I hope we are enough for you because, well, I can't entertain becoming a father again. It isn't going to be a possibility for me. And I'm at a point where I'd like for the next few years to really concentrate on my career.'

She was still frowning, drawing small tight circles with her finger on the tabletop. He watched as the circles looped slowly wider and wider.

'I don't want to mislead you,' he added.

'I don't think you have a bad bone in your body, Patrick. You couldn't deceive anyone if you tried.' She smiled a beautiful, open, gorgeous smile. Her eyes now seemed almost blue.

'I should hope not,' he said. God, she was amazing, unexpectedly, extraordinarily amazing.

'I … I know you already have two fabulous boys, and I understand if you feel that is enough. And I can see that you want us to settle as a family, get used to each other, and get your career sorted, before….' She took his hand across the table and smiled. 'Patrick, I love you. I want to spend the rest of my life with you. I'm happy not to make any plans. Let's just see what life brings and enjoy everything and anything that comes our way.'

'I love you too. I don't know what I would do … but I would understand if you wanted nothing more to do with me. I should have been transparent earlier.'

'Oh, Patrick, it's going to be fine, don't worry. I'm on your side.'

Patrick couldn't believe it had gone so well.

Later, as he lay in his bed studying the ceiling in the dark, he wondered if Margot had heard him clearly. She had taken it awfully well. He rolled over and looked at her asleep, lying next to him. He inched forward and nuzzled her. She smelt like heaven.

The Dust Settles

'So, have you told her you're damaged goods?' said Vi.

Could she read minds? It was another Friday evening, and again, Patrick was dropping the boys off for the weekend. Vi was making it hard for Patrick to like her. He struggled to recognise the person he had been drawn to when they were young. She may be the mother of his children, but she had become unbearable.

'Because that is the sort of thing you ought to discuss before you get married,' she added.

'Yes,' he said, dumping the boys' overnight bags in Vi's hallway.

'How did she take it?'

'She was fine, not that it's any business of yours. We had a good chat, and she accepted the situation.'

Was Vi smirking? God, she was deplorable.

'Are you sure she heard you clearly, Patrick? You know how obscure you can be, pussyfooting around. I bet she wants babies. I thought so when I met her. With those breasts, she's made for feeding.'

Vi had engineered bumping into Patrick and Margot, when they were food shopping one Saturday morning. She had pounced somewhere between baked goods and frozen meals.

'Oh, hello,' Vi had said, her eyes darting all over Margot. 'I'm the first Mrs Patrick Walker.'

'What are you doing here?' said Patrick. 'You're supposed to be with Ollie and Toby?'

'You must be Margot. The boys have told me all about you. What an unexpected pleasure.' Vi said, ignoring Patrick and putting some fish fingers and frozen peas into her trolley. 'How thrilling to finally meet and how unexpected. I just thought I'd pop in and get some groceries while the boys were at football.'

Just pop in and see if Margot was with Patrick while he was doing his regular weekend shop.

'Will you be taking Margaret? Is that her name? Food shopping with you again this Saturday?' Vi said now. 'Quite the cheap date.'

'That's enough, Vi. Ollie, Toby, I'm off,' he called up the stairs. The boys tore down from their bedrooms and hugged his legs. He squatted down to say goodbye. 'See you on Sunday.'

'Can Margot make cookies again,' said Toby.

'I'm sure. I'll ask,' said Patrick. He noticed Ollie glance at Vi, a sly look or perhaps he was just worried, anticipating trouble. He hoped the boys didn't learn to manipulate the situation. 'Gotta go, boys. Love you guys.' Patrick was out of the house, waving and waving again as he drove away.

Why did Vi have to do it? Why couldn't he drop the boys off, exchange a few pleasantries, and be gone? She should be happy. He didn't ask her what she was up to or how she lived her life. That wasn't his business anymore. Vi ought to be able to move on. She was a fool if she thought he wasn't going to do all he could to be happy this time around.

Vi was all angles and energy, brimming with vitality, like a wiry brillo pad on springs. It had been great when they were young, but now he needed Margot. Margot was his dream. She had poise. She had curves and shelves and softness and pillows. In the moonlight, her bare, rounded shoulders could send shivers down his spine. Margot, in her calmness, brought him peace.

'Moving a bit fast, aren't you,' said Vi when he picked up Ollie and Toby on Sunday evening. 'The boys tell me you've set a date. How long have you known her?'

'Six months or so, but we're both adults. There's no need to hang around,' said Patrick.

'On reflection, you're probably right. Good idea to grab her fast before she finds out what a disappointment you are and changes her mind.'

Patrick, on a second marriage, had arranged for them to have a civil ceremony with close family at the Morden Registry Office early in the New Year. Margot chose to have a marriage blessing at Angela's church in West Clandon in the spring. Patrick and Margot went down to meet the vicar. Although he had been at St Mary's for many years, Angela still referred to him as the new vicar.

Angela was such a stalwart member of the congregation that although Patrick and Margot were not regular worshippers at any church, they were welcomed with open arms, and in that charming Anglican way, the small fact that Patrick had been married before was disregarded. After their conversation with the vicar, a date was agreed upon for the blessing, avoiding Lent.

Margot wore an off-white, knee-length dress with silvery-coloured cuffs, belt and collar and carried armfuls of white and yellow roses opening peachy and gold.

'It's not everyone who would think of grey for a wedding dress, is it?' said Patrick's mother.

'You look lovely,' said his father to Margot, wobbling rather as he staggered from the church, his walking frame and heavy shoes bumping over the uneven gravel.

'Beautiful even,' said Patrick in Margot's ear.

Angela presided at the wedding tea, opening The Old Vicarage. The drawing room was filled with spring flowers, and the table was covered in white linen. Rows of champagne flutes stood ready beside platters piled with tiny crustless sandwiches and pretty plates of miniature eclairs.

Patrick had been worried that two rambunctious boys would be too much for the elderly Angela and her house full of antiques and whatnots, but Angela was delighted with the boys. Margot's sister, Lily and her husband were there with their three. Patrick watched through the drawing room bay as the children, he supposed they were cousins now, sorted through some old bicycles. They were soon tearing around the garden, having a great time ripping up the gravel on the roundel at the front of the house and dashing through the parterre.

'Lovely children you have,' said Patrick to Lily, who had wandered over to stand beside him in the window.

'Thanks. It's wonderful to see Margot so happy. For as long as I can remember, she has been searching for a family of her own – and here you are, with your two boys. It's perfect.'

It *was* perfect. Blue skies, beautiful bride, close family. Patrick couldn't quite believe he was the recipient of so much good fortune.

After their church blessing, Ollie and Toby went with the nanny to stay with Patrick's parents. Patrick and Margot escaped to Mauritius for ten days on their honeymoon.

It was bliss. They hired a boat for the day and had a picnic lunch in an unspoilt bay of a tiny island. They walked on white sands and swam in turquoise seas. They lay on loungers on the hotel beach and sipped cocktails under palm trees.

Patrick marvelled as Margot's alabaster skin turned rosy and then honeyed. As he lay beside her at the beach, he caressed her arm, soft as a ripe peach. She suggested he take her up to their room and stroke the rest of her. The endless days, drugged by the warmth of the sun, were over too soon.

Bliss

That first night home, Patrick and Margot relaxed in bed, their suitcases were half unpacked and laundry was scattered on the floor. Margot leaned over and pulled Patrick to her. He loved this about her - that she initiated sex, wanted to have sex with him. Patrick wrapped her up in a firm hug. He inhaled her. Her hair still smelled of the sea.

He was far away, back in a secret cove, when he heard the small thump, thump, thump of bare feet running across the landing. He quickly rolled away from Margot, who turned away from the door as it was pushed open, the nightlight from the hall silhouetting a small figure.

Daddy, are you there?' It was Toby. Patrick gave him a cuddle and took him back to bed.

Later the same night, he was woken by a small hand shaking him. Ollie was awake.

Patrick hadn't anticipated that the boys would be so unsettled by his absence. But, of course, Vi had a habit of disappearing. For his children, telling them that he would return at the end of the week was no guarantee.

Vi had gone off again on another of her long retreats. This time, she was doing the Far East. In a fit of sour grapes, she had left just before he and Margot got married.

'Don't worry, Mummy will be back very soon,' Vi had said to the boys as they climbed into the back of Patrick's car. She was leaving the next morning, early. 'You won't be upset, will you? No need to cry.'

Patrick closed the back door of the car and turned to say goodbye to Vi. She was dabbing at her eyes with a tissue.

'I didn't tell the boys, but I might go for longer this time. Travel on a whim. See where my fancy takes me. I might be away for a couple of months, or a year … or more. Keep an eye on the house for me, will you.' She passed Patrick a spare key. She smiled a strangled smile. 'So happy for you, Patrick, really.'

'Safe journey,' Patrick said, getting into the car. He gave her a perfunctory wave as he drove off. He didn't think Vi had said anything as nice to him for, well, as long as he could remember. Perhaps she was leaving the country because she couldn't bear to see him so happy.

Patrick now had full charge of Ollie and Toby just when he was starting his adventure with Margot. Now, that care would involve her input as well. Perhaps that was Vi's plan, foisting the children on the newly married couple. But Margot had taken it all in her stride.

'Do you mind having the boys here all the time?' he asked. 'It wasn't how I thought it would be. I hoped we would have some breaks on our own.'

'Of course, it's no problem. This is their home, and they're such darlings,' she said. 'But you don't want me to give up my job, Patrick? I hope you didn't marry me just because you wanted a fulltime mother for the boys?'

'No, no, nothing could be further … but you could, if you liked…,' he said. He could hear the eggshells cracking under his words. He didn't want to be patronising but wanted to be generous. 'My salary is sufficient,' he added. Not really, but he would give her the choice.

'Could we cope? Well, anyway, I'd rather not stop working, if you don't mind. It's not very well paid, but I like my job,' she said.

Patrick was relieved. With their lifestyle, two salaries were far better than one.

‘But I will miss our little weekends away together,’ said Margot, laying a warm hand on his cheek for a moment, a short reminder of delicious hours.

‘At least, with Toby joining Ollie at primary school in September, the nanny can go,’ said Patrick, another saving.

As Margot’s work didn’t start till what she called a reasonable hour, rather than at crack of dawn like Patrick’s, she was happy to get the boys out of the house in the mornings. They would get an au pair to collect them from school and help in the evenings.

It was a sunny Saturday. Patrick had picked up a coffee for Margot and was heading back to the house with the boys after football. Home with the boys to Margot. He couldn’t imagine anything more satisfying. His heart bounced, eager to be with her. He couldn’t quite believe that he had found someone who fitted into his world so seamlessly. Margot had taken over the things that needed looking after and given space in the areas where he was already coping. No toes had been stepped on. No feelings were harmed in the making of this marriage.

Only a few terse words exchanged between them about the work required on the house. But Margot had explained how important the renovations were, and, in the end, he had agreed that she shouldn’t have to live in Vi’s house. And when she said she would pay for the work with the proceeds from selling her flat, he could hardly disagree.

It was going to be chaos. Margot had suggested the house would benefit from a kitchen extension. She had sold the plan to Patrick as an external job that would hardly affect their use of the house until the knock-through. Of course, it was more complicated than that. The back of the house had been demolished in the first week. Patrick wandered around the wreckage, thinking he had owned a perfectly good house, and now, he didn’t. No doubt, it would take much longer to stick everything back together. The kitchen was reduced to a microwave and a kettle on a table in the sitting room, and having ripped the house apart, the builders seemed to have gone on holiday.

But having the kitchen renovated was a small price to pay for Margot's happiness, and if Margot was cheerful, he was ecstatic.

'The builders are only away for a week. They'll be back on Monday, and then the exciting bit will begin,' said Margot. She was on the sofa surrounded by kitchen catalogues and colour charts. 'Do you prefer this grey or that yellow with these tiles?'

'Do you promise it really will be exciting?' he asked, leaning over the brochures and avoiding tile samples to give her a kiss.

'Well, Ollie has already discussed with the foreman what sort of digger will be used for the foundations. But the really thrilling bit is that they will be finished before the summer holidays, and we will be able to enjoy the warm weather with the new windows open onto the garden. It's going to be fabulous.'

'Can't wait.' Patrick retreated to his study, sliding through the plastic wrap from one room to the next. He wasn't convinced all this cellophane worked. The sheets draped over the doors were coated with creamy plaster powder, and when he finessed his way through, there still seemed to be a layer of fine sticky dust waiting for him on the other side. He eyed the old Chesterfield as he settled at his desk, tapping his papers sharply at an angle to remove any lingering fine powder. Margot had suggested he replace the sofa with something more comfortable, but he was rather fond of it, and she had agreed that it had a certain nostalgic charm, they had both smiled when she had said that. Anyway, his study was his refuge.

Margot was right, of course. As the weather warmed the builders finished up. They had gone from being invasive strangers to best friends in a matter of months, but at last, they were done.

The kitchen was now light and airy, with a skylight over the extension where Margot had a table and chairs for proper meals. There was even room for a small sofa and chairs. A peninsula separated the kitchen from the dining area, with an incorporated breakfast bar for a quick morning coffee. The grey floor and walls were peaceful, the space clean and calm. As a bonus, the downstairs loo now had a shower.

'So, we will have somewhere to wash when we get the builders back in the autumn to do our ensuite,' said Margot.

Patrick didn't meet her eye. The advantage of Margot planning and paying for the work was that he didn't have to think about it. The disadvantage was he had no say.

How to have a baby

A Home

Margot swept her hand over the new breakfast bar. It felt cool, even where the sun rested. The diamonds on her ring sparkled as she swam her fingers back and forth. Every sunny day, oblique rectangles of light from the skylight and windows slid across the Corian top and dipped into the Corian sink. Margot loved the sleekness and the continuity, with the shiny sentinel of the tap standing straight and proud. None of the curvy, cottagey, bohemian style Vi had favoured remained. Everything was built-in, slick and clean, not a curl or a crumb anywhere. The room was filled with light, and it was spotless. Under Margot's direction, Mrs Stapleford had risen to the challenge of cleaning.

Last year, when the work was underway, Margot had thought she had made a terrible mistake. All the palaver, and the mud, but the new extension was a sun trap and looked smart with the modern, sharp sofa and chairs she'd bought. They weren't comfortable, but they looked the part.

The view of the garden across the new terrace was beginning to come. The Japanese maples she had planted in the autumn between the rhodies on the bank at the far end of the lawn, had begun to unfurl their miniature leaves, gloves of burgundy hanging like umbrellas over the pink and white of the azaleas. It was amazing what some clever planting and a good feed could do.

Margot turned back into the room and took a sip of her coffee. When the travelling sunlight lit up the stainless-steel toaster, it would be midday, and she would do something about lunch; she thought there was some salad in the fridge. Today, the boys were out with friends from their football team, at a birthday party, and they would be dropped off later. Patrick was playing golf. Jenni was coming around for coffee, but for now, Margot would read the Saturday papers and relax.

'Well, this is lovely,' said Jenni, perching on one of the bar stools. 'All minimalist, sophisticated grey. And you have a Nespresso machine … yes, please. Do you have the gold ones?'

'How are things?' said Margot, handing her a coffee. She noticed Jenni's roots needing doing, something she usually kept on top of.

Margot had already put out a small cream jug and matching sugar bowl beside the box of doughnuts Jenni had brought.

Jenni added sugar to her coffee. Margot added milk.

'Honestly, what's not to love? I'm not so keen on the army wife thing, all the hanging around. I decided not to go for that job at the local Primary, not sure I want to be surrounded by other people's children all the time. I want to do something more creative, so I'm selling kitchenware from home.'

'Like Tupperware?' said Margot.

'No, much more upmarket. I have a brochure.' Jenni scrabbled in her bag and passed Margot a glossy leaflet. 'Here, you should come to one of my events.'

Margot studied the flier. 'Looks like a domestic pyramid scheme.'

'No, no, it's not like that,' said Jenni.

'Well, good luck. How's Jack?' Margot opened the box and slid it across the kitchen counter. 'Doughnut?'

'He's back from Afghanistan. He's been around for a couple of weeks. It's great to have him home. Honestly, I've never been so happy. He's amazing, but he just gets busier and busier. He's up in London quite a bit.'

'Isn't it a bit boring stuck in the house … waiting?'

'Well, yes, but no, it's not like that. There are all these other wives,' said Jenni, biting into an iced butterscotch ring, cream oozing. 'Anyway, is married life living up to your expectations?'

‘It’s wonderful,’ said Margot. ‘Patrick is a honey, and I’m loving getting the house up to scratch.’

‘Nesting?’

‘Barely got my feet under the table,’ laughed Margot. ‘And we’ve agreed to wait, for things to settle before we try.’

She and Jenni must look like a Beryl Cook painting, though to be honest it didn’t seem to matter how many doughnuts Jenni ate she remained super slim. Still, they were two gossipy, gorgeous girls in colourful summer prints cross-legged at a bar, sipping their drinks. Burgeoning with humour, Margot always wondered what the people in the paintings were talking about. She hoped their chat was just as outrageous as the image they portrayed.

‘And how long will that take?’ said Jenni.

‘Are you and Jack?’ Margot said.

‘No! Not for a bit. Jack’s still a bit irresponsible, not ready for kids.’ Jenni sniffed and stuffed the rest of her doughnut into her mouth. While she chewed, she looked down and tapped the counter with a sharp fuchsia pink nail. ‘Actually, I’m thinking of leaving him.’

‘What! But you were just saying how happy you are. You’ve only been married … well, not quite two years.’ Margot’s idea of them being a couple of Beryl Cook’s happy gossiping girls exploded.

‘Don’t tell Patrick, will you? I haven’t quite made up my mind, but Jack’s … so unreliable … he’s still a boy.’

‘He’s over thirty.’

‘I know, thirty-two, but … he is just so wild. That’s what I loved about him. But I think Jack has realised he made a terrible mistake by marrying me. I mean, not me, anyone. He wasn’t ready.’

‘No, not you …’ said Margot, leaning across and taking Jenni’s hand, stopping the tapping fingers beating nervously on the counter.

'And now he's behaving atrociously. He can't face up to telling me it's over,' said Jenni, sniffing. 'In the army, he's renowned for being decisive and brave, but for this, he needs me to do the dirty work.'

'I'm so sorry,' Margot cooed as she pushed a box of tissues Jenni's way. It was awful to see Jenni, who always seemed so together and cheerful, slowly falling to pieces in Margot's lovely new kitchen, where she had thought only good things would happen and nothing would ever go wrong.

'It's such a shame. I love him to bits, and I know Jack loves me, or he did when we married. But now he's carrying on, out late. I don't know where he is half the time.'

'Thank goodness you don't have children.'

'It's silly, really. We just met too soon. I bet Jack will make someone the perfect husband in ten years' time … when he finally grows up.' Jenni blew her nose. 'Anyway, how are Patrick and the boys?'

'They are all well,' said Margot. 'Luckily, Ollie and Toby see me as an extra add-on grown-up, a bonus. I'm quite different and separate from Vi in their minds. So, no conflict.'

'Ha!' Jenni's tears had practically all dried up.

'Really,' said Margot. "They are lovely boys.'

'It will have helped that Vi has gone travelling again,' said Jenni.

'We are going to decorate Ollie and Toby's bedrooms together over the summer holidays. The boys will get to choose.'

'Part of the bonding as a family?' said Jenni.

'Toby's room is still decorated with bunny rabbits, for goodness' sake, he's not a baby anymore, he's five.'

'But you will need a room for your baby,' said Jenni.

'There is the little box room … but I don't want to get ahead of myself,' said Margot.

'Sounds perfect,' said Jenni, sniffing.

All Margot could think about these days was how much she wanted a baby before the boys got too much older. She hadn't told Patrick, but she had decided to jettison her contraceptives. She would decorate when she knew what sort of a small person she was welcoming into the world.

What Patrick said

'My husband loves me,' Margot said with confidence. The yoga teacher had asked them to be inspired by a truth and to voice it to the class before they started their workout.

'I'm not sure I like this instructor so much. There's too much of the breathing techniques and mumbo jumbo and not much actual exercise,' said Jenni, sipping her coffee in the adjoining cafe after the class.

Margot and Jenni had started meeting up on a Saturday morning for yoga. At first, Margot had enjoyed spending time with Patrick watching the boys at football, but it was a cold damp way to spend the start of the weekend, and she hadn't always wanted to be the one to do the Saturday shop. These things were part of Patrick's routine which she didn't want to interrupt. So, as the year turned and the weather got bleaker, Margot had found a class and persuaded Jenni, who was somewhat at a loose end now her divorce was underway, to come too.

'I don't know,' said Margot. 'I like to have something different to think about rather than how unfit and unsupple I am and how appalling my balance is.'

'I was planning my flowerpots. Have I told you about them? I'm painting Christmas designs in gold on lovely old terracotta flowerpots. You can pick them up for practically nothing. I've booked a stand at the Chelsea Christmas Fair. You should come along.'

'I'd love to,' said Margot. 'No more kitchenware?'

'God, no. I'm going to arrange candles in Oasis in the pots and decorate with moss and ribbons, so they look lovely and festive.'

'The Chelsea Fair always has such good stalls,' said Margot.

'Can you believe what the idiot said, the one who always has his mat next to the teacher? Such a creep.'

'What was it? My vibe attracts my tribe. Eugh!' said Margot. 'Well, he's the most flexible, so I guess he can get away with it.'

'And you? My husband loves me. How cheesy is that?' said Jenni.

Margot had forgotten, in the elevated moment of inner thought central to her preparation for yoga and having had satisfying sex with Patrick that morning, that Jenni, even though she had initiated the divorce process and confessed to being over it, was still mad at Jack.

'I am sorry about Jack, but Patrick really does love me.'

Margot had not seen much of Jenni over the summer, she had returned to her parents in Manchester, but she was back in London now and their friendship had picked up again.

'But how can you know for sure?' Jenni leant towards Margot over her coffee. 'You're tempting fate. I mean, I could understand if you said, *I* love my husband because that's from your heart. But what's in his heart?'

'But it's true,' said Margot. 'Every day, Patrick tells me he loves me.'

'And you think Jack didn't say that to me?'

Margot looked at Jenni, then sought the truth from the froth of milk on her coffee.

'Do you know, I found out Jack was at it with one of my bridesmaids on our wedding day. On our wedding day!'

Margot looked up, 'On your wedding day? How do you know?'

'Oh, earlier this year, Louise, you won't know her. She was my maid of honour. When I told her I was thinking of divorcing Jack, she took me out for a drink and told me all about it. She said it was to make sure I didn't change my mind.'

'Oh…'

'Yes, well, I thought he was trustworthy, to begin with, and then I guess he got bored or just couldn't pass up an opportunity – and seemed to trip over willing women at every turn. Louise could see I wasn't facing up to facts. She told me in great detail how she knew for certain he'd slept with four of my bridesmaids. She suggested it was a game or a bet …'

'Cake?' For a conversation like this, Margot could really do with something sweet.

'Alright then, carrot, please.'

When Margot returned to the table, Jenni was blowing her nose.

'How many bridesmaids did you have? There were loads…'

'Six and Louise, my maid of honour.'

'Six, well seven, goodness'!'

'But, if you don't trust your husband, where are you? So, I said to Louise that this all sounded very childish. I knew that Jack was a bit wild, but he wasn't all bad. But -'

'So, four out of the seven?'

'She could tell I wasn't buying it. I told her, Jack loves me, he tells me every day. In the morning, he gives me a kiss and says it when he leaves for work. And every evening, whatever time he gets home, he wakes me to tell me the same.' Jenni paused, considered her coffee and lifted her cup before replacing it without taking a sip. She sighed and looked at Margot. 'So that was when she told me. On the day of my wedding, if you please! In the spare bedroom at my parents' house, can you believe it … upstairs, while I was chatting with guests in the marquee!'

'Blonde?' For a moment, a face flashed through Margot's mind, a pink face peering out in alarm, from under coats.

'What?'

'Sorry, I've just remembered which one Louise was, is. She's blonde, isn't she?'

'Yes, not that that's got anything to do with anything. Jack is not fussy.'

'No,' said Margot. 'I suppose not.'

'Anyway, you would have been number eight. So, you dodged a bullet.'

'Number eight?'

'Yes,' said Jenni. 'If I could have had more bridesmaids, you would have been my next pick, but my mother said enough.'

'Oh.'

'Don't be miffed. I hadn't seen you for years then.'

'No, no, I know. I'm not.'

'It was great you came. Even though we hardly had a chance to speak, there were so many cousins and aunts to talk to. But you met Patrick there, and now here we are.'

'Yes.' Margot had met a good man, and she knew he loved her. She now had a family and a home. She had almost everything she had ever wanted.

'You know, I can't decide if I'm angry or upset by Jack.' Jenni said, pulling the plate of carrot cake towards her. 'Married for nearly two years, and half that time Jack was away! All I'm saying is, you can't trust them, husbands. All you can really know is how you feel, not how Patrick does.'

'Patrick isn't Jack,' said Margot, hoping she hadn't overstepped. At least, she had managed not to say how she had always found Jack unbearably full of himself.

'But if Patrick loved you, he'd have a baby with you, wouldn't he? That's what you want. He must know that … you have told him?'

Margot looked at her watch. She had waited more than a year; to give Patrick space and so she could have a spring baby. Then she had stopped taking the pill. She hadn't said anything to Patrick, he would just come up with some reason why it wasn't the right time. But months and months had passed and really something should have happened by now.

'Must go,' said Margot. 'Patrick will be back with the boys, and I want to get the sausages on. Vi is back, so we need to plan some strategies this weekend.'

Back home in the shower, Margot tried not to feel grumpy. After all, Jenni was going through such heartache over divorcing Jack. God, he had been a shit, and Jenni deserved sympathy.

Margot couldn't expect everyone to be sensitive about it, but Jenni was the one person who knew what Margot had been through and her hidden pain, that Margot needed to resolve her past. She really enjoyed being with Ollie and Toby. And in the circumstances, it was a blessing that Patrick had given her a ready-made family. Out of the shower, Margot wrapped herself in a towel.

It was years ago. She ought to have got over it by now. She looked at herself in the mirror. To be precise, it was eight years, eight months and eighteen days ago, and as her reflection attested, Margot was not getting any younger. She opened the drawer of the sink cabinet to find her straighteners, pushing aside the stack of pregnancy tests. It was her particular curse to be naturally irregular.

They had told her she was young; she would have plenty of opportunities to have another baby at a better, more suitable time. And here she was. The time was right. The place was right. However, she still wasn't pregnant.

Margot tried to remember what Patrick had said when she had brought up the subject of children when they were engaged. What was it? He didn't say he didn't want another baby. He said he couldn't or wouldn't. She hadn't really been listening because she knew Patrick was who she wanted to be with, and she was excited about their future together and couldn't imagine children not being part of that dream. She had been happy to wait for a while, but nothing could stop her biological urge, and she knew if she was pregnant, Patrick would come around.

What Margot did

Margot held up her hand and counted the months that had passed, the missed opportunities, but she didn't have enough fingers. Why wasn't she pregnant? Patrick seemed to physically slide sideways to avoid her whenever she tried to bring up the subject.

Having a baby should be easy, but the endless eating of the right thing and taking the recommended supplements, and nothing happening was wearing. Ticking off the days with the code she used in her diary seemed increasingly pointless. Her yearning was becoming an obsession that bordered on the abnormal, a filthy secret. She had everything she needed, the husband, the job, the home, this couldn't be happening to her. She was Margot.

Maybe something was wrong with her. Perhaps something had been damaged that last time. Margot decided to go to a private clinic on Harley Street. She could get there and back from work during her lunch break.

She almost asked Jenni to come with her, give her some moral support. But Jenni, free of Jack, had started dating again and in the first flush of meeting someone new was insufferable.

Margot was sure she could manage on her own without too many memories piling in.

On her way, sitting on the tube, swaying with the movement, watching the dark tunnel flash past, Margot thought about the last time. She remembered colourful, stackable chairs set out in rows on a green, wavy lino in the waiting room, like buoys in a harbour. Margot had sat on a blue chair in the far corner. The acrid pale green walls had reminded her of sick.

There had been an older woman with a girl about Margot's age and sitting near them, a couple with a young woman crying silently.

‘She’s never been good on the boats,’ the man with the young woman had said. He spoke in a soft Irish burr. He had motioned to the other girl and added. ‘We were on the same crossing this morning.’

‘It has been a bit of a bother getting here, for sure,’ the woman with the girl had said.

She must be her mother. What would it be like to have a mother to hold your hand at a time like this?

First, one girl had been called, then the other. Margot had watched the silent, wall-mounted television. It showed her how to brush her teeth on repeat. At last, Margot had been called for her appointment. She steeled herself, she had a problem, and she had to deal with it.

On the bus on the way back to her flat, faltering down the high street, stopping at every light. Margot had sat in a window seat in a daze, wrapped in shame. She had watched fat globs of rain slithering down the window, distorting her view of the world, pulling the streetlights this way and that. She had been aware of people on the pavement rushing back and forth, heads bent against the cold weather. Silhouettes backlit by shop windows. The world a dystopian Lowry warped by dark rain and bright lights.

The bus had juddered through a pothole, and Margot’s hands had swayed in her lap, cradling what was no longer there. Her stomach had been heavy with an empty weight that she feared might drag her down through the floor of the bus and smear her on the tarmac. There, her heart could be crushed into paste by the passing traffic. That would be just. Back then, she didn’t want a baby, but afterwards, she knew she owed the world something.

Margot emerged from the Underground and was pleased to see the sun was still shining. Her memory belonged in the dark. She crossed Oxford Circus and cut behind John Lewis.

This clinic was quite different, calm, and the furnishings were a soothing, white and pale turquoise, implying cleanliness and care.

Margot sighed, reassured. The cheerful receptionist's uniform supported the decor. This was a place that suggested hope, that helped people who were having problems fulfil their dreams.

Having checked in, Margot took a seat and waited for her name to be called. She sipped her water and thought about her lost child. It was impossible not to. Sitting here, a different clinic, a different hope. Was the little soul who she'd prevented from living, still waiting in the wings for their chance.

Margot hadn't told Patrick she was visiting the clinic. She didn't like keeping things from him, but he wouldn't be keen. For her it had become essential. A simple blood test and an ultrasound. Then she would know.

Her name was called. In the consulting room, Margot was ushered behind a curtain. She slid off her skirt and tights and climbed onto the gurney.

'Sorry, my hands are freezing, and the gel, worse,' said the technician.

Margot felt her stomach contract as the cold goo landed on her skin. The paddle slid through the gel, pressed down, and swam across her belly. The technician turned the monitor so Margot could see. A blurry black-and-white image appeared on the screen.

'So, let's see.' The paddle swept back and forth. 'Now, here you can see an ovary.' The technician's fingers clicked on the keyboard. 'Just measuring … now remind me, where are you in your cycle?'

A squirt more gel. The swooping and clicking continued in silence.

'There, all done.' The technician wiped Margot's stomach and handed her more tissues to complete the cleanup.

Margot dressed before returning to the consulting room to hear what the clinician had to say.

'No signs of endometritis, ovaries look healthy, no cysts, no thickening of the womb or narrowing of the fallopian tubes.

Everything looks .... great. You shouldn't be having any problems. When did you stop taking contraceptives?'

'Over a year ago.'

'So, your body should have adjusted. The blood test results may flag up something we can't see. We should get them back in a few days. Make sure reception has your correct details and we'll get the results to you directly. I can't think that there will be any problems, as I said we haven't seen anything unusual. There doesn't seem to be any reason for concern.'

'Good.'

'Well, as sure as we can be. It would be ideal.' The clinician glanced at Margot's rings. 'If your husband were tested too, then we would have a better idea.'

'I'll ask him,' said Margot, knowing that she never would. He would hate it and surely the two boys were proof enough that everything was in working order there.

The blood tests came back. Everything was normal, nothing was flagged. She phoned the doctor for reassurance.

'We need to get your husband in for a test. When we know if and where there is a problem, we can tailor our approach. Then, we can move to more proactive treatment. We have a great success rate with our IVF programme.'

Margot sighed. She wanted this to be easy, solvable, not a conundrum. She must talk to Patrick again, but whenever she had tried to bring up the subject, he would huff.

'You've a real bee in your bonnet, but we've been through all this, I've explained,' And he would retreat a little, and she could see him closing down and shrinking into his chair.

At the thought of him withdrawing from her, she felt a stab of pain like an ice splinter in her heart. But they should be able to talk about this. She wondered if there had been some trauma or perhaps it was boarding from a young age that had done it. She had read somewhere that could inhibit men from talking about their feelings.

Margot didn't feel she could insist. She couldn't tell him why this was such a need for her. He would be horrified if he thought she had ended a life, just for convenance. She wasn't sure where Patrick stood on these things and she didn't want to see him glancing at her over coffee on a sunny morning thinking that she could be so selfish, or of an evening with a glass of red wine looking at her, knowing that she could do something so despicable. He would despise her.

What she had done was in the past and would stay buried.

That Sunday, Margot was collecting Ollie and Toby from Vi's. Now she was back, they had reverted to the old routine. Patrick usually had the honour, but he had asked if she could go. He was halfway though some files he needed to read for work the next morning. He would be finished by the time she got back.

The boys weren't there. They were at a friend's house and would be back shortly. This was something that sometimes happened on pick-up night. Patrick had explained that Vi would apologise and offer him a drink while he waited. This evening, Vi would have Margot to entertain. Margot was given tea.

'Sorry the boys aren't here,' Vi said. 'But this gives us a chance to get to know each other better. We don't usually get an opportunity to chat. Do we?'

'Lovely,' said Margot.

'I hear you have done great things to the house,' said Vi. 'Patrick really must love you. He never spent money like that on me. He was always so stingy!'

'Well, it's been great to put our stamp on the house together.' It was the sale of her flat that had paid for the renovations, but Margot would not be disloyal, she would not give Vi any ammunition.

'It's a shame Patrick has had work over the weekend. He occasionally brought work home when we were married, but I suppose, as he's more senior now, it's likely to happen more frequently.'

'It doesn't happen that often and he seldom has to stay late; sometimes a meeting runs on or there is a dinner during the week. It's not a problem.' Margot never complained. Patrick did like to keep on top of things, but he had his study if he had work to do at home.

'Well, let's hope not,' said Vi. 'Of course, nobody knows what Patrick gets up to all day. He's so ambiguous, analytics or something, what does it even mean? And working late is such a euphemism, isn't it?'

'Is it?' said Margot. 'For what?'

'Well,' said Vi. 'You know, for having an affair.'

'Patrick doesn't have to stay late often.'

'Oh, I'm sure you're right.'

'And his work doesn't encroach on his time with the boys. He'll be finished by the time we get back.' Margot looked at her watch.

'I'm so sorry they are later than usual today. I did ask for them to be back on time, but they do dilly dally.' Vi smiled and wandered into the kitchen. 'Would you like a gin? I think I might have one.'

'No thanks,' said Margot, following her. She could see the kitchen was clean; there was no sign of food preparation. Perhaps on her nights without the boys, Vi went wild, going into town and partying.

'I hate cooking for one. I'll probably order a takeaway after you go,' said Vi.

It was uncanny how the woman could read thoughts.

'When I was with Patrick, and he started that dull job of his, if he had a busy patch and was working late, I'd get bored and sometimes arrange alternative entertainment. Usually, a spa weekend with the girls. Revenge. But sometimes, I might have a bit of fun. If Patrick cared so little, why not? He never knew, never guessed. He has little imagination, don't you find?'

'Not sure I agree,' said Margot. Really, the woman was the limit.

'But I'm sure you have noticed that although Patrick is lovely and reliable, he is not the most exciting in the bedroom.'

'That might depend on who he is with,' said Margot, looking at her watch again.

'Well, anyway, it was just a bit of fun.' Vi laughed and leaned back against the kitchen counter. She raised her chin slightly and gave Margot a brazen stare. Margot glared back. She would not rise. The woman always had an agenda.

Vi turned to look out the kitchen window and continued. 'Once In a while, I look at the boys and wonder … but of course, they must be Patrick's; they look just like him.' A car drew up at the front of the house. 'Oh, look, here they are.'

Driving home, Margot looked at the boys in the rearview mirror. Ollie and Toby were sitting on the backseat. They were playing with little model aeroplanes, and their dark heads were bowed towards each other, peas in a pod. They were eight and six. Lovely boys, still into Lego and Beano. Of course, they were Patrick's. They looked just like him. Vi was a venomous bitch.

A Shower

Weeks later, Margot was still mulling over what Vi had said. She was stirring, Margot knew that, but it had got to a point where she had to bring it up with Patrick if she was going to get any sleep. When he had finished reading to the boys, supper was over, and the house was quiet, Margot thought the moment had come. They were together on the sofa. Patrick was reading some papers he had brought back from work. Margot had her unopened book beside her and half a glass of wine.

'Darling, will you tell me something?' she asked.

‘Anything,’ he said, not lifting his eyes from his work.

‘I was wondering … it was something Vi said, ages ago.’

‘I wouldn’t believe anything that spews out of her mouth. She just wants to cause trouble.’

‘It was about the boys and you and her,’ said Margot.

‘Especially if it’s anything to do with her reimagining the past.’

‘She inferred that you might have had problems … conceiving the boys.’

‘Me?’ Patrick put down his papers and looked at her. ‘She suggested I … I had a problem getting her pregnant. Margot, let me tell you that was not the case. Vi asked for a baby and I gave her one, twice. There were no problems in that department.’

‘Oh, well then …’

‘She is such a snake. She may have had affairs later, but the boys are mine.’

‘Well, that is reassuring.’

‘Is there any more of that wine left?’ he asked.

Margot went to fetch the rest of the bottle from the kitchen. She felt like a top up herself.

‘In that case,’ she said, filling his glass and then her own. ‘If I asked you for a baby, would you give me one?’

‘Darling, we have talked about this. You know that’s not feasible, now. And anyway, I’m working hard, you enjoy your work too, the boys are demanding. We don’t need to have anything else to worry about.’ Patrick took a mouthful of wine.

‘You know, you get to a certain age and priorities change …,’ she said.

‘Not for me,’ said Patrick.

‘Patrick, will you listen to me? It’s important for me that we talk about this clearly.’

‘I’m sorry, Margot. You know I struggle with this. I find it painful, but at the end of our marriage, Vi enjoyed tormenting me. She took me for the fool I was, and I allowed her to ruin everything for me. It was humiliating. I can't bear to go over this again.' He finished his wine in one gulp. 'I really need to concentrate on this,' he added, standing and waving his papers and retreating to his study.

Margot stared at the empty cushion beside her on the sofa and wondered yet again why Patrick found it so hard to talk about the important things. Always running away. Vi was a bitch, but he was an adult. And what did feasible mean anyway? It was infuriating. He was so reasonable and therefore impossible to argue with. Tears began to slip down her cheeks. She filled her glass again and searched for the TV remote.

In the morning, Patrick was out of the house with the boys at football. He had been in a rush and hadn't brought her the usual cup of coffee and the paper. But Margot had to get up and get going, she didn't have time to laze today.

Margot opened her wardrobe. Her hand hovered over the hanging rail. What did she want to wear to Jenni's? There was her safe navy blue, but something more upbeat would be appropriate. She didn't want her dress to drag her mood down, what she needed was a lift. There was the pink dress. She pulled it out. Her nose wrinkled, perhaps too short and frilly. In the end she wore a pale green dress because she had some tortuous shoes that matched, and she felt she needed a lift.

In front of the mirror, she saw she was over-dressed, a poisoned pill, but she had run out of time to change again, so she grabbed her bag and headed out.

The traffic was appalling. Chelsea was a nightmare for parking if you didn't have a permit. Selfishly, Henry and Jenni had chosen to live, in a lovely, terraced house miles from the tube. Margot was relieved to find a space for the car near enough. She wasn't prepared to walk too far in her heels.

Jenni's baby shower made Margot feel a flame of fury, even fierier, because complaining wasn't appropriate. Being pregnant was a shared joy. Not being pregnant was a private, secret ache.

It had been impressive, the turnaround. Jenni had sorted herself out, got over Jack and on the rebound, caught Henry, a banker who was doing fabulously well. And now, Jenni was expecting.

So there had to be a baby shower. It was an Americanism, and just another excuse for people to give you a present. Of course, she would have given Jenni something anyway but being forced to do so rankled. She was trying not to be cross with her, but Jenni had got pregnant with what Margot saw as undue haste.

'Henry was very keen. I would have liked to have had a bit of time together as a couple first, but he's that much older and wanted to get on with it,' said Jenni when she broke the news. Jenni was effervescent in her joy. 'And would you believe it, I was pregnant just like that; first month of trying.'

Margot couldn't quite believe it. She had to flex her fingers, forcing them out of the tight balls they found themselves in, ready for a defensive assault. She took a deep breath. She was very happy for Jenni.

At least Margot hadn't had to organise the event. That was the job of the trusted Louise, who had recently married and already had a modest bump. Margot felt like punching someone.

Her rage did not prevent Margot from taking time off work and spending an entire afternoon in the children's department of Peter Jones. She tried not to buy anything for herself. But she was acquiring a small bottom drawer in neutral tones in expectation. As a gift for Jenni's babies, Margot bought a divine peach snowsuit and a matching pink one. The babies would look adorable and, of course, a small toy for each, a stuffed rabbit and a little bear.

'Two little girls, how wonderful,' said Margot handing over her wrapped gifts as she arrived. Jenni looked huge. She waddled in front of Margot from the front door and lowered herself with caution onto the sofa. Margot went to help Jenni's mother with the tea.

'Looking lovely, Margot, you always look so chic. Teapots in the cupboard above the toaster. We were a little worried. At Jenni's last check-up, her blood pressure was a bit high. And there's a milk jug there, too. But I'm sure it's all going to be fine,' said Jenni's mother as she reached into the fridge.

'Remind me of the due date?' Margot said, following Jenni's mother back into the sitting room with the tea tray.

'I officially have five weeks to go, but of course, with twins you never know, and babies have minds of their own. If I have any problems, the doctors will … but all good for now,' said Jenni, patting her taut stomach. 'Fingers crossed.'

'Just over a month, how exciting.' said Louise, running her hand over her still neat belly. 'It will be so lovely to have children almost the same age. They can be friends.'

Margot sipped her tea.

'Mine's a boy,' said Louise to Margot. 'I had my scan last week. Those shoes are a fabulous colour, real femme fatal stuff, how do you walk in them?'

'A boy, how lovely.' Margot's toes pinched. What would Louise's round face look like with a fist planted squarely in the middle of it? 'Would you like a biscuit?' Margot added, struggling not to think about how unfair the world was.

'Henry is keen to be very hands-on, though he has hired live-in help, we'll need it with twins. He is very excited about the babies,' said Jenni.

'The perfect husband,' said Margot.

'Well, you deserve someone who really cares for you after Jack. God, he would sleep with anyone. You are well rid of him,' said Louise to the room.

'Yes, well, perhaps you should open some of these lovely presents,' said Jenni's mother.

Margot looked deeply into her cup of tea. Jack was a likeable rogue but had been a disaster for Jenni. Henry, affluent and attentive, said and did all the right things. Patrick thought he was a nice bloke, one of the good guys. But there was something almost antiseptic about Henry that made Margot feel uncomfortable. It was such a small thing, not worth worrying about.

A Man

MoD

The war in Afghanistan was a relentless business, chaotic danger on the ground and endless headaches in Whitehall. Patrick had initially trained as a war analyst and had recently been brought onto a committee convened to look at the suitability of the Snatch Land Rover. Was it sufficiently mobile or armoured for the conditions in the country? There had been rumblings from troops on the ground and journalists were already sniffing around. Having read the reports, Patrick thought to get ahead of the game and wrote to his Senior Executive Officer.

> *Suffice it to say that in Afghanistan, there is a need for a range of vehicles for different terrains and operations. Land Rover have provided a variety of vehicles with proven use in the field. However, considering the known issues surrounding Snatch Land Rovers, I would recommend these should be withdrawn from service in Afghanistan immediately unless fitted with electronic countermeasures. In particular, those designed to jam mobile phone signals used to trigger improvised explosive devices. Alternatively, use should be restricted to solely within the bounds of a military base camp.*

He had been horrified by some of the tales that Jack had, in moments of confidence, relayed about certain equipment. Patrick did not want to be part of slap-dash supplies that might endanger troops. He would not be able to sleep at night if he thought he had not done everything he could to secure the best provisions possible.

His senior officer replied.

Patrick, your knowledge, research and enthusiasm have been noted. As you well know, ongoing upgrading of Land Rovers of all varieties is part and parcel of MoD policy. P.S. I see you are not up to date with HR requirements.

As part of his upgrade, Patrick had to attend regular courses on management, systems and innovations. But belonging to a government agency meant he was also required to show up for courses that covered interpersonal communication skills. Patrick wasn't so keen on these. Most involved pretending to believe that everyone was special, even when they were not.

He had a folder on his computer where he hid any recommended admin that HR thought essential, management suggestions and invitations to awayday group activities. He didn't want to be friends with his colleagues or get to know his team better. They were all lovely people he was happy to keep at arm's length. He didn't want to be taught how to think differently.

However, with the prompting of his boss in mind, Patrick clocked in with the HR department. It was a waste of time, but he would sign up for the courses he had been avoiding. He needed to complete them if he was to get ahead.

'Well, about time, Patrick. I was about to send you another reminder. *How to Recognise and Combat Discrimination in the Workplace* is a four-hour course. There is an introduction, slides, examples, a mock up, interaction, and role-play. You know the sort of thing. Though, maybe you don't, as you've never been to one before.'

'Four hours! When is the next one?' said Patrick.

'They are held on the last Friday of every month, in the afternoon. I'll sign you up, shall I?'

'I suppose you'd better.'

'It's current and very relevant since the new legislative framework was passed. There are too many who are unwilling to change their attitude.'

Patrick thought of all the other exhausted-looking men in his department.

It would mean having to work late. He probably wouldn't be back in time to help at home, or to drop off the boys at Vi's, if the course coincided with a weekend which they were due to spend with their mother.

The boys had a hectic schedule. Ollie and Toby seemed to sign up for any and every after-school activity going. Feeling vaguely guilty about not being more hands on with chauffeuring them around, Patrick suggested that Ollie switch to a boarding school.

'Why, as soon as I get back from my travels, are you making plans to send my children away?' Vi said.

'Only Ollie, at the moment.'

'He'll hate it. You hated it. It won't have changed.'

'I have rung my old school and asked for a prospectus. There is a new science block, and senior boys are now allowed to walk on the lawns. It will be a marvellous opportunity for Ollie. It will open up the world to him after being cosseted at Primary.'

'I like their school,' said Vi. 'Patrick, what has happened to you? You are reverting to some old-fashioned stereotype, sending the boys away for their own good. Ollie's only eight for goodness' sake. You are turning into your father.'

Reverting to type! Ollie was nearly nine, many boys went away a good deal younger. Now Winton had a junior school, it made sense. Patrick would ask Margot for her support, after all, it would make their lives a good deal easier, he felt bad about how much of Margot's time was taken up with the boys.

Margot had been somewhat cantankerous of late, asking him again to clarify what he had already explained quite plainly. It had been awkward, but he had been clear. He was not going to rake over the past in front of her again. Anyway, it was too late now, and with the prospect of the boys boarding, Patrick and Margot could get on with their lives and he wouldn't need to see so much of Vi. Margot was loyal, she would swing behind him. He was just being practical. He was nothing like his father.

Patrick's father was a tall man with a gammy leg. He was older than most of Patrick's friends' fathers and had been caught up in the final years of the war. He had been unlucky to be injured but lucky enough to survive. After he was demobbed, his father had qualified as an accountant and moved into an unassuming job at an unremarkable company in the City. The sort of undervalued post suitable for Sisyphus.

When Patrick was little, he worshipped his father, the hero, with the limp to prove it. To his disappointment, his father never talked about his war experience, but Patrick and his friends collected all the Commando magazines. They knew exactly what soldiers had to face.

In the evenings, when his father poured himself a pre-dinner whisky, he would always read Patrick a bedtime story.

'What shall we have a look at tonight then?' His father would say, picking up his glass and flicking the ash from his cigarette into the fireplace.

Patrick, in his pyjamas, would bring a book and curl up beside his father in the big chair by the fire, crawling inside the fug of smoke and feeling the comforting scratch of his father's wool jacket against his cheek.

Patrick would choose something edifying, like *The Story of Britain* or *The Myths of Greece and Rome*, which he knew would please his father, but if he sensed something of greater levity was called for, he would bring his battered copy of *Just William* downstairs.

Though he didn't laugh much, the attribute his father most admired was a sense of humour. As a small boy Patrick wasn't exactly sure how to get one. It didn't seem to be something you could learn, but he knew it was the most damaging insult of all to be told you lacked one.

'Can't take a joke,' boys would chant in the school playground when they had done something horrid and wanted everyone to think their stunt hilarious. Patrick had the sense to see that wasn't humour.

When he moved from his day school to Winton, it was no longer cool to be impressed by your parents. The war years had receded. Superheroes and robotics were the craze. Patrick felt his parents slowed him down. When out and about, they must always wait for his father with his useless leg. His father's apologies made everything worse.

Now, Patrick cringed to think how he spurned his father's kindness and generosity.

He had worked hard to provide for his family, but Patrick knew it was his mother, the beneficiary of a small trust, who controlled expenditure.

As an adult, Patrick saw his father had held down a steady respectable job, but Patrick was ambitious and determined to be more successful. However, the more he wanted to do well at work, the more hours he had to put in, and the less time he had at home to enjoy the things he could afford because he was doing well at work. It was the sort of equation that his father would appreciate. And it turned out Patrick was as susceptible as anyone to the assistance bestowed by his mother. Perhaps that's why a sense of humour was so essential.

Nonetheless, Patrick's mother's cash would not last for ever. Although Ollie and Toby were clever, competitive boys, the world was an expensive place, and they would need to study hard and choose wisely to be financially independent adults. Boarding school was the perfect place to start.

Patrick turned to Margot for confirmation that he was doing the right thing.

'He is so little,' said Margot.

'I thought you'd think it a good idea. If the boys go away, it will be less work for you. I was sent off … didn't do me any harm,' he said.

'Well … it seems a bit extreme when there is a perfectly good, very well-regarded private day school on our doorstep. You could always send Ollie there now and decide about boarding when he's thirteen. Isn't that when bigger boys get sent away.'

'He would need to pass the exam.'

'He'll need to pass an exam if he's going to go anywhere half decent. I don't think anyone gets into a good school these days just because their grandfather was a governor, and their father paid for the cricket pavilion.'

'Ah, the old days,' said Patrick, as if his family had ever had such largesse but, with opposition from both Vi and Margot, he agreed to a stay of execution. If Ollie passed the entrance exams for Kings, he could stay at home.

A Dinner

Patrick loaded the dishwasher. Margot was rinsing glasses at the sink.

'We should use the ones that go in the machine,' said Patrick.

Margot held up a glass she had just cleaned to the kitchen light as if to gauge the dazzle on the crystal. Then she turned the dripping glass, cup-side down on the drainer. 'I thought Henry would appreciate us using proper glasses.'

'You look like a TV add. In your pinny and marigolds,' said Patrick.

'It was kind of Angela to give us these,' said Margot, turning back to the sink.

'They are lovely,' said Patrick, stroking Margot's arm, brushing her hair behind her shoulder, before moving through to clear the table. 'How much did we drink, d'you think?' He raised his voice so she would be able to hear him above the noise of the tap water.

'I wasn't counting,' said Margot from the kitchen.

Patrick gathered two more empty bottles from the dining room table and took them to the utility room, where he was making a collection for recycling.

'Two white, three red, and we've drunk half of the dessert wine that Jenni and Henry brought. That seems quite a lot, doesn't it?' he said, returning to the kitchen. 'You never have very much, and Jenni was driving.'

'And there were the drinks before dinner,' said Margot, washing up a small, cut-glass tumbler.

There had been eight of them. Margot had invited Jenni and Henry, feeling it would be good if Patrick and Henry got to know each other better. Then Patrick asked Greg, from work, and his wife, Ann.

'Do you think they'll get on?' said Margot at the beginning of the week.

'Perhaps we should ask someone else as well?' he said. 'The couple at Number forty-one?'

'It's rather short notice to ask anyone now.'

By Wednesday, Margot was planning the menu.

'Prawn salad to start I think and then I'm going with that Jamie Oliver dish with the pork, parsnips and pears and to finish off, individual chocolate soufflés.'

'Sounds ambitious,' he said.

'Well, I'll be organised. The tricky bit is adding the egg whites at the last minute, but I have a foolproof plan for that,' she said. 'I think I will call number forty-one after all.'

'Rather last minute, isn't it?' said Patrick.

'If I'm cooking for six, it may as well be eight and … do you think Henry and Greg will get on? We might need to mix things up.'

'They can always say no, I suppose.'

The neighbours at number forty-one were delighted.

Patrick had been laying the table, using napkins Margot had bought for the occasion. They were a rather insipid apricot, but they went with the rest of the table decorations. Margot was still upstairs finishing getting ready when the doorbell rang. Jenni and Henry were on the step, smartly dressed and brandishing a bottle and some chocolates.

'Apologies for being prompt. The babysitter arrived early, and as we were ready, we thought we should head out,' said Jenni.

'And there was no traffic to speak of,' said Henry.

'Thank you for these,' said Patrick as he ushered them inside. He noticed the bottle was a rather fine dessert wine. He must remember to serve it.

'This is our first time leaving Julia and Molly,' said Jenni.

'The babysitter seemed efficient,' said Henry.

'But very young,' said Jenni. 'So, would you mind if I keep my phone out, on the table? I told her to call if there was a problem.'

'Of course not,' said Margot, joining everyone in the sitting room.

'You look gorgeous, Margot,' said Henry. 'You're a lucky man, Patrick.'

'Margot always makes an effort,' said Jenni.

'I am indeed,' said Patrick, smiling at Margot.

'As am I,' said Henry, pulling Jenni into a sideways hug and kissing her on the cheek. 'I think my darling Jenni could have been a model. A super model.'

'You do look amazing,' said Margot to Jenni, exchanging a welcoming kiss.

'I'm still struggling to get into my good clothes.'

'What do you mean?' said Margot. 'It's only been a few months.'

Jenni looked as statuesque and as slender as she ever had been. Patrick couldn't understand what they were talking about.

'What would anyone like to drink?' he said.

'Thought you'd never ask,' said Henry.

Ten minutes later, Greg and Ann arrived. Greg entered the house rubbing his feet on the door mat and shaking his coat as he took it off, as though he bore both a grudge.

Margot called Greg, a history buff, the train spotter, but Patrick enjoyed his dry humour. They had adjacent desks at the MoD and on quieter days, between phone calls and meetings, they would entertain each other exchanging bizarre facts usually about arcane military details. However, although Greg looked like a mellow librarian in his Fair Isle tank top, he could be belligerent. Patrick handed Greg a whisky, hoping a drink would calm him.

'What is happening? No one has any manners anymore. I don't know what is going on with the world,' said Greg.

Henry finished his whisky and proffered his glass for a refill.

Ann told Patrick there had been a minor altercation on the drive to Wimbledon. Something about lane protocol at one of the large roundabouts.

'He just needs to vent,' she said quietly to Patrick, accepting the gin he proffered. 'He'll calm down in a minute.'

The neighbours were late but reliably uncontroversial. They would keep the conversation flowing when he and Margot were out of the room. They all moved through to dinner.

After the first course, Jenni followed Margot and Patrick into the kitchen helping to clear the table. She brought her phone with her and made a quick call.

'Everything alright?' said Margot as she strained the vegetables.

'Oh, yes. Just wanted to make sure,' said Jenni. 'The twins are asleep.'

Margot handed Patrick the filled serving dishes to carry through.

'The starter was delicious. You always make it look so easy.' Jenni slid around the kitchen picking things up and putting them down again.

The scraping of her nails along the counter set Patrick's teeth on edge.

'I love the peach-coloured candles on the table,' said Jenni

'These are a bit hot,' said Patrick, juggling the serving dishes. Margot handed him a dishcloth.

'So good of you to have us over,' said Jenni. 'Generally, we see more of Henry's friends. It's good to get a chance to even things out and such an adventure coming south of the river.'

Margot opened the warming drawer to retrieve the plates.

'What's this,' said Jenni, lifting an upside-down bowl on the counter.

'Oh!' said Margot, rescuing the dish and passing Jenni the warm plates for the table. 'Those are my egg whites.'

'Sorry,' said Jenni. 'They look a bit runny. Will they be okay?'

'I'm sure they'll be fine,' said Margot. 'I just need to pop pudding in the oven and I'll be through with the pork.'

She sounded in control. Patrick was balancing the hot serving dishes using the cloth Margot had given him as oven gloves. Jenni must have something she wanted to go over with Margot. Patrick left them to it and went back into the dining room to the furious sound of the electric whisk.

'… and of course, last year, before the babies, we were in Cannes for the festival. Amazing weather and fabulous cocktails.' Henry said.

Patrick placed the dishes he was carrying on mats in the centre of the table.

'Did you meet anyone famous?' asked Ann.

'It's in May, isn't it? It always seems a bit early in the season to have truly hot weather,' said Greg.

Patrick returned to the kitchen to fetch a bottle of red and the corkscrew while Margot, having put the soufflés in the oven, brought the casserole through, followed by Jenni with the plates.

'God, that smells good,' said Henry.

'We have been hearing about your fabulous holiday in the South of France,' said Ann to Jenni.

'Nothing wrong with Cornwall,' said Greg, tugging at his bowtie.

'Jenni tells me you normally go to France,' continued Henry as Patrick filled his glass.

'My parents sometimes take a house in the Dordogne,' said Patrick. 'But last summer, we took the boys to Wales.

'Patrick used to go there every summer as a boy,' said Margot.

'My aunt's husband's family have a small estate, more a farm really, in Gwynedd. When I was young, all the cousins would decamp there for August. I hadn't been for years.'

'The weather was atrocious, of course, one wouldn't expect otherwise, but the boys had great fun. Ollie and Toby haven't seen much of their cousins on that side, and there are some splendid castles in the Welsh Marches,' said Margot.

'Ah,' said Greg. 'Now, Harlech Castle was the home of Owain Glyndwr and is one of the best preserved and a splendid example.

'Clearly,' Henry broke in.

'I think Ollie and Toby would vote for Caernarfon,' said Patrick. 'Possibly because of the dungeons and the adventure playground.'

'Now, Caernarfon …,' said Greg

'Could you pass that bottle?' said Henry to Patrick.

Patrick handed the wine down the table.

When Greg was rambling, Patrick's mind wandered. Their trip to Wales had been great. Margot, of course, had made it all happen, liaising with Jack's sisters.

Apart from visiting castles, there were long, soggy walks and games of rounders on the smooth front lawn and endless evenings of Monopoly. Margot won much admiration for her stamina for snap and go-fish when the weather was too wet for the children to go outside.

Patrick had been disappointed Jack had not been there, away on manoeuvres or something. But it had been fun, and Patrick hoped they would be invited another year.

'Right,' said Margot, breaking into Patrick's reverie and halting Greg's monologue. 'Let me collect these plates, and I'll bring pudding through.'

'Anyone like a top-up?' said Patrick, waving what was left in the bottle.

'Well, I could help finish that before you open the dessert wine,' said Henry.

Patrick filled his glass then took the hint and followed Margot into the kitchen to get the narrow bottle of rich golden wine and fresh glasses.

'I don't know whether to laugh or cry,' said Margot, glaring at the unrisen souffles on the cooling rack.

'No good crying over spilt milk. I'm sure they'll taste good,' said Patrick. 'With delicious ingredients, you can't go wrong, surely.'

'I love your confidence. I think I'll quickly whip up some cream,' said Margot. 'A swirl on top and no one will be any the wiser.'

'A success, don't you think?' said Margot later as they cleared the table. 'Despite a comprehensive guide to the castles of Wales.'

'A triumph,' said Patrick. 'Particularly the chocolate melt-in-the-middle puddings.'

Margot laughed, relaxed now the guests had gone. Patrick kissed her as they passed in the kitchen doorway. He watched her shimmy away from him gliding between the dining room chairs as she picked up dirty napkins. Her dress was a symphony of engineering that emphasised every curve and movement. Margot was always game, but it had been a busy evening, and she did like to clear everything away before they went to bed. He hoped she wouldn't be too tired by the time they got upstairs.

An Unreasonable Man

Patrick was at his desk when a memo flashed up on his screen. He rootled inside his jacket, hanging on the back of his chair, for his phone. He needed to call Margot, a message notifying him of an essential meeting, something about policy change, had bounced into his work diary.

'Would you be able to drop the boys at Vi's on Friday? I'm going to have to work late.'

'Not this Friday. I can't. I'm meeting Jenni in town, remember? Straight after work. She's got tickets for some play,' said Margot. 'She's arranged a babysitter. I can't let her down.'

'Shit,' said Patrick. 'A meeting has been scheduled for the afternoon, and there will be a team discussion after, and then I will need to write it up. What about the au pair?'

He tried not to feel put out. He did remember. She had told him. It was just that he had become so used to relying on her to pick up the slack.

'You know she's off this weekend,' said Margot. 'You will have to get home and run Ollie and Toby over. Then you'll have the whole evening to catch up on your work. Or you could ask Vi to pick up the boys.'

'It's a running meeting. And I'm not asking Vi a favour. I'll never hear the end of it.'

'I'm sorry I can't help.'

Sometimes, it was possible to set up a conference call. He would need to enquire. He could get home before it started and run the boys over. He wouldn't be needed for the whole meeting, but he hated missing anything.

Patrick wanted to be included in any decisions. His work was engrossing, despite distracting and apparently random alterations in policy, but the vicissitudes of those in charge had less impact on his small cog of special interest in the MoD than some other areas of the civil service. The war in Afghanistan was losing public enthusiasm at home but was broadly supported by those in authority.

Margot had become a buffer between his work, and the rest of the world, freeing him up to concentrate on his career. She had gradually taken over the day-to-day management of the boys, the house, the au pair, and Mrs Stapleford. The renovations had been a nightmare, but Margot had shielded him from the worst of it, and she had been right. The changes had made a positive improvement and added value to the house. There really wasn't a price to be put on the joy of successful mutual collaboration with someone you loved. So, it was always a surprise when she couldn't help.

Patrick had happily surrendered his responsibilities and had come to rely on Margot's cool efficiency. She was rarely demanding, but occasionally she became sentimental. He had become adept at sidestepping the usual topic. He did not want to disregard her wishes, but he had gone through it many times and it was futile to wrangle over the impossible.

Of course, Margot was also reluctant to engage when their lives overlapped with Vi. That he could understand.

Patrick fussed and complained when he dropped Ollie and Toby off that Friday.

'I have to rush, I'm in the middle of a very important meeting,' he said hustling the boys and throwing their bags into the house.

'Patrick, what has come over you? I thought Margot was supposed to be a calming influence, but you seem to have turned into an angry, little man. That's not what our boys need as a father,' said Vi.

Driving home, Patrick tried to slow his breath. He did not recognise Vi's description. The family all knew she was the volatile one, not him. He was not an angry, little man. His blood boiled just thinking about it. He would have to calm down if he was going to get any work done when he got home.

Back at the house, he made himself a G&T. The ice cubes rattled in a seductive way. He almost relaxed. Patrick took a slug and carried it through to his study. He turned on his computer and logged in to catch the end of the meeting, surreptitiously running through all the emails that had arrived while he had been on the road. The phone in his pocket had buzzed as every message dropped.

'Am I an angry, little man?' he asked Margot the following morning when he returned from the corner shop with the paper.

'Well, if you are, you are *my* angry, little man,' she said, pulling him back into bed.

'It's a serious question.'

'You are definitely a man. But you are not little, average to tall, I'd say. You are even-tempered and cheerful … though sometimes recently, you do seem to have let things get to you a bit more,' said Margot. 'Why do you think that is? Perhaps turning forty?'

'God, forty! Not till next year.' How had this happened? Life had been moving at a steady, reasonable pace, but time had been slipping away while he was busy commuting to work.

Patrick had met Jack recently for one of their lunches and Jack, just about to head off somewhere on deployment, had been more pensive than usual.

'Big birthday looming, how does it feel?' Jack asked.

'Forty is hardly considered middle aged anymore and anyway, I'm still thirty-nine.'

'I just feel, well, I suppose it's all these stints abroad, but sometimes, life just feels so short. Do you ever feel that?'

'With a father who is in his late eighties and still enjoying life, I still believe there is time to make an impression. I still like my job and there is a ladder to climb,' said Patrick.

'But have you done all you meant to do? When we left school, forty seemed so far off. Did you have a plan? The army has taught me a lot, and I've seen the world – or at least the most screwed up bits of it. But there are still things I want to do before I'm too old.'

As he left Jack and headed back to Whitehall, Patrick found Jack's mood had rubbed off on him. Patrick wasn't sure that he had set himself any concrete objectives to reach before forty. But if he wanted to achieve something in his fifth decade and beyond, he should perhaps think about his health. By the time he reached the office he was dreading his birthday.

'I was thinking we should have a party to celebrate,' said Margot. 'If the weather is good, we could be in the garden.'

'I'm not sure I want to broadcast my age to everyone.'

Over the years, since the work on the house, the garden had settled. Patrick had been sceptical that they would ever sit outside, let alone one day have a party out there, but Margot had made a fantastic haven, a sheltered sun trap surrounded by colour and fragrance.

He had been horrified when she had hacked at the roses leaving nothing but bare, dead stalks.

'Are you sure you know what you're doing.'

'It called pruning,' she had said. 'They've got far too leggy. Once the tree surgeons have cut back the overhanging trees, they'll come again.'

Margot had been right of course. The garden was much brighter, and the roses had grown tall and were now covered in blooms. Though his favourite orange rose didn't seem to have made it. Margot had replaced it with a soft pink one, that she said fitted much better with the other colours in the garden. She had been kind enough to leave an area of grass for the football net, but now the boys were older, they had grown out of knocking a ball around.

'Rugby,' said Ollie. 'Is the game to play.' And once his older brother had pronounced, Toby didn't pick up a football again either.

One weekend, Patrick noticed the old football net had gone, and there was a tasteful new area of planting at the end of the garden with a statuette rising from the greenery.

'I found it in the gallery on the High Street. It's by a local artist. I thought it improved the view from the landing window,' said Margot. 'Angela always says a focal point is important in a garden.'

'Aren't you worried about your new plants?' said Patrick, taking his coffee and joining her on the terrace in the sun as she read the morning paper. Under the spreading branches of the chestnut, the only tree that had been allowed to remain intact, reaching its spring-green, hands of leaves out over the garden, Ollie and Toby were throwing a rugby ball around.

'I thought I might, but they are rather good at catch, aren't they?'

'Passing,' said Patrick.

'Pass what?'

'In rugby, it's passing the ball, not catch, it's a skill, with the shape of the ball and the spin ...'

'Well, I can see they are very skilful, whatever the terminology.'

Patrick bathed in the warmth of the sun. He closed his eyes and listened to the rustle of the Saturday paper as Margot turned the pages, the chink as she placed her coffee cup back on the table. The shouts of Ollie and Toby, the woosh and the thump as the ball was caught. It seemed implausible that he should have sons who were good at sports. He could hear the noise of some birds twittering high in the lime trees. Further afield, the sound of a mower and fainter still an aeroplane somewhere overhead.

He smiled. Life was under control. Ollie had got into Kings and was doing well. Toby had also passed the entrance exams and would be joining his brother at the end of the summer. Margot was all he wanted and needed. He opened his eyes and stretched out and took her hand in his, and pulling her towards him, kissed the back of her hand. They had fitted together with a gratification akin to the snap of Lego bricks. Margot could do everything. He didn't have to worry about anything anymore.

Contentment

A Mistake

Margot was in the shower, surrounded by the glistening bottle green tiles, struggling not to feel as though she was being swept into some deep, dark chasm as she tried to wash away the imperfections of her empty, useless body. She rinsed the shampoo from her hair and felt the thick foam heavy on her body as it slid toward the plug. She lifted her head into the spray and pulled away again she felt an errant drip land on the centre of her forehead and glide down and over her nose. She was bleeding again.

She was back on unrestricted caffeine in the mornings and sharing a drink with Patrick at the weekend. In truth, she had never been that strict about denying herself, she was a firm believer that no harm would come if she subscribed to the tenet, all things in moderation. Of course, she hadn't given up trying to get pregnant, that wasn't about to happen, but she had become more philosophical about her situation. She had always said to Patrick let's just wait and see what comes our way, but she had waited so long, it now seemed pointless being good all the time. She had been checked. She was ready. She was beginning to think she might be being punished for her sin. Though all she wanted to do was right the wrong.

Really, she shouldn't worry, there was no need to get so wound up about it, she was only thirty-four, she had plenty of time. But she must find a moment to talk to Patrick about her frustration again. She didn't want to worry him, but she needed reassurance if not answers. He was very involved with his work, gearing up to get a promotion and signing up for all the necessary courses and by the time he got home, he was not in a mood to think about anyone else's problems, but however fatalistic Margot would like to think she was, she needed to make this a priority.

On the weekends, now that they were older, the boys stayed up with Patrick and Margot for supper and to watch television. It was as it should be, a natural progression and Margot enjoyed the boys' company, but it did mean she had less time to have Patrick to herself.

'Can't it wait, Margot? You're like a dog with a bone. I'm being pulled every which way,' Patrick had said the last time she had brought it up.

It irked that Patrick could so easily dismiss her concerns. She would need to find a moment to pin him down, she couldn't wait forever.

The following weekend, when Patrick was getting soaked on the side lines watching the boys at their school matches, Margot was on her way to see Jenni. She tried not to take anyone's eye out with her umbrella as she snaked through the shoppers on the King's Road.

Jenni had asked Margot over for tea to see the twins.

Margot was playing with Julia, her goddaughter, sitting on the carpet building colourful bricks into a tower together to be knocked down by Molly, a game both girls thought hilarious, while Jenni making the tea.

Where's Henry? Is he playing golf?' said Margot, shouting through to the kitchen. 'The weather's not great.'

'No, no, he's not playing golf today. Well, he might be. He's not here, as a matter of fact.'

'He's away?'

Henry was often away travelling for business, but not generally at the weekend.

'No,' said Jenni, bringing two mugs of tea through and putting them in the centre of the table out of the twin's reach.

'What's this?' said Margot, joining Jenni at the table and eyeing the mug of pink tea that Jenni presented her with.

'This is rhubarb and ginger tea, from my latest project,' said Jenni. 'I'm designing ethically sourced leaf tea. What do you think?'

Margot took a tentative sip. 'Wow, it's ... different,' she said.

'If you like, I'll order you some.'

'That would be great,' said Margot, pushing her mug aside. 'Bit hot. No more flowerpots?'

'That was only ever a one off.'

'Henry's out?' said Margot

'Actually, I asked him to leave,' said Jenni.

'Again?' Margot looked at Julia and Molly. The little girls were playing nicely, unaware of the seismic changes that were happening in their life. They sat on the rug, bouncing on padded bottoms, waiting for Margot to build the blocks again. Margot couldn't quite believe that Jenni was thinking of destroying her family, she was running through marriages as though eligible men could be disposed of in two bites like a biscuit.

'Asked him to leave? When?'

'Oh,' said Jenni. 'The weekend before last.'

'But... but, why?' Henry had seemed great. He was supportive, involved with the children and doted on Jenni.

'I know it's a bad look, throwing out a second husband. But it became apparent that .... that he has a problem.' Jenni sniffed.

'What sort of a problem?' Margot didn't think she'd met anyone who didn't have a problem of one sort or another. She thought of Patrick prioritising work, his desire to get ahead. The way he sometimes wrapped himself up in his thoughts and she couldn't break through. How, if he didn't want to engage, he would bury his head in the sand. It was just a matter of what you decided you could live with.

'He drinks.'

'Everyone does.' Margot knew that wasn't what Jenni meant, but did Henry really have a problem or was Jenni looking for an excuse.

'All evening … every evening.' Jenni picked up Julia, who had started to grizzle.

'Wow! I mean, really?'

'I didn't realise it was a problem at first.' Jenni bounced Julia on her knee.

Julia's chubby, little arms flew out with every landing, and she started to cry in earnest.

'Gently,' said Margot, wary of criticising a new mother, before turning to Molly who had also started to wail.

'I mean, when we first married, I knew he liked a drink, nothing wrong with that. And his work is not humdrum like Patrick's. Henry is very senior at the bank. His job has long hours and is high powered and demanding. I could see he'd want to relax when he was home.'

'Poor Henry, how very stressful.'

Margot took the whimpering Julia from Jenni and rocked her before she sat her down on the mat next to Molly and gave them a toy. Then she gave Jenni, who was also sobbing, a hug.

'There would be a whisky before supper and then we'd have a bottle of wine, like anybody else. I hadn't clocked that I would only have a glass, and he would have the rest. It didn't seem like anything to worry about. He could carry it.'

'So, what went wrong?' said Margot.

'It was so gradual. It wasn't apparent until after the twins were born. I think as a mother one is more aware and sensitive to danger,' said Jenni through sobs.

'That's probably true,' said Margot, shaking a rattle at the gurning twins.

'Then some nights, I noticed he'd have a whisky while he gave the girls a bath. I was terrified he'd lose concentration and drop his drink on the tiles and there would be glass everywhere and someone would get hurt. Often, he'd open a second bottle of wine during supper. By the end of the evening, he'd be out for the count, and somehow, I'd have to get him up to bed.'

Margot felt her jumper damp on her shoulder from Jenni's tears. Jenni raised her head and pulled away.

'Sorry, sorry,' Jenni said, getting up and pulling a fistful of tissues from the box. 'I guess if you have that sort of disposition, it just eventually takes you over. I mean, one day it was fine, and then it wasn't.'

'I'm so, so sorry. I can't imagine how you were able to look after the girls with all that going on. It must have been impossible.'

'Henry's drinking didn't affect his work. But, in the end, I couldn't bear watching him falling to pieces while I papered the cracks, and I was worried about the girls.'

Julia had caught her mother's mood and had pulled herself upright and was now clutching Jenni's leg, howling, Molly was joining in.

'I had no idea.' Margot was bemused, Henry had always seemed urbane and charming, never out of control.

'Well, how could you?' said Jenni. 'In the end, I just had to ask him to leave, sort himself out … I couldn't look after him as well as two babies, not if he wasn't prepared to help himself.'

'No, of course not.'

'He promised. He's signed in to The Priory. When he dries out, he'll be back.' Jenni smiled a weak smile, more hopeful than certain. She picked up the crying Julia.

'But at least I've got my darling little girls.' Jenni bounced Julia on her hip until the sobs gave way to hiccups.

'Shall I put the kettle on again? We could do with a hot cup of tea,' said Margot.

Goodness', it never rained but it poured. She may not have had two darling little girls like her friend, but Jenni hadn't been lucky with her choice of men. Patrick was a paragon of virtue compared to what else was out there.

An Empty Nest

'Dinner was divine, thank you.' On the way to the car park, Margot's narrow heels kept slipping into the cracks between the cobbles.

'Well, five years is something,' said Patrick, holding onto her arm and helping her back into the car.

Margot leant back against the leather seat allowing her head to relax against the headrest. She felt replete and slightly giddy. She had drunk more than her fair share of the wine, a sign she had given up hope. Patrick was driving.

'Your fortieth will be the next celebration,' she said as Patrick manoeuvred himself into the driving seat.

Then, she must have dozed off, she had no memory of the motorway, until she heard the tick, tick of the indicator as Patrick inched the car off the M4, down to the roundabout and onto the south circular to cross the bridge at Kew. Margot took a deep breath and sat up straighter. It was difficult to keep upright in Patrick's car, the slippery seats induced reclining. But now she was awake she wanted to stay that way, or she wouldn't sleep when they got in.

They drove past the brilliance of shopping parades clustered around traffic lights with their chippies and kebab shops still serving customers. Between junctions, there were long stretches of dark streets. The occasional house with the blue light of a television leaking around the curtains, or a light at an upstairs window. Margot thought of a waking child, imagining the mother walking back and forth rocking her baby on her shoulder, gently patting their back and crooning, eager to get them back to sleep.

Back home in bed, the alcohol churning her brain, Margot stared at the ceiling feeling too dizzy to sleep. She hadn't brought up her concerns over dinner. It was too special an occasion to ruin the mood. But she must get back on track, be good about her diet and persuade Patrick to get tested.

Margot thought about what Vi had said, 'They look like Patrick; they must be his.'

She hadn't mentioned this poisoned dart to Patrick. She never would; how could she? Vi knew that. This barb had been for Margot to mull over in the middle of the night.

Vi probably slept like a baby, with a notepad by her bed just in case something malicious occurred to her as she was dropping off. A book for all the drops of venom, or perhaps she had a cauldron in the garden shed.

Of course, Vi had dark hair too. Or, perhaps, Vi had a type: dark hair and blue eyes. But what if Vi was telling the truth? What if the boys were not Patrick's? What if Patrick was the problem?

Unusually, Vi came to collect the boys the previous Friday. She rushed in from the gym, her wiry hair looking like it was trying to escape from her head, her skinny legs stork-like in leggings.

'Extraordinarily tidy as always.' Vi followed Margot into the house. 'I don't know how you manage it, working full time. I suppose having a cleaner must help,' she said making herself comfortable on a kitchen stool.

'Tea? The boys are ready. Their bags are in the hall,' said Margot. 'All I need to do is give them a call.'

'Thanks, I could do with a cup,' said Vi. 'I've been in such a rush. I haven't stopped since my first class this morning. Not even for lunch!'

'Earl Grey?' Margot always asked, even though she knew what the answer would be. It was the meanest she could be face-to-face with Vi, who was scary in her vividness.

'Builders if you have it.'

Margot filled Vi's mug straight from the boiling tap.

'Swanky,' said Vi.

Margot let the teabag brew while she fetched her leaf tea and the small pot, with the matching cup and saucer that Angela had given her. She only used the set when Vi was there. Margot warmed the pot before making her tea. Then she squeezed Vi's teabag and added milk from the fridge before pouring her own tea.

'Proper tea always tastes better from porcelain, don't you think?' Margot said.

'Oh, you have great taste. The house is a triumph. It wouldn't be my choice, well it wasn't. But at least you kept most of the original features. Grey, of course, can seem cold, but I think you get away with it,' said Vi, looking round the room before she sipped her tea.

'Thank you,' said Margot. 'I think a calm environment is good for the boys.'

'I've always appreciated what you do for the boys,' said Vi. 'But … I wonder … are you pregnant yet? I thought you were of an age where you wouldn't want to hang around.'

'That's not really any of your business.'

How did Vi keep it up, it was a literal stream of invective. Margot called the boys even though Vi hadn't finished her tea.

'Send my regards to Patrick. His fortieth is looming, isn't it? How's he taking it? He was always terrified of the big birthdays,' said Vi as she followed Ollie and Toby to her car.

Patrick had been grumpy lately, protesting about his age, avoiding talking to her about the things that mattered, hiding in his work.

Margot had read all about the war in the papers. Surely, it was unnecessary for Patrick to feel so responsible and be so embroiled. He often told her he was just a civil servant with a tedious job in administration, a small cog in a vast machine. If nothing he did made a difference, why did he invest so much energy in the MoD? Patrick liked a puzzle, of course, 'if there are two tanks in Aldershot and four captains in Catterick, how does the sergeant make an omelette?' Margot hated those sorts of problems. She preferred simple equations. Patrick plus Margot equals a baby.

Now, lying in the dark, a nightmarish memory flashed into Margot's head, like an unwanted dream. She remembered walking through the vanilla ward, moans and muted chat had escaped from the rooms on either side.

Margot's shoes had squeaked on the floor, as she had approached the high desk that protected hospital staff. Reaching over, Margot had showed her admission letter to the nurse.

'You've come in the wrong door. There's a separate entrance for terminations.' The nurse had said.

Margot had followed her terse instructions and headed down the hallway past mothers and babies. She had paused outside an open door. In the room there were rows of cots, each with a perfect bundle lying within. Like a box of all sorts, blankets crinkled around infants like pleated paper cups holding sweets. She had watched the babies, some wriggling and waving, but most sleeping. It was a different world. Margot's heart had been quite still. A nurse entering the room with bottles of formula had broken Margot's trance and ushered her away.

Margot had turned towards the termination unit, where she had been met by another nurse, who had asked Margot her name and date of birth and had handed her a clipboard and pen. Margot had blindly signed the forms. She didn't need to read them. She already knew what they would say. They would be standard. Everyone who had this procedure would have to sign. Margot had given her sister's name as next of kin. Nothing would go wrong, so Lily would never find out.

The room had been white and smelt of clean. Behind the curtain, the bed, angled like a dentist's chair had seemed to float. She had undressed and in a hospital gown, had climbed up onto it.

Margot had lain back with her feet in stirrups. It was humiliating. For a moment, she had an impulse to run for the door, away from this sterile room with its instruments of torture. But she knew every day mattered, there could be no delay. Her hands had grasped, crumpling the paper sheet on the bed. The tears had rolled down her cheeks and her innards had clenched as the doctor approached with a speculum.

'Try to relax,' he had said. 'It won't take long.'

Margot had concentrated hard on the wall behind the doctor, soon she would be clean, and the mess she had made would be all vacuumed up. Soon, this moment would be in the past. Margot had closed her eyes and tried not to feel.

Afterwards, the nurse had patted Margot's shoulder. 'You're young, you'll have plenty of chances ... later... when the time's right.'

When she had arranged to have the procedure, Margot had been focused on getting rid of a problem, she had not thought there would be an emotional cost, but when it was all over, she had this overwhelming sense of loss. She remembered thinking that nobody should have been nice to her. She should have been held to account, she had stolen something, an opportunity for someone to be, she had destroyed a soul, and she deserved to be scolded. She had been too ashamed to tell anyone. It had not been the time or the place for a baby, but she had known she would feel responsible forever.

And here she was lying by Patrick, ambushed by the past, by something she thought she could forget. A one-night stand, over ten years ago, with a man she barely knew and had never seen again, and barely thirty minutes to end the life, a little girl, she was sure, that nobody would ever know or see.

Now she was ready to make amends, and yet Patrick was refusing to engage with her. Perhaps he didn't love her anymore. Of course he did, but Margot regretted that yoga truth she had spouted years ago, 'my husband loves me'. She had been tempting fate. They were married, so Margot had presumed his love, but there was no guarantee that just because she loved him that he loved her, or that they would have a child.

Margot turned in bed dragging her share of the duvet. Lack of sleep was driving her to ridiculous assumptions. Of course, Patrick loved her. But they had been married for five years; how could she not be pregnant?

Margot looked over at the bulk of Patrick's sleeping form, breath so gentle she couldn't hear it. She nudged him, snuggled up against him.

'What now?' he muttered as she roused him.

Margot needed to reassure herself that she was doing all she could. Postcoital and drowsy, she would be able to get back to sleep.

'Love you,' he mumbled into her ear, before rolling over and falling back asleep.

'Love you too.' Feeling satisfied and replete, she knew she would be out in a moment.

Pockets

Margot knew exactly what she wanted. She hated that. It was easier to buy a dress by accident. Find the perfect coat when shopping for boots and buy amazing shoes for yourself when you are supposed to be Christmas shopping for someone else. To have something in your mind's eye was a disaster.

As it was a summer party, the dress should be light and airy, but no frills. She didn't want too much fullness in the skirt. A narrow silhouette, finishing on the knee.

She wanted a subtle pattern with colour, in greens or blues. A V-neck was more flattering with maybe a bit of a collar. The sleeves could be loose, but they must have a cuff. Trailing sleeves were too impractical. They were for people without children, not for someone who would be doing the washing up.

Margot didn't feel she was being difficult. Her dress was striking, but feminine. It was contemporary with an edge, while being age appropriate. She had absolutely outgrown cute.

Finding something suitable should be the easiest thing, something she could get done in advance, a dress she could keep ready, waiting in her closet. But somehow the days had run together, and the lunch hours slipped by.

Margot had started her search around the office, but Covent Garden had become so touristy. She ventured north to the Seven Dials, but the shops were super trendy. So, she had looked further afield, up Regents Street to Oxford Circus and another time all the way to Knightsbridge and Harvey Nicks.

She had no luck, so Margot convinced herself she had plenty of dresses, she didn't need a new one.

Then, a couple of weeks before the party, as she was driving home with a food shop, out of the corner of her eye, in the shopping arcade off the bypass, she saw a flash of blue in the window of a boutique she hadn't noticed before. Margot did a U-turn. There was a parking space right outside the shop. It was meant to be.

Margot studied the dress in the window. It was blue with flashes of green. It had a straight skirt, a raised moulded collar, with a slit to the breastbone, and three-quarter length sleeves with turned back cuffs. Bodycon, she thought it would be called. It was her dress.

From the street, behind the window display, the shop seemed dark, though a brightness glowed from the depths. There was a tatty A4 poster in the corner of the window, tape peeling brown from the glass, advertising alterations and tailoring. On the door hung an open sign.

Margot entered the narrow shop, a bell tinkled, and a shop assistant rose silently from behind the lit desk at the rear of the shop. The upward light from the lamp highlighted the frills on the collar of her blouse and caught strands of frizzy hair escaping from her bun. She had a tape measure hanging around her neck along with a chain and reading glasses. The assistant clasped and unclasped her hands. Margot hesitated.

'Can I help,' said the assistant turning on an overhead light.

Margot glanced at the door, but now she was here, she might as well make the best of it.

'I spotted the dress in the window as I was passing. Could I try it on?'

'We don't take display items down, but anyway, that's a size ten, love. That's not going to fit you.'

'Oh,' said Margot, deflating.

Now she took it in properly, the dress on display did seem neat. That was probably why it looked so smart.

'Unfortunately, that is the only size we have in that design. We only carry one or two of any style. These dresses are exclusive, made by an artist in the West Country who prints her own fabric,' said the assistant.

'It's just what I was looking for.'

'We do have a different frock by the same designer.'

The assistant drew Margot into the back of the shop. She selected a dress from a rack, pulling it out from between other rainbow dresses for Margot to see. 'Would you like to try this one on.'

The dress had an abstract flowery print in mainly the same blue and green but also with dashes of pink, red and yellow. Margot could see the pattern was like the dress in the window, but the style was quite different. This dress was made from a fine, woven fabric, not silk or jersey, and hung lank like a tissue from the hanger. It was a basic shirtwaister, but everything about it was exaggerated, too colourful, too long, too full in the skirt. This was not her dress.

'I think someone like you could carry it off,' said the assistant. 'Not everyone could. This style is for someone with height and flair.'

Seduced, Margot took the dress from the shop assistant and swept into the fitting room, as she pulled the curtains behind her the hooks rattled on the chain. The flimsy, cambric fabric almost covered the opening. Margot was undressed, exposed, looked at the fine cotton dress, wondering whether to step into it or to pull it on over her head, when the disembodied voice of the assistant asked from beyond the curtain. 'How are you doing?'

'Not quite there yet,' said Margot.

'This will give the skirt a bit of oomph,' said the assistant, pushing a net petticoat through the edge of the changing room curtain.

Margot hadn't worn a net skirt since she had taken ballet classes in primary school. She stepped into the petticoat and then pulled the dress over her head. Margot ran her hand over the smooth, polished fabric. The cotton was so fine it had a sheen.

She came out into the shop to look in the full-length mirror. With the net, the dress was transformed. It now had the New Look of a '50's Dior dress. The assistant stood behind Margot and looked at her reflection critically.

'You could really do with something to emphasise your waistline,' said the assistant, producing a royal blue belt.

At two inches, it was much wider than Margot would normally wear, but the belt sat neatly on her waist. She looked in the mirror. The bodice fitted perfectly.

'You'd get the proper effect if you put on some heels.'

The assistant gave Margot a pair of royal blue shoes. They were higher than Margot liked and had a wedge with a peep toe, which she always found tricky, but she put them on just to get the effect.

She twirled in front of the angled shop mirrors. Refined and floral, chic and fancy. As she swirled, enjoying the swish of the full, long skirt against her legs, she knew she looked fantastic. The skirt was long and floaty, but the deciding factor was the large patch pockets carefully matched to the pattern. Margot was enjoying herself. She didn't give a thought to the prawns and peas defrosting in the boot of her car. This dress was summery *and* sophisticated.

The assistant laid the dress on the counter, wrapped it in crisp, pink tissue paper and slid the parcel into a smart, rigid shop bag. She snapped the flaps over and pulled the ribbon handle through the designated slots. As Margot passed over her credit card, the shop assistant handed Margot the bag with a smug smile.

Margot walked out into the late afternoon sunshine, the bag with the shop logo hanging from her arm. She had bought the floral dress, the petticoat, the belt, and the shoes. She was ready for the party.

Guest List

A 40th PARTY
to celebrate Patrick's Birthday
Saturday 22nd May 2010

A week before the party, they were having coffee out on the terrace, bathed in sunshine and the sweet scent of the lime trees. She held Patrick's hand while he read some work papers. After a while, Patrick wriggled his fingers free to turn a page.

This early in the morning there was a slight, cooling breeze. Margot shivered, pulled her cardigan over her shoulders, and sipped her coffee. She could hear the murmur of the bees busy in the limes and birds about their business, chattering, a flicker in the bushes. The wind pulling at the tips of the birch trees at the back of the garden, was an intermittent background fussing. So much going on, and yet so peaceful. Through half closed eyes she almost saw the sunlight filter through wafts of pale blond hair lifted by the breeze at the seat next to her. The ghost of her little girl.

The wind rustled the paper in front of her, Margot picked up her teaspoon and pinned the sheet to the table. It was her list of names with ticks and crosses. The invitations had been sent out two weeks before and nearly everyone had replied. Patrick's father probably wouldn't make it, but they all had to pretend he would. Close family, the aunts, uncles and cousins, mutual friends, and one or two of Patrick's work colleagues, anyone who was important to Patrick was invited.

Margot wanted the garden to have the feel of a village fete, with games on the lawn for the children. Patrick would help her hang bunting on the morning. She made a note to call the caterers later to see if they had been able to source the crayfish she wanted.

The weather was set fine; it would be perfect for next weekend. There were alliums and early day lilies out under the lilac tree. The roses were on the brink, covered in buds. A day or two before the party, she would pick some closed buds on short stems and display them in tealight glasses. If she placed them in a warm window they would open in time.

The boys came out into the garden, they had brought bowls of cereal, which hardly hit the table before their breakfast was slurped down. Then without a moment to digest, the boys raced each other to the bottom of the garden and began a pseudo-rugby game, calling to each other as they ran and dodged, skirting around the flower beds. Their shouts melding with the other sounds of a garden at play.

Ollie and Toby were uncomplicated, easy to love. There had been few problems at home or at school. Of course, the dreaded teenage years loomed, but Margot felt confident there wouldn't be too many issues. She and Patrick agreed on the ground rules. She would never undermine his authority, apart from that one time when he thought of sending the boys to boarding school. What was the point of having children if you sent them away just when they were becoming interesting. That was the only time she had ever seen eye to eye with Vi.

Margot often thought about how difficult it must have been for Angela to look after two rebellious, distraught teenage girls, when she was well into her sixties. She had selflessly given Margot all the care and attention she needed. She was Margot's inspiration.

From her childhood loss, through those awful years of growing up with grief, only to face the catastrophic choice that had coloured her twenties. It was extraordinary that, here she was, sitting in the sunshine in her own garden with her own husband, and Ollie and Toby. And this year, they had the party for Patrick, and who didn't enjoy a party?

Margot studied her list once again, her eyes sliding through the names, when she had a thought. She went inside to find her phone.

'Jenni, hello! I just thought I should ring you about the party.'

'Perfect timing. I was about to call you. I have a favour to ask,' said Jenni.

'What about?'

'You go first it's your party, and I feel a bit embarrassed to mention mine.'

'OK,' said Margot. 'I only just realised that we have invited Jack to the party. We have, of course, asked all Patrick's first cousins. And I suddenly thought, well, I didn't want it to be a problem for you.'

'Oh, Margot, is that all? Jack is ancient history. Honestly, I haven't thought about him for years, but thanks, good to be forewarned.'

'Are you sure?' said Margot.

'Yes, yes, that was such a long time ago, I've moved on. There's been Henry, after all, and the twins,' said Jenni.

'And how is my Goddaughter?'

'Julia and Molly are on good form. Looking forward to seeing Ollie and Toby at the party. And that's what I wanted to ask you … could I bring Richard?'

'Richard?' said Margot.

'After Henry's defection, and his meeting someone new in rehab who really understood him,' said Jenni. Margot could hear the cynical sigh and imagined the eye roll that went with this comment. 'Richard has come to be my rock. He's helped me understand the personal weaknesses that have led me to make such bad choices in the past.'

Jenni had met Richard recently at the gym and bounced into a relationship with him.

'I don't think they've been all bad, have they?' said Margot.

'You are probably sensitive about numbers, but I thought I would ask anyway. Nothing ventured ...,' said Jenni.

'Of course, no problem. We should have included him from the off.'

Margot had only met Richard once and had taken an instant dislike to him. She would have been hard pressed to explain why. She wished she could give him the benefit of the doubt, but he had seemed so severe and unfriendly. Margot went outside to join Patrick'

'Jenni asked if she could bring Richard next weekend,' she said.

'And you said yes? I thought you said he was unbearable.'

'Of course, I said yes.'

'Of course. Now I can't wait to meet him and see how ghastly he really is.'

'Oh, you'll probably think he's an excellent sort of a person.'

'Really, in what way?'

'In the way that he's organised and punctual and somehow clipped …. well, just not like Jack, who is wild and fun, or like

Henry who is an alcoholic and fun. Richard is methodical and sensible.'

'You mean logical. It sounds like he will be the perfect antidote. I suspect Jenni has had about as much fun as any one person can take.'

The Party

The lawn was cut and looked like baize, firm like a dance floor. The ladder Patrick used to hang the decorations was back in the shed. Single, freshly opened roses sitting upright in different coloured tealight glasses adorned the tables in clutches. The caterers had arrived and taken over the kitchen, the family was washed and pressed.

Margot saw Patrick's father teetering up the path to the front door supported by his Zimmer, the taxi driver, and Patrick's mother. They were the first to arrive. Patrick went to help his parents up the steps. After saying hello, Margot went through to the kitchen to gather some eats for them. She found Ollie and Toby hanging around, eyeing up the canapes, getting under the caterer's feet.

'Come on boys, your grandparents are here, come and say hello.'

When her sister, Lily, arrived with Aunt Angela, Margot suggested her aunt might like to join Patrick's parents where they had settled on the sofa in the calm of the sitting room, but after a cheerful wave to one and all, Angela moved through the house.

'I do so want to see your garden,' she said as she picked up a sherry from a tray and manoeuvred her way towards the sunshine and noise.

'How does she do it?' said Margot, greeting Lily and her family.

'She's been chatting to the kids all the way in the car. She has more energy than I have,' said her sister.

Lily did not look as though she had just climbed out of a people carrier either. She wafted into the garden in diaphanous silk, followed by her children, who were eager to find Ollie and Toby. Patrick handed over his old camera to Lily's eldest daughter and asked if she could take some photographs of the day. She was a bit older than the other children and was taking an 'A' level in Art and was a keen photographer. She was happy to have a task to keep her busy.

Later, through the open terrace doors, Margot saw Patrick weaving through family and friends. He was carrying a large jug of Pimm's, topping up drinks, getting waylaid and moving on. At that moment, he stopped to catch up with Angela, resting the jug on an outside table.

The boys, Toby, now almost as tall as Ollie, saw Angela with their father and ran up to give her a hug. Ollie and Toby delighting in her confusion as Angela pretended not to know which was which. Margot's most favourite people in the world sharing a moment in the sunshine.

There was a crash and a clatter. One of the younger children had spilt juice on the pale carpet in the sitting room.

'Whoops,' said Margot. 'Not to worry.'

She scuttled through the house to get a cloth.

'I didn't expect to find the hostess with the mostest in a cupboard.'

'Oh! Hi Vi.' Margot extracted her head from under the sink, where she had been looking for some kitchen paper. Where had the woman come from? She had not been on Margot's list.

'I think Ollie and Toby are in the garden,' Margot said.

'Is this a surprise?' Vi beamed. 'Did he tell you? I overheard the boys discussing his birthday. I wasn't sure I should, but Patrick insisted I come along. And I thought why not. Even if I didn't get a formal invitation … come and see what all the fuss was about.'

Vi, sipped her Pimm's. 'I'm enjoying seeing Patrick turn forty,' she laughed, following Margot around.

'How are you, Vi?' Margot found some kitchen paper after scrabbling under the sink in the utility room.

'Good, thank you. Oh, you've kept the old height chart going.' Vi ran her finger up the marks on the door frame that showed the boys' heights over the years. 'I thought you'd eradicated every trace of me.'

'Who doesn't like a growth chart, family history in the making,' said Margot.

She left a roll of kitchen paper for the caterer and took the other through to the sitting room.

'It's so lovely to catch up with Patrick's relations. I haven't seen them all in years,' said Vi, trailing behind Margot as she moved through the house. 'And the garden is looking beautiful; you've done a great job there.'

At least Vi was not in the usual gym gear but was wearing a bodycon dress in a similar blue to Margot's floaty frock. It was uncanny. Margot was almost positive it was the dress she had seen in the boutique window where she had bought her own dress. But Vi couldn't have known what Margot would be wearing.

In the sitting room, a server was already mopping up the spill with a wad of napkins. Margot hid her roll of kitchen paper on the side table behind a large pot containing a sweet-smelling gardenia that someone had brought as a gift.

'And I think the tiles in your ensuite look fabulous. It's a bold choice, dark green,' said Vi.

When had Vi slipped upstairs? The woman was unconscionable Margot left Vi with Patrick's parents and stepped out onto the terrace to escape.

The swirling bunting, bright summer clothes and colourful roses made a carnival of the garden. Relatives and friends rippled back and forth, seeming to coordinate with the warm breeze swirling the tops of the lime trees. The sun shone, the children gambolled, and everything moved together in a gentle sway, like a carousel at a fairground.

To one side, under a parasol, Margot saw someone she took a moment to recognise, it was Richard. Jenni was beside him, waif thin, and wrapped around her legs, half hidden in her skirt were Julia and Molly.

'There you are, so glad you could come. And you too, Richard, welcome,' said Margot, giving Jenni a kiss and Richard her hand, arm's length was close enough.

'Lovely to see you again and thank you for including me.' His smile looked as though it was being wrenched from his face.

'Of course.' Margot turned and bent down and spoke to the little girls. 'And don't you look like gorgeous little dolls. Too cute in your smocked dresses.' Margot gave her goddaughter a hug. 'Why don't you and Molly go and find Ollie and Toby. Look, there they are over there. They can find you some toys to play with.'

'Or if you are feeling a bit shy, with all these big, noisy children running around, you can stay here with Mummy,' said Richard.

Julia and Molly didn't move, looking at their mother.

'You can stay with me for a bit,' said Jenni, brushing Julia's fringe of her forehead and taking Molly's hand.

'Whatever you like,' said Margot, glancing at the girls. 'But it's a lovely day to run around with the other kids. Toby, can you come here a moment?'

'Hi Julia, Molly, remember me?' said Toby, and, with a wide generous smile to the adults, he took the little girls by the hand, and within minutes, they were absorbed in the gaggle of children.

'Shall we mingle,' said Margot and before Richard could complain, she took them both by the arm and led them into the party. 'Let me get you a drink. Richard, what would you like?'

'Richard doesn't drink,' said Jenni.

'But there are some soft options too.'

The garden table on the terrace was covered in a long linen tablecloth and set out with drinks and glasses. Too late, Margot realised Jack was by the table, filling a tumbler of Pimm's for himself and asking Angela what she would like. Ready to make a diversion Margot's step faltered, and then she smiled. How endearing it was to see Jack bending to her birdlike aunt and pouring her a thimbleful of sherry. Anyway, it was too late to steer Jenni and Richard in the opposite direction, Jack had spotted them.

'Margot, mwah, mwah.' Jack kissed the air. 'I've just been having a fascinating chat with your aunt. And look who it is! Jenni, Darling!' He gave Jenni a kiss and a Pimm's.

'This is Richard,' said Jenni.

'Oh, good to meet you,' said Jack, pumping Richard's arm. 'I'm the dastardly first husband.'

'I know who you are,' said Richard, picking up a bottle of sparkling water.

'You're looking gorgeous by the way Margot, ... and the garden is enchanting. Love the roses.'

'Thanks,' said Margot. 'We were just circulating.'

'Don't let me hold you back,' said Jack, theatrically holding his hands up, his Pimm's sloshing wildly. 'Let's catch up later,' he said to Margot, trailing his free hand across her shoulders as he backed off into the throng.

'Well, really!' said Richard.

'Jack was always full on,' said Jenni.

The rest of the afternoon was a whirl of smiles and cake, and birthday wishes.

Later, when the guests had left, the caterers had swept up and gone, and the boys were watching TV, Patrick came to chat with Margot while she got some soup on for supper.

'A fabulous birthday party, thank you.'

'You are very welcome. I'm glad you enjoyed it,' said Margot, turning to give Patrick a kiss. She slipped her arms around him and pulled him close.

The sun was now low behind the lime trees, glints flashed through the foliage and sparkled on two highball glasses as though fairies were dancing on the crystal rims.

'You couldn't fetch those tumblers for me from the table outside,' she said releasing him.

'Sure, it's amazing how things have moved around the place. I found a roll of kitchen paper behind a pot plant,' said Patrick.

'Oh, that was me. There was a spillage crisis, but someone had already dealt with it.'

'Talking about things turning up in odd places, I'm sorry about Vi,' Patrick said as he returned from the garden with the stray glasses.

'That certainly was unexpected.'

'She wheedled the details out of me the other day.'

'She said you'd insisted she come.'

'You don't for a moment think I did, do you?'

'Vi knows when to make an entrance and I'm sure she had a ball going through all our things. She admitted she'd been upstairs in our bathroom. The woman has no shame.'

Later still, when the boys were getting ready for bed and Patrick was in his study, Margot gently wandered around the kitchen, putting a few final things to rights. With the last of the sun sliding into the kitchen, she rearranged glasses and jugs in the cupboard where the caterers had stacked things indiscriminately. Then she gathered the wilted flower arrangements and threw away the truly sad and sorted the flowers that could survive another day. Amongst the tealight glasses was a small jug which had no reason to be amongst the vases. Another case of something turning up where it didn't belong. Margot took the creamer back into the kitchen, gave it a rinse and dry, and reached up to put it away in the high cupboard where it belonged. As she leaned against the countertop, she felt a crinkle in the pocket of her dress. With the jug safely stowed, Margot reached into her pocket and pulled out a piece of paper.

It looked like a sheet torn from the magnetic pad for lists that lived on the fridge. In blue black ink was written a number, smudged somewhat by her damp washing-up hands. How unusual it was to still use a fountain pen. The exchange code was the same as Peter Jones. None of her friends lived in that area. And how had the number got in her pocket?

She turned the note over and read the slanting hand.

I believe this is your preferred method of communication. If you ever feel the need, please do call. Jack.

Really! The gall! How outrageous. What was he thinking? She didn't think about Jack that way, he was Patrick's cousin, and to think he thought she might be casting her eye.

At that moment, she had never been more content. It had been a glorious day, a celebration. She and Patrick had something special, surely it was obvious.

Jack had kissed her on the cheek as he left. She remembered the feeling of his hand slipping down her arm. He must have slipped the note in her pocket then. An invitation to get in touch. She laughed. It meant nothing. Everyone knew she was happy. Nothing would get in the way of what she had with Patrick and the boys, her family. Margot scrunched up the note, dropped it back into the pocket of her dress and went back to clearing up the flowers.

Photographs

Feeling Forty

'Keep your cool, Patrick,' Vi had said as she left the party. 'No need to see me out. And no need to get worked up. Everyone will think you and Margot are saints for having invited me.'

'Are you sure you should be driving?'

'Are you sure you should be out here while Jack and Margot are in there unsupervised?'

Vi laughed too loudly as she got into her car.

He turned from the front door and stomped back through the house. The woman needed to pull herself together. Vi should have interests other than him. She should have remarried; meditation and yoga weren't a substitute for living life.

Life, he was forty, halfway. All these friends, and relatives, had been here to celebrate the passing of his years. Now, he was no longer young and promising, he was officially middle-aged. He didn't feel any older, but the thought struck and persisted, he had reached a turning point.

Margot had put out some disposable cameras on the tables at the party. Patrick had tried to use them, but it was an intrusive business. He hated stopping the flow of conversation for everyone to pose.

Post party, as a family, they looked through all the photographs, those Lily's daughter had taken and the more candid shots from the disposable cameras.

There were some good ones of his parents, which Patrick had taken before he handed over his camera. There was a picture of Margot and Vi with icy smiles.

'Why is Mummy wearing the same dress as Margot?' said Toby.

'It's not exactly the same,' said Margot. 'Mine is fuller and has more colour, and I'm wearing a blue belt not red.'

The dresses were remarkably similar. Patrick hadn't noticed on the day. They could have been made by the same company. Ollie shuffled his feet.

'Sorry,' he said. 'Mum asked me what you were wearing for the party, and I saw you unpack the bag and hang up your dress. That shop - it's next to the games shop. Is it a big deal?'

At eleven, Ollie had no idea about dresses, but he did know his games. Patrick was rather impressed Ollie had described Margot's dress so well.

'Ollie, darling, of course it's not important,' said Margot. 'Look, I think this is my favourite photo.' Margot pointed to a picture of Angela smelling roses surrounded by the children.

There were photographs of quite formal groups taken in the garden and then a slew of happy images of friends laughing and some of Patrick in mock amazement as Margot presented him with his surprise cake. The one he had seen her bake and ice that morning. So many candles. A couple more of Patrick giving a speech, just thanking them all for being there. The final pictures from the disposables were taken by Ollie and Toby with googly kids' faces doing handstands and larking around.

'He really is a pillock,' said Patrick, pointing to a picture of Margot's goddaughter, Julia, throwing a beach ball to Toby. 'Such a killjoy,' he added. In the background, Richard was caught unsmiling, his arms crossed, a bottle of water dangling from the fingers of one hand.

'Perhaps this is why,' said Margot, showing Patrick the following picture, a photo of Jenni open and laughing talking to Jack.

When Patrick scanned all the pictures, his handsome cousin didn't seem to have just sought out Jenni. He was featured in quite a few of the photographs chatting with sunny, smiley women who seemed to enjoy his attention, even Angela. Patrick couldn't understand why he felt uneasy, almost jealous.

Later, Patrick rifled through the photographs on his own. Margot looked lovely. In every picture, she was stunning, smiling her beautiful smile. Here she was with his parents. He remembered taking that one. Another with her aunt and sister. Then Margot with Julia on her knee as she sat chatting with Jenni, who had Molly on her lap, not that he could tell the girls apart. Yet another looking radiant, this time with Jack. Jack again, lean and good looking. Margot was facing the camera, but the look in Jack's eyes as he gazed at Margot was of more than mere admiration. Then Margot looking delighted to be talking to Richard. She really was a saint.

In the photographs of himself, he seemed so much older. Wrinkles at the eyes and mouth, laughter lines, though he wasn't amused. And what had happened to his chin? He was developing jowls. He did look better when he smiled, pulling everything up and in. There was another photo where he looked pensive. It was black and white but rather a good, moody shot. He was in the hall, silhouetted, by the front door fanlight. That one must have been taken after he had escorted Vi off the premises. There was another of him next to Jack, both with a glass in their hand, both laughing. He looked pale and flabby, as though he had more than just the two years on his cousin.

One night, while he slept, he ceased to be in his thirties, young and promising. From now on, he would be viewed as middle aged and middle management. Patrick put the brooding photograph of himself next to the one of Margot and Jack. He mustn't let destructive thoughts about Jack or Vi get to him.

Not Irrelevant

Forty was only a number. Patrick could remember the disdain he had felt for his father when, after a certain age, he had conceded defeat and gradually shrunk from the world into a riser recliner armchair of irrelevance.

That was not going to happen to Patrick. If he worked on himself now, he could avoid the same fate.

He had been an insufferable teenager. Not the sort that screams and yells and slams doors. Patrick anxious at school, had dripped with contempt at home.

One evening, on the long summer before Patrick left for university to study Modern History and Politics, he was lounging on the small sofa by the open window of the study, surrounded by shimmering dust motes and listening to the chirruping birds outside. He was supposed to be reading a book from the university reading list for the new term, but he was aimlessly watching the sparrows squabbling by the bird table.

There was a click as the front door closed. His father must be home. The house was more than halfway up the sunny slopes of Wimbledon Hill, a steep climb for his father with his recalcitrant leg.

Patrick became aware of a hush from the hall. He waited, then lifted himself from his comfortable seat, reconnected his loose limbs that cascaded over the arm of the sofa and went to see what all the silence was about.

His father stood crumpled in the hall. As Patrick watched from the doorway, his father uncurled his fingers from his briefcase handle, and the bag dropped from his hand with a weary clump. His father didn't move but stared at the case slumped on the parquet at his feet.

'Hi… I thought it was you,' said Patrick.

His father, started, squared himself into a man and looked at Patrick. 'Yes, I'm afraid it is I.' He took off his coat, abandoning it on top of his briefcase, and then he limped past Patrick and down the back hall towards the kitchen to greet his wife.

Over sherry, his father complained about the large, square magnolia computer with an accompanying keyboard that technicians had installed on his desk. His father had attended the compulsory course, but how to use the thing remained a mystery. His secretary had shown him how to turn it on. His mother glanced at Patrick; they had heard all this before.

'The worst of it is not the space it takes up on my desk, and the trailing cords and all that electrical gubbins left for anyone to trip over.'

'I hope you haven't fallen,' said his mother as they moved through to the dark red, north-facing dining room that always felt cold.

His father rearranged his place setting, making sure the cutlery was square, and didn't meet their eyes.

'Now, I'm not supposed to send memos through my secretary anymore. I'm expected to communicate by typing into that flashing, green dash thing that pulses expectantly. It's like it's laughing at me. I write my note out, and then I have to copy it into the machine. A blithering waste of time.'

Patrick saw the tortuous process. His father reading his own note, finding the corresponding key letter by letter with a hesitant, wavering finger. Then, his eyes searching the screen to make sure the word was correct. Then sliding back to his note to find the next character.

'The cursor.' said Patrick, who was hoping there would be some computer options on his degree course.

'The … what did you say?' said his father.

'The dash … it's called the cursor.'

His father looked at him. Patrick could see the confusion. The chasm opening between them over a lifted fork, the fish dropping back on his father's plate from the prongs, and the raised glass of water Patrick held stalled in mid-air.

'My secretary has been reallocated,' said his father, having managed to regather his fish on his fork. 'I rather fear she may have been let go.'

Were all those assistant-type positions and entry-level placements going to be replaced by a computer? Patrick hoped there would still be a job for him by the time he completed his degree.

'But the worst of it,' said his father over coffee in the drawing room. 'Is now that I no longer have a secretary, if I want a cup of tea, I have to go down the corridor to the company kitchen and make my own.'

His father looked at them to make sure they agreed with the unreasonableness of it all. Then he let out a deep sigh. He seemed to deflate as the air left his body. Patrick thought his father never stood up quite as tall again. Gone was the upstanding war hero. Who remembered the war anyway? The scales had tipped, now he was archaic. Someone the tech guys had to explain things to. Someone whose office had become a backwater.

'Well, I'm pushing seventy, now there are no more school fees, I can retire,' his father said as Patrick made plans for university.

That summer, to celebrate his A level results, Patrick and Jack met for lunch at the Rose and Crown. Even though Jack was underage, they were not challenged, and both had bitter with sausages and mash.

'I'm just worried he's going to fade into the upholstery,' said Patrick.

'That's their job, isn't it? Their lives are over now. My father is old, over fifty and yours is ancient. It's time for them to step aside. It's our turn now,' said Jack.

Patrick remembered how grown up he had felt standing at the bar ordering another round. He had seldom felt as mature, talking to Jack, man to man, contemplating their shiny futures.

Before Patrick finished his degree, his father had his first mini stroke and ceased to be angry. He settled into a state of charming bewilderment.

At forty, Patrick was hardly at retirement age, but if he didn't want to decay like his father. It was important to be active, be attractive for Margot, relevant for the boys and engaged at work. He should join a gym, he was always saying he was going to get fit, but now he really must. His father had never done any exercise beyond the walk back and forth to the train, but Patrick didn't even do that, jumping in the car whenever he wanted to get anywhere.

Angela

An Angel Falls

Later that year at Advent, Lily telephoned Margot at work.

'It's Angela, she's had a fall… on the ice.'

As soon as she got home, Margot sorted out the boys and drove down to the Royal Surrey. She found a parking space and traversed the slippery hospital car park with care. At the reception desk, she enquired about her aunt and went to find Lily.

'How is she?'

'Quite chipper. I'm more worried than she is. She's in triage now,' said Lily.

'I hope she's alright,' said Margot. 'What was she doing? It's lethal out there.'

They were in a corridor outside the triage ward that could be anywhere or nowhere, swept clean of personality or purpose by the traffic of muffled healthcare personnel. Margot joined her sister on a flip-chair attached to the wall. A place for waiting where no one stopped.

'Angela was calling on an elderly neighbour to give them a lift to the Christingle service when she slipped on the steps up to the front door,' said Lily.

'I remember, the oranges with the candles and all those unsingable modern carols that no one knew the tunes for.'

'A children's service for the elderly.'

'Wickedly, I always used to hope something would catch fire. All those shaky hands, the music sheets, the old and the young. But nothing ever did.'

Now Margot had arrived, Lily left to get some fresh air.

Margot waited, feeling at a loose end. Heel, toe, heel, toe, she tapped her feet then lined up her shoes with the edges of the flooring tiles. She hoped Angela was getting on alright. No one had as yet told them what was going on. Margot regretted not bringing a book to distract her. She wondered if Patrick had received her text and would know where she was.

Lily returned with two paper cups of bitter, milky tea.

'How old was this elderly neighbour?' said Margot. 'Angela is eighty-five?'

'Angela is eighty-six, and the neighbour is ninety-one.'

'Will we be so intrepid at that age, do you think?'

'Or so civic-minded.'

A blue-clad, blue-capped, blue-slippered medic stopped to let them know they should go home.

'Can we see her?' asked Lily.

'If you like, but your aunt is currently sedated. She will have a hip replacement in the morning. If we can get her up and moving and can confirm a care package, you should look to be getting her home in a week or so.'

Without the energy she normally radiated, which the sisters when they were younger had alluded to as her force field, Angela looked small and frail in the hospital bed.

Out in the freezing air, returning to their cars in the dark, Margot said. 'We had better find a live-in nurse. She going to need help getting back on her feet, but Angela will be furious if we don't get her out of there as soon as possible.'

'It shouldn't be a problem,' said Lily, who had power of attorney. 'I'll look up an agency when I get home. There is plenty in her account. She has been prudent.'

Thankfully, Angela's operation was successful, but the sisters knew it would take some organising to give Angela the sort of independence that she was used to when she got home.

The sisters spent the weekend preparing the house. They wanted to move a bed downstairs to the morning room where Angela had done her sewing. Margot spent the day moving furniture around, making room, clearing space, winding up fraying tape measures, tidying away old patterns into shoe boxes and sorting and stacking tobacco tins of pins and boxes of fabric ends.

Margot recognised the old tea caddy and sitting in the nursing chair, low to the ground, emptied the contents into the bowl of her skirt. She sifted through, pulling out the strings of spare, white buttons from forgotten shirts and the brown scale-like, unremarkable buttons that, threaded together on a fine wire, looked like a snake. She put them to one side. The buttons left in her lap were individual, some made of Bakelite were rainbow-coloured, others flaky mother of pearl slithers, and some cut glass, like chandelier drops, others made of brass were dented, and there were a few, fat braided leather buttons, like acorns.

This had been a favourite teenage pastime, to sift through the buttons as if looking for clues, searching for treasure while her aunt sewed. Margot's fingers stirred through the buttons one last time before pouring them all back into the tin and putting it away. Then she covered the sewing machine with its box lid and hid everything in the cupboard, softly closing the doors. Meanwhile, Lily had been cooking meals-for-one for the deep freeze.

Lily and Margot modified their lives to fit in visits to West Clandon. The nurse was lovely and caring and helpful, but always there. At Angela's insistence, she left after a couple of months.

'I'm walking again,' she said, clutching at her Zimmer with shaking hands as she staggered from room to room. 'I don't want to be mollycoddled.'

It was all possible between Angela's friends, the church ladies, and Lily and Margot. The sisters would leave each other notes as they dashed in and out, passing each other's shadows in the door, the hints of familiar perfume, seeing fresh bunches of flowers in the hall, before they headed back in different directions to their busy families and home duties.

Patrick was going through one of those phases when he was distracted by work and keeping erratic hours. So, Margot dropped the boys off, picked the boys up, cajoled about homework and washed sports kits. She cooked meals and dashed to and from the Old Vicarage. The only time she seemed to be still was at work or in the car driving up or down the A3. But then her mind would be turning over what she had forgotten and what she still had to do. She hardly seemed to see Patrick.

Driving home from West Clandon one evening, she was looking forward to a quiet house. It was the right time of the month. She had arranged for Ollie and Toby to have a sleepover with friends that night. So, when she got back from seeing her aunt there would be no shoes abandoned in the hallway or crisp packets in the creases of the sofa. Tonight, she would cook up the boeuf bourguignon she had taken out of the freezer that morning and relax with a glass of red wine. Hopefully, Patrick would be there to join her.

And Breaks

Then Angela took a turn for the worse.

It was late spring, and the azaleas and lilacs were over. Angela, who had been able to manage without a walking stick for some months, had come in from the garden, sat down and ceased to engage with life.

'Hello,' said Margot, arriving that weekend with a huge bunch of peonies wrapped in pink tissue paper. Lily had been in touch to warn her their aunt seemed a bit down.

'Oh, darling, how gorgeous,' said Angela, touching the flowers as though the blooms were the cheek of a child, before turning away.

Margot took the flowers to the cool pantry beyond the old kitchen. By the Belfast sink, there was a tall, green cupboard. This was where her aunt kept her collection of vases. The shelves were covered with yellowed, curling, sticky-backed plastic. Most of the vases were glass, piled like cups, they sat inside each other at all angles. Margot pulled out a few before selecting a fat-bellied vase of thick, distorting glass that had the effect of a myopic lens. With the use of a green glass rose Margot arranged the flowers, hoping a cup of tea would help to lift her aunt's spirits. Margot wasn't sure where to start, she had not had to worry about this before, Angela was straight forward, no nonsense and not given to melancholic moods.

Margot placed the peonies on a side table. She would usually talk about family. Her aunt was always interested in what Ollie and Toby were up to, but today even the under 13's cricket teams' potential didn't seem to distract.

'Lily said you were not feeling yourself?' Margot said.

Her aunt looked small. Angela was staring into the empty fireplace where a fan of pleated white paper filled the grate. Margot had set the tea tray on the side table near her aunt and, pulling a chair close, poured the pale, clear liquid, dropping a semi-circle of lemon into each cup.

'Oh, nothing to worry about, I'm sure,' said Angela.

'If you are anxious about anything, we should talk about it.'

Angela fussed with the embroidered handkerchief in her lap for a moment or two before turning to Margot.

'When I went for my check-up last week, the doctor said he had some test results back. He was sorry … but there was cancer. They had taken some samples when they were doing the operation.'

'Oh,' said Margot. She reached out to take her aunt's hand. 'What else did he say? How bad is it? What are the treatment options?'

'I listened carefully, and I've read through all the leaflets, but I'm not sure anything makes much sense. Have a look, would you? The papers are on the table over there.'

Angela's cup and saucer tinkled in her hands as Margot fetched the doctor's letter and handouts.

'So, the cancer in the bone is a secondary cancer, from a probable undiagnosed breast cancer.'

'Hmmm.'

'And the recommended course of action is chemo and possibly radiation therapy, but they want to do more tests to confirm.'

'It all sounds very … disruptive,' said Angela.

'But the prognosis is not terrible.'

'If you do all the advised invasive treatments,' Angela sighed. 'You know, when I was young, cancer was never mentioned. To speak of it was worse than swearing.'

'But then, there wouldn't have been the variety of treatments we have now.'

'You know, I always thought if I kept moving, if I didn't sit about, I'd avoid all this troublesome stuff.'

They sat in silence and drank their tea. Margot's half-moon of lemon looked like a silvery, yellow fish swimming in a briny sea. After a while, she said. 'On my way here, I was thinking how good you were to us as children, Lily and I, when we were so sad after our parents died. It can't have been easy taking in two distraught teenagers.'

'Darling,' said Angela, turning to face Margot. 'I had to beg to be allowed to have you. I had the space, but your guardians and the executors thought you would be better off with strangers, someone younger. But family is everything. I had to put them right.'

'You were so good to us and for us.'

'It was a challenge but so worthwhile. Lily was desperate to go and be an adult somewhere, get on with her life. I had to create a bubble for her where she could feel grown up but had the time to finish growing up.'

'Lily always seemed to be halfway out the door,' said Margot.

'I appealed to her better nature and her compassion for you to influence her to stay until she was ready to go.' Angela sipped her tea. 'You were different, desperate for a home, and I was more than happy to give you one. I never felt I could quite do enough; you were a lost little soul.'

'You were the best.'

'Well, you were both a source of joy. And it's a delight to see you both now happily married with your own families.' Angela put down her cup. 'I had rather hoped you and Patrick might have a baby. They bring such joy. Everyone draws near a newborn, like to a candle, to be included in the wonder.' Angela held her hands in her lap as if she were holding a cup of some precious delight.

'Yes, it is a shame. Still, you never know. And we have Ollie and Toby.' Margot smiled, reached out to her aunt, and held both her hands in hers. 'I would have been lost without you when I was young.'

Angela gently pulled her hands free and turned back to the clean grate.

'I have been thinking things over since I saw the doctor. I can see that I have done with being able to help others, and from now on, I will only become more and more dependent on people to look after me.'

'Isn't that how life goes,' said Margot. 'It is our pleasure to return the favour.'

Angela turned towards Margot and leaned over as if to share a confidence. 'You know I was in the garden yesterday, wobbling between the flower beds, and I was thinking, I should do this, and I must remember to do that. You know, moving plants, digging stuff up, trimming things back, and it came over me that I couldn't do any of those things anymore.'

'But you have Burr to help in the garden. We could ask him to do more hours if you like. It's not a problem ...'

'No, no, darling. That's not my point.' Her aunt patted her hand. 'I had a bit of a revelation about what it meant to be me. I am not the sort of person who wants or needs care. I was put here to be useful, not to be a burden. After I lost Charles in the war, I decided to focus on the church and my Christian faith. I feel strongly that I was put here to help others, not the other way around.'

Margot felt her body still.

'So, you see, I have decided not to have any medical treatment apart from palliative care. I don't want months and months of painful, invasive treatment to live for an extra week in excruciating pain.'

'Oh…, but …,' said Margot, the breath leaving her in a long, sad sigh.

'I'm old, I've had a good, healthy, active life. Now, it's over.'

'But.' Margot needed time to think this through. She finished her tea and put the cup back on the tray. She held Angela's frail, listless hands in hers.

'You can't, you know. How will we cope without you?'

'You'll be fine.' Angela smiled for the first time that afternoon, patting Margot's hand.

'Whatever you wish, of course,' Margot chewed her lip for a moment. Ultimately, it was her aunt's choice, and she was capable enough to decide. 'But could I come with you to the doctor, to see what treatment he advocates. It might not be as awful as you think. Then, if you still feel the way you do, we can work out the best course of care. How we should manage things.'

'Good idea. The doctor did say something about a Macmillan nurse.'

After Margot had cleared the tea things, her aunt walked with her to the door.

'Can I ask you something?' said Angela as she kissed Margot goodbye. 'Will you promise me not to be falsely cheerful. I couldn't bear it. Promise to tell me the truth.'

Margot would respect her aunt's request, but it would be hard. She admired Angela's faith and the meaning it gave to her life and was awed that she had such a clear understanding of what it meant to be her.

As Margot drove home, she wondered what it meant to be Margot. Why was she here? What was the point of her?

When she got home, Patrick was there. He was making a risotto, and the house smelled of warmth and wine. She gave him a kiss. Then she called Lily.

'We need to get that nurse back.'

The Change

Relevant

Margot went through the films, selected the best of the photographs from the party, had them made into a book, and presented it to Patrick. He was thrilled to have a memento of the day but found it hard to look at the pictures.

With his parents and the boys, his father looked frail but charming, nearing ninety. His mother was still attractive, just verging on the well-preserved. Ollie and Toby, at eleven and nine, were human versions of puppies. But Patrick had retained none of his boyish looks nor gained the gravitas he might have hoped for. Patrick looked closer at the photograph. Was his hair beginning to recede?

Photographs didn't lie. He couldn't blame it on the light, it had been a gorgeous day, or on the angles because everyone else looked fabulous, summery, glowing. There were the stunning photographs of Margot. He could look at those over and over. What did Margot see in him? Really, he was the luckiest of men.

His friends had aged too, but they seemed to have grown into who they ought to be. They seemed more like themselves. There was Jack, in a photograph with Jenni and Margo, an arm around each. His cousin had gathered a few more wrinkles over the years, but he had matured into himself and appeared more charming than ever.

Patrick wondered what his sons thought of him. Probably as some boring old fart. His own father was always ancient, but Patrick had been born when his father was forty-eight. Imagine having a child at that age?

'I hadn't realised how much older we have all got,' Patrick said to Margot as he flicked through the album yet again. 'Though my friends seem to have aged more than yours.'

'Well, she's had a bit of a touch-up. Botox, I should think, and maybe some fillers,' Margot said, looking over his shoulder and pointing to the photo of the wife of one of Patrick's work colleagues.

'No! Surely not,' said Patrick, peering closely at the photograph. 'I can't see any cracks.'

'It's good work. But I had a chat with her. You could tell when she moved.'

Patrick was astounded. He looked at Margot. 'But you don't, you wouldn't …,'

'Darling, what do you think.'

Patrick knew Margot had regular facials, but he was sure that was all. She was only thirty-five, too young to need any work. He would have noticed if she had changed, like all those terrible women with lips that couldn't close and foreheads that couldn't frown. Margot was a happy person. She never frowned.

In the album, Margot hadn't included the picture of herself with Jack sitting together chatting, unaware of the camera. Patrick looked for the box of spare photographs in the cupboard. He rifled through and found it. It was a gorgeous candid shot of two attractive people. They looked good together.

Now he had crossed the Rubicon of forty, he really must improve his diet, stop having sandwiches at lunch, and eat salad instead. He should get in shape. He didn't want to let Margot down. He wouldn't want people to think he didn't deserve her.

Vi had always been going on at him about getting healthy, but he was in his twenties and early thirties then, he had been invincible. Now, he was haunted by thoughts of advancing decrepitude. He would find the gym at the office and renew his membership at his local tennis club. He could never be as tall, but he could try to be as fit as Jack.

But it would be hard to keep up any fitness regime, as it was, there weren't enough hours in the day.

At work, Patrick was under pressure. On the one hand, the MoD must ensure the correct supply of the right equipment, and enough of it, even if they didn't have it. Body armour had been an issue initially and then transport. Surely, any Land Rover was better than none. Obviously, the right Land Rover would be best of all. The objective was to wrap everything up as soon as possible but leave the Afghan people with a credible government and a chance at autonomy. But also, the British must not let their allies down.

It was a conundrum of political and diplomatic complexity, and that was just within Patrick's department. He tried not to let the arguments keep him late at work or awake at night. He would lie still, trying not to toss or turn or pull the duvet. He didn't want to disturb Margot. He was worried about her. She had been so taken up with her aunt's care. Her resolve to give Angela, who had given her so much, a decent, dignified end to her life, had exhausted Margot. So, although he wished he could give her more of his time, she probably hadn't noticed that he was a little preoccupied.

The next Monday at lunchtime, he signed up at the Whitehall gym, it was in the basement. He needed to book a trainer to show him around and make him do the graft. He could see through the glass wall behind reception, a room of heavy, matt black and shiny steel equipment, the machinery of torture. The keenest huffed and puffed, others strolled between the contraptions with purpose, towels hanging around their necks, a sign of dedication, muscles and sweat displaying their craft. At an unfocused glance, the cut of bodies, machinery and mirrors, was like a moving monochrome cubist artwork with splashes of bright and neon colours. Patrick committed. Soon he too would be part of this dystopian world.

Patrick was encouraged to book three sessions a week, which was a couple more than he thought necessary, but he would do what he had to do to look fit and stay relevant. By booking a lunchtime slot, it wouldn't impinge on his working day, and he would still be able to make it home for the boys' bedtime. They were older now, but he still liked to catch up with them at the end of the day if he could.

Ninetieth

Ollie should start boarding. He was almost thirteen. It was the right moment for a change, many of his school friends would be setting off for somewhere new too. When Patrick brought the subject up again, Margot was horrified, but he persevered and took her to look around his old school.

'It's a fabulous school. I can see that, and it has a wonderful history, but Ollie is far too young to be sent away,' said Margot on the way home in the car. 'I shall put my foot down over this.'

'I love it,' said Ollie, who had accompanied them. His voice carrying over from the back of the car. He was flicking through the school prospectus. 'All the sport! I'm going to have so much fun.'

'You'll have to pass the entrance exam,' said Patrick.

'No problem,' said Ollie.

Patrick would love to have had that confidence at the same age. Each generation tries to build something more into the next, make it stronger, better able to deal with the world. If his boys were confident. Patrick couldn't ask for more.

When Toby heard Ollie was going away to boarding school, he demanded to go too.

Vi was planning one of her trips and had already told Patrick she would be away for at least three months. So, when he broke the news, she didn't confront him, as she might otherwise have done.

'Well, it's up to you Patrick. If you want to send our little boys away to be brought up by strangers - go ahead. You're the one footing the bill. As the ex-wife, I shall just do as I'm told. I shall expect to see them at half term, of course, make sure they are happy and settling in. Then I shall be off before Christmas.'

Patrick couldn't remember when Vi had done anything he had asked. And he didn't think he had ever told her to do anything. The woman lived in a fantasy world. But in this instance, it made his life easier.

Margot took more persuading, but it was a practical solution. It had been a challenging year for her, spending time with her aunt, dashing madly between Wimbledon and West Clandon. All the time with her sister looking after Angela. Then the inevitable end and the subsequent time spent sorting out The Old Vicarage with all the emotional upheaval that engendered. Lily and Margot spent an age going through everything. It was all the memories; Angela was the last link to their parents. On top of that Margot had the boys to contend with, trying to keep their home life normal. She deserved a break.

'But we won't be together as a family anymore,' she said.

'Apart from the long school holidays.'

'And how are we going to afford it?'

'It's all sorted.' Patrick hadn't told Vi or Margot that his mother, keen for the boys to go to Winton, had offered to pay the school fees.

In early September, before Ollie and Toby were due to go away, Patrick and Margot took the boys to lunch at their grandparents'. It was Patrick's father's ninetieth birthday. He was more or less an invalid, spending most of the day in his riser recliner, but his brain was still sharp, even if he was shy about sharing his thoughts. Patrick and Margot brought champagne, and after they had raised their glasses in a birthday toast, his father said to Patrick.

'It was the happiest day of my life when you arrived in our lives. Apart from my wedding day, that is.' The old man tipped his glass to his wife.

'I always thought I must have been the most atrocious sort of child.'

'No, you were a joy, kept me young,' said his father.

'But you were atrocious,' said his mother.

Patrick smiled and turned to look at Margot. She was smiling too. She looked radiant. Her eyes were unfocused for a moment as though chasing some ethereal thought. She must have felt him looking at her as she turned and transferred her smile to him. She was wearing that pretty, floral outfit she wore for his birthday.

After lunch, they looked through an old album with photographs of his father as a young man. The boys were interested in a picture of Patrick's father before he went off to war.

'Did you have a gun?' asked Toby.

'Of course, he had a gun,' said Ollie.

In the black and white photograph, Patrick's father stood tall in his uniform, proud. He hadn't filled out yet. Eighteen, trying to look a man, wanting to be confident in front of the camera. His parents must have been anxious about him enlisting. He must have been terrified. Whatever the opinion in the press, Patrick's father would have known it was not going to be a picnic.

The phoney war was over, Dunkirk was being hailed as a success despite the losses, and now the real war was underway. This photograph was potentially the one that would sit forever on the family sideboard, a testament to his parent's sacrifice to the war effort. His father had defied the odds.

Patrick shook his head to banish his morbid thoughts and drew everyone's attention to a different photograph, his parent's wedding day. His father looked distinguished, his salt and pepper hair beginning to recede. He had waited until he was worthy of his bride and had achieved a suitable income before getting married. In another photograph, his father looked joyous, holding Patrick as a baby.

'Dad, you're wearing a dress,' said Toby laughing.

'That is the family Christening gown,' said Patrick's mother.

'You wore it too when you were christened. It is a family tradition to wear it.'

Toby looked horrified. 'There aren't any photos, are there?'

'Are you looking forward to going to your new school?' Patrick's mother asked Ollie. 'It is where your father, and your great grandfather went to school, as well as my brother and your father's cousin Jack. Your first cousin once removed. Winton is also a family tradition.'

A Beginning

A Note Recovered

Margot had brought a cake, and, with Toby's help, Patrick's father blew the candles out.

'There aren't ninety candles,' said Toby.

Patrick's father didn't seem concerned. He beamed at everyone, happy to have his family with him, happy to share his day, happy to celebrate being alive for another year.

She couldn't help but think of her aunt. Margot had spent most of the previous summer and autumn at the Old Vicarage. She had read aloud old favourites while Angela lay uncomfortable, staring into space with teary eyes. If her aunt slept, Margot would wander around the garden in the gloom, circling the lawn again and again, listening to the screams of the last swifts. And later, when the birds had gone, she kicked at the rotten apples lying in the long grass and watched Burr sweep up leaves.

When Angela was up to it, she liked to reminisce about life, her hopes and dreams. Sometimes, she spoke about Margot's parents. It was like time travelling, sitting with her aunt in the old house surrounded by swirling memories.

'I am trying to hold onto my faith,' Angela said through the pain one day. 'But it's harder than I imagined. As though there is a final test as one reaches the door.'

Margot wept. If her wonderful aunt couldn't die peacefully but was hounded by agonies of belief, what chance would Margot have? When it was her time, she wanted to feel she had done all she could and achieved all she conceivably should.

Angela had faded with the old year, and the day of her funeral the previous November had been wreathed in fog. Without her aunt, Margot found her days empty and without purpose. She had lost a link to her past and her parents and she felt shaky.

Margot and her sister had cleared out The Old Vicarage. It had been hard and had taken months and months. Every object held a memory and had to be assessed. Now, they had been granted probate. All that was left was to clear the last bits and pieces before the house finally sold. They had a completion date in November.

Patrick's father was now ninety and had been frail for years, Margot couldn't help but remember how full of life her aunt had been in comparison, and yet, Angela had gone first. Feeling emotional, as Patrick's father blew out his candles, Margot rootled around in her pocket for a tissue and found a crumpled piece of paper instead.

For a moment, Margot couldn't think what it was, some rubbish she should have thrown out. She hadn't worn this dress since Patrick's party, full and floral, it needed an occasion for an outing. It was a dress for celebrating a birthday tea. Margot glowed with the memory of that idyllic summer's day. It had been a moment of perfection, a slither of time when Margot had felt that anything was possible.

Then it hadn't been. The months had passed, and nothing had changed, just everyone getting older, Angela had gone, and soon the boys would be going to boarding school. Margot felt bereft.

On the way home from Patrick's parents, Ollie and Toby, in the back of the car, had their headphones on, and Patrick seemed more thoughtful than usual, hardly answering her chat. From what she read in the newspapers, the war in Afghanistan was winding down, but that didn't seem to make Patrick's work easier. Apparently, a good exit strategy was the most critical thing of all. The conflict consumed all Patrick's time and thoughts.

Once the boys started boarding, her evenings were quiet, and the weekends empty. While Patrick was working late or playing golf, part of his new fitness regime, Margot wandered around the house in a dream-like state or sat in the little upstairs spare room, folding and refolding the baby clothes she had accumulated. She was now thirty-seven. Perhaps she should give up on her dream. She swept her hand over a super soft Babygro, in a soft pearly sea green for ages newborn to three months, before she returned it to the drawer.

At half term, Ollie and Toby were back, full of noise and energy. Margot and Patrick took time off work, and they all went to Disneyland Paris for a long weekend. Back home, the boys were busy catching up with school friends, enjoying bonfires and fireworks and visiting their mother, before she set off on her travels.

Margot went to pick up Ollie and Toby from Vi. When he got back from golf, Patrick would drive them back to their schools. Margot stood in the porch, reluctant to move further into Vi's house, waiting for the boys to get their bits and pieces together and hurtle down the stairs and out and into the car.

'By the way, I did so enjoy Patrick's party,' said Vi, standing in front of Margot, arms folded across her chest, guarding the entrance to her home. 'I know it's ages ago, but I have such fond memories. It was a fabulous chance to hook up with some of Patrick's cousins I hadn't seen in years. I must say, his father was in a bit of a state. He turned ninety this summer, didn't he? But what was so very lovely was to see all the children. Everyone growing up and getting on.'

'It was rather glorious to have the garden filled with the happy young, wasn't it,' said Margot. She glanced up the stairs. What were the boys up to? And where was Vi going with this?

'I always thought it a shame for you not to have children. You seemed just the sort of woman who should have a brood.'

'Some things are just not meant to be.' Margot threw a rictus smile at Vi and her eyes narrowed. Vi never made a casual comment without some motive.

'You could put it like that,' said Vi snorting.

Vi was on a whirlwind of goading, starting small and obtuse, then gaining momentum, before the reveal.

'I've always known Patrick didn't especially want anymore,' said Margot.

Vi laughed, showing her teeth.

'Didn't want! You haven't listened to a word I've said. I've tried to tell you before -,'

'I'm not interested in your take on Patrick,' said Margot.

'You should be.' Vi seemed determined to have her say. Her eyes shone. 'He's not capable,' she spat. Vi paused, watching Margot, her eyes widening with glee.

'But …,' said Margot.

'Obviously, it suits me to have you in the boys' lives. You are much more maternal than I am, but when I was at Patrick's party, I saw all those pregnancy tests in your bathroom … all that wishful thinking – so pitiful. I thought I really must say something. I wanted to say something sooner, but somehow there just wasn't the opportunity.'

'Oh…,' said Margot. She tried to keep breathing. She felt violated as though Vi's sticky fingers had torn literal babies from her arms. She hugged herself, nursing the absence. Not only had Vi invaded her private space, but also her dreams. Vi was forcing her to face an awful truth, something she had avoided for years. Margot took a deep breath and straightened her shoulders. She didn't want to appear disconcerted in front of Vi, who looked so immensely pleased with herself that Margot wanted to hit her.

'He didn't tell you, did he?' said Vi.

'Not in so many words.'

'I should have been clear earlier, what are you now? Thirty-seven?'

'Yes, thirty-seven.' Margot knew what Vi was insinuating. Like a big cat hiding in the bushes, waiting for the right moment to pounce. Vi had waited to tell Margot, waited until she knew it would be almost too late.

'Knowing Patrick, he probably thought he had been clear but was so circumspect it would have been hard to divine what he was trying to say.'

What had Patrick said? Margot couldn't recall, it was so long ago. She remembered being thrilled, getting married, having a ready-made family with Ollie and Toby and the implicit possibility of more, she would have read into any declaration whatever she pleased.

'Well, I realised everything wasn't …, but …, so the boys …?'

'The boys look like their father – that's true,' said Vi.

At that moment, Ollie and Toby careered down the stairs with their bags, hugged their mother goodbye, and they left with Margot sleepwalking behind them to the car. All the years of hoping and the recent years of despair. Breathe, she must breathe. She felt desperately sad and disillusioned.

By the time she was home with the boys, she was livid. Had Patrick not noticed how wound up she was about having a child, the special salads and vitamins, the days set aside for sex? Had he been oblivious? Why hadn't he been more honest with her?

Patrick was waiting for them in the kitchen putting supper together. The boys were rowdy, excited about going back to school. Everything was ready their bags were by the door.

'You seem very quiet,' said Patrick as he served the shepherd's pie.

'Lots to think about. Just running over what's been packed. If I've left any washing in the utility room. That sort of thing.' She didn't want to speak in front of the boys.

Margot studied Ollie and Toby as they larked around, chatting noisily about the friends they were about to see and what would happen in the next half term.

Patrick was enjoying joshing with the boys, as he dished out seconds to Ollie, who seemed to be a bottomless pit these days.

When they had finished, with hugs, and tears on Margot's part, all the clobber was bundled into the car and Patrick drove Ollie and Toby back to school.

The silence in Margot's life resumed. She tidied up, wondering what to say to Patrick when he returned.

Back and forth, from the front bay window to the terrace doors, Margot paced and any anger she held against Patrick, fizzled out. She was as much to blame as he for this misunderstanding. She had on occasion tried to question Patrick, but he never quite answered clearly, he deflected. It must be difficult for a man to admit being sterile. And she, perhaps fearing his answer, had allowed him to wriggle free.

But he had the boys, didn't he? Had Vi been about to reveal more? Years ago, she hinted that they might not be Patrick's. But if Patrick wasn't their father, who was? They both looked so very like him. Apart from the strong resemblance, they had the same mannerisms, but maybe that was learnt behaviour. Or perhaps something had happened later, after they were born.

All these years together, and yet it seemed she knew so little about Patrick's inner life.

Margot went through to the kitchen and collected a bin bag from under the sink. She marched upstairs and opened her bathroom cupboard. She took all the stockpiled pregnancy tests and bottles of vitamins and threw them out, right out into the black bin outside. In the narrow side passage by the house, it was already dark. The weekend before the clocks had changed and a clean, sharp coldness was gathering in the air. There would be a frost. Margot closed the bin with a decisive clang, and returned to the house, she sighed. That was that.

When Patrick got home, it was late.

'Patrick, I need to ask you something.' She intercepted him in the hall. 'We need to talk. Something Vi brought up.'

'You shouldn't worry about anything that woman says. She just comes up with whatever, guessing what will hurt the most. I'm sorry if she's upset you.'

Margot paused, losing the thread of her rehearsed confrontation. Patrick was right Vi was always saying hurtful things for effect.

'Work,' he said, gesticulating towards his study door. 'I just need to go over some papers. I'll be up in a moment.'

She hesitated. Patrick kissed her on the cheek before retreating to his lair. The door closed behind him with a quiet, firm click. Margot alone in the hall, had once again missed her moment.

She wended her way upstairs as if in a dream, her hand holding on to the roundel of the newel posts for a moment longer than necessary, leaning her weight out, she swung around the turns in the stairs, like she did as a child. She had that empty Sunday evening feeling as though time was standing still, only it wasn't.

She sat on the bed in the small yellow bedroom. Patrick's indifference relit her fury. How dare he avoid her concerns and brush her off. All the days, weeks and months she had waited. She was furious with Patrick and his evasions.

If he had been clear at the beginning, would she have married him? She loved Patrick, he was her all, she didn't want to answer that question. Perhaps he was right, Vi *was* lying, but what she said had the ring of truth and explained much.

Margot wept silent, furious tears and picked at the knobbly candlewick fabric on the bedspread until all the hurt had trickled away. She was such a fool. She looked at the little chest of drawers that housed the clothes she had hoarded and thought of the little hats, mittens, and soft toys. She brushed her tears with her sleeve. Margot knew the empty room would make her feel wretched, yet here she was, still drawn to her shrine to unfulfilled dreams. She spent half an hour shaking out all the tiny Babygro's and refolding them and putting them away again, smoothing the soft fleecy and terry fabrics. Her reflection in the long wardrobe mirror radiated dejection. Through the open door, she listened to the clock ticking in the hall downstairs.

Patrick was still in his study.

Before she could stop herself, Margot opened the door to the wardrobe and sorted through her summer clothes, packed away in this unused room. The dresses rustled with excitement. She could hear the piece of paper crinkle and crackle in the pocket of her party dress as she pushed the garment bags aside. A whisper of a promise to fill the long, lonely, purposeless evenings that stretched before her. What had unerringly brought her here rifling through her own pockets? Was it Patrick? Was it Vi? Was it Jack? But she knew. It was something else that she would never acknowledge, even to herself. The moment her hand closed on the note it was as if she had always known what would happen next.

If Patrick didn't want a confrontation, she wouldn't challenge him. She would take matters into her own hands and wouldn't think about this too hard. It might give her what she wanted, perhaps even if she didn't get pregnant.

As soon as she had a moment at the office the following day, Margot reached into her bag for her phone and the smoothed note. The ink had faded, but she had been able to decipher the number. As the ring tone sounded, she imagined Jack rolling over through rumpled bedclothes to take a sip of last night's wine from his bedside table before picking up the phone.

'Hullo,' he said, long and drawn out as though his voice was in itself an invitation. Margot paused, suddenly timid. She was intruding. It had been years since Jack had dropped the note in her pocket. He would have forgotten all about it.

'Hello, hello,' said Jack again, more briskly.

'Oh, yes, well, hello Jack, it's me.'

‘Me who?’

‘Me, Margot.’

‘Oh, … hullo there, Margot. How very good to hear from you.’ His voice was warm again, languid. ‘I’m working now, but shall we meet for a drink later?’

‘Well … actually, I’m not sure why I’m ringing.’ A wave of second thoughts, such shallow motivations fluttered through her. What was she doing?

‘I’m sure you are sure, really. Otherwise, you wouldn’t have called,’ said Jack.

They agreed Margot would come to Jack’s flat off Walton Street that Friday afternoon. She could slip away from work early, and Patrick would doubtless be working late. He would never notice if she was home later than usual.

A Course of Action

Unit One

Patrick had run out of excuses. He needed to complete those wretched tick-box courses that HR was so keen on. He had had to cancel the previous one at the last minute. He turned off his computer and headed to the lifts, he had warned Margot he would be late.

The course was being held in one of those airless, underground, honey-coloured conference rooms with no windows and fake cornices trying to convince the inmates that they weren't in a cell, but a place of refinement.

The space was set up like a wedding reception, with eight round tables. If the course was full, which it looked as though it would be, half the room would not be able to see the speaker. Patrick quickly took a seat facing the main desk.

He looked around. He was among the more senior grades in the room. He really had left it till the last minute to sign up. But he mustn't moan about having to attend, all government employees were required to have completed this bureaucratic exercise. He was sure he would glean helpful information that would equip him for the daily struggle of office politics. He was prepared to have his mind blown away by the new directives, but it was already very warm in the conference room. Patrick would need more than the one small coffee he had picked up on the way in, if he was to stay awake for the next two hours and fifty-five minutes. He tipped his cup, but it was empty.

The woman from HR, arrived. She introduced herself and connected her laptop to a projector. The screen at the end of the room lit up. It was a government issued course titled, *The Basic Principles of Discrimination, based on recommendations following the Equality Act of 2010.*

'Sounds like it's going to be a thriller,' said the woman sitting next to him, leaning towards him so she wouldn't be overheard by the room.

Patrick recognised her. She was one of the gaggle of lawyers who held court at the far side of the large open plan office on the third floor.

'I'm surprised you have to sit through this too,' said Patrick.

'No one is exempt. That, by the way, is just the sort of comment that this course will tell you is sexist and racist,' she said, sitting back up in her chair and turning away from Patrick.

He felt chastened. He had thought as a lawyer … but never mind.

When the first talk and set of slides had finished, and a tea break was announced, everyone took the opportunity to stretch their legs. Patrick, hoping to make amends, asked if he could get his neighbour a tea or coffee.

'Do I look as though I need a drink, or do you think I'm incapable of getting one for myself?' she said arching her brows. She was tall, the same height as Patrick.

'Not at all,' said Patrick, who wondered if she was already getting into character for the role-play session later in the afternoon. 'After that introduction, we all need refreshments. I am merely heading that way myself and would be delighted to collect something for you, if you would like,' he added.

'Well, in that case, I'll have a tea with lots of milk but no sugar. I'm Charity, by the way, one of the law officers on the third floor.'

'Patrick.'

'I've seen you cross my floor,' she said.

'Yes, on the way to the gym.'

'Three times a week, that's keen.'

'Yes, well, need to keep fit.' He nodded and headed for the queue at the urn, thinking he had wasted valuable minutes on his exchange with Charity. He hoped some biscuits would be left by the time he got to the front of the table.

He returned with the tea and proffered the final pack of biscuits, some custard creams.

'Perfect, thank you,' she said, taking the pale tea and all the biscuits.

Disgruntled, Patrick sloped off to see if he could find someone else he might know, someone to chat to or cadge a biscuit off, but he was unsuccessful.

He had barely done a circuit of the room before the presenter called them all together again. The idea was to split the room into smaller breakaway groups to work on projects. Once again, Patrick found himself sitting next to Charity. As the afternoon progressed, he found her friendlier than before. Those custard creams had obviously hit the spot. He smiled at her cautiously, he was wary of anyone who had that much milk in their tea.

There were ten of them on his table, he was the most senior, and despite the collusion of the other nine to find fault with him, Patrick quite enjoyed the role play as the sins of unconscious bias were hammered home.

'You're not as stuffy as I thought,' said Charity at the end of the afternoon leaning towards him, her thigh pressing against his.

'Ah, well,' said Patrick, nudging his chair back slightly. 'You need to be wary of making assumptions.'

'We could get a drink sometime?' she said.

'Er ...,' He stopped his right hand from reaching to brush his hair forward over his receding hairline.

At that moment, the woman from HR approached them. Patrick took the opportunity to stand, Charity rose too.

'I have signed you up for the follow-up course, Patrick. Best to complete all the units in one and get your certificate.'

'There's more! How many units are there?' said Patrick.

‘Four, it will take three more afternoons, also run on the first Friday of the month.’

Patrick was astounded.

Charity smiled. ‘Looks like we’ll be spending lots of time together, with or without that drink.’

‘Oh yes.’ Patrick wasn’t used to being singled out by flirtatious, younger women.

‘See you around,’ said Charity.

On the way back to his desk, Patrick calculated how many hours he would have to make up. He would explain to Margot, she would understand.

‘I’m sorry, I’ll be a little late this week, making up the hours from that wretched diversity course last Friday. There will be more too, there’s a whole set of them, apparently. And it looks like I have a dinner on Wednesday as well this week,’ he admitted the following Monday morning as he headed off to work.

‘No worries,’ said Margot. ‘My work looks to be getting busier too. Fridays I might be a little late going forward.’

Patrick was glad to see Margot was keeping busy and seemed happier.

A Change of Heart

An Assignation

Margot was cutting through the streets behind Sloane Square, heading towards Walton Street. She passed a carmine rose still in bloom. Sheltered by the white stucco houses, its ragged flowers were held high, defiant against the cold November wind. The leaves on the trees in the street were turning. They had already fallen at home in the colder suburbs.

The note with the address was in her handbag, she didn't need to look at it, she knew it by heart. All these years, Margot had only thought of Jack as Jenni's husband or Patrick's cousin. Life had been busy, and there had been things to do, but at this point in her life, there was nothing more important than getting what she knew she had always needed.

Jack was an attractive solution to her problem. He came from the same genetic pool as Patrick, so there would be no surprises. Jack was arrogant and known for being a lothario. The string of girls he was supposed to have slept with was legendary. Yet he was discrete. Margot had never heard him bragging about some woman or other. And he was good-looking; it would be no hardship.

Jack had left her his number. He was interested. She didn't love him, so she could get herself a baby and walk away. This would be fun.

Margot didn't want to do anything that would jeopardise her family and didn't want Patrick to get hurt, she was sorry he was unable to give her what she wanted - through no fault of his own. She didn't want to ruin what she had, but this was the price for all those squandered years. It would be tricky to explain her pregnancy when it happened, but she would find a way that he could live with. Perhaps persuade him he still had it in him, nothing was absolute. And after all, she had not been misleading about wanting a child of her own. When he understood how she felt, whatever he thought, he would forgive her - wouldn't he? They would still have a family, and she would have her baby.

Margot's stride shortened; her footsteps slowed. At the corner Margot halted altogether. She checked the address, listening to her anxious heartbeat, thinking about what she was about to do. Could she really go through with this? Could she risk everything she had and go behind Patrick's back just so she could have a baby?

Despite her calculations, despite what she had decided, Margot wavered. Marriage wasn't meant to be easy. Just because she and Patrick had their ups and downs didn't mean that they didn't have something worth working on. They were very happy, and she loved Ollie and Toby. The life they had made together, all the little everyday things, added up to something important. She didn't really need her own baby. She was about to imperil the family she had - for a craving.

Margot couldn't do it. She pivoted and headed back the way she had come, towards the chichi shops and Sloane Square.

The pavements were slippery with swirling leaves, she shook her head to order her thoughts, but the motion only seemed to twist her decisions into a knot. She couldn't decide if she was missing the only opportunity she would have or whether she was escaping with her marriage intact.

At a corner an icy gust of wind caught her unawares and she pulled her coat to. She was doing the right thing. Head up, marvelling at her close shave, Margot turned into one of the smarter streets with bigger red brick houses and apartment buildings behind Peter Jones. She stopped.

A man at the other end of the street was paying off a taxi. He looked just like Patrick. She was sure it was Patrick. She almost called out, her hand was half raised in a wave, but she paused. What was he up to? He should be at work.

Patrick paid the cab driver, looked up and down the street, without seeing her, and went up the steps of a tall apartment building, and rang a doorbell. Margot heard the click of the lock as he was admitted. Patrick vanished into the building. For a moment, Margot couldn't move. Her arm was still midway to a wave.

Patrick never left work early. It didn't look like he was going to a meeting. She knew it was dress down Friday, but even so, Patrick looked far too casual and relaxed. He almost had a skip in his step. She blinked a couple of times to grasp what she knew she had seen. What was he up to? He couldn't be meeting someone, having an affair. Patrick loved her.

Margot's centre seemed to come unstuck and drop, leaving her winded. Then, bit by bit, the beat of her heart picked up until it hammered. She had persuaded herself to preserve the sanctity of their marriage, to be honourable. Meanwhile, Patrick was playing fast and loose with her trust. Did he think so little of her? It would explain all the excuses and the late nights and the business dinners. She had fallen for the old cliché.

Margot turned and walked back to Jack's flat. Two could play at that game. She noticed half the petals from the brave rose had fallen, caught by the sharp wind, only a few remained grasping onto the green hip.

'Hello, Margot,' said Jack, buzzing her up. 'Second floor.'

Margot let herself into the dark, unfamiliar hall and climbed the steps up the narrow communal staircase. She rounded the turn in the stairs and saw Jack's door was open. He was waiting for her, leaning against the jamb. Tall, lean and tanned, his dark hair rising in careless spikes.

Margot stood up a little straighter with each step as she came up the final flight.

Despite herself, she arched her back and dropped her chin as she looked up at Jack, trying to dispel the enormity of what she was about to do. She put her hand out onto the wall as she took the last few steps, so he wouldn't see her shake.

'What took you so long?' he said.

About Turn

A Change of Plan

When he looked back on it, it was at his father's ninetieth the previous August, that Patrick had his damascene moment.

He had passed his father a plate with a piece of birthday cake and as he turned back to the tea table, he had ruffled Toby's hair.

'Geroff,' Toby had said cheerfully through biscuit crumbs.

Toby was ten, Ollie twelve, they would be teenage before he knew it. Patrick relaxed back into his chair and picked up his cup of tea. He looked at the insipid concoction. He had absentmindedly added milk, forgetting his mother only served very weak china tea. He had not been paying attention, as usual. He was always trying to get ahead, without really concentrating on what was going on around him, without living in the moment. He had only thought about what he wanted, not what he needed.

Patrick thought his angst, had to do with his health, but in fact, his life had become one dimensional. He looked around the room as he sipped his cup of perfumed, warm milk. If he, like his father, could bring as much happiness to his small family in his dotage, that would be something truly worthwhile.

His father was describing to the boys how pinhole cameras worked, his mother was refilling his tea, and Margot was doing whatever magic she did to hold the whole family together, prompting the conversations, passing the cups and cake and giving the room a hug. She was the epitome of motherhood.

It was then the lightning bolt struck. Ollie and Toby brought Patrick immense delight and pride. He was ashamed of how selfish he had been to deny Margot this personal joy. He knew she loved the boys, but he had always known she wanted a baby. She had been a bit down since her aunt died. A warmth spread through him. It wasn't too late. This would be the best gift he could give her, a thank you for all the happiness she brought him. Why hadn't he thought about this before? He believed a reversal was possible, if not always entirely successful. He would look into it.

In the end, it had been simple. Patrick had found a consultant off Sloane Street and booked an assessment. He had managed to get away from work early on a Friday afternoon.

When he arrived at the clinic he had been startled for a moment, when out of the corner of his eye, he thought he saw Margot at the end of the street, but he realised how ridiculous that was. Margot worked in Covent Garden. She started at ten and didn't finish till six. It must be a coincidence. He had shaken his head, bounded up the steps of the converted mansion block and pressed the bell. He was called up for his consultation.

Patrick went through the motions of weighing up the odds, so the consultant would think he was being vigilant in his decision. Then he booked the op for the next available Friday afternoon. It happened to be a weekend when the boys were at school, and Margot was going to be away with her sister, for a final visit to The Old Vicarage.

Patrick felt good about himself. It wasn't often he did something truly altruistic. He hoped she was still keen. She hadn't mentioned it for a while. Anyway, he decided not tell Margot what he was up to, he was enjoying having a secret. Also, if she was charged with expectation and the reversal didn't work, he wouldn't be able to bear her disappointment.

Afterwards, he had a quiet weekend planned. He cancelled his golf. The consultant said to take it easy for a day or two. He said it might take months for Patrick to produce sufficient sperm, but outcomes were generally good. He was to go back in three or four months to see if all was well.

Patrick decided he would be philosophical about the procedure. Either it would work, or it wouldn't, and as he hadn't spoken to Margot, she wouldn't be anxious one way or the other. It would be a lovely surprise. He could watch her amazement when she found out she was pregnant. It would be a moment to cherish.

Once home, he saw that Margot had filled the fridge with food for his weekend. She really was an angel. Patrick selected a Caesar salad. There was a note on the cover, which he didn't notice till he was settled on an icepack wrapped in a towel at the table, *dressing in the fridge door*. Patrick shuffled back to the kitchen and fetched a bottle of proper mayonnaise. Despite what he had told her about being good and eating well, he hoped all the meals she had prepared weren't quite so healthy.

On Saturday, from the comfort of the sofa, Patrick watched two games of rugby and a football match back-to-back. Only getting up to toast the crumpets Margot had bought for him to have with his tea. The following day he watched cricket between two teams in the southern hemisphere for whom he had no affiliation. At lunchtime, he took a short tour of the garden in his dressing gown and slippers. There seemed no point in getting dressed. His footprints left a trail through the cold, damp, autumnal grass. He thought of Ollie and Toby playing rugby at school, naked knees in freezing mud. He lifted his face to the grey, smoky sky and took in the sweet scent of a bonfire.

Beneath his feet, through the soft soles of his slippers, Patrick felt hard round chestnuts imbedded in the lawn. Usually, when they were home, the boys would collect them for playing conkers, as he had used to do with Jack when they were young. A late half-rotted brown leaf swirled down onto the grass beside him. He really should do something about all the leaves. He kicked at a few and felt a twinge. Perhaps this year they could be left to rot down into the lawn.

When Margot returned, he would claim to have a bout of flu. He had already booked Monday and Tuesday off and would work from home. That should be enough of an explanation to give him space for a week or two, by which time Christmas would be on the horizon and Margot would be preoccupied, busy getting ready for when the boys came back from school.

Patrick was excited with his plan. He felt joyous at the prospect. It was what Margot needed. What with Angela dying and Ollie and Toby starting boarding school, Patrick thought Margot would welcome having time to herself, but it didn't seem to have worked out that way.

'I don't know what to do,' she had said. 'The evenings are so … quiet.'

She was understandably sad the night the boys went back to school after half term. He was too. He had been miserable all the way back in the car and rushed into the privacy of his study as soon as he could when he got home. He didn't want his being upset to affect Margot more than she already was.

Then Angela's estate had finally been wound up and Margot seemed happier. Though to Patrick's dismay, she filled a storage unit with pieces of furniture and bric-a-brac she would probably never look at again.

'The storage costs will mount up, month by month and over the years,' he said, but he didn't want any more stuff in the house.

'There are too many memories to just throw it all away. Lily and I have already got rid of so much. It has been so hard. It's like every piece of furniture, picture, or vase tells a story,' Margot said.

Patrick liked his life spare, clean and tidy. Margot was always smart and neat, but she was a bit of a hoarder. Patrick had seen her carrying bags and boxes into the small spare room. She had probably filled the wardrobe with mementos.

He found it hard to believe it had taken him so long to work out how to make Margot happy. He felt mortified that he had only been concerned with how Margot could meet his and the boys' needs. He thought it was the same thing, if he was happy, she would be happy too. As soon as he felt confident, he would cuddle up to Margot. He was hopeful she would be pregnant soon. The doctor said to be patient, that it could take up to six months. Patrick was sure it wouldn't take that long.

Nothing happened. A cold New Year was followed by a ghastly February and an unusually dreary March and still nothing happened. Patrick encouraged Margot to give a couple of dinner parties, something she always enjoyed, she was such a great cook, but her mood seemed to have deteriorated like the weather, and nothing seemed to lift her spirits.

Thwarted

Jack Away

In the lead up to Christmas, Patrick had said he had a bug and seemed withdrawn, disinterested in her. She thought of the moment she had seen him entering the red brick mansion block on Cadogan Gardens. It suited her that he was distracted but she couldn't help feeling a little peeved that he might be having fun with someone other than herself. Particularly as she was finding it so hard to meet up with Jack.

Starting an affair was one thing, but committing to it was harder than Margot could have foreseen. It became a pedestrian process, trying to find time when they were both free with their work schedules, and when Margot wouldn't arouse Patrick's suspicion. Then Margot was away with Lily at The Old Vicarage for a final weekend before the sale went through, a cathartic experience. Then, she only managed to see Jack once more before it was the boys Christmas break, and they were home for three weeks of school holidays.

Patrick and Margot had driven down to the school to hear Toby sing a solo in the carol service. They kept their coats on in the cold church, rustling with hymn sheets, whispered conversations, and expectation. Margot was so proud when the choir arrived. She didn't know when she had felt so moved. Toby's beautiful voice rising and falling in the school chapel seemed to embody the possibilities for all the children who raised their voices to fill the stone arches.

Over the next few weeks, with all the festivities and parties with family and friends, there was no chance for Margot to be with Jack. Their paths crossed at Jack's parent's annual Christmas drinks, but they managed to avoid each other, skirting the room, each keeping an eye on where the other was. It was exciting and frustrating in equal measure. Jack had kissed her goodbye, a cousinly peck on the cheek almost touching, but not quite.

Margot had a negative test. It was not that she was late, really, just a day or two, but she had been so sure she would get what she wanted. She had pinned all her hopes on that last time she had seen Jack before Christmas. Later that day, she started to bleed. What a way to start the New Year. When she got in from work, she took a long hot shower to wash away the feeling that she was flawed. Maybe she was the problem after all. She sighed and looked at her peaky winter reflection in the mirror as she dried herself then went downstairs in her pyjamas to make a hot chocolate.

Then, when the snowdrops were joined by the first daffodils and everyone's hearts were lifted at the prospect of spring, the weather closed in, a cold wind blew, the heavens opened, the days were hemmed in by darkness, and Jack was sent away on a training course.

She wouldn't miss Jack exactly, he was a means to an end, but she was frustrated. How was she ever going to have a baby if her lover was in Yorkshire.

That night as she lay in bed next to the sleeping Patrick, she imagined that her body was sinking into the mattress heavy like a corpse, and the bedclothes rose up and folded around her like a shroud, engulfing her. As if waking from a bad dream, she fought her way out of bed and slunk to the bathroom to feel the cool tiles under her feet and to splash her face with cold water.

'You seem a bit put out,' said Patrick, coming into the kitchen, back from golf a cold Sunday early in March. 'Anything the matter? It's not the wrong time of the month, is it?'

How could he not know how irritating that phrase was?

'Oh, no … nothing… forget it. Just the time of year I expect. I'm completely fed up with this weather. I want longer days and warmth. Tea?' How dare Patrick. She could be in a filthy mood whether she was having her period or not. She found some mugs and banged them down on the kitchen counter, so he would know how infuriating he was, but he didn't seem to notice as he peeled off his wet weather gear and hung it up in the utility room.

'I feel invigorated after that,' he said. 'Forget what?'

'How was the game? It's a bit wet out, isn't it?' she said. He was far too cheerful. She rootled in the shelves for some teabags.

'Shocking, but it's good to start the year as I mean to go on doing some exercise in the fresh air. But … I was thinking, as you are so fed up with the miserable weather, would you like to go away somewhere warm? We could go with the boys over the Easter holidays.' Patrick fished the milk out of the fridge.

'I hate skiing,' said Margot. That would be Ollie and Toby's choice. She squeezed the teabags and flung them into the bin. Besides, Jack was due back at the end of March, Margot didn't want to be away then. 'You must be soaked,' she added.

'It got worse as we went around. Luckily, I have the right equipment. There's no such thing as bad weather, only bad clothing.'

Margot resisted the urge to say something. At first, she had found Patrick's use of aphorisms endearing, they had been a part of the parcel, but today her exasperation at Jack being away was making her irritable.

'I've lit the fire. Shall we move through,' said Margot.

'Good idea. I am still a bit chilly.' Patrick came back into the kitchen having emptied his golf bag in the utility room so his clubs could dry. Margot had heard the clatter and clunks.

'Are you playing next weekend too? I might give Jenni a ring. I haven't seen her for ages.'

The following Saturday morning, it was raining again. Such fine drizzle you could hardly tell it was wet until you were outside and drenched. Margot met Jenni at a soft play centre. Julia and Molly had brought friends.

‘The girls are enjoying school so much. Now they’re busy all day, I don’t know what to do with myself,’ said Jenni, looping her coat and bag over the back of a chair on a free table.

‘I was at a loss when the boys went off too,’ said Margot. She also secured a seat before turning to help Jenni with the girls. ‘It seems just moments since the twins were babes in arms.’

‘I know, I know, time flies.’

Jenni took Julia’s friend’s coat, and Margot helped Molly take off her shoes.

‘What gorgeous girls you are.’ Margot gave Julia a hug.

‘It’s so much easier now, I’m thinking about going back into teaching actually,’ said Jenni. ‘But there are still all the activities to organise with all the toing and froing that involves.’

‘Well, you never really got into teaching, as I remember. What happened to the tea leaf business.’

‘Oh, golly that was ages ago. Teaching would fit in with the school holidays.’

‘Twins must be quite a handful even when they are in school,’ said Margot.

Julia, Molly and their friends disappeared amongst the blue and red tubes of the apparatus, reappearing on a yellow slide, landing in the ball pit. As Jenni prattled on Margot’s mind wandered. How old would her baby be? She counted the years, nearly a teenager, slouching around the perimeter of life, grumbling. What a delightful concern that would be. A puzzle easier to solve than her current predicament. She mustn’t give up hope, Jack would be back at the end of the month.

‘These places must be a godsend when the weather is so awful,’ said Margot, a non-sequitur that could fit anywhere in the conversation.

Her lack of attention hadn’t been noticed. Jenni had no brain space left for anything else but Julia and Molly. Margot sighed. Her problem had become so mundane that, for her friend, it had ceased to exist.

'I'm always trying to find different interests for them, so they're not always doing the same thing. But they both need to learn to swim, it's essential. Ballet, they both insist on, all that pink. You'll have to come to their next recital. It's not till July, but you'll love it. The children are just so adorable.'

'Yes, I'm sure I'd adore that.' Margot couldn't think of anything worse. All the parents doting over their children, she would be the token spinster, the Godmother, again.

The twins and their friends had extracted themselves from the play area and, having collected some pocket money from Jenni, headed over to the shop to get some sweets.

'I'm so lucky to have such sweethearts. Being married to Henry was a bit of a disaster, but if there is one good thing to come out of it, it's the twins. Well two good things! Henry pushed me to have children. I wasn't sure if having a baby so quickly was a good idea, but it is such a joy. You must feel nearly the same sort of thing with Ollie and Toby.'

'The boys have always been a delight.' Really, they had. It had been a privilege for Margot to be part of their lives.

'Don't get me wrong, it's hard being a single mother, but I wouldn't give Julia and Molly up for the world ... they are such a blessing. You know they made me these lovely cards for Mother's Day at nursery. I've stuck them up on the fridge with magnets. I think Julia particularly shows real artistic promise.'

Margot tried not to be uncharitable, but the house Henry had given Jenni at their divorce and the financial settlement, couldn't make being a single mother too difficult.

'And how's Richard?' said Margot. Why, oh why, couldn't she have her own child to talk about incessantly. Was it too much to ask? When Jack was back, and she was pregnant, she would talk the socks off Jenni.

'Oh, he's great. He dropped us off this morning and will come and pick us up. I'll need to keep an eye on the time. Honestly, it's good to have a man around the place. I don't want Julia and Molly to grow up scared of men because they don't know any.'

'I find Richard rather scary,' said Margot.

'You don't... he's, well, if anything, a bit boring and predictable. But I like being organised, having a routine. I think I might marry him.'

'That's a big step, are you sure?' Margot put her hand on Jenni's arm, hoping to get her full attention. 'He's not a little … overbearing sometimes? What does Henry think?'

'You know me. I like having a partner. Honestly, I think just having a man around outweighs trifling shortcomings, don't you? How's Patrick?'

'He's playing tennis this morning. He's on this health kick. No more doughnuts and sport, sport, sport.'

'That sounds dull. What are you doing to cheer yourself up?'

'Well, you are right there. I'm all for eating healthily, but extreme exercise is not for me. I preferred the Patrick who wanted to take me out to fancy restaurants.' Margot brushed the hair from out of her eyes and retied her ponytail.

'We don't get out much either. Children are such a tie, and Richard likes to stay in.'

'And now the boys are away, and Angela has gone and … I'm at a bit of a loose end, really. I did have a plan, but it's fallen through for the moment.'

'You are so lucky. I'd love to have the time to do something for myself. A class, pottery maybe, I've always fancied that, or getting my French up to scratch. Something improving.'

'Hmmm,' said Margot, suddenly desperate to leave.

Back home, Margot unpacked her grocery shop. It wouldn't be for much longer. Jack had said he would only be away for six weeks. Six weeks! The way it worked out, that covered two opportunities, two chances to get pregnant. Two more weeks to go. Perhaps she should take up a class, as Jenni suggested. Maybe bridge, people who played bridge never had time for anything else. No, she would save that for later, when she knew there really was no hope.

Margot counted the days Jack was away as fervently as she counted the days between her periods. She missed him more than she had expected. Margot had never had that feeling before: physical yearning.

Sex

Margot thought about the first time, way back in November. She had never asked Jack if he was surprised that she had eventually got in touch. He certainly didn't seem so. When she arrived at his flat, he had opened a bottle of champagne with a flourish. She was still in her coat in the centre of his sitting room, not knowing where to look, hardly taking in the warm decor. Her motivation deserted her. She had not initiated sex with a stranger for so long. She wasn't sure she remembered how.

Seeing her discomfort, Jack put down the bottle and came to her. He took her bag and then her coat and laid them on a chair in the hall. Then he poured the champagne and placed the glass in her hand, closing her fingers around the stem, his warm hands enveloping hers. All the while, he talked about a large, embroidered panel that hung on the wall. She took in the decorative fabric, and tall bookcases crammed full of hardbacks and paperbacks jostling together, trying to grab the reader's eye.

Then Jack led her through the flat, talking about the Middle Eastern artists he was interested in. They passed a gorgeous painting of a hunter on horseback dressed in burgundy and gold his spear raised, menacing the viewer.

'Love this guy,' said Jack. 'He's Persian rather than Islamic. There's a real energy.'

Margot picked up a small, notched stone from the side table below.

'What's this? Is it old too?' she asked, turning it over in her hands, her thumb feeling the ridges worked into the surface.

'Quite,' he said, taking the artefact gently from her hold, his hands cupping hers as he did so, before he replaced it on its stand.

Margot had never thought of Jack as being cultured. She had not moved her ideas on from that picture that Jenni had painted of her wild, untameable, young husband. But Jack had grown up while Margot had been busy in her life with Patrick and his boys.

When they finished the tour of the flat, Jack took her back to the sitting room and had shown Margot some beautiful, illuminated manuscripts that he had collected, and he laughingly showed her some of his own attempts at replication. Then she admired the few decorative tiles and shards of painted pottery that he had accumulated over the years. Jack even asked her to take off her shoes so she could feel the texture of the rug with her toes.

Every little thing that Jack showed her, with a measured explanation, showed his interest and passion for the bits of the world he had explored and with each item he showed her, he opened a part of himself.

They were at the table, deep in conversation leaning over, heads together, Margot admiring a small antique ceramic bowl, when an alarm went off, loud and persistent, burring rudely.

'Shit,' said Margot. 'Sorry, sorry.'

She fumbled in her bag to find her phone. That first time, she had set a timer so she wouldn't stay too late, so she wouldn't miss her train, so, she could get home before Patrick. so, he would never guess what she was up to.

She left a bemused Jack with a peck on the cheek. It wasn't how she had thought she would start her affair.

In early December the second time she went to Jack's flat, Margot stopped off and went into the loos at Peter Jones. She wriggled around in the cubicle, unhooked her bra and pulled it off shoving it deep in her bag. In the long mirror by the door, she adjusted herself and undid the top-most button of her blouse. This time she wasn't going to leave anything to chance.

Margot had hardly got in the door before they had tumbled into each other, and it seemed as though she felt every twist and knot of the Turkman wool beneath her as she and Jack wrestled out of their clothes and touched and felt and found each other. As they rolled, she placed her hands on the carpet on either side of his head, her fingers pleasingly covering symmetrical, geometric designs. She rather wondered she could think of such a thing. Her hair had fallen forward. She arched back up to tie it up out of the way and Jack sat up and pulled her to him and laughed as though just for the joy of being with her. After all the years of counting and calculating, initiating sex on auspicious days, although she was only here for a baby, this was liberating. It had been a long time since Margot had thought of sex as spontaneous.

Then there was the Christmas break. They had been busy as a family, and it had been almost possible to put thoughts of Jack to one side.

But when the frustration broke through, she channelled her upset at missing Jack into a frenzy of indignation at Patrick's perceived betrayal. It might take time, but she would find out what he had been up to. Before Christmas, Patrick seemed keyed up and over solicitous but also shied away from sex. Proof, she felt, of his infidelity. She didn't reveal that she had seen him in Cadogan Gardens. It suited her that Patrick had withdrawn just as she was getting to know Jack. It gave her a certain power, and a secret validation for her own behaviour.

After the boys were back at school, Margot arranged to see Jack again. She arrived at the flat ready to continue where they had left off, but the sofa and chairs had been removed from the ochre sitting room.

'Are you moving?' she said.

'What, no. Coffee?'

While Jack made some coffee, he talked about the provenance of the rug that she was standing on and the adventures he had bringing it back to London, and where he had learnt how to brew Arabic coffee. Jack clearly had an idea of how the afternoon would play out. Margot dropped her coat on the chair in the hall and settled herself modestly on one of the large, patterned cushions on the Persian rug.

When the coffee was ready, Jack placed an antique Arabian coffee pot along with a plate of syrupy pastries on a ceramic tile of intricate blue, turquoise and red design on a low curved-legged table between them. Jack sat facing her, one leg crossed and the other with the knee raised. He rested his elbow on his knee and gazed at her.

'God, I've missed you,' he said. 'I usually enjoy Christmas, but this time, the festivities seemed to go on forever.'

'I missed you too.' Margot smiled, what was this ritual about? Was Jack trying to woo her?

The room smelt of a rich, burnt earth and of sweet cinnamon. Jack served the coffee in tiny, thick, handleless cups. She felt the round heat of the small pot in her hand. She took a sip under Jack's gaze. She felt the grit of stray coffee grounds as they sieved through her teeth. The coffee was strong.

'Is this how Arabs have their coffee,' she asked, her breath ragged.

'No! They sit on chairs in cafes like anyone else.' Jack smiled. 'This … is theatre.'

Low sunlight filtered through slatted blinds, crossing the room with bars of light, knife-like in its precision. Shredding the rich gloom with brightness, catching slithers of dust sparkling in the air. Jack held up the plate of pastry and offered them to her. Margot took one and ate it, licking her sugar-coated lips and fingers.

She started to speak, but he reached across and put a finger to her lips.

She finished and Jack proffered the plate again.

Margot ate the pastries, one after the other, slowly, sipping the bitter coffee to counter the sweetness. Jack watched her. After each one, she licked the residual honey and icing sugar from her mouth, her tongue darting out flickering over her sticky fingers. Jack's eyes never left her. They hardly exchanged a word. Whenever Margot began to say something, she couldn't help trying to fill the void, he would lean towards her and wipe any flakes of pastry from around her mouth with a linen napkin, pressing her lips, silencing her as he did so. It became mesmerising, her watching Jack, Jack watching her. Shards of light slicing over the velvets and tassels and fringes in auburn and gold. The thick air seemed saturated with the sensation.

She hadn't known that eating pastry could take so long or be so beguiling.

The coffee ceremony was the most protracted and sensuous foreplay Margot had ever endured. It was time to leave, but she was trembling and had trouble getting to her feet.

There was still one piece of Turkish delight left on the plate, but there was no time.

'Never mind,' said Jack. 'There's always another day.'

He followed her to the door. She struggled into her raincoat, rushing because she was unsettled. In the narrow corridor, he reached past her to open the door. As he dropped his arm, he encircled her waist and pulled her back into him, hugging her from behind. The side of her neck warmed as he breathed deeply against her.

'Till next week,' he said, then, then let her go.

That evening, Margot got home just before Patrick. She ditched her coat, kicked off her shoes, and tried to make it seem as though she had been back for ages.

'I was a bit late and haven't cooked. I thought we could order a takeaway. What do you fancy?' Margot said as Patrick came in the door.

She placed the order.

'We've got twenty minutes. Let's go upstairs.'

'What's got into you?' said Patrick, following her.

Margot was still thinking of Jack and wanted gratification. Also, she and Patrick had not had sex for a while. Their abstinence had gone on too long, and although Margot didn't like to think of herself as calculating, if she did get pregnant with Jack, she would like Patrick to believe there was a slight chance the baby could be his.

What with one thing and another, there wasn't another day to finish the Turkish delight with Jack. Then Margot received the text.

Sorry, orders, I'm off to the frozen North for training for the blazing Middle East – if you can believe it! 6 weeks. It will fly by – perhaps. x J

A Portrait

A View

It had been Patrick's shout. He chose somewhere within easy walking distance of the office, the restaurant at the top of the Portrait Gallery.

'This is great. Haven't been here for ages,' said Jack.

'It's one of my favourite places in London. I love the view. Untidy roofs, glimpses of landmarks and tourist attractions, all hugger-mugger. And being able to see what Nelson sees is extraordinary,' said Patrick. 'Though the weather isn't great today.'

'I was a bit early, so I had a run around downstairs,' said Jack as they took their seats at their window table. 'It's like catching up with old friends. All the iconic portraits that filled our history books at school are here for real.'

Dark clouds gathered and rain spattered the window.

'So, how's things,' asked Jack.

'All good, busy. Boys thriving, loving their new schools. Turns out Toby has the most amazing singing voice. We're hoping he'll get a choral scholarship when he joins Ollie at the senior school in the autumn. You're going away, aren't you? Catterick?'

'Yes, standard stuff. A prelude to deployment. But I'm hoping I won't have to go anywhere.'

'I thought you loved the adventure.'

'I'm beginning to think it might be time to settle down.'

Patrick ordered drinks and they looked through the menus.

'How's Margot?' said Jack. 'Angela's estate has been wound up, hasn't it? It must have been quite painful for her.'

'Yes, wretched. Margot's been a saint throughout. She was a bit down for a while there but seems more cheerful now the whole thing has been settled.'

'Moving on,' said Jack.

'A time of readjustment. She's had some time on her hands. Especially with Ollie and Toby away. But she's pragmatic. Angela was a good age and made the choice not to have treatment.'

'At your party, Angela was delightful, she made sure she talked to everyone and loved being with the children. Margot has some of the same joy about her.'

'Yes.' Patrick had not forgotten the photograph of Margot with Jack taken at the party. He trusted Margot one hundred percent, but he didn't trust Jack one iota. Patrick felt a wave of paranoia wash over him. He hoped Jack wasn't interested in Margot.

'How long are you away? And when are you off?' asked Patrick.

'Soon,' said Jack. 'Six to eight weeks, probably not back till after Easter.'

Why did Patrick feel Jack was laughing at him?

'We're thinking of taking the boys skiing over the long bank holiday weekend.'

'They'll love it. Does Margot ski?'

'It's not her favourite, but she loves being with Ollie and Toby – being a part of their adventure.' Margot had a heart of gold and would never betray him, but there was something about Jack's attitude that worried Patrick.

Their food arrived and they ate in silence for a moment. Patrick gazed out of the window hardly taking in Nelson or further away, glowing in an isolated ray of sunshine, Big Ben.

'I would take the medicine every time, I mean if I had cancer. Who knows what advantage time might give. What about you?' said Patrick.

'I don't know. I don't know that you can ever know what choice you'll make unless you are in that place.'

'I suppose not. Why do we make any choice one way or another? But you must know how it feels to make life or death decisions, having been in dangerous situations with the army. I'm assuming there have been such moments.'

'You have to be there, to know what it's like,' said Jack. 'The reaction every time is different. Why do we make the choices we do? Turn left, turn right, disaster or safety. Life is in the lap of the gods.'

Back in Whitehall, Patrick turned left and right as he strode through the corridors of power, wondering what impact any of the decisions he made might have, that is if he could get anyone to listen to him. Unfortunately, he wasn't the only one who thought they knew best.

When Ollie and Toby were home for the holidays at the end of March. Patrick did take them skiing. Easter was early that year, there would still be snow. It was unlike Margot, but she didn't accompany them.

'I'm a bit worried about you,' he said, kissing her as bags packed, he headed out to the car with the boys. 'I'll miss you when we are away. I hope you'll keep busy and not mope.'

'You'll have fun with the boys – bonding. It's only five days. I'll be fine. I've had enough of the cold weather this year. I'll catch up with friends and go to Lily at the weekend.'

A Long Weekend

Two Hearts

Easter loomed and he was back, and she was waiting. Patrick was away with the boys, and she had two whole days with Jack, then Sunday lunch with Lily and her family. On Monday, Margot was meeting Jack again for a walk on Hampstead Heath, far away from anyone they knew. Margot had all the time in the world. The whole of the long bank holiday stretched in front of her.

When Margot arrived at Sloane Square feeling excited, she told herself there was no good reason for her to behave like a teenager. She was having an affair for a calculated reason, and she would be in control. She was going to enjoy Jack's company while it lasted, but she wasn't going to let her emotions get in the way.

She climbed the narrow stairs and saw the door to Jack's flat was open. She wondered what Jack had in mind this time. It was an exciting game.

The sitting room was back to normal. The velvet sofas were littered with the embroidered scatter cushions. On the central wooden coffee table was a pewter plate with a beaten rim. On the plate was a single piece of Turkish delight. Margot laughed and felt her insides begin to melt.

'There you are,' said Jack from the kitchen through the hatch.

'What's this?' She gestured to the plate.

'Unfinished business ... gin?' He held up a bottle.

'Later,' said Margot, not wanting to lose the initiative. She dropped her coat and bag on a chair. Then she took off her wedding and engagement rings and left them with the keys on the hall table. Her engagement ring, she viewed as a beautiful promise of her budding romance with Patrick. Her wedding ring sometimes flooded her with joy but also reminded her of slave bracelets, evidence that she belonged to Patrick. Either way her engagement ring's winking eye seemed to reproach her when she was with Jack, so she had taken to leaving it at the door. A sign she was free to make her own choices. She wanted to feel free, that she had no responsibilities. This weekend was hers to be who she wanted to be. It felt safer to leave Patrick's rings at the door.

She picked up the plate with the Turkish delight from the table and moved deeper into the flat down the jade green hall.

She paused outside the bedroom door, running her finger over the dimples in the pewter of the plate. She could hear Jack mixing the drinks, then the ice cubes tinkling in the glasses as he walked down the hall behind her. She pushed open the door.

The richness of colour gave the bedroom a sumptuousness. The oriental patterned curtains hung loosely obscuring the window and subduing the light from outside. Margot put the beaten plate down on the bedside table. As she turned around, Jack was there, right behind her. Surprised for a moment, the breath left her. They were so close, so still, and then Jack was gently peeling off her clothes.

After the Turkish delight, one small square shared in a slow nibbly kiss and a dusting of icing sugar, sprinkled and licked, Margot needed a shower. Jack joined her.

Another time, she must bring a bottle of her own shower gel, or Patrick would notice she smelt of neroli.

Afterwards, she saw the gins, their cold dampness making rings in the wooden hall table, the ice gone.

They changed the sugary sheets and ordered in.

'So, Margot, tell me, why are you here? What brought you to my door and why now?' said Jack the next morning as they lay curled together postcoital in bed.

'Because I have a whole weekend and no one I'd rather spend it with.' She never mentioned Patrick by name in Jack's flat. It wouldn't be right.

'Hmmm. You know that's not what I mean.' He stroked her hair brushing it off her face. 'After sitting on my note for years ...

why now? I'll let you think about your answer while I get us something to drink,' he said, slipping out of bed.

Margot had expected the question since the first time she had rolled up at his door. She hadn't known what she would say then, and she was no nearer an answer now.

Jack was not always a comfortable person to be with. She didn't always know what he was thinking or what he would do or say next. Margot was mesmerised by his unpredictability. Being with Jack opened something in her, an unfolding, like a child's paper fortune teller, a game to tease, flicking the paper corners to reveal emotions or feelings or maybe even the future.

Margot was not about to break the spell and tell Jack the actual truth. Besides, she was enjoying watching him wander around the flat naked. She stretched under the duvet warm and cosy. It was a long time since Margot had experienced such a feeling of freedom, such a lack of responsibility.

'I thought this would be more fun than coffee,' said Jack, returning with a bottle and two glasses. 'Now, I've never made it a secret that I'm very fond of you and have been desperate to get my hands on you for some time.' He knelt on the bed and poured her a glass and laughed before continuing. 'Though I might have been a bit circumspect about that with Patrick.'

He passed her a glass before slipping under the duvet beside her. She sipped the cool, crisp white. How did Jack know what wine went with rumpled cotton sheets? Was there a directory somewhere that told you such things, *Wines for all Occasions*.

She knew her motivation, but what about Jack? Was Margot, Jenni's eighth bridesmaid, part of a tally, or perhaps she was just part of the rivalry between Jack and Patrick that had been going on for years. What did Jack really feel about sleeping with his cousin's wife? It couldn't just be because he fancied her.

'But you, what impulse pushed you to call?' he said, sinuous beside her. 'Why me, why now?'

‘Well …. I can think of a few reasons.’ She reached for him looping her leg over his thigh.

‘I don’t believe you’ll ever be open with me,’ he said, rescuing her glass before rolling and pinning her to the bed, his hands either side of her head holding her wrists on her pillow.

‘Does there have to be an ulterior motive, can’t it be just because…I’m having fun,’ she said, wriggling her arms free and encircling him.

‘I think,’ he shuddered. ‘That you don’t like telling the truth. Don’t like being made to have an opinion. You’re good about life and the everyday, but about what you’re feeling … I wonder if you are even honest with yourself.’

Afterwards, Margot took a call from Patrick, reassuring him she was keeping busy, that she was fine. When she put down the phone, Jack said. ‘I imagine you and Patrick talk and talk but never say anything important. You are both too considerate. I see you side by side, meandering through life, misunderstanding each other at every turn and always being too polite to say what you really mean.’

‘You are being offensive,’ she said, gulping down the last of her wine too quickly.

’She speaks to me,’ he laughed. ‘That’s better. But I’m right, aren’t I? Do you know what Patrick thinks about you at this moment?’

She didn’t, of course. For the first time, she really didn’t. It was a frightening thought. She had always known exactly where she stood with Patrick. But they had both flipped a coin and now were flying blind. She had a feeling Patrick’s fling had fizzled out, had not lasted long, but that didn’t mean he wasn’t re-evaluating what she meant to him. Though she trusted, that for them both, being part of a family, was the most important thing. Neither of them wanted to lose what they had.

'Am I just a passing amusement for the lady about town who has everything and is bored?' said Jack.

Margot began to sob. It was not what she meant to do, but unbidden, the tears slipped down her cheeks. Jack took her empty glass, placed it on the bedside table and dabbed at her face with the corner of the duvet cover.

'Forgive me,' he said, kissing her. 'I didn't mean to upset you. I just look forward to our time together and wanted some reassurance that you perhaps felt the same about me.'

Margot sniffed and hoped she didn't look too blotchy. It was a joy to be with Jack, but she wasn't about to tell him that.

Drinks

Post Vasovasostomy

Back from skiing, Patrick made a follow up appointment at the clinic. He was confident. He felt back on form. The consultant had said that although it could take as long as six months, there was no reason that in time Patrick shouldn't be able to get his wife pregnant. Patrick had been holding his breath, waiting to hear if his reversal was successful. He initially booked an appointment for mid-March, but he had to reschedule.

He had been distracted. Work had been hectic. The focus had shifted in Afghanistan; security responsibility was being transitioned to local forces. Somehow, this required more operational involvement from the MoD. Patrick had been looking into setting up training and support for Afghan troops on the ground. Also, the monthly DEI course had been running concurrently, creating more work and subsequent late nights to catch up. Then he had taken time off to get away skiing with the boys over the Easter holidays.

So, what with one thing and another, it had been over five months before he managed to get an appointment. He was eager to be told his life was back on track and that he would be able to give Margot a baby and seal their relationship. Though he had some work to do there. Margot had seemed preoccupied, distant. All too often recently, they had hurried by each other on their own trajectories, forgetting to interact on their way.

He should pick up some flowers for Margot. There was a new florist by the off-licence in the arcade near the by-pass. He would stop off on his way home, buy Margot something pretty, and show her that he really cared.

Patrick knew he wasn't very good at demonstrating how he felt. He loved Margot. He wanted to stand up and be the man she had married and live up to her expectations of who her partner should be. He would woo her all over again. Perhaps he could buy her a present too, something expensive.

Vi had always accused Patrick of being parsimonious, but being careful had been something his father had taught him. They counted the pennies in Patrick's father's family. His mother often mentioned that she had married down and to a catholic. She had her own money and came from an old family, CofE, thanks to Henry the eighth. She controlled the purse strings when he was growing up and still supported Patrick in ways she felt would make a difference. In contrast his mother's younger sister, Jack's mother, had married up, to someone fabulously wealthy. The cousins never mentioned this discrepancy in their family fortunes and Patrick fought hard not to feel the impoverished cousin. Being well off wasn't everything.

He was meeting Jack for one of their lunches. Jack's choice, in Chelsea. Patrick remembered Jack had a flat off the King's Road, that he had inherited from some great uncle or other. The Bluebird would be ideal for him, a leisurely stroll. It was inconvenient for Patrick, nowhere near his work, but as he had managed to book his follow up appointment at the clinic for that afternoon, it all fitted in rather well.

Jack stood as Patrick entered the terrace, late and flustered. Patrick had forgotten how far the restaurant was down the King's Road. They sat outside. It was an unusually warm day for this coldest of cold springs.

'Good to see you. How're things?' said Jack, shaking his hand.

'Sorry I'm late … work, tube, sorry,' Patrick hated it when he sounded like this, an eternal apologist. His sweaty hand was clammy in Jack's cool grip. 'Good …you?' he asked.

'Never better,' said Jack, calling the waiter to order gins. 'Still waiting to hear where I'll be going next.'

'Hoping for somewhere exciting?'

'Well, you know, I have no say in the matter, but as I think I mentioned before, I'm hoping for something in London.'

'Are you sure? You have always thrived on adventurous postings,' said Patrick.

'Not this time … things have changed,' said Jack. Their drinks arrived. 'Cheers!'

'Cheers,' said Patrick. 'So, what's new?'

'I've met someone.'

'Someone special? I mean you are well known for new, er, new and, er, numerous relationships. Always a different girl on your arm.' When Patrick considered it, he had never heard Jack confess to any conquest. He had only listened to scandalised women defaming their peers. Jack's reputation was hearsay.

'Am I? Well, maybe when I was young. Appetites change, don't they?'

'What makes this time different?'

'She's exceptional, something about her … fits me well,' said Jack. 'The eggs benedict is good, but I think I'll go for the steak frites?'

'Sounds great, no need to think.'

'Steaks, rare,' said Jack to the waiter.

'Medium rare, for me,' said Patrick. 'Anyone I know?'

'She's someone I've known for quite a while. Always carried a bit of a flame for. And now, things have brought us together.'

'Things?' For no reason he could think of, Patrick felt defensive.

'I haven't examined the reasons. I'm too happy enjoying myself. Sometimes, perhaps one should just accept what the fates bring.' Jack was looking rather pleased with himself. Patrick didn't like it.

'I'm glad for you and happy you're feeling … settled. But you're due off somewhere soon, for what, a year?'

'Probably only six months, if I go. But, as I said, I'm going to ask to be transferred to Whitehall. I want to be here now.' Jack leant back on the banquette and stretched his long arms along the back in either direction.

'Wow, Jack is coming down to earth. I hope you have a smooth landing. Do you really want to give up your decadent lifestyle? I always thought you liked your independence too much to commit to anyone.' Patrick could hear the sneer in his voice, the lack of empathy. He didn't like it, but he was alarmed by Jack's calm confidence. He oozed happiness.

'Selfish, you mean? You know, I have always been jealous of what you and Margot have.' Jack leaned in.

'But you have to be me, to have what Margot and I have,' said Patrick. Was there an undercurrent here, a subtext he was having trouble reading? Patrick didn't want to overreact.

'I suppose, there are lots of happy couples out there,' said Jack.

'What's the saying, all happy families are alike … But what holds any two people together is singular to them, like magic. Unspoken, intangible,' said Patrick.

'You don't want to put too much store in the belief of magic. Always need to work at a relationship to prevent the cracks from gaping … I should think,' said Jack. 'Anyway, I've found some of that mysterious glue. I am enchanted.'

'Well, I wish you all the best,' said Patrick, tipping his glass at Jack without smiling. 'Love is … more precious than rubies. Margot and I are very happy, and I would like to feel that you, too, had found a relationship of real meaning.'

Jack beamed back.

Corinthia

By the time the boys went back to school after the Easter break, the weather had improved, and Patrick was back on the golf course. His four was well matched, and it was good to get out and get some fresh air. He had felt a bit bad abandoning Margot for so long over the Easter weekend, but she seemed to enjoy herself at her sister's. Now, he was abandoning her to play golf.

'No, of course you must go, you will have fun. Of course I don't mind,' she said. 'I might go up to town. Do some shopping.'

He gave her a kiss before stashing his clubs in the boot of the car and driving to the Golf Club for lunch and a game.

She really was kind. He wasn't sure what Margot got up to when she went shopping. She rarely came back with many bags, but she seemed to have a good time.

They were both generally late home on a Friday these days. Then, he had his tennis on Saturday morning and golf either later that afternoon or Sunday if they weren't having lunch with his parents. All fine-tuned to fit around any sport on TV. They might ask some friends around on Saturday night, and Margot would cook something delicious. Then, when everyone had gone, sex before bed - the perfect weekend.

The following week was the final session of the diversity and inclusion course. He was glad it was almost over. He needed to complete the programme to be eligible for the next level of promotion, now he would have everything in place. After the concluding talk and the certificates were handed out, Patrick needed to check his desk but agreed to join the group for a celebratory drink an hour later. They were meeting around the corner in the ground floor bar of the newly opened Corinthia.

The program had been better than he thought it would be. Some of the ideas were new to him. What became apparent was that the etiquette of the workplace had changed. He had always lived by the adage, manners maketh man, there was a certain irony in discovering that wasn't strictly true anymore. It all depended on interpretation.

As it was a Friday, the Corinthia bar was already busy. The DEI group had found a seating area of leather armchairs and padded sofas in a corner and were already enjoying themselves. Charity rose and gave up her chair for Patrick and then settled on the wide arm next to him. She leaned behind him and draped herself along the high back of the chair. Patrick found this proximity to a slightly intoxicated Charity slightly alarming but was determined to be affable. They had got on well throughout the course and always sat next to each other. Charity would rib him on his old-fashioned views, and he would cautiously tease her about her feminism. All in all, they had a good laugh, and he felt flattered by her friendship.

Charity leaned in to reach for her drink. She put her hand on his knee to balance. Patrick sat very still, trying not to flinch. It seemed that respect for personal space wasn't something that was applied universally. Every time she reached for her wine glass on the central table, Patrick would lean back into the chair and nervously twiddle his wedding ring. Apart from feeling uncomfortable at her closeness, he feared she would fall off her perch.

Patrick offered to get the next round of drinks. Even though there was waiter service, it was an excuse to change the dynamic of the group. He took orders as he straightened and inched away from his chair.

'Come back soon, Patrick,' said Charity, waving her wine glass at him and sliding into his vacated seat.

While giving his complicated order to the bartender, Patrick noticed a man leaning against the bar. He looked to be on his own. Patrick vaguely recognised him. A friend of Jack's, perhaps.

'It's Will, isn't it?'

'Yes! Good to see you … er… remind me….'

'Patrick. I think we met years ago at Jack's stag. I'm the older cousin.'

'Yeah, right, right.'

There was a pause.

‘To be honest with you, I don’t remember much from that night.’

They laughed.

‘Staying here?’ said Patrick. ‘They’ve done an amazing job with the revamp, haven’t they?’

‘Yeah, it’s fab. No, I’m staying round the corner in more modest accommodation. I’m here for five days, for work … meetings, next week, but thought I’d come down early, have a bit of a jolly over the weekend.’ said Will. ‘A rare visit to London for me these days. I’m still in the army, but based in Glasgow, Personnel.’

‘Interesting,’ said Patrick, trying to sound as though he really thought it was. ‘I’m MoD.’

‘Procurement, right?’

‘Well remembered!’

The group’s drinks were accumulating on the bar. Patrick hovered, asking for a tray. He was reluctant to return and take his seat next to Charity. This aspect of discomfort had not been covered on the course.

‘All for you?’ Will nodded at the drinks.

‘Works do, but informal. Care to join us?’ Perhaps the not bad-looking Will would distract Charity. ‘You could do me a favour,’ continued Patrick. ‘Despite wearing this.’ He held up his left hand to show his wedding ring. ’Someone is not getting the message. Nice girl … just not for me. Can I add a drink for you?’ Patrick nodded to the loaded tray.

‘Ah, well, yes, OK, why not. Gin, thanks. I mean, if I’m not intruding. That would be great. I’m on my own this evening.’ He smiled. ‘I’m available and happy to distract and be distracted.’

Patrick added Will’s drink to the order, and between them, they carried the round back to the table. Patrick introduced Will. Other groups in the bar had moved on to dinner, so it wasn’t too difficult to find more seats to drag into their circle. He was careful to put Will between himself and Charity.

Patrick slipped away an hour later before another round arrived. As he had managed to stick to one gin and tonic, he would be fine to drive. He just needed to grab his gym kit and check his emails, and he would be on his way home. A few others left simultaneously, but a core group were set for the evening. Patrick waved goodbye to Will, happily chatting to Charity.

Back on Track

A Test

Last minute, Patrick had let Margot know that he had a dinner and would not be home until late. She didn't know whether to believe him anymore, and although she had not seen him skulking round the streets of Chelsea again, it gave her an excuse and an opportunity. Margot phoned Jack as she was leaving the office on the off chance, and here she was, deliciously cosy and content, wrapped up with Jack in his duvet and the beams of evening sunshine that stroked the room.

She was so relaxed she was almost asleep. Here, she had no commitments, her real life was left at the door. For Margot, it had all been about the sex and, it was still. Sometimes, Jack wanted to make their assignations more of a date, but she preferred to get down to business, without too much chat. She wasn't there to get to like Jack, and she hoped he wasn't getting fond of her.

He had a reputation, and she was relying on it. He was a notorious bachelor and wouldn't want more from their affair. Every time she went to see him, Margot reminded herself that this, what they were to each other, meant nothing. This little interlude was not going to affect her relationship with Patrick. When it was over, when she had what she wanted, and she was back in Wimbledon, Jack would be over her in a moment. He would be on to the next woman, and she knew she wouldn't feel a thing, make a fuss or bear a grudge. She was using him, just as he was using her.

Having dawdled drowsily, Margot needed to leave in a rush. Jack was waiting, ready to kiss her as she left. Always in the door, offering a way in or blocking her way out, as if to entice her to stay with him for longer, part of the merry dance they played.

On the tube home, Margot grabbed a seat next to a window where, in the crowded carriage, she could fold her thoughts together, treasuring her hours with Jack. She stared through her dark reflection in the glass, memorising the feel of him, the smell of him, the way he touched her. Until the train surfaced and her phone buzzed.

Next week, we should take time to talk. It would be good to share more than sex.

Not till I've had enough, she texted back. She would not get side tracked by charm. The Easter weekend had been a one-off fabulous rendezvous, when they could pretend they were in a proper relationship, but she wasn't about to lose her head. Patrick was her life's companion, her family. She must remember that she needed Jack for just one thing, but he was making it very hard for her to remain indifferent.

Another text pinged through.

On my way – see you soon x P

She should make it back before Patrick, just. It was raining but not cold when Margot got off the train. She left her brolly at the bottom of her bag, glad to walk up the hill, letting the drizzle soak her hair and seep under her collar. Wash away any traces of Jack. She wouldn't need an excuse for looking as though she had just stepped out of the shower when Patrick got home. She checked her watch when she got in. She didn't have much time.

With a little care, Margot could keep things separate, she would get what she wanted and there would be no need for her to lose anything at all. Patrick was her mainstay. Jack was a bit of fun, an opportunity, and a sperm donor, that was all. She had a plan, and she was going to stick to it.

Since he had got back from his skiing break with the boys, her connection with Patrick had perked up too. She had been so miserable after Angela's death, that Patrick's withdrawal the previous winter might have been considered thoughtful, allowing her to rebuild. Until she realised it had given him a freedom, too, but now, Patrick was more attentive than he had been for an age, but his renewed interest smacked of contrition. He had even brought her flowers the other day, his dalliance must be over.

Perhaps Patrick subconsciously knew he had a rival and was staking his claim. Was there something about her, had something changed because of her relationship with Jack, that made her more attractive to Patrick. It might have been because Margot felt more alive than she had for a while, and that filtered through. She was juggling but so far, all the balls were under her control. If anything did happen, it would make things much easier if Patrick thought he was part of the equation. If the boys were his, and he certainly believed so, surely, there was a slim chance something could happen again.

The following week, on the tube going into work. Margot had a seat, but noticed a young couple strap-hanging near her, swaying with the motion of the carriage. It had to be a first love, their heads nodded towards each other in harmony, like horses in a sun-kissed field. His arm around her, protective, as they rode with the flow of the train. There was something endearing in their stance. They shared something that held them together apart from everyone else, as if only they understood how the world truly worked.

Margot felt a warmth, a bit of a glow. She smiled, she was hardly late but had been counting every hour. The train doors opened, the couple got off, leaving some of their joy in the carriage, and more people got on. Margot did the sums again. The train moved off and she felt a ripple of delight. She had waited thirteen years for this moment.

On her way home, she would pop into the chemist by the tube station. There were plenty of tests at home, she had bought more just in case, but the situation demanded a new one, then there would be no reason not to believe the result. The day dragged on. Only a few hours and she would know. As she walked home from the station, she decided she would wait till the weekend to take the test, that way more time would have passed, and she would know for sure. Two slow days, but it would be worth it.

Margot cancelled her tryst with Jack that Friday. She didn't want her excitement to give her away. She wanted to hold herself still while she waited for the hours to pass. She looked in her handbag, the test was still there, of course it was. She couldn't face disappointment again, so she would wait. She would be patient.

On Saturday, Patrick was up early to get the papers before breakfast and his tennis. He always made an excuse about how important it was for small traders and how he wanted to keep the corner shop busy, but he enjoyed this weekend ritual. Margot listened as he got himself ready to go. He seemed to take forever guddling about downstairs. When she heard the front door click shut, she slipped out of bed, retrieved the test box from her handbag on the chair and went into the bathroom.

Margot read the instructions three times, even though she knew them by heart. It was easy, really; these tests were foolproof. She read through the leaflet again. She peed and waited. Time teased. Breathe in, breathe out. Gradually, the moisture seeped across the display. And then, faintly at first, a lovely blue line appeared. Margot motionless, looked and looked again, the blue line was really there. She let out a sigh of relief, of disbelief, of gratitude. Then, her heart seemed to inflate filling her chest, lightness bubbled up inside her. At last! Her reflection in the bathroom mirror, was bed hair and face a blaze of utter joy. Margot laughed. Then, she took one of her old tests from the stockpile in her drawer under the bathroom sink and did the test again. It wasn't that she wasn't sure, but she wanted it to be indisputable. She wanted to feel the excitement again, and watch the line appear once more. It was extraordinary. Margot stood for far too long, just staring at the blue line. It was true. It was really happening.

'I'm back. I've got your coffee,' called Patrick from downstairs. 'I'll bring it up.'

Heart beating, Margot swept the test sticks and boxes into the drawer under her sink. She knew she should tell Patrick immediately, but she wanted to savour the moment. It would be fun to hold this knowledge to herself. She would give it a week or two, do another test and show him then. Besides, it would seem more natural if she allowed some time to pass. So, it didn't seem as though she had been expecting to be pregnant.

She wondered how Patrick would take the news. He would be surprised, she was sure of that, but with a little persuasion, he would support her and be happy for her. She had never made any pretence about the fact that she loved children and would like one of her own. She knew that was part of the equation for Patrick in marrying her, because she would make a home for him and be a mother for Ollie and Toby. Surely, he would at the very least take joy in repaying the favour.

When Patrick went out to play tennis, Margot had a shower and dressed. Downstairs, she made herself another coffee, sat at the kitchen bar, and looked out at the garden. She loved this time of year. It was early yet, but the promise of all that would come was nascent in the garden. The first riot was not long away. The daffodils and cherry trees had led the way, the azaleas looked stunning under the unfurling maples, and the roses wouldn't be far behind. Then, as the weather warmed up, the garden could settle down into a steady flourishing. Margot revelled in the life outside and the life within. She placed her hand on her stomach, still flat, and thought of all that was to come. She would blossom too, nothing would go wrong, this was meant to be, she was good at nurturing. She pushed her coffee away. She probably shouldn't and smiled at the thought of the changes to come.

Charity

Emails

After Iraq, the support of the public for military involvement abroad was no longer a given, even if there was a humanitarian component. Afghanistan was a country of factions and competing warlords. It wasn't that Patrick felt they were on a fool's errand, that was not his job, but a peaceful form of government of a Western type seemed an illusion, particularly with the Taliban lurking in the shadows.

Patrick had seen the headlines. Of course, positive stories didn't sell papers, but it was disheartening after all that had been achieved. It was unfortunate but support for the war in Afghanistan was collapsing.

Following the leaking of unedifying classified documents about coalition forces and civilian casualties and the immensity of information available on the internet, politicians were more inclined to pay attention to public attitudes. The Monday after the diversity drinks at the Corinthia, Patrick was reading new information that had been submitted for evaluation. There was a timetable for British troops to withdraw. Many felt it couldn't come soon enough, but without a planned exit, there would be chaos.

It was midmorning, Patrick felt good, even from behind a desk there was a chance he could influence outcomes, change even in the theatre of war could be seen as advantageous. First thing, he had sent in his application to move to a post in a higher pay band and was now halfway through analysing the report and mid write-up, when an email dropped into his inbox.

Hey Patrick,
Hope you don't mind me getting in touch. Great to see you last Friday.

Seeing as you set me up with Charity, I wondered if you could give me her contact details? She mentioned she might be around this week and wrote her number on a napkin, but I seem to have lost it. I was hoping to see her again this evening.
Hope you got home OK. Thanks for the drink and the introduction.
Will

Patrick didn't like to hand over personal information without consent. So, he resorted to what he had to hand, open information, he searched for Charity's details in the MoD system. Will had helped him out, and he was happy to be helpful in return.

Hi Will
Of course, here is Charity's work email ...
Charity is great fun if a bit of a flirt. Even though I've tried to be clear that I'm not interested. I was mortified on Friday night, and concerned things might get out of hand as she had had quite a bit to drink, and she was coming on strong. Given what we spent the day doing, you would think a female lawyer might take DEI a bit more seriously! I was delighted you were able to step in and save my bacon.
When I left, Charity looked to be very much enjoying your company. Woman is ever fickle ...
Patrick

P.S. You mentioned you were in personnel. Jack was just saying how much he was looking forward to his next deployment. It's been a while since he's been anywhere interesting, and he's hankering after an adventure. He was worried he'd be thought to be past his best and would be sidelined into an office job. Don't know if you could help?

Patrick pressed send and returned to his urgent report.

It was only later, on his way to the gym during his lunch break, that Patrick had a niggling thought. He looked across to Charity's desk to give her a wave as he often did when he passed through the large open office where she worked. Today, she was talking to the girl at the neighbouring desk and didn't look up.

Patrick was almost out of the room when it struck him. He half turned but thought better of it. Shit. He needed to check his emails, but he couldn't miss his gym session. He always paid for the trainer in advance to ensure he didn't wimp out. He didn't have time to go back to his desk now. He'd just have to continue as though nothing had happened. And nothing would have happened - until he checked.

'Slow down. You seem to have some stress that needs venting,' said his trainer as Patrick huffed over the weights.

'Not a good day,' said Patrick between sharp breaths, rushing to complete his reps.

Maybe he was mistaken. Maybe it would be fine. Shit, he couldn't be that stupid, could he?

There was nothing he could do about it one way or the other. He would check as soon as he had showered and was back at his desk.

When he got to his computer, Patrick was horrified to see that he had cc'd Charity. He had typed her name into the cc box, copied the auto-completed email address into the body of the email, but had forgotten to delete the cc! He read through the emails. Nothing too awful, but nothing he was happy about sharing. He read the exchange again.

When he tilted his head to the right, it seemed just a bit of fun, but when he leant to the left, there seemed to be far too much that could be misinterpreted if one was sensitive or unsympathetic to banter or had just spent four monthly Friday afternoons learning about discrimination. How embarrassing, a rookie error. At least Charity didn't know Jack, so his postscript was irrelevant.

The sensible thing would be to email Charity directly and apologise, but the first email might have gone into her junk folder. If she hadn't opened it, he would just be drawing attention to himself.

He was late for a meeting, and this would take careful thought. He would sit on it overnight. He wouldn't sleep, but instead of digging a deeper hole, he would wait and see if he had a response from Charity in the morning.

The next day, when he logged in, there was nothing from Charity. Had he got away with it? He didn't know if a lack of response was good or bad. As the days passed, all was quiet. Patrick decided that if he bumped into Charity, he would be bright and breezy, polite and genial, acknowledging her without making eye contact.

When he did see Charity in the corridors of power, she wasn't quite as friendly as before. Now, she never looked up and waved when Patrick crossed her floor on the way to the gym. It was ominous, but for Patrick, preferring to take the most innocent interpretation, it was a positive. On reflection, Charity had been far too friendly before this fiasco.

He emailed Will mid-week to ask if he had met up with Charity and to find out if she had admitted to seeing the email trail and whether she had been upset. Patrick saw Will had replied.

Hi Patrick
We had a lovely evening, thanks. I took Charity out to dinner at that art deco place at the Savoy. Very civilised, oysters, steak, the lot.
I popped Charity in a cab shortly before midnight.
No mention of emails – it looks like you are off the hook.
Will

P.S. I'll see what I can do for Jack. He is the consummate soldier and very knowledgeable in his field and his familiarity with the region makes him a good fit. I'm sure the Adjutant General would like to use him if he can. I don't suppose you can get your hands on his file.

If Charity had turned her attention onto Will, that was a good sign and could explain her coolness towards Patrick. And what better way for Jack to close his distinguished career. Someone might argue that Jack's seniority and exemplary contribution had earned him a desk job if he wanted it. But if Patrick could quietly pass Jack's file to Will, and he had an opportunity to make sure it was seen by the right people, the chances were that Jack would be deployed far, far away from Margot.

Perhaps there was nothing to worry about after all.

A Decision

A Spanner

Now she had what she wanted, she should break off with Jack, but Margot still visited him at his flat again, and again. He was a habit that was hard to break. She thought she could resist the temptation of him and that when it came to it, she would be decisive. She had even stumbled over the words in her mind, practicing what she could say. But still she found herself ringing his doorbell on a Friday afternoon. It must stop. Patrick might not notice she was pregnant, but if she left it too long, she was sure Jack would. The next time she saw him, she would say something.

'I mean it. It's over.' Margot dressed and stomped down the stairs to the street, before he could stop her. She knew he didn't believe her, but it really had to stop.

Then she had to climb back up the stairs as she had forgotten her rings. They were on the side table in the hall beside all Jack's keys. She should keep them in her handbag, but there was something wonderfully reckless about pulling them off and casting them on the tabletop as she entered Jack's flat, a confirmation that she was up to no good.

'This is absolutely the last time,' she said.

'I love it when you are so determined,' said Jack, pulling on his coat as she gathered her rings. He followed her down the stairs.

They walked together through the blossom-strewn streets towards Sloane Square. Margot could feel Jack move beside her, his easy lope, long legs shortening their stride to keep level with her. At the corner, they turned for a long look at each other. She knew he thought she didn't really mean it. How could she, they had such fun. He held her hand and gave her a chaste peck on the cheek before they parted to go their separate ways. It was the restraint, the smallest touch, that was almost as enthralling as a full embrace.

'I mean it,' she shouted after him.

Margot paused, basking in the moment, watching till he disappeared with a wave around the corner in the street. As she turned, cherry blossom swirled along the pavement in the wake of a passing car and ended up in a puddle over a blocked drain.

Deep in thought, Margot ran into Vi outside Peter Jones.

'You're back!' said Margot. 'And looking very smart and summery.' Vi was wearing a tailored, eau de nil coat. It was curious to see her out of her usual sportswear.

'Well, yes … this is a surprise. I have a moment, why don't we grab a cup of tea,' said Vi, and Margot, in postcoital absentmindedness, was too slow and dim-witted to escape. They went up to the sixth-floor café and managed to get a window table as the lunch crowd had left.

After the normal preamble about the weather, there was a pause in the conversation. Margot looked out the floor length window to the street below. Cherry blossom was falling off the trees and drifting like snow. That was Housman, wasn't it? They had done the poem at school.

'I wonder … are you having an affair?' said Vi, pouring milk into her tea.

'What? Why would you say something like that?' Margot was glad she hadn't been holding her cup; she would have spilt the tea. Was it obvious, or was Vi up to her tricks and trying to unsettle her?

'Well, yes, I saw you at the far end of the street, and you were skulking along as though you didn't want to be noticed. And you just seemed so shocked to see me,' said Vi. 'And you are … glowing.'

'Of course, I was shocked. I thought you were in the Far East. When did you get back?'

How long had it been between the corner and bumping into Vi. Had Vi seen Jack saying goodbye to her. It had been a restrained kiss, but Vi's sharp eyes would have seen there was more to it than that.

'Oh, I got back weeks ago. I may be doing some skulking of my own.' Vi picked up her cup with the fingertips of both hands, took a sip, and smirked at Margot. 'So, who is he?' she added.

'Um… why on earth do you suppose I'm seeing someone? I could just be meeting a friend and shopping. In fact, I am … was … just meeting a friend and now have some shopping to do.'

Vi guffawed. 'Really?'

'You are looking very smart.'

'Oh, just dressing for the West End.' Vi patted her curls, then smoothed the fabric of her skirt. 'Ollie seems to be loving Winton, but you know that, Patrick will have spoken to him too.'

'Yes, he does seem to be enjoying himself,' said Margot. 'I was surprised Toby wanted to go away too. I suppose he didn't want to miss out.'

'Oh, I know, nothing worse than being left alone with boring, overly attentive parents. They don't warn you how harrowing these big life moments are for those left behind. I feel quite lost and desperate, knowing my little boys are growing up and growing away. And there is nothing like boarding school to cause separation and aggravation. You only have to look at Patrick and Jack. A perfectly good childhood friendship ruined by the system,' said Vi.

Why did Vi have to bring up Jack? Margot hoped she wasn't blushing. She took a sip of her too hot, green tea and hastily returned the cup to the saucer, misplacing it so that it banged and scraped.

'Well, this has been lovely. I had an hour to spare, and this was much more fun than browsing through haberdashery,' said Vi, not disguising her haste to leave now she had shot her dart.

'Are you sure you won't have another cup of tea?' said Margot, gathering herself and smiling her sweetest smile. She could hardly ask Vi what she had seen and if she recognised Jack.

'No, I must be off. I'm meeting a good friend of mine…' Vi checked her watch, 'In fifteen minutes. Oh, not that we're not friends … and don't worry, your secret is safe with me.' Vi patted Margot on the arm as she stood and smiled down at her.

'How lovely. Goodbye then,' said Margot.

She half rose as Vi bustled off, her bag swinging over her arm. Margot settled back to finish her tea, feeling most unnerved. Surely Vi hadn't seen anything, and Margot hadn't admitted to anything. She hoped Vi wouldn't report back to Patrick. Not that Patrick believed anything Vi said, but her jibes always set one wondering.

Five minutes later, glancing out the window again, down below on the pavement, she saw Vi, in her smart eau de nil coat, hurrying down Symons Street in the direction from which Margot had come not an hour earlier. Vi could be going anywhere. Thousands of people lived in the flats and houses in and around Chelsea. As Margot watched Vi teetering on the edge of the curb, she couldn't help but imagine a black cab hurtling round the corner, out of control and wiping Vi off the pavement and into oblivion, carrying her suspicions with her.

Margot gasped. A speeding taxi *was* coming around the corner of Cadogan Gardens. Vi had just reached the spot where Margot and Jack had said their goodbye. As the cab sped past, its back wheel spun dangerously close to the edge of the road. It didn't mount the curb but rolled into the blossom-flecked puddle. A wave of water shot up splashing the pavement. Vi, stepped back quickly, the water sloshed back onto the road.

Margot pressed her hand to her lips. She should be careful what she wished for. Vi paused before continuing on her way, disappearing around the corner unharmed, turning left, away from Jack's.

Margot let out a long sigh. A close call. She hoped she never saw the woman again. Some hope! She returned to the last dregs of her green tea, now tepid and bitter. She couldn't read the leaves, but this would be a good time to know a bit about the future. She sat for a long time, watching the remnants of her tea get cold.

When Margot got home that evening, Patrick wasn't there. How could he not be there? There had been some courses at work, but he must have finished those by now. She looked at her phone. He had texted her to say that he would be very late and not to wait up.

Margot dropped her bag and keys in the hall and kicked off her heels. She went through the dark house to the kitchen and slid her hand along the smooth kitchen countertop. Perhaps she should eat. She pulled on the heavy fridge door, cold light spilled out. She looked at the clear glass shelves, she must do a shop in the morning. She pushed the door to, before wandering into the sitting room and looking at the photographs on the shelves. Patrick and the boys, all of them together, the one with Patrick's parents. She moved through the house, trailing her fingers touching the familiar furniture, thinking of all that she and Patrick had built together.

She had to make Jack believe it was over. Margot had been furious with Patrick and his little fling and livid about his dissembling, and that had made the decision to have an affair easier, but she was no longer angry with Patrick. She wasn't going to jeopardise everything she had with him, now she had what she wanted. Patrick was a kind man. They didn't really have different ideas of what family meant.

That is, if Margot could present her case in a favourable way. It would be entirely different if Vi told Patrick that Margot had been having an affair. Patrick would be furious and if he thought she had slept with his cousin Jack, there would be no going back.

The Price

Margot was on the clock and not just because she was pregnant. She would have preferred to take her own time and pick her moment, but Vi was holding a grenade without a pin and could lob it towards Patrick at any minute.

The sex was great, and Jack made the most delicious coffee, but it was time to end it, settle back with Patrick and give her baby a proper family and home. For whom would be the better father? Patrick had the track record. She must stick to her plan.

Margot arranged to meet Jack one afternoon the following week, not at his house, but in a small cafe round the corner, where net curtains obscured the patrons from the street beyond, and they wouldn't bump into anyone who knew them.

Tea was a safe option. She could say what she wanted to and leave. There would be no chance of Jack wooing her back into bed for one last time.

'So, what is this about, Margot? Are you going to cast me off for real?' said Jack as he joined her at the small table at the back of the room.

'I'm feeling dreadful about Patrick. I suppose I should have understood that from the start… it has been thrilling being with you, Jack,' Margot patted his hand. She assumed he was rarely turned down and didn't want Jack to feel worse than needed. 'But yes, it has to stop,' she added.

They ordered tea from the waitress. Margot also asked for cake, she would need sustenance. They said nothing till the tea arrived.

'What if I don't want to stop? Perhaps I don't want to give you up. What if I enjoy your company, our …. liaisons?' Jack leaned back in his chair and played with his teaspoon, twirling it until it thudded on the tablecloth beside his cup and saucer.

Margot had not expected Jack to disagree or be this upset. Surely, she was one of many. Why was he being difficult? To see if she would react. She knew he enjoyed playing the devil's advocate. She had seen him winding up Patrick at family get-togethers. But when she looked at Jack, he seemed genuinely disappointed.

'I had begun to think that I might persuade you to leave Patrick.' Jack tossed aside the teaspoon and leant across the table towards her, reaching for her fingers. 'I like being with you, Margot.'

'I … I don't think I could do that to Patrick,' said Margot, sliding her hands under the table before he could catch them.

A spark of audacity flashed through her mind. Might that even be an option? She wondered if Jack wanted children. They had never discussed it. They hadn't talked about a future that couldn't be. That wasn't the sort of relationship they had.

She licked her top lip with the tip of her tongue. 'Patrick has always been envious of you; it would be devastating for him.'

'Jealous of me.' Jack laughed. 'Patrick was always the clever one. I was always being told to study hard, like Patrick. To be good, like Patrick. To cultivate sensible friends and take life seriously, like Patrick. God, by the time I was fifteen, I was sick of Patrick.' Jack sipped some tea. 'I decided to live in the moment. Take whatever opportunity came my way.'

'Well, you seem to have enjoyed your life and have had a successful military career to boot.' Had he only seduced her to get back at Patrick? If Margot felt she was part of a game, she would have no qualms about walking out the door.

'Being wild and not achieving much academically didn't endear me to anyone. That's why I joined the army. At the time, no one else would take me on.' He paused and studied the teaspoon, picking it up and flipping it this way and that, before looking up at her with his entrancing, blue eyes.

'Oh, Jack, you have so much to celebrate.'

'I don't know, you get to a certain age, and suddenly you have different priorities. Now, I feel more reflective.' His teaspoon tinkled against the edge of his saucer. 'I should never have married Jenni, of course. I feel bad about that. I was too young and irresponsible. But I had made Captain and was trying to be sensible and grown up. It was a mistake. But now I want -'

'Actually, I wanted to talk to you about Jenni.'

Margot didn't want to hear whatever it was Jack was going to say. He was the very devil to tempt her. She had her plan, and she couldn't ditch it now. She didn't need a dilemma. She didn't want to have to think about a new strategy. She didn't want to have her heart opened and be forced to examine how she felt. The only way she had been able to come up with this plan was by being objective and she was going to stick with it because of the growing baby within and the looming shadow of Vi. She couldn't be distracted by either Jack or her own emotions now.

'Classic diversionary tactics.' He almost smiled. 'Oh, yes, why?'

'I feel she is making a terrible mistake getting engaged to Richard.' said Margot. 'I wondered; would she listen to you? Could you persuade her not to do anything foolish?'

'Just because she wants to marry a stuck-up prig isn't reason enough to intervene. And I thought you, of all people, would understand her need for family.'

'When you put it like that, I do sound like a nosey busybody, but I am getting such bad vibes about the whole thing.'

'Hmmm. Maybe … but I would rather you thought about what I said to you, not what I might say to Jenni.' Jack caught Margot's hand which had strayed onto the table while she was talking. He held it firmly. 'I have another tour coming up. I've applied to stay here, but if I must, I'll have to go. But either way, I don't want to stop seeing you. I want us to stay in touch. I would like us to think about our options, as a couple.'

Jack's blue, blue eyes seemed to be searching for her soul. Margot tried to remember to breathe. How could she say no.

'It's … it's a lot to ask… all the unravelling. Of course, I will consider, but …. I need to think about all this …. and what it will mean for everyone.' Margot felt like crying. This meeting was not going how she had imagined. Jack was holding her hand as though if he let go, he would be lost forever, and she could think of nothing but her desire to be with him.

She couldn't be in love with Jack. She had purposefully kept her heart out of their arrangement. She hadn't wanted a complicated relationship, and yet here she was. She still loved Patrick, of course, he was her family, whatever he had done. 'You must see what a very difficult decision it is for me,' she continued. 'I have to look beyond myself, us, to Patrick, to Ollie and Toby too.' And her baby.

Jack let go of her hand. She felt bereft. He sat back and sipped his tea, watching her fidget. He must have sensed he had pushed her far enough.

'I don't think I'm ready for this. It wasn't what I had in mind,' said Margot.

'Those boys, very charming boys, I might add, are safely away at boarding school and are at an age where their peers will be more important than their parents. You've brought them up amazingly well. You'd hardly think they had such a bumpy start. Little credit goes to Vi, such an odd woman, quite unhinged.'

'How well do you know Vi?' said Margot, wondering about that old jibe. Had Vi come to the same conclusion as Margot, that he was a good genetic match. She should be asking Jack what he would do if she was pregnant, not about what he might have done in the past with Vi.

'Do you mean have I slept with her.' Jack laughed sadly. 'How little you must think of me. Understandable, I suppose. But God, no. Wouldn't touch her with a barge pole, dreadful woman. The trouble with Vi is that half of what she says is lies, and the rest of the time, she reads minds.'

The tube home rumbled over the points into Earls Court, where it waited for an irritating long time with the doors open and people hopping on and off. Finally, the train began to move in earnest and, at last, emerged above ground. Margot stared out the grimy window for the rest of the journey, glancing at the gathering rain clouds. She had forgotten her umbrella. She watched as the rain began to slap down with seeming vengeance.

Deadheading

The heavy summer shower during the week had given the weeds a boost and surprised the first early roses, turning their promising buds to mush. Margot had been distracted by Jack, spending too much time with him. Now she had given him up, she was back in the garden. May was a good month to make an impression, clear everything out before the weeds got bedded in.

She wore her pink gardening gloves and had her claw to hand for any troublesome, deep roots. The weed trug was within tossing distance. She was deadheading the roses and clearing beneath. By the time she reached the end of this bed, near the kitchen, she would have cleared her mind.

Through the open window she could hear the television. Patrick was watching the rugby. She couldn't understand how he could loaf inside when the sun was shining. But it did mean she could be busy in the garden and knew she would not be disturbed. Patrick wouldn't come out and see what she was up to, in case she asked him to help. So, her mind was free to soar.

She should be happy. The sun was shining, and she was almost six weeks pregnant. That was all she had ever wanted, a baby and a happy family.

Years ago, Vi had planted the seed that Patrick might be infertile and repeated the charge. Snip, snip, Margot tidied a nearby rose deadheading soggy buds that would never open. Then she raked the claw over a tenacious nettle that had sent roots out into the surrounding border. Now it was loose, if she grabbed it near the base and yanked, she should get the whole thing out.

Patrick had told her Vi was a troublemaker. But was he saying that to protect himself. Margot hated taking anything Vi said into account, but in this instance, she had concluded Vi might be right, after all she had been there. Margot was furious with Patrick, for at best being weak at most duplicitous. He should have been clear. She felt her marriage was based on a false premise.

But then again, Margot had never told Patrick what she had done and why she needed a baby. She hadn't wanted him to think less of her, after all, it had all happened so long ago, years before she met him. Margot threw the pulled nettle into the weed bucket. She had just turned thirty-eight, this could be her last chance to right the wrong. Three mouldering rose heads joined the nettle.

She should go ahead with a second test this weekend and surprise Patrick with her news. She could innocently say. 'But I thought you couldn't have children,' and see what he said. That might work. Hopeful fingers of vibrant lime green poked through the potentilla. As she pulled at them stray tendrils clung to Margot's jeans. She could never get all the fine roots of sticky willie out, but it had this habit of climbing through everything, the potentilla would be overwhelmed if she didn't try.

If she had not sought out Jack, if she had not acted, she would not be pregnant and wouldn't be expecting to be. She should wait for another couple of weeks, a month even, until it was obvious. She would need to look amazed; her surprise must mirror Patrick's. She picked out a few, final strands of the sticky willie. It was the best she could do. It would come back, but she would just have to keep on top of it. She heard a roar from the open window. Someone must have scored a try.

Margot hated keeping anything from Patrick. Her first pregnancy didn't count, and if she was honest with herself, Margot hadn't worried about lying when she had made the arrangements to meet Jack and was unlikely to be found out. Now, it was different, there would be no hiding if Vi raised her suspicions with

Patrick. Margot pulled at some couch grass with her claw. It was so unfair, Vi, with her warped and twisted perspective, had moved the goalposts.

If Vi introduced the possibility of Margot having a lover, Margot and Patrick's marriage would be over. She used the claw again to attack a clump of creeping buttercup, hacking away at the earth and roots to free the intruder. She and Patrick must have sex on average three times a week, more when they were first together. Things had tapered off somewhat recently. But they had been married for over seven years and been together more than six months before that. Margot straightened, arching her back to ease the stiffness while she did the maths. That must mean they had had sex nearly two thousand times. Margot sighed. Surely, the chances were, even if he was just a little short of what it took, that she would naturally be pregnant by now. She worried Patrick wouldn't see it that way. He had a clear understanding of how probability worked. Margot pulled the weed free and chucked the yellow flowers in the bin and pushed a stray strand of hair back off her face with the back of her hand, hoping her muddy glove didn't leave a streak on her forehead.

If Patrick rejected her and the baby, would she turn to Jack? He had been merely a convenience, but now she had ended their Friday meetings, Margot felt bereft. He said he wanted to continue their arrangement when he returned from Afghanistan, but she would be hugely pregnant by then. He would be horrified. And she wasn't sure he was steady family material.

Snip, snip, snip, she threw another handful of clipped deadheads into the bucket. She loved working in her garden, but it didn't give her quite the satisfaction an afternoon with Jack would have. When they met at the café and Jack asked her to consider being with him, he had not told her he loved her, so she had not taken him seriously, and had not wanted to. She would need to hear him say that if she was to contemplate giving up everything and commit to him. But there was nothing to think about, it was the last thing she wanted to hear and wouldn't fit in with her plans at all.

If she were to open her heart, would she realise that Jack had moved in. She crushed against the budding lavender, green flower spikes waving as she moved through the bed, and she was surrounded by the fresh, clean scent. She rubbed her hands through the leaves to release more of the perfume and breathed deeply. She would like to believe in Jack, but she was too afraid to go there.

Whereas Patrick was her bedrock. At the back of the border near the wall, Margot spotted bind weed climbing through the philadelphus. It was hard work. She got quite sweaty pulling out the worst of it.

As she tackled it, thorns from the arching branches of the climbing rose raked at her head. Each year, new growth had put pressure on the too thin wire she had used to tied it up with when it was first planted. Then, she had not imagined what a monster it would grow into. She had avoided pruning it over the winter and the wire had snapped. She sighed and shook the strands of hair pulled lose by the thorns and her exertions from her face so she could see what she was doing. Taking off her muddy gloves she re-tied her ponytail. She would tie back the stems of the wayward rose with twine when she had finished the weeding.

Patrick was everything, and Jack had filled a temporary need. Jack had been so inconsequential she didn't feel she had done anything wrong by having an affair with him. Margot sighed as she pulled her gloves back on. Was she so fickle that all it would take would be a declaration of intent from Jack and her world would be upended? It must be her hormones muddling her thinking.

Margot had enough, she straightened and rubbed her lower back. Looking back down the border, she could see she had made a slight impression. She picked up the weed trug and emptied the already putrid petals and waste into the compost bin. Then she fetched some string to tie up the fallen rose and returning to the shed, she put her gardening bits and pieces away and peeled off her gloves and dropped them in an old flowerpot.

In her heart she yearned for the immediacy and engagement of Jack. But it was time to go in and see if Patrick would like a cup of tea. She couldn't hear the television anymore, she wondered where he was.

A shadow obscured the light from the shed door.

'I've just had Vi on the phone,' Patrick said.

'Oh?' She turned her back to him, so he wouldn't see her face. She had the ball of twine in her hands and taking special care rewinding the loose ends fiddling with a stray length. 'Did she have anything specific to say?' she added.

'She was wittering on about this and that. She said she saw you in Peter Jones the other day.'

'Oh, yes, I did bump into her,' said Margot, putting the ball of string back on the shelf and turning to him. 'Didn't I say. She was looking unusually smart. I rather wondered if she was meeting someone special. You know, had an assignation.' She smiled at Patrick raising her eyebrows at the revelation.

'Anyway, she wanted to know when the boys are off for half term. I told her I hoped she didn't have any plans, as they are home next weekend.'

'Was that all?' Thank goodness, Vi was just teasing. 'I managed to get the whole of the long bed done by the kitchen.'

'A weed is just a flower growing in the wrong place. Isn't that what they say?'

'Something like that.' Margot sighed.

'How are your roses?' he said.

'A bit battered after the rain, but better for some attention.'

'I was thinking… let's go away … perhaps the weekend after next,' said Patrick as they walked back to the house. 'Golf has been cancelled, and Greg mentioned this gastro pub near Bath. We could drive down on Saturday morning, back Sunday evening. A mini break when the boys have gone back to school after half term. I'll see if they have a room.'

The Age of Bewilderment

An Outing

Patrick had been feeling a growing unease about his relationship with Margot. On the face of it, everything was good. But there was something wistful about Margot recently, something absent-minded, that alarmed him. He shouldn't look for problems that weren't there, but he couldn't get out of his mind that something was off key.

His lunch with Jack the other week had compounded his disquiet. Jack enjoyed provoking him. He was always digging in the ground around Patrick, making him feel unstable, talking about Patrick and Margot's marriage as though it was fallible like any other ordinary marriage. Patrick wasn't having it. He had never trusted Jack. How dare he talk about Margot. That was trespassing.

Patrick hoped that was all it was, talk.

Now, despite the long hours at work, Patrick was trying to re-engage with Margot. She seemed surprised at his enthusiasm, and if anything, it was she who now seemed preoccupied. But what was he expecting? He had not been the most attentive of husbands. He wanted to make it up to her. So, he booked the bijou pub with an excellent restaurant and took Margot away for the weekend.

The pub was a couple of hours drive down the M4. As they neared their destination, Patrick decided to take the smaller roads, hoping it would add to the mystery and romance of the occasion. Margot, however, seemed a little queasy by the time they arrived, and although she put a brave face on things, Patrick could see that she was struggling through dinner.

'It's all so lovely, Patrick,' Margot said, but she had only picked at her food. 'Perhaps I should have chosen more conservatively, given I'm not feeling my best.'

It wasn't turning into the romantic evening Patrick had imagined, but he had enjoyed his meal, foie gras followed by pheasant and an outstanding red. He had done very well.

'It's a shame you're not feeling great. This is delicious.'

Margot looked green. He reached across the table and took her hand. His thumb rested against her rings. The triple diamond engagement ring that they had chosen together, at the jeweller that his mother had recommended, and the matching thick gold band that Patrick had placed on her finger in the registry office in Morden.

'I'm so sorry I'm not up to enjoying this treat.' Margot pulled her hand away.

'You may not be feeling great, but you look as beautiful as ever…. I had hoped this might be an opportunity to … reconnect. You've seemed a bit preoccupied lately.' Margot may not be eating, but she looked very lovely this evening, perhaps it was the candlelight. She might even have put on a little weight, but he knew better than to mention that.

'I, distant? You're the one who … It's not my fault I'm not feeling well, Patrick.' She sat back in her chair.

'No, I didn't mean that.' Patrick, an arm on each side of his placemat, leaned towards her across the table. 'It's me, I know. It's a difficult time, and I've been working too late too often. Though you have not been … I feel that lately, we've been drifting.'

'Perhaps … I should have realised I was coming down with something. I shouldn't have come.'

'Well, it is a great pity you haven't felt well enough to share this delicious St Emillion.' Patrick finished the last of the wine. 'But I am happy that you are here with me.'

'I need to go to bed,' said Margot.

The following morning, they were woken by church bells. Margot was, if anything worse, and she sent Patrick off to breakfast on his own. He returned to their room with a cup of mint tea, and Margot rallied.

It was one of those beautiful sunny, high, pale blue days. They went for a walk into the village, passed the big grey manor house and the lynch gate of the neighbouring lichen-covered graveyard. The square tower of the church and the customary ancient yew in the churchyard were both reaching up to the high cobalt heavens. Patrick wondered if it was a race, the belfry had the edge currently, but the growing yew was bound to win, a defeat of Christianity by ancient beliefs? Either way, it was the dark of the cedars in the garden of the manor behind that towered in tiers of green above them all.

Patrick and Margot made a loop past a field where small lambs were skipping, white and innocent, tails waggling, close to their mothers. It was bucolic, but the yellow, sinister stare of the sheep nearest the gate made Patrick uneasy. They returned to the pub over the cobbled road through the village. Was it his imagination, or was Margot walking slightly further away from him than usual? Normally, they would hold hands. He hoped his efforts to reconcile any misunderstandings last night had been successful, but perhaps he had got the tone wrong, or maybe she just needed space. Poor Margot, he had hoped the fresh air would help her feel better.

The buildings in the village were all made from the same soft grey stone. The roofs of adjoining houses were all at different heights and angles. The old houses were well preserved. That was the sort of thing that Patrick's mother would say about a good friend. These houses looked like comrades and had been here long enough to look comfortable in each other's company, their edges blurred by climbing roses and softened by mature trees. The village exuded a harmony that Patrick couldn't echo.

Back at the pub, Margot managed some lunch and professed to feeling much better, just in time for the journey home.

'We should do this again,' he said in the car on the way back. 'We should spend more time together.' He should treat her, make her feel special. Their marriage was something to cherish, a treasure.

The Graveyard of Empires

Since 9-11, British troops had been deployed in Afghanistan. Patrick was a small cog, part of the chain of command. Sitting at his desk in Whitehall, he could see the whole mess unfold before him. Afghanistan had been a bad idea in 1842, in 1879, and again in 1919. What made anyone think that they would be successful this time around? The more troops were deployed abroad, the more troubles seemed to spring up at home. The world had become a dangerous place. Patrick went to get himself a coffee. He had five minutes before his next meeting started.

The office had also become a dangerous place. Patrick had attended all the compulsory courses. He did see the irony that the men and women in charge of the men and women being sent to fight were being told they needed to get acquainted with their sensitive sides. He had been lectured on how to embrace change to become a useful part of the workforce, and he could do it, drag himself into this brave new world where nothing seemed to be quite what you thought it was.

Once, Patrick could stride into work with a plan for the day. He had places to go; things to achieve. That business with Charity preoccupied him. Whenever he saw her, she was civil, distant and horribly polite. He had hoped Will's charm offensive and the expensive dinner he treated her to had poured oil on that one, but at the back of his mind, Charity's ongoing behaviour towards him seemed a timebomb.

These were not the sort of problems Patrick had envisioned being an issue in his career, but Greg, two desks along, had been asked to move to a different department over some off-hand comment. Patrick missed Greg. He stumped back along the corridor to his desk with his coffee to collect his brief.

Patrick paused in front of the bank of filing cabinets. He flicked through the files selecting which to take into the meeting. His hand hovered and swooped as he picked out those relevant to the agenda, hovered, then swooped. The adjacent area seemed bereft without Greg's jovial though misplaced bonhomie. Along the far wall were ranged the cabinets that held staff files. It was not Patrick's prerogative to be concerned with personnel, but he sidled over towards Greg's cabinets and pulled open a door. The drawer grated on metal runners. Patrick looked around. The office was quiet. He located Jack's folder, plucked it from the cabinet, and added it to his bundle, attaching a note with Will's name on the cover.

Patrick entered the lift that would take him down to the basement meeting rooms. He stabbed the button for his floor. You had to have faith. He wanted to stay relevant at work. He wanted to be an example for Ollie and Toby. It was his responsibility to keep his family together. It was a strange world the boys were growing up in. Perhaps every generation thought that the next was foolishly unprepared and uninterested in what was truly important. He remembered his parents being horrified by the music he listened to. But Patrick would not be like his father, emasculated by technology and a change in culture.

The lift doors opened. Patrick looked at the pile of files in his hand. He had read the agenda. He knew what he was going to do.

Patrick entered the meeting room. *Personnel, Deployment and Essential Equipment* was the topic of the meeting. He placed his files and notes in front of him on the table and listened to the preamble. They were still sending people out to Afghanistan, for goodness' sake. The meeting ran smoothly, battalions were put forward, companies discussed, accepted or rejected. Today, Patrick didn't have to say much beyond various specifications of mandatory supplies and implementation of recommended equipment. He made suggestions and took notes. Later, he would compile reports for securing the required kit and check and confirm everything agreed, was collected and delivered.

Files were opened, closed, and shuffled like cards in a deck. Patrick slipped Jack's folder amongst the personnel files being sent to Glasgow for consideration for deployment.

It probably wouldn't make any difference. Who ever made these decisions would already have the men they wanted in mind. Returning to his desk, Patrick felt a cold sweat. He hated any form of manipulation. It was a type of cowardice.

Perplexed

About Jack

Margot lay beside the reassuring bulk of Patrick, with whom she could not imagine being without, and thought about Jack. She stared at the dark ceiling, like an effigy of a medieval lady lying next to her husband in a church crypt. Unlike a stone knight, Patrick's measured breath was like a metronome, counting along with her thoughts, I could do this, I could do that...

She had not seen Jack for a couple of weeks. Her body betrayed her, yearning for him, the sensation of him, the excitement and possibility. Fragmented images floated through her mind, that wink with his half smile, his hands, elegant long fingers resting on the arm of a chair, or on her thigh, the smell of him, his imprint in bed.

He said he wanted her and suggested she leave her happy home for him. She was carrying his child. It was hard not to feel something for someone who wanted to … what exactly? To be with her? But her instinct was, without a proper commitment, Jack's words meant nothing. Then again, the thought of being with him, even for one more afternoon, was unbelievably exciting.

But it was over.

In the dark, her phone pinged and lit up the room with a ghostly light, a text.

Missing our regular hook ups. I LOVE YOU! We need to be together. x

Jack was incorrigible. What if Patrick had been awake. Margot pushed up on an elbow to open the text and read it again. In the middle of the night, she had questioned his commitment, and he had met the challenge. It was what she had been waiting for, but now she had his declaration she wasn't so sure. All the time she had spent with Jack had felt like a fabulous dream, but now, with a text, their relationship had become real.

Margot didn't text Jack back immediately. She tossed, pulling the duvet away from Patrick. She had been able to prevaricate because she had conditions. Now, all other excuses fell away. She couldn't deny the happiness she felt when she thought of Jack and how much she wanted to be with him. How shallow she was, so easily flattered. But she wasn't ready to throw her life into turmoil, was she?

I love you too x

Terrified of the power she had unleashed, she muffled a laugh. The idea of such a pure emotion. Patrick stirred beside her, grunting in his sleep. He whistled half a snore, and Margot gently slid her arm beneath him to encourage him to turn on his side. She didn't want him to wake and witness her excitement. She hoped this feeling would not vanish in the morning light like some enchanted dream.

Jack texted back.

When can I see you? Let's make plans. x

Now she was scared. Was she about to throw everything away? She would miss Patrick and the boys, of course, but not in the same urgent way that she yearned for Jack. She was used to Patrick being around and out, or late and slightly taking her for granted, but she felt a surge of excitement at the idea of being with Jack.

This Friday x

In the morning, as soon as Patrick had left for work, Margot sat on the bed in the little spare room that she had always secretly called the nursery. Patrick never came into this room. He had no need to, and the door was always closed.

She thought about what she could take with her and what she would have to leave behind. If she went, there was almost nothing she could keep from this life. Not Patrick, not Ollie, not Toby. Just the clothes on her back, well, maybe from her wardrobe too. But even so the fantasy of Jack seemed to call like a siren on the rocks luring her to drown her reality. She knew if she answered Jack's request and went on Friday, she might never come back.

'Are you alright? You seem a bit preoccupied,' said Patrick that evening. He was sitting at the kitchen counter, catching up with some work emails. Margot had just burned the onions and was scrapping them into the bin.

'I am a bit, aren't I.'

'You don't have to start again. I rather like a bit of charcoal,' he said.

'No, with the fish we're having, it won't work. The sauce will end up dirty and bitter.'

Margot wiped out the pan and chopped another onion. Patrick clattered at his keys.

'Oh,' he said.

'Oh, what?' said Margot.

'I've just had an email through from an old, well a new friend, Will. I bumped into recently, but we hadn't met since Jack's stag. He's in the army, based in Glasgow, in the personnel department.'

'Is that interesting?' she said.

'Well, I asked him to let me know if he heard anything and he says … he says, Jack is to be deployed in Afghanistan.'

'Again? I thought he was after a desk job,' said Margot, turning towards him at the dreadful news.

Patrick looked at her. Had she given herself away? She hoped not and she hoped she didn't look as upset as she felt.

'I'm sure you mentioned it,' she said. Was that true? She could hardly admit she had heard it from Jack.

'Did I?' he said. Patrick shook his head as if he was shaking what he must know to be the truth, and the untruth Margot had just spoken into something he could believe.

'Or maybe it was Jenni. To be honest, I can't remember where I got that from.' She turned back to her onions.

'Either way, he is off … on the 21st of June,' said Patrick.

The knife trembled in her hand. That …. that was in only ten days. This couldn't be true. This couldn't be happening. Jack couldn't go, not now. She didn't want him to leave. She felt a tear slip down her cheek and she blinked to clear her vision.

'Apparently, they were looking for people with experience and language skills, which of course Jack has,' said Patrick. 'It's to do with training the local Afghan forces. We are preparing for withdrawal … those onions really do seem to have got to you.'

'I know,' said Margot, dabbing at her eye with the heel of her hand. 'It's not like me. I'll just get a tissue.' She seemed to be dissolving, becoming liquid in her misery. She retreated to the downstairs loo, wiped her eyes and blew her nose with a wad of loo paper. She glanced at herself in the mirror. 'Get a grip,' she said to her reflection, better to be angry than upset. It had all been whimsey, it would never have worked, and she knew what she had to do. She was married to Patrick.

On Friday afternoon, when it would be too late for her to get there, Margot texted.

Sorry.

She had to be realistic. She wasn't prepared to walk out into a void. If Jack was away, she would be on her own to field all the opprobrium. And where would she live? She could hardly move into Jack's flat if he wasn't there, whatever he suggested. If she told him she was pregnant, what would he say? They were lovers, they had never talked about children and how would he cope, going away knowing she was vulnerable? It would leave him exposed. But if she didn't tell him she was pregnant, she would meet him on his return merely weeks from her due date. But all this was unnecessary conjecture, she saw she was merely infatuated with the dream of Jack. She had been tempted by the excitement, but that was all it was an alluring mirage.

Margot decided to pretend none of her interchange with Jack had happened, it had been foolhardy, hardly a day old. She would revert to her plan and put her faith in Patrick's compassion and understanding. The family she had was the best outcome for her and her baby.

About Patrick

Margot's hand stumbled to turn off the alarm. The early morning sun somehow managed to squeeze around the edges of the material to light the heavily curtained room. She must get up, it was Monday. She had agonised all weekend wondering if she had made the right decision, but she had to do what was right for the baby. Still, she had struggled to drop off the night before, her thoughts spiralling in the small hours, thinking of all the what ifs.

She stretched an arm out across the bed feeling the emptiness, Patrick was already up and away. While she had paced the bedroom late into the night, cool toes digging into the soft carpet, twitching the curtain at a sound outside to see a baleful fox pad down the street, Patrick slept. He was much more relaxed now he had handed in his application for promotion. As soon as his head hit the pillow, he was out. Then, he was up before the dawn. They must have shared the bed for all of a couple of hours.

At the weekend, he had been up before her too. After bringing her the paper, Patrick had disappeared off to the tennis club instead of joining her in bed. When the boys were away, Margot loved a lazy Saturday morning where sex, papers, coffee and crumbs were part of her start to the weekend. She had hoped Patrick might stay. It would have reminded her how much she enjoyed their time together, reinforcing why she had chosen him.

She pulled herself out of bed and into the shower. If she moved slowly, she might not feel queasy.

On his way back from tennis, Patrick had bought some flowers, lovely, strong stemmed lilies in bud that she had stood in a tall, green glass vase that she had brought from The Old Vicarage. She had become suspicious of flowers, but she was confident Patrick's fling was over.

The lilies opened over the warm weekend. Margot came down on Sunday morning to the suffocating perfume and opened the terrace doors before she gagged. It was an insidious scent, and she could faintly smell the lilies still, her stomach churned.

After her shower, Margot dried herself and looked through her clothes. If it was going to be warm, she should wear something loose. She smoothed a hand over her still flat stomach and then counted on her fingers, April, May, it was now mid-June, she was nearly three months. She needed to think through how she was going to break the news to Patrick. There wasn't much time. It wouldn't be long before her belly spoke for her, if Vi didn't get there first.

Vi had been quiet, but with her poison, could ruin everything. It was a miracle she hadn't already raised her suspicions with Patrick, but there wasn't any reason for their paths to cross as the boys were at school. The summer holidays loomed, but by then, Margot would have spoken up, and it would be obvious what was happening.

Downstairs, Margot made herself a coffee, breathing in the bitter, burnt smell. The capsule coffee didn't have the same depth as Jack's home ground, but it was almost strong enough to counter the scent of the lilies. She had heard nothing from him. She hadn't expected to, had hoped not to. On Friday evening, missing their rendezvous, she sniffled, tissue in hand to stem the flow, all the way home in the privacy of the tube everyone had looked the other way.

She hadn't really been upset, she had made up her mind, she knew she was doing the right thing, she just had to mourn the dream.

Then there had been a deluge of messages in the middle of the night, and she had blocked his number. She lifted her coffee and replaced it without taking a sip, she looked at her fingers, she had been crumpling a dropped lily petal, its moistness repelled her and where it was once pure white it was now an odious, soggy brown. She flung it in the bin and washed the stickiness from her fingers.

In her original plan, she imagined that even if he wasn't enthusiastic, Patrick would be happy for her, knowing she had always longed for a child. She would present her pregnancy with amazement as that one in a gazillion chance. He would want to believe the baby was his. He was a good man and Margot knew that, somehow, he would be able to accept the gift of a baby.

Now, instead of going straight to Patrick with a positive pregnancy test and astonished joy in her eyes, all she could think of were the negatives and she prevaricated. If, for a moment longer, she didn't share, nothing bad could happen, she could continue blissfully immune to the disruption the future might bring. Her hand stroked her abdomen, she was enjoying holding her secret to herself and she wasn't quite ready to share. What if Patrick knew the baby wasn't his? He would demand to know the truth. It would destroy him if she confessed that she had slept with Jack. Patrick would rightly feel betrayed. He wouldn't be able to forgive her. He might throw her out or insist she get rid of the baby.

She could counter, confront Patrick about his affair, then he would have to be more forgiving. But maybe he would be ready for a permanent change. That would be dreadful, Patrick was hers. She didn't want anyone else to have him, and how would the boys cope if Patrick divorced for a second time? Their prospects of having lasting relationships when they were older would plummet. She was sure there were statistics to back that up. Besides, she wouldn't want to lose contact with the boys. She had brought them up since they were tiny. They were hers as much as Vi's. They would always bring their washing home to her.

Margot finished her toast using it to chase away the remnants of her nausea and dropped her plate into a slot in the dishwasher, bending she felt a tightness at her waist. She had her share of Angela's estate. She could survive on her own if she had too, but it would be a struggle, and that wasn't the life she wanted her baby to have.

She sipped her second cup of coffee, the one she didn't really have time for and knew she shouldn't drink. She would drive to the station and save a few minutes. Torturing herself like this was doing no good. This was the baby that was supposed to right the wrong, not cause disruption. She breathed deeply, when she could no longer do up the button on her jeans, she would tell Patrick she was pregnant. It would be fine.

Parking the car at the station, lucky to find a space, Margot wondered if she should have told Jack she was pregnant, but it hadn't been that kind of love. She didn't mean love. Margot had to believe she didn't love Jack for this to work. She couldn't love two people at the same time. She loved Patrick. Everyone knew that. They had the perfect marriage.

Resolution

Having left a little later, the tube into London was busier than usual. Hanging from the rail, Margot knew she had made the right choice. She thought about the life within her and the lost life she had never known. The little person that she had left behind in the termination ward had trodden by her side throughout her life. Her child would have been friends with Ollie and Toby and grown up with them. With each milestone the boys had reached, she had wondered what her lost baby would have achieved if Margot had given them the chance.

This baby, tiny though it was, was already affecting her life, it made her queasy and kept her too long in the bathroom and made her late. Margot stroked her stomach tenderly with her free hand, the child she owed the world. This child would have every opportunity, Margot would make sure they were brought up in a secure home and showered in love, just as Ollie and Toby had been.

At twelve-thirty, Margot was looking for her handbag, on the point of going out to get some lunch, when the office manager popped her head round the door.

'Don't forget the meeting at two.'

'Of course not,' said Margot.

'I thought I'd mention it as on occasion you take longer than the statutory hour for lunch and you often leave early, especially on a Friday. It has been noticed.'

'Only periodically, and I always make up the hours. Anyway, it won't be happening again.' Margot hated being put on the back foot. She grabbed her bag and rose from her desk. 'I won't be late,' she added, smiling at her manager as she passed her in the doorway. Margot headed for the lift. Now, she had no reason to be late. She would have no reason to make excuses and skip meetings ever again.

Patrick, she was only going to think of Patrick.

It was raining, Margot quickly crossed the wet road and ducked under the shelter of the colonnade, marvelling at the number of tourists who thronged Covent Garden. She crossed through to the other side of the square. In the cafe, she queued at the counter and placed her order, paid, then turned to wait for her meal at the end of the bar. That was when she saw him. He must have been there, behind her in the queue. She should have felt his presence, somehow known he was there, he must have been waiting, watching her office door. That felt unnerving. Having placed his order, Jack came to wait beside her.

'You've blocked me,' he said.

'Yes.'

'Not very friendly. I was expecting you.'

'I know …' They stood awkwardly side by side, waiting for their orders, waiting for the other not to speak. Jack broke first.

'I didn't mean to surprise you. I thought I might watch you from afar. Not disturb your day. That it would be enough, then I realised I wanted to be with you. For a moment or an hour or an afternoon … before I leave. I go on Friday morning.'

Her order was called. She collected it and took it to a full, benched table. Jack followed her with his sandwich and pushed himself into a non-existent space opposite her, causing the other diners to groan and squeeze up.

'Jack, I can't see you anymore.'

'And yet, here we are,' he said.

Margot opened her lunch and began to eat. She ate without looking up, refusing to meet his gaze. She knew he was watching her. They sat in silence. She ate slowly. Jack unwrapped his sandwich but barely touched it, crumbling the bread with his fingers. Part of her wanted to run away, and part of her wanted this time to last forever. She had rejected him, and yet still, her heart beat for him.

But she was married to Patrick, he was her all, there was no room for Jack in her life.

The cafeteria was modern, with too many hard surfaces that intensified the din. The room was full of busy diners, everyone rushing through their meals. The people at their table left, and another group arrived. Margot finished every last grain of rice in her bento box. It was amazing how she could move and eat without seeming to breathe. A tear slipped into her empty box.

'When I come back…' he said, as they waited to place their rubbish in the trays and bins provided.

She had her back to him. His voice grazed her ear.

'While I'm away … it won't be long. Will you consider…'

Having stashed her tray, Margot moved to the door and stepped out into the drizzle, mindful of the time.

Jack caught her arm as she paused to cross the road and return to work. He shook her slightly, and she glanced at him in surprise. He had never touched her roughly. His blue eyes were dark.

'Think about it, will you, about being with me, about us being a family, having children.'

Margot, caught in his gaze, suddenly rose up on her toes and whispered in his ear. 'We *are* having a baby.'

She heard Jack's breath, sharp and short. Why had she said that? Margot hadn't meant to say anything. She was undoing all the work she had done to remove him from her life. The words had come out of her unbidden. It was as if an angel had come between them and uttered the words.

Jack released her but remained beside her, very close, looking down at her, giving her his half smile.

'What a deliciously dark horse you are,' he said at last, pushing a damp strand of hair off her forehead. He took her right hand in his and kissed the fingertips.

'I wonder… would you let me give you this?'

Before she could stop him, he slipped a ring on her fourth finger.

'Oh Jack, I can't accept it, and I have to go I'm late.' She moved to take it off and give it back, but he wrapped his hands around her fingers closing them in a fist.

'What a shame we have no time to celebrate.'

'You really think it's a good idea then?' Having been ambushed by a romantic gesture, Margot had lost focus and seemed unable to stand firm.

'The very best of ideas. Though, as I'm away, what we do about it all, I'm not sure.'

He took out his phone and, stepping beside her, took a selfie of them together.

‘For the road,’ he said. ‘I’ll write with a plan, I promise, we will be together Margot. Unblock me, so we can sort something out. I can’t bear the thought of you being with Patrick.’

‘Jack, I really can’t keep this.’ She handed him back the ring. It was beautiful, a deep ruby flanked by single diamonds, but to accept it would be the worst sort of deception. ‘I’ll never be able to wear it.’

‘I have this for you.’ He slipped an envelope into her jacket pocket. ‘For you to read later. It is all the things I want to say to you, but, when we are face to face, I seem to lose my nerve.’

He kissed her on her forehead, winked and turned. She watched him walk away from her towards the tube, tall, lean and straight, not seeming to notice the rain.

Margot glanced at her watch and turned and rushed back to her work, she almost wasn’t late. And what a nightmare, what was she going to do? She had successfully disentangled herself from Jack, only, when he was in front of her, to capitulate all over again. She was stupid and spineless and unbelievably susceptible to Jack’s charm. She mustn’t let this be a disaster.

It wasn’t till the end of the day that Margot had a moment to read Jack’s note. She dreaded what it might say, but also, she was excited. As soon as she pulled the envelope out of her jacket pocket, she felt the weight of the ring and her heart sank. The enclosed card had a single line of script.

You have my heart, Margot, keep it safe against my return, yours forever x

It was delightful to be loved, but Margot knew she was not the person to take care of Jack’s heart, as soon as he returned, she would need to break it.

That evening, Patrick was very sweet.

‘I thought I’d cook,’ he said. ‘I picked up some salmon on the way home.’

Margot sat at the breakfast bar watching him scrub new potatoes, twisting a tissue in her hands. It had been exhausting seeing Jack and now she faced a real dilemma. He had pledged himself to her, she had his ring and held his heart.

'You don't seem yourself,' said Patrick. 'I hope you're not coming down with something.'

'I just feel a bit out of sorts, as though a sword of Damocles is hanging over me.'

'I wonder why that would be,' said Patrick, putting down the peeler and coming to give her a hug. 'I can't see that there's anything to worry about,' he added.

'I know it's foolish, everything is quite settled really,' said Margot.

That night, Margot lay awake scanning the dark ceiling for answers, listening to the calming sigh of Patrick's dependable sleepy breath. He was the best of men.

She would not unblock Jack's phone. She would not be charmed back into his life. She loved Patrick and was married to him. If Margot had any integrity, she would message Jack and tell him, but she was a coward and she was scared she would be sucked back in. She would not be swayed from her original plan by promises of what if and if only. A life with Jack was a lovely, errant dream, it was not reality, and she didn't want it to be. She had Patrick and the boys, and they were her family. Margot was where she was meant to be.

She should write to Jack and tell him she couldn't be with him, ever, but she knew she wouldn't. It could wait until he returned from Afghanistan. It was the coward's response, but she could hardly dash his hopes when he was so far from home. Why had she been so stupid as to tell him about the baby. He was so mesmerising, when she was with him, she lost her senses. But he was away for six months, and that was plenty of time to come up with a plan.

All Margot wanted was to have a happy family with Patrick, Ollie, Toby and her newborn child. It couldn't be that difficult.

JACK

He had been there for three weeks. Previously, when he had been out, it had been spring, not this dry, or dusty, or hot.

They had been driving for over an hour and seen nothing and nobody. The driver slowed. They had been skirting potholes and hugging the edges of the track where the road had been washed away. They were driving in convoy, Jack, his driver and interpreter in a Snatch, accompanying a patrol. The team was in two Mastiff troop carriers. They were in Nahr-e Saraj, just north of Lashkar Gah.

Their Land Rover had been surrounded by a ball of dust for miles. Grit that made the air the colour of the land. The convoy turned onto a better, less sandy road, the haze cleared, and Jack could see, low on the horizon, a line of distant hills pock-marked with caves, like eyes that seemed to follow them as they drove, closing in, observing.

After an age, the road turned away from the ridge and they drove through the flat, dry land, gravel, rocks, rubble, mile after mile, all shades of the same pale sand. They drove past some deserted looking windowless buildings that seemed to grow out of the earth. Outside the hamlet, they passed a lone palm tree verdant in the dryness and approached a dry riverbed. The trucks turned off the road to cross the wadi.

Before, Jack had seen the rivers in spate, sweeping down the valleys, washing everything before them and making roads impassable. Floods that, when tamed, would keep the crops growing. Back then, there had been farmers in the fields, green with pink poppies. There were people in the streets, and at the side of the road stalls sold melons. By this time of year, the crop had been harvested, and the sun had dried everything out. The land was empty. There was not a trickle, nothing to keep the ground green.

The first Mastiff crossed the riverbed and climbed back onto the road on the other side. Jack's driver, following, manoeuvred the Snatch, turning the steering wheel to catch the gradient and pull the Land Rover back onto the paving. The pale sandy scree forced the vehicle to slide back down off the track. The driver found traction, and the Snatch slowly climbed back towards the brow of the gulley.

They reached the surface of the road with relief. No need for a tow. They waited for the second troop carrier to make the incline before setting off again. As the Snatch accelerated, Jack spotted something unusual about the rocks at the side of the road, something so slight that it took Jack's brain a moment to compute. His driver had noticed too and turned the steering wheel hard. They shot each other a look.

There was a noise so loud he could only hear silence, and he was in the air, turning too fast, sky, sand, mountains, the flash of a green palm. That's it, he thought as the rocky earth caught him. He landed in a pit like a baseball mitt, jagged rocks rising around him. He was in a morass of pain. He thought he could hear rain, pitter, patter. Lifting his head a little, he saw hard sand and small rocks falling around him. Someone was crying. He tried to look around, but he couldn't turn his head.

Just when his life had been coming together. He cracked a laugh, but there was too much grit in his mouth, and he couldn't wet his tongue to do it any justice.

He looked up at the sky, a perfect blue, with no clouds, just faint contrails. Someone was watching.

The crying stopped.

The sky was still and wondrously clear and seemed to go on forever.

Improvised Explosive Device

The Beginning of Summer

Ollie and Toby were home for the final exeat of the school year. Patrick and Margot had driven down to collect them. There was a school family day, a chance to get to know other parents. Patrick had parked under the trees at the edge of a large, green pitch, with faint markers for the boundary line and a mown rectangle in the middle, bails at either end.

It was a lovely day. They set up their folding chairs and table beside the car. Margot had made a picnic, which the boys demolished in moments. They watched an endless cricket match played between the current school team and old boys. Patrick hadn't volunteered, instead, he drank too many glasses of warm rose in the sunshine while he walked around the playing field, talking to other parents. Margot drank iced tea. She was driving home.

The next morning, Patrick had a crashing headache. He had woken to a glass of water and some paracetamol on his bedside table, placed there by an angel. He was late downstairs. He could hear the boys messing around in the garden. Margot was checking the roast. He winced as the oven door banged closed.

'Good of you to join us,' she said, giving him a kiss. 'How are you feeling?'

Patrick tried to think of something upbeat to say, but his mind was still in pause mode.

'Coffee?' he asked as he clicked a pod into the machine.

'Not for me,' she said.

'How much wine did I have yesterday?'

'I wasn't counting,' said Margot, chopping some leeks. 'But enough for you to sleep in the car on the way home.'

‘I never sleep in the car,’ said Patrick, filling his glass with chilled water from the fridge. ‘What are the boys up to?’

‘Some basic form of cricket. Could you call them in to lay the table?’ said Margot.

After lunch, Patrick settled down to watch the Grand Prix with the boys. It was lovely to spend time with them. They were turning out to be good company.

When Patrick had taken them away at Easter, they had fun, all skiing together now the boys were older. He had agonised at the resort, regretting leaving Margot behind. He knew she didn’t like the cold, but he missed her. Patrick woke in the night in his stuffy chalet room, having had a nightmare, nothing specific, but a sense of unease. In the morning the memory seemed like a symptom of a greater disease, he felt he was losing Margot. He gave her a call later that day.

‘Oh, hi Patrick. How are you getting on? How are the boys? What’s the snow like?’

‘All good here. Back for the day. I was just thinking about you, missing you.’

‘Well, I’m here… a bit busy actually. About to go out.’

‘Ah well yes. I won’t keep you. We’ll speak again soon.’

‘Of course. Love to Ollie and Toby.’

‘I love you,’ said Patrick, but the phone was already dead.

When he got back from skiing, both he and Margot were busy, days seemed to pass without them having a proper conversation. As the weather improved, he became obsessed with his golf. The concentration required was a good way to turn off any troublesome thoughts, but perhaps he should spend more time with Margot in person rather than thinking about her.

He had his own preoccupations with work, but he was feeling generally upbeat. Initial feedback for his application for promotion was positive. There was only the interview to go.

Whereas Margot seemed particularly sensitive of late. He couldn't say she was avoiding him, but recently she had been pensive and distant. He didn't know if her erratic behaviour was because of work, he wasn't sure what she had to be upset about, but Patrick was glad Jack was out of the picture for a bit. And it was good to have Ollie and Toby home for the weekend. It was fun being together, they felt like a family again.

'What's going on?' Margot asked, coming through to join them, handing him a tea.

'Budge up,' she said to Toby as she settled between the boys on the sofa and took a sip from her own mug.

They had been sitting in companionable silence, mindlessly watching the cars circle the track, but as soon as Margot joined them, Ollie and Toby leapt into life, vying to give the best explanation to Margot of the race, the drivers and the difficulty of the track.

The commentator said it was hot, well over thirty degrees. Jack wasn't a million miles from Bahrain. Patrick wondered how much hotter it would be in Afghanistan. He was sorry Jack might be finding it unpleasant in Helmand, but Patrick knew he had done the right thing. He was prepared to fight for his family. He drank his tea, mesmerised by the cars looping around, droning like cartoon bees roused from their hive.

Bad News

Patrick was at the office when the news came through. He was called to a meeting room ten minutes before the given time.

'Sorry to tell you like this but thought you would want to hear this first. We lost a land rover, one of those crap Snatch jobs. Thought we'd phased them out. Anyway, three were lost.' His supervisor said handing Patrick an envelope. 'An officer was among the passengers … your cousin…'

Patrick stared at the man. 'What? Jack… Jack was in a Snatch?'

'Yes, 'fraid so.'

'Oh…,' said Patrick. He felt as though he was shrinking down a rabbit hole. The room seemed huge, his boss far away. Patrick was struggling to understand. 'Are you sure? When?'

'All the details are in the envelope.'

'Right …' said Patrick, his voice fading out. His feet had found the ground again. He should have questions, but instead, there wasn't anything else to be said. He looked around the bland room as if to find meaning, then lifted the tab of the envelope but didn't look inside. He searched his feelings. Nothing, a huge, vast hole was opening and opening inside him. He knew right away that this was his fault. He had wished Jack gone, and now he was. Patrick felt himself in danger of crumpling into the void that had opened within himself. He was about to swallow himself alive.

'Exemplary soldier, they all were. Special reconnaissance group. I shall get the letters sent out tonight, they should arrive in the morning. Take the rest of the day off… rest of the week. We'll keep it out of the papers for a couple of days, till the family has been informed. HR will be in touch about a counsellor.'

The man patted Patrick on the back and pushed him out of the meeting room just as Patrick's colleagues arrived.

Patrick went back to his desk, and packed up his bits and pieces, and, sleepwalking, left the building. He would call his mother this evening and ask her to accompany him to see his aunt in the morning. They should be with Jack's parents. He didn't want to break the news, but he wanted to be on hand when the letter arrived. He would take the report. Perhaps he would be able to give some details or memories that would be of some comfort. Jack's parents would be stoic. Patrick wouldn't be able to bear it, it would be worse than if they cried hysterically. Nor did he want to witness Margot's reaction, she still seemed a bit fragile.

He marvelled that the world seemed to be turning. People were busy. Hadn't they heard? The clocks should stop. Jack was gone.

Patrick had sent Jack to his death and at that moment, there seemed nothing of consequence left. He should be struck down by some avenging hand. His conscious self, seemed to have evaporated in the meeting room back at the office, this body driving his car was just his shell.

Patrick spent the afternoon moving around the house in a dream, doing unnecessary odd jobs. He walked into the village and bought some chops for supper and, on the advice of the florist, picked up some purple lilacs for Margot. Patrick usually loved the clean and vibrant little shop, but today, the scent of the flowers was overwhelming. He stumbled home in a trance, wondering why he had chosen the strongest smelling flowers in the shop. His mother would never have lilacs in the house, he couldn't remember why, he knew Margot would love them. It was a warm day, almost too hot, and on the way home Patrick in a jumper waded along the pavement forging a path through the dense air that strangled his breath. As he walked, he absentmindedly slapped the flowers in their wrapping against his thigh, leaving an intermittent trail of purple petals on the pavement.

The boys should be told. He would drive to their school later in the week and tell them himself. He didn't want them to find out any other way. Jenni would need to know too. That marriage was long ago, and Jenni had moved on, but it would be the thing to do.

'We need to phone Jenni,' Patrick said when Margot got home. He had a gin and tonic ready and waiting for her and supper on the go.

'Thank you, but you know I've given up for the summer,' she said, pushing the glass away, having ditched her cardigan and bag on one of the bar stools, she slipped out of her shoes and perched on another.

'Gosh, it's hot today. The office was stifling.'

She looked rosy, smiling. She leant out to touch the flowers he had arranged in a large artisan jug he had found in the utility room.

'These look lovely,' she said.

He pottered around the kitchen. He was glad she was cheerful and hated that he was about to break her mood.

'You're home early,' she said. 'What are you cooking? And why do we need to call Jenni?'

'I was sent home after lunch.' He had just drizzled oil into a frying pan, but he stopped what he was doing to come and take her free hand across the bar. She looked at him with cautious eyes. 'A nasty piece of news came through at work. And we ought to let Jenni know.'

'Nasty? What?'

'I've been feeling wretched all afternoon.' He came round the breakfast bar to be beside her when he said the words. 'Jack's gone.'

She seemed O.K. He touched her arm gently then pushed that wanton curl of hair behind her shoulder. She was very still. He stood beside her, waiting for her reaction, but she seemed frozen. The frying pan was beginning to spit, and he could smell the hot oil. He left her and added the chops to the pan. He had to raise his voice. 'He was in Lashkar Gar, on patrol. It was an IED, a roadside bomb. It took out a Land Rover. Three died.'

Margot was awfully quiet. Time seemed to stand still for the second time that day. Patrick looked up from the sizzling chops to see Margot had gone very pale. He recognised this need for stillness as if by being motionless, one could stop everything and maybe force time back to a point when the world had been whole.

'Gone?' she said at last as if she didn't understand. Her eyes had filled with tears.

'Yes, they gave me a few details, but there will be a full inquiry.'

'Not Jack,' Margot said with a long sigh. She pulled the gin towards her and picked up the glass. The ice cubes caught the light and gave a cheerful tinkle. She downed her gin with a steady fatality as though some things, like death, were inevitable. She looked up at Patrick, brushed a tear from her cheek and disappeared upstairs. She only reappeared when he called out that supper was ready.

'Sorry,' she said. 'I don't know what happened there. I just needed a moment. It is just such sad news and so out of the blue. Why was Jack even in Afghanistan?'

Indeed, thought Patrick.

'I'll call Jenni after supper if you think it is a good idea, but I'd rather tell her in person. I could go and see her tomorrow after work.'

Hay Fever

All About Jenni

Margot dreaded going to see her, but Jenni did deserve to be told in person. She had only been Jack's wife for about eighteen months and almost ten years ago now, and it had been ghastly, but despite it all, she remained fond of Jack, and she would be devastated. Margot just wasn't sure how to appear less distressed than Jenni.

Jack's death was inexplicable, shocking. When Patrick told her, Margot went upstairs and locked herself in the bathroom. The note Jack had written before he went away was tucked under her makeup. She pulled it out and read it through, letting her finger trace the words as if to reassure herself that Jack had ever lived. Then, she tucked the letter away and sliding to the floor howled into a towel. She had felt like breaking something, but instead, when all the tears were spent, she went into the bedroom and looked for the ruby ring. It lay inconspicuous amongst her own jewellery. She held it up, the central stone dark and red like a drop of blood seemed to absorb the light. Tears slipped down her cheeks again.

Margot heard Patrick call her name. She carefully slipped the ring back where no one would find it and went back into the bathroom. She filled the basin with cold water and submerged her face hoping to snap out of her misery. She kept her eyes open in the water, as if seeing would help her understand what had happened, but it was impossible to imagine that she would never see Jack again.

When she surfaced, she wiped her face and patted any wet strands of her hair with a towel. She looked in the mirror. The reflected woman looked damp and ashamed. She knew, for all that she missed Jack, her life had become much, much easier. Now her plan was safe, Margot wouldn't have to worry about Jack coming back to claim her and their baby. She had wanted to be free of Jack, he had become a complication, and now he had gone. The guilt only added to her grief.

Downstairs, she had found it hard to keep the depth of her feelings from Patrick, but he was deeply dismayed too. After cooking supper, Patrick, who was usually so stoic, seemed overwhelmed and didn't seem to notice what was going on around him.

After their silent meal, Patrick shut himself in his study to mourn in private, and Margot wept in the kitchen over the washing up, huge sobs lurching from her, masked by the running tap. It was a relief not to have to hold them in.

The next morning, Margot filled her handbag with tissues and headed for work. It would be good to be busy, she may be ineffective, but at least she would be distracted. She phoned Jenni from the office at lunchtime to let her know she was coming over. At the end of the day Margot took the bus to Chelsea. She was glad that Jenni's girls were out on a play date with a friend.

'Jack? Are they sure?' said Jenni, her voice sounded tinny.

'It doesn't seem real, does it?' said Margot.

'I wouldn't put it past Jack to pull a stunt like that for a joke.' Jenni sounded hopeful.

'No, I'm afraid not,' Margot said. 'He really is gone.'

'I hope you don't mind me howling. It's so difficult hiding my pain,' said Jenni, putting the kettle on. 'And I will need to get the grief out of my system now. In front of Julia and Molly, I shall have to be careful. I don't want them to think terrible things can happen to grown-ups at any time. I'll just say, Mummy has lost a friend and is a bit sad.'

'It is dreadfully sad,' said Margot, looking at the tissues in the bottom of her handbag. 'I hope you don't mind if I join you in some howling.'

Jenni brought the tea over.

'On reflection, I can honestly say that Jack really was my first and greatest love.'

Jenni could put Jack on a pedestal if it made her feel better. Now he was gone, it was easy to forgive the philandering.

'Oh, Jenni, I'm so sorry,' said Margot, sniffing.

'I know I was cross at the time, and we didn't really keep in touch or anything. But there was a bond, you know, a lifelong connection.'

'I know,' said Margot, opening the packet of biscuits she had brought and pushing them towards Jenni. Margot felt her grief was safe, camouflaged by Jenni's mawkish anguish.

'Anyway, I hadn't seen him for ages, and there he was at your party.'

'I'm glad we gave the party, since then, Patrick's father has declined, Angela has died, and now Jack.' Margot swallowed a sob.

'It is so awful,' said Jenni. '… it was the most gorgeous afternoon. I remember you warned me Jack would be there. I was a little apprehensive as I was bringing Richard.' Jenni picked up a cookie and began to munch.

'I'm so glad you called that off,' said Margot.

'Oh, me too' A few crumbs fell on the countertop. 'It would have been a disaster if I'd married him. It was Jack who put me straight. He got in touch just after Richard and I got engaged. Jack said we had to meet.'

'Really,' said Margot, not really wanting to hear what Jenni had to say.

'I know, I was surprised. We met during a lunchtime, Jack came to the school, so I didn't have to explain myself to Richard. He did like to know what I was up to all the time.'

'Richard did seem a little … controlling.'

'That's what Jack said. He said you can't possibly marry him. What are you up to? Even if you don't mind being pushed around, think about the girls. Well, I said, Richard is just a little overprotective, it's fine. I'm so disorganised, it's great having someone in my life to sort me out. But Jack wouldn't let me get away with that.'

'I did wonder if I should say something too,' said Margot. 'When you got engaged, I was concerned. But once a relationship is formalised, it's hard to intervene… well done, Jack.'

'He wouldn't let me off the hook. He said, you're a strong woman Jenni, you can do the right thing. Just watch Julia and Molly … see how they behave around Richard. I saw them together at Patrick's party, it's not good. So, I did. The following Saturday, when Richard came over, I watched him with Julia and Molly, and I saw how tense the girls became when he walked in a room, how polite. It was like…. something just clicked for me, suddenly, I saw it all and Richard was exposed. I broke it off that weekend. Once you've seen something, seen it properly, you can't unsee, can you, you can't go back.'

'No, you can't,' said Margot, thinking of Jack's jaunty walk as he had left her standing in the rain in Covent Garden. 'Jack was ever brave. Always doing the thing that had to be done, however hard.'

'I had to change the locks.' Jenni attacked another biscuit. 'Then we get to the intriguing bit…'

'Oh?' said Margot.

'About a month later, Jack took me out to dinner to see how I was getting on. He congratulated me, said he knew I could do it. That it couldn't have been easy. He ordered some bubbles to celebrate.'

'A breakup is not always a reason for champagne,' said Margot.

'Well, that's what I thought. And Jack was so lovely, you know, building me up, and well, after a few glasses, we were getting on like a house on fire. Just like old times.'

Margot tried not to stiffen, tried not to react. She took a sip of her tea, thought of her yoga, and breathed deeply.

'So, I said it … said what I wanted to say,' said Jenni. 'I was a little tipsy by then.'

'What was that?' said Margot. She must be kind. This was hard, but in quite a different way from what she had expected.

'Well, I said, how about us then, Jack? Getting together again. I always thought we were onto a good thing, we just hooked up too soon. We were too young. And you've always wanted children. We could have one before the twins get much older and be a family.'

'Did he? Want children?' Margot's hand dropped and brushed her stomach. She was over three months. She was wearing a loose shirt, but she wouldn't be able to hide her condition much longer. 'What did Jack say to that?' Her voice sounded strangled, but Jenni didn't seem to notice. She was munching her way through another biscuit.

'Aw, he was sweet. He said he was so sorry, but he was in love with someone else.'

'Really?' said Margot. 'Did he say that? Who?'

'I was curious too because I had heard, I'd done some background research, phoned some of his friends from the old days, and they all said the same thing, that Jack wasn't playing the field anymore. That's why I thought it was my moment, I had a chance. Nothing ventured, nothing gained, right?'

'Right…,' said Margot.

'He told me how brilliant and capable he thought I was. How he knew I'd make a good home for the girls. How I shouldn't rush to find someone new like I had in the past.'

'Sound advice.'

Jenni was perfectly competent. She would be able to bring up Julia and Molly on her own, if need be.

In the same instant, Margot saw that it was not for her. A baby was her need, but it was important that her child was brought up within a family unit. And that was Patrick. It was a clarifying thought. She had done the right thing.

'Yes, easier said than done, but Jack made me realise I already had everything I needed.'

'So, who is this mystery woman?'

'He wouldn't say. But he said this time, it was the real thing. That hurt a bit, I can tell you. But he said she was married. She didn't know about his feelings for her, not the true extent of how much he cared or for how many years. He said he was prepared to hold a flame, in case one day she was ready to commit to him.'

'He was maybe just saying that, so he didn't seem rude ... declining your suggestion,' said Margot taking a biscuit while there was still one left.

'That occurred to me too. But Jack looked so melancholy, I felt quite sorry for him. I think he really meant it. Romantic isn't it. I thought, well here's a challenge, I wanted to know who the mystery woman was. I asked if I knew the person, probed, but he wouldn't budge, wouldn't say a word.'

'How intriguing,' said Margot. Thank goodness Jack hadn't revealed anything, Jenni would have confronted Margot if she had an inkling about her involvement with Jack. When he wrote in his note that he had always loved her, Margot thought he was being apocryphal, poetic. She mustn't think about the possibility of being his great love, it didn't fit in with her intention. She fished out a tissue from the pack in her handbag and blew her nose.

'Are you alright?'

'Wow, what a turn up. Yes fine. Must be hay fever.'

Jack really meant all those things he said that they should be together, that he would write and come up with a plan. At first, Margot made sure she always got to the post before Patrick, but with the days passing and no letter, she had begun to relax. Jack wouldn't have time to think of her or make plans.

He was gone, she missed him horribly, but she had wanted her problem solved, and now Margot despised the relief she felt that he would not be coming back. A great wave of grief swept over her again.

'I didn't know you suffered. Anyway, what we have to do, at Jack's funeral, is we must keep an eye out for someone, a stranger, a married woman, who seems more cut up than expected. It'll be fun. I'm looking forward to the funeral now. Gosh, you really are streaming.'

'Must be something in the garden, said Margot. 'Perhaps I'd better go.'

Press Briefing

PR

The following week, back at work, Patrick was called to join his supervisor in his office on the sixth floor. A formal space that combined modern practicalities with reassuring tradition. There were several people there that Patrick didn't recognise. He was introduced to members of the MoD PR team.

'Don't know if you saw the papers this morning?' said his boss.

'No,' said Patrick. 'I have been a little inattentive lately.'

'Understandable, understandable.'

There was a heavy pause in the room. Patrick supposed it was to be respectful.

'Anyway, there is an article in the Mail about Snatch Land Rovers and their unsuitability in Afghanistan. Public Relations here have had the brilliant idea that as you have been involved in procurement and as … a family member was involved, your endorsement of the Land Rover despite what has happened would greatly help with the optics going forward.'

Patrick stared at the man. He was being asked to be the face of the disaster that had killed Jack. And to deflect deficiencies in the Land Rover, that soldiers in the field called mobile coffins.

'After all,' continued his boss. 'There's nothing wrong with the Snatch if used in the right circumstances. And in this instance, there was no reason to believe the men would need a stronger armoured vehicle. They were in a safe area and escorted.'

Patrick knew there were no safe areas in Afghanistan. The Snatch was controversial, but he had been told you can't replace everything overnight, and … God, what was Jack doing in a Snatch?

Patrick would do it. Of course he would. It was apt, the least he could do.

The next day, Patrick sat at an insubstantial desk protected from the press by a row of enormous microphones arrayed in front of him. He was flanked by a couple of the people from PR. The room was full of journalists. Patrick was hot from the lighting the film crew had set up. He blinked. He hadn't thought there would be this amount of interest, and the journalists hadn't started asking questions yet. He supposed it would only help the process and validate his opinion to the press if he looked a little shaky. Afterall, he had lost his cousin, his boyhood friend.

The PR woman, whose name he had already forgotten, leaned in towards him, turning her head so the microphones would not catch her voice.

'No need to be nervous. I'll have your back and divert anything inappropriate,' she whispered.

Margot had been appalled when he had told her what he had been asked to do.

'You can't do that!' she said. 'What about Jack's legacy? Are you going to suggest he should have known better … whatever you say, you know they'll make mincemeat out of you.'

Patrick knew that. No one ever came out of a press interview in one piece. He could see where the MoD stood and what his remit was. He was there to distract and defend, he would do his best. He hadn't really had a choice, but anyway it seemed appropriate apropos of what he had done.

The PR woman on Patrick's right opened the proceedings.

'Good morning, everyone. Right, if we are all here …if you could settle down, we can make a start. I would like to introduce Patrick Walker, our representative from procurement, who will explain the uses of different Ministry equipment in the field. Patrick's first cousin was one of the men lost in this most recent incident. First question, please.'

There was a pause, in deference to the dead, Patrick supposed. Then the questions started, gently at first. The reporters were full of sympathy for him and his loss. Patrick was beginning to feel he might have got the hang of this, might have got away with answering benign questions with a tear in his eye. He was starting to relax.

'Right, from The Mail,' said the PR woman.

'Hello, Patrick, sorry for your loss, but can you tell me, how many Snatch Land Rovers are currently in use in Afghanistan? And were you aware of the flaws with the vehicles?'

'Land Rovers have been successfully used by the Armed Forces since 1949. At the Ministry of Defence, we rigorously assess all equipment for appropriate use. The Snatch Land Rover was used successfully in Northern Ireland and subsequently approved for use in Iraq and latterly Afghanistan,' said Patrick.

A woman rose from the middle of the audience.

'Could you then explain the following? I have seen an email you sent on the 12th Aug 2010, that's over two years ago, now. It seems to contradict what you have just said. I quote,

In the light of the known issues surrounding Snatch Land Rovers, I would recommend these should be withdrawn from service in Afghanistan immediately.

That never happened, did it? You didn't follow up on your recommendation? Was there ever an investigation?'

'Um.' There was a long pause while Patrick stared into the lights and realised there was no good answer. Of course, he could say he was merely a small cog, but that was not why he was here. He had understood this was not so much a cover up as an opportunity for a show of confidence. Now he realised that if that failed, he was the scapegoat.

'I think you might be quoting that out of context. I'm afraid we don't have time for any more questions,' said the artful PR woman, before Patrick could incriminate the MoD. She pulled the stunned Patrick to his feet and hustled him out of the door.

‘Little bitch, I wonder where she got that information. We seem to have a leak,’ said the PR woman to her associate as they left the room. ‘Ah, here is our legal representative.’

Patrick looked up. Charity was coming towards them down the corridor.

‘We had to finish a little earlier than expected. An awkward moment, an old email of Patrick’s seems to have got into the wrong hands. Nothing I’m sure you legal bods can’t sort out for us,’ said the PR woman to Charity.

‘Oh dear,’ said Charity. ’How difficult.’ She turned to Patrick. ‘I am sorry. You do have to be so careful with emails. Perhaps you cc’d someone in on an exchange you shouldn’t have. It’s easy to do.’

‘That sort of thing can happen, but you wouldn’t have emailed someone outside the organisation with that sort of information, would you?’ asked the woman from PR.

‘No,’ said Patrick, aghast.

‘No, it must be a malicious leak then.’

‘But who would do something like that at a time like this?’ said Patrick, looking at Charity.

‘Perhaps someone with a grudge,’ said the PR associate.

‘Well, at your level, you would certainly be expected to know how fastidious you need to be.’ Charity smiled.

As Patrick moved away, released from the media circus, Charity followed him down the hall a short way.

‘But Patrick, don’t worry. I have your back, and the department will do everything it can to ensure there won’t be any more embarrassing disclosures.’

He stared at her in horror, Charity was enjoying wielding power, she knew she held sway over his career. He shivered.

Patrick returned to his desk and stared at his computer screen, hoping that if anyone noticed him, he would look busy. He had worked so hard and for so long to build his career. All the days and evenings spent at his computer screen, reading reports, evaluating situations and now, it might be over in a moment. He was contemplating the end of his time at the MoD and wondering whether he would be shuffled sideways to some back water or if he should start looking beyond to the great outside world for a new position. An awkward situation as his name would be all over the press by this evening and in all the mornings papers, alongside his photograph no doubt.

When he got home, Margot was sympathetic. She had picked up a Standard outside Covent Garden tube on her way back from work.

'I can't believe they threw you to the wolves,' she said. 'You've just lost Jack; we've all lost Jack.' She seemed unduly distressed at his misfortune, but perhaps she could see his career unravelling too. She pulled a tissue out from the sleeve of her cardigan and wept softly. 'How could they?'

'It wasn't how it was supposed to pan out. The powers that be didn't know about the leak of the old emails. They were just as horrified as I was,' said Patrick, wrapping his arms around her quivering shoulders. 'No need to be so upset. It will blow over … eventually.'

'They only printed your emails, not the responses. Doesn't anyone else share the blame? Did anyone commit to replacing the Land Rovers?'

'I noticed that too and they quoted snippets, not the whole. But that's the way these things go.'

Now was not the time to say he'd had trouble with a girl at work, and she was exacting revenge. How would that sound to Margot? Or to confess that he deserved all the opprobrium. He couldn't get away from the fact that it was his fault Jack was in Afghanistan in the first place. It was a heavy burden to hold on his own.

He would wait, wait until after Jack's funeral, when the dust had settled. Margot would be back to her normal calm self, and he would confess then. If he hadn't been suspicious of Jack's intentions, and on what evidence, if Patrick hadn't snubbed Charity, if he hadn't sent Jack's file to personnel, perhaps none of this would have happened. Jack might have been given the desk job he wanted and still be alive.

Patrick would tell her everything, and Margot would sympathise. She would tell him it was alright, that Jack was the commander's favourite for the job, he would have been selected whether Patrick had interfered or not, and Patrick would be able to sleep at night.

A Pattern

Knit one, Purl one

It was a hot July day. Patrick was playing golf. Margot didn't know how he could at a time like this, but old habits die hard, and it was good he was out of the house. She had come out to the village to buy some fruit from the grocers that she had forgotten to get on her weekly shop. Her bag wasn't heavy and not having anything particular to be getting on with at home, nothing to distract her, she was browsing the shops. Absentmindedly trailing along, with this whole business about Jack, she had lost focus.

She went into a small haberdashery shop on a side street she had never been into before. As the door closed behind her, the cramped room enfolded Margot in a welcoming, musty smell coming from the hanks of twisted yarn that covered every surface. She ran her hands over the coiled bundles, the fluffy mohair that always made her want to sneeze, the scratchy northern wool that prickled like heather, and the smooth soft wool, tightly wound that reminded her of socks. There were colourful adverts for funky sweaters, rotating stands with needles and buttons, and a whole wall with diamond shelving of brightly coloured wools.

Margot flipped through the racks, found a pattern, and asked the assistant for help finding suitable wool and needles.

As it was so lovely she would not return home yet. She walked down the street, past the butcher and baker and Patrick's newspaper shop. Beyond the war memorial that rose on a triangle of green just down the road from the pub, there was a children's park.

Margot crossed over onto the common, entered the bark strewn playground, and found a bench in the sun. There were only a few mothers there, half a dozen children. It was still early in the day.

Ollie and Toby had loved coming here after school with their friends. She used to bring them sometimes at the weekend too. She hadn't been here for years, it was just for little ones, and the boys grew out of it quite quickly.

Margot opened the haberdashery paper bag, took out the needles and wool and started to cast on. Angela had taught Margot and her sister to knit when they were teenagers. Lily had not been interested and was out of the door in no time.

'Better things to do, I expect,' Angela had said to Margot. 'But you and I will make something exciting.'

Margot was cack-handed, but her aunt had persevered. They had not made anything very exciting, but the afternoon had passed, and they had fun, and for two minutes Margot didn't think about her parents, and Lily had been given a scarf for Christmas that year.

Now, Margot sat in the sweet sunshine and unravelled what she had already done. It was too tight and then too loose. The wool lay crinkled and unhappy in her lap like a bleached bird's nest fallen out of a tree. Perhaps she should do a tension square. Margot pulled out the pattern. She had never been good at reading instructions. She started again.

'What are you doing?' said a small voice.

'Just knitting,' said Margot.

'What?'

'I don't know, really.'

'It looks like a cardigan in the picture.'

'Yes, I suppose it does. But my knitting doesn't really look like the photograph, does it?' said Margot holding out her misshapen square.

'It could be a scarf.'

'I suppose. If I keep going.'

'Who's it for?'

'I'm not sure about that either,' said Margot.

'Come away,' said a voice. 'Don't bother the lady.' A woman pulled the child away.

‘Just asking,’ said the child before rushing off to the slide and the other children. Their voices chirping like so many birds.

‘Who are you with?’ the woman asked Margot. ‘Which is your child.’

‘Oh, I’m not here with anyone … yet. I’m waiting and knitting and enjoying the sunshine.’

‘Well, it’s not really done to come into the playground if you’re not accompanying a child,’ said the woman, giving Margot a steely look before stomping back to the other mothers.

She wasn’t allowed to join the club without a baby. That’s how these playground games went, but Margot knew that already.

Margot watched the mothers watching her with suspicion, the childless one. It made her smile, well half a cynical smile, but it was more of a smile than she had done for days. Then another smile for the knowledge of the child within. Soon she would be allowed to join in.

Margot started to cast off her square. The pattern leaflet had a tape measure printed against the spine. She lined up her square and counted her stitches. Her knitting had become more even despite the interruptions. She was getting better, but at what cost. She had lost Jack even though she didn’t want him.

She had managed to avoid Patrick those first few weeks after she said goodbye to Jack, wanting a separation between her attraction to Jack and her commitment to Patrick. Margot needed to reboot her emotions. Then, when the news broke, they had clung to each other. Margot hated lying to Patrick, but she would never be able to confess why she felt so disconcerted. But her problem had been resolved. She was now clear to rebuild her relationship with Patrick and make sure her family was strong for the new baby.

She wouldn’t unravel and use the wrinkled yarn again. She would begin the baby’s cardigan with fresh wool, a new start. Margot had bought a small pair of scissors, shaped like a reaching stork, at the wool shop. She sniped the wool joining the tester square from the ball, like the cutting of an umbilical cord.

Knit one, purl one for the hem, to hold the fabric flat and give a ridged edge, a good foundation. She would switch to the larger needles for the main body of the piece. One row plain, one row purl. If she could finish this small sweater and it worked out, she would get more wool and try some fancier stitches, but for now, she was happy to keep it simple.

Was she happy? As happy as she could be. The sun was warm, a new person was growing inside her, and she was relearning a skill. She was making something. It would be a productive morning. For one moment, she could build on the present and not think about what had happened.

Oh, Jack! There he was, popping into her thoughts again. Just when she had supposed his memory to be safely stored in a box in a safe part of her brain. She couldn't believe he wasn't ever coming back.

Margot blew her nose and dabbed her eyes and glanced at the knitting pattern measuring her work against the gauge. It was such a tiny cardigan she was knitting. It was already time to cast off for the armholes.

She needed to remember Jack, for the pleasure he had brought her and then put him aside. Patrick was and always had been her future.

After the funeral, when all the family had left, and they were alone, she would tell Patrick about the baby. After they laid Jack in the ground, and she saw for herself that he really had gone, then she would state, calmly and without emotion, what she had done. She would say she was pregnant, by then she would be nearly four months, and let him know the baby was Jack's.

Then Patrick could decide what he wanted to do, and she would accept his decision.

Outcomes

Repercussions

The rest of the week passed slowly, and the next started slower still. Patrick finished the work he already had. Gradually, his computer grew silent. No new queries or reports were sent his way. He gazed into the blank eternity of his screen. He took long lunches and wandered around St James' Park. No one seemed to notice if he was at his desk.

Patrick read all the newspaper reports on his interview, over and over, and as more email snippets were released in a trickle, the story seemed to run and run. No mitigating circumstances, budget restraints, availability of alternatives, or use limitations to excuse him were published. If he knew the Land Rovers were unsuitable, why hadn't he done more to ensure they were replaced. If he had kicked up a stink, he may have lost the possibility of a promotion, but maybe Jack would still be alive.

At the end of the week, a blip and a flash of his cursor announced an email had landed in his inbox. Patrick roused himself and clicked on it, a summons from his boss.

'Well, Patrick, here we are.'

'Indeed,' said Patrick, there was not much more he could say.

'Didn't go as we expected. No idea about the leak up front, as I'm sure you gathered. We don't normally send our loyal servants to the gallows without a heads up. But don't worry, our legal team are on it.'

Patrick groaned inside. How long would Charity drag this out? She was enjoying twisting the knife. Well, nothing he could do about it now. He just had to weather the storm.

'I need you to sign this form, if you will.'

Patrick looked at the document in front of him.

The decision to deploy Snatch Land Rovers on operations in Iraq and Afghanistan took account of a range of factors, including the nature of the mission and the theatre specific threats at the time. Given that these vehicles were already available in our inventory, no EU regulatory or financial factors applied. As written statements made evident at the time, senior operational commanders were clear that they needed a vehicle of the size, weight and profile of the Snatch Land Rover, capable of transporting men, to fulfil their tasks in theatre. A series of modifications were carried out to enhance the Snatch's mobility, and it has the highest levels of protection for its size and weight class.

Patrick signed.

'That should do it. You took the rap. You didn't hesitate. Kept your head. Good man. I think we've avoided further questions being raised in Parliament. Don't worry, Patrick. It will be quiet for you for a while, but we old Wintonians look out for each other. I have your back. There will be more and better opportunities in the pipeline.'

Should Patrick say thank you? He didn't know the special handshake, if there was one. He just nodded in what he hoped was a thoughtful manner.

'Unfortunately, I've had to rescind your name from the next round of promotion opportunities. And perhaps it would be advisable to lay low for a couple of weeks, even months. We'll call it compassionate leave. On full pay. I'll give you a call when the dust has settled.'

Jack's Funeral

A Service in Celebration of the Life
of
MAJ. JACK ROBERT WEATHERSTONE, DSO, MC
9th November 1972 – 16th July 2013

'Jack was always larger than life. He was adept at hunting, fishing, and shooting, but he was also a natural linguist with an extraordinary thirst for life that took him beyond normal human experience. He wanted to ride faster, climb higher, and laugh longer and louder than anyone else. These qualities made him not only a superlative human being but also an exemplary soldier and officer. We have all lost something with the loss of Jack; his was the quintessence of an exuberant life, a life well lived.'

Patrick looked up from his notes at the congregation. His words followed the military eulogy, which had been given by Jack's commanding officer.

Patrick had been to Brize Norton with Jack's family for the repatriation of Jack's remains. It felt disingenuous to be there, but apart from Jack's father, who was now in his eighties, Patrick was the nearest male relative and his connection to the MoD added gravitas. Patrick had to stand tall. It was there that Jack's sisters had asked him to speak at the funeral.

From the lectern, Patrick could see Margot and Ollie in the fifth row of the church. The boys had broken up for the summer holidays. He had collected them from school the week before. Patrick hadn't wanted them to come to the funeral.

'It will give them closure,' Margot said. 'They are serious boys and loved Jack. And Toby has said he would like to sing.'

Patrick didn't think it appropriate but didn't want to argue with Margot over this. She had been thirteen, the same age as Ollie was now, when her parents died.

Margot sat like a stone, the only sign she was paying attention was the quivering of the black feather in her hat. Jack's immediate family were in the pews in front of her. His parents, unable to comprehend their loss, his sisters and their families and Patrick's mother. His father had been considered too frail to attend. Jenni sat the other side of Ollie and behind them numerous cousins.

Army officers, associates, and assorted friends sat to the left and filled every spare pew at the back of the church. The army knew how to do things properly. Even through his work, Patrick had never seen so much glittery braid or so many medals. Everyone was dressed in their finest to honour the passing of a fellow soldier. Beside him, on trestle legs, was Jack's coffin, draped in a Union flag. Jack's cap, medals and belt, and a wreath had been placed on top. Patrick finished up his speech.

'Close by is the house where Jack's parents live. Where Jack grew up with his sisters. This is the church where, as a child, Jack attended Sunday school, where he was dragged as a teenager, and where he worshipped as an adult. It is now where he is to be buried.'

Patrick stepped down from the lectern as the congregation rose to sing Jerusalem. He walked back towards his seat next to Margot. He glanced at her as he turned to sit in the pew. She gave him half a smile and dabbed the corner of her eye under her veil with a handkerchief.

'Well done,' she said in his ear and squeezed his hand.

As the military bearers lifted the coffin and followed the vicar out of the church, from the balcony high up behind them over the church door, hesitant at first, came Toby's beautiful treble voice singing the Panis Angelicus, a song to lift all hearts to God.

In the churchyard, the burial was accompanied by a salute and Last Post. The mourners stood on freshly clipped grass. After the cool of the church the air was warm. An ancient yew dark in the bright sunlight seemed to lean against the church for support. Afterwards, the crowd set off to the family home for the wake. It was a short walk from the church. Patrick took Margot's hand, Ollie and Toby in tow, they followed the crowd. It was easy to see where they were headed, a huge marquee hired for the occasion covered the garden and from the road, the white canvass could be seen rippling in the breeze.

'A good send off,' said Jack's superior, clapping Patrick on the back as he passed through the throng, having picked up glasses of champagne to take across the tent to Margot and Jenni.

'What an emotionally draining service, so moving. And the end! Toby has an amazing voice,' said Jenni, looking svelte in clinging black. Patrick handed her a glass. 'All the singing was good. I expect you always get that when you have a congregation of soldiers, trained not to hold back. I do like your dress, Margot, not your usual style, rather floaty.'

'It was all I could find,' said Margot. 'I don't ever really wear black.'

'I can see it isn't your colour,' said Vi, appearing through the crowd with a young man in tow. 'It makes you look terribly pale. But black hides a multitude of sins, don't you think?'

'Oh hi, Vi,' said Jenni. 'You look well. Who's this?'

'This is Jason, my toy boy.' She smiled, triumphant at their astonishment. 'You don't mind me calling you that, do you?' she added snuggling into Jason, stroking his arm.

'Lovely to meet you,' said Margot to Jason, who was blushing.

'And slimming, black, don't you think, when you're carrying a few extra pounds. Oh, don't look so horrified. It's sexy to have a bit of a jiggle.' said Vi with a clipped hiccup of a laugh. 'At least that's what it says in all the magazines for women of a certain age.'

'What are you doing here?' Patrick had arranged to drop the boys off with Vi on their way back after the service.

'Oh, Patrick. I couldn't resist coming. Afterall, I have known Jack for years too. And this way, you won't have to make a detour on the way home.' She turned to Margot. 'Partly, I wanted to hear Toby sing. He was marvellous, wasn't he?'

Before anyone could say anything else, Vi added. 'We really must mingle.' And she turned on her heel and left with Jason, smiling sheepishly, following in her wake.

Trust Vi to make an entrance, even at a funeral. He wondered if she had pre-loaded, but she was driving the boys later, so probably not. Margot and Jenni looked a little stunned.

'Do you think Jason … and Vi? Really?' said Margot.

'He seems frightfully young. I saw him earlier and thought he was one of the wait staff,' said Jenni.

'How are the girls?' Patrick asked, reaching for a safe topic.

'Good, thanks. Both are enjoying school, and Julia has taken up riding …'

Patrick tuned out. Jenni could talk about her daughters non-stop for hours. He didn't know how Margot put up with it. He glanced round the room, letting Margot take the strain of keeping Jenni going with the odd, 'Really!', or 'Marvellous!'.

'So, do you think she's here?' Patrick paused. Jenni was whispering.

'Who?' said Margot.

'The lover, the married woman.'

'That, now? I haven't seen anyone we don't already know.' Patrick was glad Margot seemed reluctant to take part in this tasteless tittle-tattle.

'Maybe she was sitting at the back of the church and hasn't come to the reception.'

'Maybe,' said Margot.

Patrick moved away. He wanted to find Jack's parents. He had greeted them when he had arrived, but he should talk to them again. He nodded to Margot and Jenni and set off across the marquee.

By the bar, there were a gaggle of Jack's fellow officers, he wasn't sure if that was the correct collective noun. They were recounting tales of Jack's daring. Patrick smiled as he passed and raised his glass to join a toast they were making to salute their fallen comrade. God, it was too awful. He must confess to Margot when they were on the drive home, how he had ensured Jack would be sent to Afghanistan, he couldn't bear the truth alone any longer.

He found his mother with Jack's parents in the drawing room of the house.

'Darling, there you are,' said his mother, drawing him into the conversation, not that Jack's parents had much to say. Patrick sat next to his mother on the sofa.

'Well spoken,' said Jack's father. 'The eulogy… I know you and Jack haven't been so close in recent years, but you were the best of friends when you were boys.'

'The least I could do,' said Patrick. 'You're right, as adults, we never managed to rekindle that easy friendship we had as children, but we used to meet for lunch fairly regularly. I saw him a couple of months ago, just before he went out… I always respected Jack, and I was envious of him. He was twice the man.'

'Aww, darling.' His mother patted his knee.

Patrick tried to smile, but he knew Jack had had it all.

Ladies

A Queue

Margot caught her reflection with her stupid hat with its ridiculous feather. It was the only one she could find with a veil of sorts. Dark glasses would have been too dramatic, and she had felt the need to have refuge from the glare of grief.

She was in the queue. It wasn't so much that she needed to go, but she wanted some respite from the social pressure. She didn't think she could hear another word about Julia and Molly, much though she loved the girls, and she didn't want to hear any more about how wonderful Jack was, it was all too terrible. Margot's emotions were stretched thin and taut, burdened by the past weeks, like the thin wire she had used for her rose that had snapped under the burden of new growth.

She would tell Patrick about her baby when they had dropped off his mother on the drive back home. She couldn't withhold the truth anymore and she would live with the repercussions.

She was worried about Patrick. On top of everything to do with Jack and the funeral, Patrick had been devastated to be asked to leave his work, even if it was only temporarily. The added loss of his chance of promotion rankled. She watched as he brooded, pacing, in limbo, not knowing when his life would pick up again, time following him slowly from room to room. Though, it did mean supper was waiting for her in the evening when she got back from work, feeling guilty for being employed.

'I thought it was you,' Vi said, pushing through the line to stand next to Margot, ignoring the huffing and tutting. 'I spotted the feather in your hat above the crowd,' she added.

'Oh hello,' said Margot.

'You sound exhausted. It can take it out of one, an occasion like this, all the emotion and the endless standing around. Especially for someone in your condition.'

Margot was astounded, how did Vi know. 'Jason seems nice, if a little young,' she said.

'Well, yes.' Vi looked smug. 'He's gorgeous, isn't he? I was on my way to meet him that time I bumped into you outside Peter Jones. We hooked up on social media, can you imagine, so I didn't really know what I was getting into, but he's proved so much more than I could have hoped for. That's why I knew you were meeting someone too. You looked just like I felt.'

'I was picking up a few things on my way home from work,' said Margot. 'Nothing more.'

'And it occurred to me… your skulking and rosy appearance and now the loose but cleverly cut dress.'

'Honestly, I don't know what you're talking about,' said Margot.

'In fact, the more I think about it, the more obvious it seems,' said Vi. 'You know, I've spent a lot of my life searching to find myself, trying to work out what is the essence to being me. All that yoga and travelling to foreign lands … as if the idea of who I was, was hiding under a rock in the sub-continent. I thought I had to discover my true self … and then I realised, I don't know what sparked the idea, perhaps the boys becoming more independent, that I was here all along, that life was right here on my doorstep, hence Jason. It's so refreshing. So, good on you for taking things into your own hands,' said Vi. 'Have you told Patrick?'

'Really …,'

'Well, you couldn't do anything else after I told you about Patrick's vasectomy, could you? You look shocked, it's quite funny really. Don't worry your secret is safe with me. I won't breathe a word and will be suitably surprised when I read the announcement in the papers. Do people still do that?'

'Do what?' Margot felt numb. She was finding it hard to keep up, but she was sure she would have remembered if Vi had told her Patrick had a vasectomy. She shouldn't have drunk that glass of champagne, but Patrick had handed it to her, and it didn't seem the moment to say she would rather have tea. 'A vasectomy?' she added.

'Yes, I've told you this, I persuaded Patrick to get the snip after Toby. Two was enough and anyway I wanted to see if he would really go through with it.' Vi's eyes sparkled at the memory of the dare.

'It all makes sense,' said Margot.

If there had been anything left inside her to break it would have shattered. Patrick had made a choice. He had chosen not to have a child with her. It hadn't been a lack of protein or too much stress at work, he knew he couldn't get her pregnant and had deceived her. She ought to feel anger, but all she felt was an endless emptiness.

Standing in a queue for the loo was not the place to have an existential crisis, but then again, she could lock herself in a cubicle and refuse to come out till the world had wound back to a time and place where she thought she had control and understood everything.

She believed her marriage had been founded on love and trust, but Patrick had not respected her enough to tell her the truth. Would she have married him if he had been honest? She wasn't sure. Perhaps that's why he never said.

'Of course it does. I can't wait to see how you persuade him that the new addition is his,' sad Vi.

'Vi you're way ahead of yourself here. There's nothing to see. I'm extremely upset about Jack, who isn't, and this was the only dress I could find at short notice. There aren't many black dresses in the shops in July.'

They moved slowly forward. Margot now had to prop the door from the hall open with her foot. She saw the black feather coyly bobbing many times over in the angled mirrors in the ladies. She tore off the hat and tossed it in the nearby bin. She was no longer in danger of weeping and wailing; she was too angry.

Aftermath

Confessions

On the way back from the funeral, Patrick and Margot first dropped his mother home and went in to have tea with his father, who wanted to hear all about the terrible day. His mother enthused about Toby's singing and commended Patrick's eulogy and called him and Jack the best of friends. It was an ordeal to hear such false praise and to go over every detail again.

It had been a long day and a slow drive back. With his mother in the car, Margot had been chatty, keeping the conversation general, but now they were alone, driving home she seemed preoccupied, silent. She looked tense and held herself turned away from him. He reached his arm over to pat her shoulder, and she flinched. Margot was definitely not herself.

'I… I wanted … there's something you should know,' she said.

Patrick took a left turn onto the slip road to the bypass, taking the sharp curve too fast as he accelerated to join the traffic. Margot didn't continue, but turned to look out the window again, not that there was anything to see. On this stretch of the road there were only massive, new warehouses, not a tree or any living thing in sight.

The evening was impressive, a yellow and purple wash to the end of a blue day. The shadows stretched long and low, and the light that was left was sharp and demanding. Patrick was glad he was not driving into the sun.

'There's something I want to discuss with you too,' he said.

Patrick was holding onto his terrible knowledge. Now the funeral was over, he needed to talk to Margot. What he had done was eating away at him, destroying him, and without work to go to, he constantly ached with self-reproach. It never occurred to him that Jack would die. He had just wanted him out of the way - for a bit.

What a fool he had been. He convinced himself Jack was interested in Margot, but just because Jack liked to provoke didn't mean anything had happened. Anger rose inside him just thinking about it. But his rage quickly turned into a burning self-loathing. He trusted Margot. He didn't believe she would have an affair or give in to the wily charms of Jack… even if Jack was very charming. Had been! God, it was all so appalling. Could he burden Margot with his crime and what would he do if she didn't forgive him?

The person he really needed to talk to was Jack.

Margot was still silent. What could be so difficult for her to talk about. He hoped it wasn't more bad news. Had she been hiding an illness, some recent diagnosis that she didn't want to talk about? She had perhaps been a bit secretive lately, keeping herself to herself. He was concerned about her but hadn't been able to separate the issues, there had been a lot going on. They were both overwrought.

Patrick indicated left and pulled the car into the slow lane, if this was going to be emotive, he might not trust his reaction if he was driving too fast.

'You know you can tell me anything.'

'I know, but I don't know how to …' He could see Margot's fingers in her lap out of the corner of his eye. She was pulling the tissue in her hands into tiny pieces, shredding it onto her black dress in a distracted manner. Margot was a great communicator; she never had a problem talking about anything.

'Now you really have me worried. Shall I go first?'

Patrick pulled off the bypass and cut down between a hotel and a petrol station, trying to find somewhere he could pull over.

'I've wanted to tell you for a while,' said Margot. 'But somehow…'

Patrick found a layby and parked behind a lorry. Wrappers and empty bottles were drifting by the bin, and a bleached plastic bag waved at him from the hedgerow. When he had stopped the car, he turned to Margot.

'It's been a terrible time,' he said, brushing her hair back where it had fallen forward and hid her face. 'With the funeral and everything. It's not been easy for anyone. We've all been preoccupied.'

'I … Jack … I,' she said.

'Darling, it's been a long and exhausting day. Now the funeral is done, we have paid our respects and can move on.'

'But I ….'

'What? What is this about?'

'I'm pregnant!' said Margot, turning away from him again.

'Oh.'

Patrick's chest felt hollow, and his heart seemed to float. He had had the reversal, but when he went back to the clinic to be assessed, they told him that, unfortunately, in his case, the procedure was not successful. It happened sometimes. His sperm count might increase over time, but they would have hoped for a better result at this stage if that were to be the case. He was just unlucky, they said.

Patrick felt the air leave his body. He was careful not to sigh out loud. This baby couldn't be his, or it was extremely unlikely. As he stared out the window at the bleak layby, now, he saw everything clearly. His assumptions had been right after all, but although he searched his feelings, he no longer felt resentment. He felt a lightness.

His beautiful Margot, his succour and strength, looked so fragile. He knew his initial reaction was paramount. He needed to say something. He hoped he hadn't already hesitated for too long.

The lorry parked in front of them pulled away, revealing a lone wild rose straggling through the barbed wire of the layby fence, its pale pink single blooms delicate in the blast from the passing traffic. Patrick turned back to Margot; tears were slipping down her face.

'But this is the most marvellous news,' said Patrick, hitting his hand on the steering wheel in what he hoped wasn't too theatrical a move. This explained everything, he had been slow. Patrick glanced at Margot. He had been blind, the nausea, the weight gain. Why hadn't he put two and two together sooner?

'It is?'

'It's fabulous.' Patrick leaned across the car and kissed Margot on her temple. 'I didn't know if I should tell you. I wasn't sure it would be successful. I didn't want you to hope too much, but now, here we are. How fantastic!'

'Tell me what?' said Margot.

'I had my vasectomy reversed. It's called a vasovasostomy or something ridiculous. Wow! I can't believe it has been successful.' Margot had brought up Ollie and Toby and been a wonderful mother to them. Surely, he could bring up Jack's child for her.

'Really… why didn't you tell me? When?'

'What, well, about six months ago, end of November, at a private clinic off Sloane Square. It was shortly after I started going to the gym at work. I decided I ought to be healthy and give myself every chance for the procedure to be effective.'

'I thought, I think I saw you … in Cadogan Gardens?' Margot said.

'Yes, that's right,' he said. 'I didn't say anything about it because I was worried it wouldn't work. If it hadn't been successful, it would have been too disappointing.'

'I remember, I rather wondered if you were seeing someone else,' she said.

'Oh, my darling, only ever you. Why do you ask?'

'I don't know really, just curious. About that time, you seemed a bit depressed and not terribly interested in me. Then latterly, you seemed to be caught up in what was going on at work, all those courses … and then what with the Land Rover scandal…,'

He could not undo what he had done, but perhaps he could stop the past from derailing his and Margot's future. 'When did you find out. How far along are you?' he said.

'I guess, I must be about three months,' said Margot. 'I'm sorry I didn't say something sooner.'

'I'm so sorry you have been worried, that you felt you couldn't tell me. My darling, nothing could make me happier.'

'You know, it just never seemed a good time to say…. I knew you didn't want more children, and I wasn't anticipating this … I wasn't expecting …'

'You must know you can always tell me everything. Our own baby! I didn't realise…. how much I wanted this.'

'I know, me too,' said Margot, turning to him and smiling at last. The remnants of her tears made her eyes seem larger and brighter than usual. He really was the luckiest of men … to have this second chance at happiness.

Margot reached over and placed her hand on his, where it rested on the steering wheel.

'Together forever, no more secrets,' she said.

'No more secrets,' he replied as he started the car and eased back out into the traffic.

A Voice echoes in a vaulted chapel
Secrets buried with the dead
Nothing is said
Silence is better.

\- *Mike Marlin*

Printed in Great Britain
by Amazon

e5a9f53e-3ded-4296-ae22-1669a7d4b438R01